Introduction

Chaza"l (Misechtas Shabbos 149a), on the *pasuk al tifnu el haelilim,* expound it to mean that one should not turn towards matters that are the creations of one's own mind (i.e fictional works and the like). While this *issur* (among others) is mentioned *in Shulchan aruch* (307:16), many poskim rule that fictional works are permitted to read as long as they are kosher and the topics have value from a Jewish perspective. My saintly Rebbe, Rav Chaim Yisroel Belsky *zatza"l,* used to say in this regards, that heimishe Jewish novels usually have some kind of Torah based message and are therefore permitted to read. It would seem though that non-Jewish works of fiction, which **on the surface** do not add clear benefits to the reader from a Jewish perspective, and oft times are filled with objectionable content, would be subject to the restriction mentioned above.

With this in mind, this modified 20000 Leagues Under the Sea attempts to resolve those issues. The book has been modified to remove objectionable content and has been overlayed with questions that frame the story through the lens of the Torah and Jewish ideals adding value to it from a Torah perspective. Perfect for the *frum* high school student, each chapter is followed by general, and Torah-based, reading comprehension questions that demand of the reader to put on his or her Torah glasses and see the story and its characters through the light of *Halacha, hashkafa,* and *middos tovos.*

Besides for the halachic improvments mentioned, line numbers have been inserted on each page allowing the student to quickly search and find what he/she is looking for in the story. Additionally, any outdated language or technical terms have been elucidated and some more advanced vocabulary terms were placed in a separate section after each chapter giving students the opportunity to focus on vocabulary that are found throughout the story.

Every book is a product of hundreds of hours of effort and work. Countless hours were put into this work, to ensure a work that is useful and at the same time enjoyable and pleasant to read. Toward that end, a few names of those who helped out in the production of this book are in order.

First and foremost, I would like to thank Hashem for allowing me the zechus to provide the Torah world with classic literature in a halachically acceptable way. If not for the siayata dishmaya-it wouldn't have been possible. I would also like to thank my parents, for without their financial and technical help, this book would not have seen the light of day. I would also like to thank the board of the Limudai Yisroel Institute and specifically to Mr. Hillel Adelman for his support in the production of this book. To Mr. Howie and Indira Moskowitz for their continuing support, to Mr. Aron and Abby Brody for their continuing support and to the many others who have contributed and continue to support this project-now in its 10th year!

May this book provide the answer that many schools have been looking for-classic Western literature in the Torah way.

20,000 Leagues Under the Sea

By Jules Verne

Chapter 1

A SHIFTING REEF

1 **The year 1866** was signalized by a remarkable incident, a
2 mysterious and puzzling phenomenon, which doubtless no one
3 has yet forgotten. Not to mention rumors which **agitated** the
4 maritime population and excited the public mind, even in the
5 **interior** of continents, seafaring men were particularly excited.
6 Merchants, common sailors, captains of vessels, skippers, both
7 of Europe and America, naval officers of all countries, and the
8 Governments of several States on the two continents, were deeply
9 interested in the matter.

10 For some time past vessels had been met by "an enormous thing,"
11 a long object, spindle-shaped, occasionally phosphorescent, and
12 infinitely larger and more rapid in its movements than a whale.

13 The facts relating to this **apparition** (entered in various log-
14 books) agreed in most respects as to the shape of the object or
15 creature in question, the **untiring** rapidity of its movements,
16 its surprising power of locomotion, and the **peculiar** life with
17 which it seemed endowed. If it was a whale, it surpassed in size
18 all those hitherto[1] classified in science. Taking into consideration
19 the mean of observations made at divers{e} times—rejecting the
20 timid estimate of those who assigned to this object a length of
21 two hundred feet, equally with the exaggerated opinions which
22 set it down as a mile in width and three in length—we might
23 fairly conclude that this mysterious being surpassed greatly all
24 **dimensions** admitted by the learned ones of the day, if it existed
25 at all. And that it DID exist was an undeniable fact; and, with

---

1 Until then

that **tendency** which disposes the human mind in favor of the marvelous, we can understand the excitement produced in the entire world by this supernatural apparition. As to classing it in the list of **fables**, the idea was out of the question.

On the 20th of July, 1866, the steamer Governor Higginson, of the Calcutta and Burnach Steam Navigation Company, had met this moving mass five miles off the east coast of Australia. Captain Baker thought at first that he was in the presence of an unknown sandbank; he even prepared to determine its exact position when two columns of water, projected by the mysterious object, shot with a hissing noise a hundred and fifty feet up into the air. Now, unless the sandbank had been submitted to the **intermittent** eruption of a geyser, the Governor Higginson had to do neither more nor less than with an aquatic mammal, unknown till then, which threw up from its blow-holes columns of water mixed with air and vapor.

Similar facts were observed on the 23rd of July in the same year, in the Pacific Ocean, by the Columbus, of the West India and Pacific Steam Navigation Company. But this extraordinary creature could transport itself from one place to another with surprising velocity; as, in an interval of three days, the Governor Higginson and the Columbus had observed it at two different points of the chart, separated by a distance of more than seven hundred nautical leagues.

Fifteen days later, two thousand miles farther off, the Helvetia, of the Compagnie-Nationale, and the Shannon, of the Royal Mail Steamship Company, sailing to windward in that portion of the Atlantic lying between the United States and Europe, respectively signaled the monster to each other in 42° 15' N. lat. and 60° 35' W. long. In these simultaneous observations they thought themselves justified in estimating the minimum length of the mammal at more than three hundred and fifty feet, as the Shannon and Helvetia were of smaller dimensions than it, though they measured three hundred feet over all.

Now the largest whales, those which frequent those parts of the sea round the Aleutian, Kulammak, and Umgullich islands, have

62 never exceeded the length of sixty yards, if they attain that.

63 In every place of great resort the monster was the fashion. They
64 sang of it in the cafes, ridiculed it in the papers, and represented
65 it on the stage. All kinds of stories were circulated regarding it.
66 There appeared in the papers caricatures of every gigantic and
67 imaginary creature, from the white whale, the terrible "Moby
68 Dick" of sub-arctic regions, to the immense kraken, whose
69 tentacles could entangle a ship of five hundred tons and hurry
70 it into the abyss of the ocean. The legends of ancient times were
71 even revived.

72 Then burst forth the unending argument between the believers
73 and the unbelievers in the societies of the wise and the scientific
74 journals. "The question of the monster" inflamed all minds.
75 Editors of scientific journals, **quarrelling** with believers in
76 the supernatural, spilled seas of ink during this memorable
77 campaign, some even drawing blood; for from the sea-serpent
78 they came to direct personalities.

79 During the first months of the year 1867 the question seemed
80 buried, never to revive, when new facts were brought before the
81 public. It was then no longer a scientific problem to be solved,
82 but a real danger seriously to be avoided. The question took quite
83 another shape. The monster became a small island, a rock, a reef,
84 but a reef of **indefinite** and shifting **proportions**.

85 On the 5th of March, 1867, the Moravian, of the Montreal Ocean
86 Company, finding herself during the night in 27° 30' lat. and 72°
87 15' long., struck on her starboard quarter a rock, marked in no
88 chart for that part of the sea. Under the combined efforts of the
89 wind and its four hundred horse power, it was going at the rate
90 of thirteen knots. Had it not been for the superior strength of the
91 hull of the Moravian, she would have been broken by the shock
92 and gone down with the 237 passengers she was bringing home
93 from Canada.

94 The accident happened about five o'clock in the morning, as
95 the day was breaking. The officers of the quarter-deck hurried
96 to the after-part of the vessel. They examined the sea with the
97 most careful attention. They saw nothing but a strong eddy

98   about three cables' length distant, as if the surface had been
99   violently agitated. The bearings of the place were taken exactly,
100 and the Moravian continued its route without apparent damage.
101 Had it struck on a submerged rock, or on an enormous wreck?
102 They could not tell; but, on examination of the ship's bottom
103 when undergoing repairs, it was found that part of her keel
104 was broken.

105 This fact, so **grave** in itself, might perhaps have been forgotten
106 like many others if, three weeks after, it had not been re-enacted
107 under similar circumstances. But, thanks to the nationality of the
108 victim of the shock, thanks to the reputation of the company to
109 which the vessel belonged, the circumstance became extensively
110 circulated.

111 The 13th of April, 1867, the sea being beautiful, the breeze
112 favorable, the Scotia, of the Cunard Company's line, found
113 herself in 15° 12' long. and 45° 37' lat. She was going at the speed
114 of thirteen knots and a half.

115 At seventeen minutes past four in the afternoon, whilst the
116 passengers were assembled at lunch in the great saloon, a slight
117 shock was felt on the hull of the Scotia, on her quarter, a little aft
118 of the port-paddle.

119 The Scotia had not struck, but she had been struck, and seemingly
120 by something rather sharp and penetrating than blunt. The
121 shock had been so slight that no one had been alarmed, had it
122 not been for the shouts of the carpenter's watch, who rushed
123 on to the bridge, exclaiming, "We are sinking! we are sinking!"
124 At first the passengers were much frightened, but Captain
125 Anderson hastened to reassure them. The danger could not
126 be imminent. The Scotia, divided into seven compartments by
127 strong partitions, could brave with impunity any leak. Captain
128 Anderson went down immediately into the hold. He found that
129 the sea was pouring into the fifth compartment; and the rapidity
130 of the influx proved that the force of the water was considerable.
131 Fortunately this compartment did not hold the boilers, or the
132 fires would have been immediately extinguished. Captain
133 Anderson ordered the engines to be stopped at once, and one of

134 the men went down to ascertain the extent of the injury. Some
135 minutes afterwards they discovered the existence of a large hole,
136 two yards in diameter, in the ship's bottom. Such a leak could
137 not be stopped; and the Scotia, her paddles half submerged, was
138 obliged to continue her course. She was then three hundred miles
139 from Cape Clear, and, after three days' delay, which caused great
140 uneasiness in Liverpool, she entered the basin of the company.

141 The engineers visited the Scotia, which was put in dry dock.
142 They could scarcely believe it possible; at two yards and a half
143 below water-mark was a regular rent, in the form of an isosceles
144 triangle. The broken place in the iron plates was so perfectly
145 defined that it could not have been more neatly done by a punch.
146 It was clear, then, that the instrument producing the perforation
147 was not of a common stamp and, after having been driven with
148 **prodigious** strength, and piercing an iron plate 1 3/8 inches
149 thick, had withdrawn itself by a backward motion.

150 Such was the last fact, which resulted in exciting once more
151 the torrent of public opinion. From this moment all unlucky
152 casualties which could not be otherwise accounted for were put
153 down to the monster.

154 Upon this imaginary creature rested the responsibility of all these
155 shipwrecks, which unfortunately were considerable; for of three
156 thousand ships whose loss was annually recorded at Lloyd's, the
157 number of sailing and steam-ships supposed to be totally lost,
158 from the absence of all news, amounted to not less than two
159 hundred!

160 Now, it was the "monster" who, justly or unjustly, was accused of
161 their disappearance, and, thanks to it, communication between
162 the different continents became more and more dangerous. The
163 public demanded sharply that the seas should at any price be
164 relieved from this formidable cetacean[2].

---

2   Name of the order of Whale, Dolphin or Porpoise

Vocabulary for Part 1 Chapter 1

agitated, interior, apparition, untiring, peculiar, dimensions, tendency, fables, intermittent, quarrelling, indefinite, proportions, grave, prodigious

Questions for Part 1 Chapter 1

1. Why does the author go to such lengths to give exact dates and places where the first encounters with "the monster" take place?

2. What types of debates erupted over the existence of such a monster?

3. What does the author feel regarding the debate between the skeptics and science? How do you know?

4. What does the author feel regarding the existence of such a monster and what event finally settles the matter that this "creature" is real?

5. What is the international response to this creature? Why is this the response?

6. At this point, do you think it is wise of the international community to try to do what they wish to do? Why or why not?

Chapter 2
PRO AND CON

1 **At the period** when these events took place, I had just
2 returned from a scientific research in the **disagreeable** territory
3 of Nebraska, in the United States. In virtue of my office as
4 Assistant Professor in the Museum of Natural History in Paris,
5 the French Government had attached me to that **expedition**.
6 After six months in Nebraska, I arrived in New York towards the
7 end of March, **laden** with a precious collection. My departure
8 for France was fixed for the first days in May. Meanwhile I was
9 occupying myself in classifying my **mineralogical**, **botanical**,
10 and **zoological** riches, when the accident happened to the Scotia.

11 I was perfectly up in the subject which was the question of the
12 day. How could I be otherwise? I had read and reread all the
13 American and European papers without being any nearer a
14 conclusion. This mystery puzzled me. Under the impossibility
15 of forming an opinion, I jumped from one extreme to the other.
16 That there really was something could not be doubted, and the
17 incredulous were invited to put their finger on the wound of the
18 Scotia.

19 On my arrival at New York the question was at its height. The
20 theory of the floating island, and the unapproachable sandbank,
21 supported by minds little **competent** to form a judgment, was
22 abandoned. And, indeed, unless this **shoal** had a machine in its
23 stomach, how could it change its position with such astonishing
24 **rapidity**?

25 From the same cause, the idea of a floating hull of an enormous
26 wreck was given up.

27 There remained, then, only two possible solutions of the question,
28 which created two distinct parties: on one side, those who were
29 for a monster of colossal strength; on the other, those who were
30 for a submarine vessel of enormous **motive** power.

31 But this last theory, plausible as it was, could not stand against
32 **inquiries** made in both worlds. That a private gentleman should
33 have such a machine at his command was not likely. Where,
34 when, and how was it built? and how could its construction have
35 been kept secret? Certainly a Government might possess such
36 a destructive machine. And in these disastrous times, when the
37 **ingenuity** of man has multiplied the power of weapons of war,
38 it was possible that, without the knowledge of others, a State
39 might try to work such a formidable engine.

40 But the idea of a war machine fell before the declaration
41 of Governments. As public interest was in question, and
42 **transatlantic** communications suffered, their **veracity** could not
43 be doubted. But how admit that the construction of this submarine
44 boat had escaped the public eye? For a private gentleman to keep
45 the secret under such circumstances would be very difficult, and
46 for a State whose every act is **persistently** watched by powerful
47 rivals, certainly impossible.

48 Upon my arrival in New York several persons did me the honor
49 of consulting me on the phenomenon in question. I had published
50 in France a work in quarto, in two volumes, entitled Mysteries of
51 the Great Submarine Grounds. This book, highly approved of in
52 the learned world, gained for me a special reputation in this rather
53 obscure branch of Natural History. My advice was asked. As
54 long as I could deny the reality of the fact, I confined myself to a
55 decided negative. But soon, finding myself driven into a corner,
56 I was **obliged** to explain myself point by point. I discussed the
57 question in all its forms, politically and scientifically; and I give
58 here an extract from a carefully-studied article which I published
59 in the number of the 30th of April. It ran as follows:

60 "After examining one by one the different theories, rejecting all
61 other suggestions, it becomes necessary to admit the existence
62 of a marine animal of enormous power.

63 "The great depths of the ocean are entirely unknown to us.
64 Soundings cannot reach them. What passes in those remote
65 depths—what beings live, or can live, twelve or fifteen miles

66 beneath the surface of the waters—what is the organization
67 of these animals, we can scarcely **conjecture**. However, the
68 solution of the problem submitted to me may modify the form
69 of the dilemma. Either we do know all the varieties of beings
70 which people our planet, or we do not. If we do NOT know
71 them all—if Nature has still secrets in the deeps for us, nothing
72 is more **conformable** to reason than to admit the existence of
73 fishes, or cetaceans of other kinds, or even of new species, of
74 an organization formed to inhabit the **strata** inaccessible to
75 soundings, and which an accident of some sort has brought at
76 long intervals to the upper level of the ocean.

77 "If, on the contrary, we DO know all living kinds, we must
78 necessarily seek for the animal in question amongst those marine
79 beings already classed; and, in that case, I should be disposed to
80 admit the existence of a gigantic narwhal.

81 "The common narwhal, or unicorn of the sea, often attains a
82 length of sixty feet. Increase its size fivefold or tenfold, give
83 it strength proportionate to its size, lengthen its destructive
84 weapons, and you obtain the animal required. It will have the
85 proportions determined by the officers of the Shannon, the
86 instrument required by the perforation of the Scotia, and the
87 power necessary to pierce the hull of the steamer.

88 "Indeed, the narwhal is armed with a sort of ivory sword, a
89 halberd, according to the expression of certain naturalists. The
90 principal tusk has the hardness of steel. Some of these tusks have
91 been found buried in the bodies of whales, which the unicorn
92 always attacks with success. Others have been drawn out, not
93 without trouble, from the bottoms of ships, which they had
94 pierced through and through, as a gimlet[3] pierces a barrel. The
95 Museum of the Faculty of Medicine of Paris possesses one of
96 these defensive weapons, two yards and a quarter in length, and
97 fifteen inches in diameter at the base.

98 "Very well! suppose this weapon to be six times stronger and the
99 animal ten times more powerful; launch it at the rate of twenty

---

3   a small T-shaped tool with a screw-tip for boring

miles an hour, and you obtain a shock capable of producing the catastrophe required. Until further information, therefore, I shall maintain it to be a sea-unicorn of colossal dimensions, armed not with a halberd, but with a real spur, as the armored frigates, or the `rams' of war, whose massiveness and motive power it would possess at the same time. Thus may this puzzling phenomenon be explained, unless there be something over and above all that one has ever conjectured, seen, perceived, or experienced; which is just within the bounds of possibility."

These last words were cowardly on my part; but, up to a certain point, I wished to shelter my dignity as professor, and not give too much cause for laughter to the Americans, who laugh well when they do laugh. I reserved for myself a way of escape. In effect, however, I admitted the existence of the "monster." My article was warmly discussed, which **procured** it a high reputation. It rallied round it a certain number of partisans. The solution it proposed gave, at least, full liberty to the imagination. The human mind delights in grand conceptions of supernatural beings. And the sea is precisely their best vehicle, the only medium through which these giants (against which terrestrial animals, such as elephants or rhinoceroses, are as nothing) can be produced or developed.

The industrial and commercial papers treated the question chiefly from this point of view. The Shipping and Mercantile Gazette, the Lloyd's List, the Packet-Boat, and the Maritime and Colonial Review, all papers devoted to insurance companies which threatened to raise their rates of premium, were **unanimous** on this point. Public opinion had been pronounced. The United States were the first in the field; and in New York they made preparations for an expedition destined to pursue this narwhal. A frigate of great speed, the Abraham Lincoln, was put in commission as soon as possible. The arsenals were opened to Commander Farragut, who hastened the arming of his frigate; but, as it always happens, the moment it was decided to pursue the monster, the monster did not appear. For two months no one heard it spoken of. No ship met with it. It seemed as if this

136 unicorn knew of the plots weaving around it. It had been so much
137 talked of, even through the Atlantic cable, that jesters pretended
138 that this **slender** fly had stopped a telegram on its passage and
139 was making the most of it.

140 So when the frigate had been armed for a long campaign, and
141 provided with formidable fishing apparatus, no one could tell
142 what course to pursue. **Impatience** grew **apace**, when, on
143 the 2nd of July, they learned that a steamer of the line of San
144 Francisco, from California to Shanghai, had seen the animal
145 three weeks before in the North Pacific Ocean. The excitement
146 caused by this news was extreme. The ship was revictualled[4] and
147 well stocked with coal.

148 Three hours before the Abraham Lincoln left Brooklyn pier, I
149 received a letter worded as follows:

150 To M. ARONNAX, Professor in the Museum of Paris, Fifth
151 Avenue Hotel, New York.

152 SIR,—If you will consent to join the Abraham Lincoln in this
153 expedition, the Government of the United States will with
154 pleasure see France represented in the enterprise. Commander
155 Farragut has a cabin at your disposal.

156 Very cordially yours, J.B. HOBSON, Secretary of Marine.

---

4   Stocked with foods and other provisions

𝔙ocabulary 𝔓art 1 𝔠hapter 2,

disagreeable, expedition, laden, mineralogical, botanical, zoological, competent, shoal, rapidity, motive, inquiries, ingenuity, transatlantic, veracity, persistently, obliged, conjecture, conformable, strata, procured, unanimous, slender, impatience, apace

Questions Part 1 Chapter 2

1. Why does the narrator decide against the theory that this monster could be a submarine?

2. The author writes: "Upon my arrival in New York several persons did me the honor of consulting me on the phenomenon in question". Why was he consulted, and why is it an honor to be asked?

3. What does the author think the beast is, and why do you think he tries to put the beast into the classifications that he does?

4. Why does the author back off his assertion that it's a narwhal, and why does he struggle with that decision? Do you think it was a wise decision?

Chapter 3

I FORM MY RESOLUTION

1 **Three seconds before** the arrival of J. B. Hobson's letter I
2 no more thought of pursuing the unicorn than of attempting
3 the passage of the North Sea. Three seconds after reading the
4 letter of the honorable Secretary of Marine, I felt that my true
5 vocation[5], the sole end of my life, was to chase this disturbing
6 monster and **purge** it from the world.

7 But I had just returned from a **fatiguing** journey, weary and
8 **longing** for **repose**. I aspired to nothing more than again seeing
9 my country, my friends, my little lodging by the Jardin des
10 Plantes, my dear and precious collections—but nothing could
11 keep me back! I forgot all—fatigue, friends and collections—
12 and accepted without hesitation the offer of the American
13 Government.

14 "Besides," thought I, "all roads lead back to Europe; and the
15 unicorn may be **amiable** enough to hurry me towards the coast
16 of France. This worthy animal may allow itself to be caught in
17 the seas of Europe (for my particular benefit), and I will not bring
18 back less than half a yard of his ivory halberd to the Museum of
19 Natural History." But in the meanwhile I must seek this narwhal
20 in the North Pacific Ocean, which, to return to France, was
21 taking the road to the antipodes[6].

22 "Conseil," I called in an impatient voice.

23 Conseil was my servant, a true, devoted Flemish boy, who had
24 accompanied me in all my travels. I liked him, and he returned
25 the liking well. He was quiet by nature, regular from principle,
26 zealous from habit, **evincing** little disturbance at the different
27 surprises of life, very quick with his hands, and apt[7] at any
28 service required of him; and, despite his name, never giving

---

5   job
6   Australia and New Zeland
7   good at

29   advice—even when asked for it.

30   Conseil had followed me for the last ten years wherever science
31   led. Never once did he complain of the length or fatigue of a
32   journey, never make an objection to pack his portmanteau[8] for
33   whatever country it might be, or however far away, whether
34   China or Congo. Besides all this, he had good health, which
35   defied all sickness, and solid muscles, but no nerves; good
36   morals are understood. This boy was thirty years old, and his
37   age to that of his master as fifteen to twenty. May I be excused
38   for saying that I was forty years old?

39   But Conseil had one fault: he was **ceremonious** to a degree,
40   and would never speak to me but in the third person, which was
41   sometimes **provoking**.

42   "Conseil," said I again, beginning with feverish hands to make
43   preparations for my departure.

44   Certainly I was sure of this devoted boy. As a rule, I never
45   asked him if it were convenient for him or not to follow me in
46   my travels; but this time the expedition in question might be
47   **prolonged**, and the enterprise might be hazardous in pursuit of
48   an animal capable of sinking a frigate as easily as a nutshell.
49   Here there was matter for reflection even to the most impassive
50   man in the world. What would Conseil say?

51   "Conseil," I called a third time.

52   Conseil appeared.

53   "Did you call, sir?" said he, entering.

54   "Yes, my boy; make preparations for me and yourself too. We
55   leave in two hours."

56   "As you please, sir," replied Conseil, quietly.

57   "Not an instant to lose; lock in my trunk all travelling utensils,
58   coats, shirts, and stockings—without counting, as many as you

8   A large trunk or suitcase

59 can, and make haste."

60 "And your collections, sir?" observed Conseil.

61 "They will keep them at the hotel."

62 "We are not returning to Paris, then?" said Conseil.

63 "Oh! certainly," I answered, **evasively**, "by making a curve."

64 "Will the curve please you, sir?"

65 "Oh! it will be nothing; not quite so direct a road, that is all. We
66 take our passage in the Abraham, Lincoln."

67 "As you think proper, sir," coolly replied Conseil.

68 "You see, my friend, it has to do with the monster—the famous
69 narwhal. We are going to purge it from the seas. A glorious
70 mission, but a dangerous one! We cannot tell where we may go;
71 these animals can be very **capricious**. But we will go whether or
72 no; we have got a captain who is pretty wide-awake."

73 Our luggage was transported to the deck of the frigate
74 immediately. I hastened on board and asked for Commander
75 Farragut. One of the sailors conducted me to the deck, where I
76 found myself in the presence of a good-looking officer, who held
77 out his hand to me.

78 "Monsieur Pierre Aronnax?" said he.

79 "Himself," replied I. "Commander Farragut?"

80 "You are welcome, Professor; your cabin is ready for you."

81 I bowed, and desired to be conducted to the cabin destined for
82 me.

83 The Abraham Lincoln had been well chosen and equipped for
84 her new destination. She was a frigate of great speed, fitted
85 with high-pressure engines which admitted a pressure of seven
86 atmospheres. Under this the Abraham Lincoln attained the

87 mean speed of nearly eighteen knots and a third an hour—a
88 considerable speed, but, nevertheless, insufficient to grapple
89 with this gigantic cetacean.

90 The interior arrangements of the frigate corresponded to its
91 nautical qualities. I was well satisfied with my cabin, which was
92 in the after part, opening upon the gunroom.

93 "We shall be well off here," said I to Conseil.

94 "As well, by your honor's leave, as a hermit-crab in the shell of
95 a whelk[9]," said Conseil.

96 I left Conseil to stow our trunks conveniently away, and
97 remounted the poop in order to survey the preparations for
98 departure.

99   At that moment Commander Farragut was ordering the last
100 moorings to be cast loose which held the Abraham Lincoln to
101 the pier of Brooklyn. So in a quarter of an hour, perhaps less,
102 the frigate would have sailed without me. I should have missed
103 this extraordinary, supernatural, and incredible **expedition**, the
104 **recital** of which may well meet with some suspicion.

105 But Commander Farragut would not lose a day nor an hour in
106 **scouring** the seas in which the animal had been sighted. He sent
107 for the engineer.

108 "Is the steam full on?" asked he.

109 "Yes, sir," replied the engineer.

110 "Go ahead," cried Commander Farragut.

---

9   A type of predatory snail-mollusk with a spiral shell

Vocabulary Part 1 Chapter 3

purge, repose, fatiguing, longing, amiable, evincing, ceremonious, provoking, prolonged, evasively, capricious, recital, scouring

Questions for Part 1 Chapter 3

1. What is the main reason for the professor's change of heart? What do you think it says about the character of the professor?

   ____

   ____

2. How does the professor describe the character of Conseil?

   ____

   ____

3. Why does the professor feel obliged to tell Conseil about the true intentions of his detour?

   ____

   ____

4. The professor makes no mention of having a wife and children waiting for him at home. How does this fact seem to assist the storyline?

   ____

   ____

5. The author describes Conseil in line 25 as "quiet by nature, regular from principle," what does the last part of this phrase mean?

   ____

   ____

6. The author in lines 28-29, writes about Conseil's character, "and, despite his name, never giving advice—even when asked for it" what is the intended pun that the author makes?

   ____

   ____

7. The author writes in lines 88-90 "under this the Abraham Lincoln attained the mean speed of nearly eighteen knots and a third an hour—a considerable speed, but, nevertheless, insufficient to grapple with this gigantic cetacean." What is the meaning of the word "mean" here?

a. Angry,
b. explaining,
c. regular
d. average

Chapter 4

NED LAND
(abridged and amended)

Captain Farragut was a good seaman, worthy of the frigate he commanded. His vessel and he were one. He was the soul of it. On the question of the monster there was no doubt in his mind, and he would not allow the existence of the animal to be disputed on board. He believed in it, as certain good people believe in the leviathan[10]—by faith, not by reason. The monster did exist, and he had sworn to rid the seas of it. Either Captain Farragut would kill the narwhal, or the narwhal would kill the captain. There was no third course.

The officers on board shared the opinion of their chief. They were ever chatting, discussing, and calculating the various chances of a meeting, watching narrowly the vast surface of the ocean. More than one took up his quarters voluntarily in the cross-trees[11], who would have cursed such a **berth** under any other circumstances. As long as the sun described its daily course, the rigging was crowded with sailors, whose feet were burnt to such an extent by the heat of the deck as to **render** it unbearable; still the Abraham Lincoln had not yet entered the suspected waters of the Pacific. As to the ship's company, they desired nothing better than to meet the unicorn, to harpoon it, hoist it on board, and **dispatch** it. They watched the sea with eager attention.

Besides, Captain Farragut had spoken of a certain sum of two thousand dollars, set apart for whoever should first sight the monster, were he cabin-boy, common seaman, or officer.[12]

---

10   The Leviathan is the English word for the לויתן (the *Livyason*)-the giant fish mentioned at the end of sefer Iyov.

11   Two horizontal crosspieces of timber or metal that spread the upper shrouds of a ship in order to support the mast.

24 I leave you to judge how eyes were used on board the Abraham
25 Lincoln.

26 For my own part I was not behind the others, and, left to no one
27 my share of daily observations... Only one amongst us, Conseil,
28 seemed to protest by his indifference against the question which
29 so interested us all, and seemed to be out of keeping with the
30 general enthusiasm on board.

31 I have said that Captain Farragut had carefully provided his ship
32 with every **apparatus** for catching the gigantic cetacean. No
33 whaler had ever been better armed. We possessed every known
34 engine, from the harpoon thrown by the hand to the barbed arrows
35 of the blunderbuss, and the explosive balls of the duck-gun. On
36 the forecastle[13] lay the perfection of a breech-loading gun, very
37 thick at the breech[14], and very narrow in the bore[15], the model of
38 which had been in the Exhibition of 1867. This precious weapon
39 of American origin could throw with ease a conical **projectile** of
40 nine pounds to a mean distance of ten miles.

41 Thus, the Abraham Lincoln wanted for no means of destruction;
42 and, what was better still she had on board Ned Land, the prince
43 of harpooners.

44 Ned Land was a Canadian, with an uncommon quickness of
45 hand, and who knew no equal in his dangerous occupation. Skill,
46 coolness, **audacity**, and **cunning** he possessed in a superior
47 degree, and it must be a cunning whale to escape the stroke of
48 his harpoon.

49 Ned Land was about forty years of age; he was a tall man
50 (more than six feet high), strongly built, grave and **taciturn**,
51 occasionally violent, and very passionate when contradicted.
52 His person attracted attention, but above all the boldness of his
53 look, which gave a singular expression to his face.

---

13   the forward part of a ship below the deck, traditionally used as the
crew's living quarters.
14   The part of the cannon behind the bore
15   The hollow part of the cannon

54 Who calls himself Canadian calls himself French; and, little
55 communicative as Ned Land was, I must admit that he took a
56 certain liking for me. My nationality drew him to me, no doubt.
57 It was an opportunity for him to talk, and for me to hear, that
58 old language of Rabelais, which is still in use in some Canadian
59 provinces. The harpooner's family was originally from Quebec,
60 and was already a tribe of hardy fishermen when this town
61 belonged to France.

62 Little by little, Ned Land acquired a taste for chatting, and I loved
63 to hear the recital of his adventures in the polar seas. He related
64 his fishing, and his combats, with natural poetry of expression;
65 his recital took the form of an epic poem[16], and I seemed to be
66 listening to a Canadian Homer[17] singing the Iliad of the regions
67 of the North.

68 I am **portraying** this hardy companion as I really knew him.
69 We are old friends now, united in that unchangeable friendship
70 which is born and cemented amidst extreme dangers. Ah, brave
71 Ned! I ask no more than to live a hundred years longer, that I
72 may have more time to dwell the longer on your memory.

73 Now, what was Ned Land's opinion upon the question of the
74 marine monster? I must admit that he did not believe in the
75 unicorn, and was the only one on board who did not share that
76 universal conviction. He even avoided the subject, which I one
77 day thought it my duty to press upon him. One magnificent
78 evening, the 30th July (that is to say, three weeks after our
79 departure), the frigate was abreast of Cape Blanc, thirty miles
80 to leeward of the coast of Patagonia. We had crossed the tropic
81 of Capricorn, and the Straits of Magellan opened less than seven
82 hundred miles to the south. Before eight days were over the
83 Abraham Lincoln would be **ploughing** the waters of the Pacific.

84 Seated on the poop[18], Ned Land and I were chatting of one

16   An elaborate story about an adventure or important event
17   Famous Greek storyteller who told over in poetic fashion, epic
stories such as the Iliad and the Odyssey
18   Highest deck in a ship

85 thing and another as we looked at this mysterious sea, whose
86 great depths had up to this time been inaccessible to the eye of
87 man. I naturally led up the conversation to the giant unicorn,
88 and examined the various chances of success or failure of the
89 **expedition**. But, seeing that Ned Land let me speak without
90 saying too much himself, I pressed him more closely.

91 "Well, Ned," said I, "is it possible that you are not convinced of
92 the existence of this cetacean that we are following? Have you
93 any particular reason for being so **incredulous**?"

94 The harpooner looked at me **fixedly** for some moments before
95 answering, struck his broad forehead with his hand (a habit of
96 his), as if to collect himself, and said at last, "Perhaps I have, Mr.
97 Aronnax."

98 "But, Ned, you, a whaler by profession, familiarized with all the
99 great marine Mammalia[19]—YOU ought to be the last to doubt
100 under such circumstances!"

101 "That is just what deceives you, Professor," replied Ned. "As
102 a whaler I have followed many a cetacean, harpooned a great
103 number, and killed several; but, however strong or well-armed
104 they may have been, neither their tails nor their weapons would
105 have been able even to scratch the iron plates of a steamer."

106 "But, Ned, they tell of ships which the teeth of the narwhal have
107 pierced through and through."

108 "Wooden ships—that is possible," replied the Canadian, "but I
109 have never seen it done; and, until further proof, I deny that
110 whales, cetaceans, or sea-unicorns could ever produce the effect
111 you describe."

112 "Well, Ned, I repeat it with a conviction resting on the logic
113 of facts. I believe in the existence of a mammal power fully
114 organized, belonging to the branch of vertebrata, like the
115 whales, the cachalots, or the dolphins, and furnished with a horn
116 of defense of great penetrating power."

19   Mammals- branch of living creatures

117 "Hum!" said the harpooner, shaking his head with the air of a
118 man who would not be convinced.

119 "Notice one thing, my worthy Canadian," I resumed. "If such an
120 animal is in existence, if it inhabits the depths of the ocean, if it
121 frequents the strata[20] lying miles below the surface of the water,
122 it must necessarily possess an organization the strength of which
123 would defy all comparison."

124 "And why this powerful organization?" demanded Ned.

125 "Because it requires incalculable strength to keep one's self in
126 these **strata** and resist their pressure. Listen to me. Let us admit
127 that the pressure of the atmosphere is represented by the weight
128 of a column of water thirty-two feet high. In reality the column
129 of water would be shorter, as we are speaking of sea water, the
130 density of which is greater than that of fresh water. Very well,
131 when you dive, Ned, as many times 32 feet of water as there are
132 above you, so many times does your body bear a pressure equal
133 to that of the atmosphere, that is to say, 15 lb. for each square
134 inch of its surface. It follows, then, that at 320 feet this pressure
135 equals that of 10 atmospheres, of 100 atmospheres at 3,200 feet,
136 and of 1,000 atmospheres at 32,000 feet, that is, about 6 miles;
137 which is equivalent to saying that if you could attain this depth
138 in the ocean, each square three-eighths of an inch of the surface
139 of your body would bear a pressure of 5,600 lb. Ah! my brave
140 Ned, do you know how many square inches you carry on the
141 surface of your body?"

142 "I have no idea, Mr. Aronnax."

143 "About 6,500; and as in reality the atmospheric pressure is about
144 15 lb. to the square inch, your 6,500 square inches bear at this
145 moment a pressure of 97,500 lb."

146 "Without my **perceiving** it?"

147 "Without your perceiving it. And if you are not crushed by such
148 a pressure, it is because the air penetrates the interior of your

20   Levels, layers

149 body with equal pressure. Hence perfect equilibrium between
150 the interior and exterior pressure, which thus **neutralize** each
151 other, and which allows you to bear it without inconvenience.
152 But in the water it is another thing."

153 "Yes, I understand," replied Ned, becoming more **attentive**;
154 "because the water surrounds me, but does not penetrate."

155 "Precisely, Ned: so that at 32 feet beneath the surface of the
156 sea you would undergo a pressure of 97,500 lb.; at 320 feet, ten
157 times that pressure; at 3,200 feet, a hundred times that pressure;
158 lastly, at 32,000 feet, a thousand times that pressure would be
159 97,500,000 lb.—that is to say, that you would be flattened as if
160 you had been drawn from the plates of a hydraulic machine[21]!"

161 "The devil!" exclaimed Ned.

162 "Very well, my worthy harpooner, if some vertebrate, several
163 hundred yards long, and large in proportion, can maintain itself in
164 such depths—of those whose surface is represented by millions
165 of square inches, that is by tens of millions of pounds, we must
166 estimate the pressure they undergo. Consider, then, what must
167 be the resistance of their bony structure, and the strength of their
168 organization to withstand such pressure!"

169 "Why!" exclaimed Ned Land, "they must be made of iron plates
170 eight inches thick, like the armored frigates."

171 "As you say, Ned. And think what destruction such a mass
172 would cause, if hurled with the speed of an express train against
173 the hull of a vessel."

174 "Yes—certainly—perhaps," replied the Canadian, shaken by
175 these figures, but not yet willing to give in.

176 "Well, have I convinced you?"

177 "You have convinced me of one thing, sir, which is that, if such
178 animals do exist at the bottom of the seas, they must necessarily

---

21   A machine that uses liquid to do work

179   be as strong as you say.”

180   “But if they do not exist, mine obstinate harpooner, how explain
181   the accident to the Scotia?”

𝕭ocabulary for 𝕻art 1 chapter 4

berth, render, dispatch, apparatus, projectile, audacity, cunning, taciturn, portraying, ploughing, incredulous, fixedly, perceiving, neutralize, attentive, obstinate

Questions for Part 1 Chapter 4

1. In lines 5-6, what does the author say about the *Livyason* that reflects the author's opinion regarding those who believe in creatures found in the Torah?

   ____

   ____

2. In lines 13-15 the author writes how sailors willingly accepted to sit in the cross trees. Why did they sit there willingly?

   ____

   ____

3. What did Captain Farragut do to incentivize people to find the Narwhal? What did the people on the ship want more than anything else?

   ____

   ____

4. Name three items that the the ship is equipped with to fight and destroy this dangerous beast.

   ____

   ____

5. In line 41 what does the author mean when he writes: "Thus, the Abraham Lincoln wanted for no means of destruction..."

   ____

   ____

6. What was so special about Ned land? Why was he worth everything on board?

   ____

   ____

7. What does the author mean in line 54: "Who calls himself Canadian calls himself French"…

   ____

   ____

8. Based on lines 68-70: How do shared experiences of extreme danger cement friendships, and what does that say about the nature of friendship?

   ____

   ____

9. How does the fact that the giant sea creature must sustain enormous pressure (see lines 163-169) to live at such great depths prove the professor's point?

   ____

   ____

Chapter 5

AT A VENTURE

The voyage of the Abraham Lincoln was for a long time marked by no special incident. But one circumstance happened which showed the wonderful **dexterity** of Ned Land, and proved what confidence we might place in him.

The 30th of June, the frigate spoke some American whalers, from whom we learned that they knew nothing about the narwhal. But one of them, the captain of the Monroe, knowing that Ned Land had shipped on board the Abraham Lincoln, begged for his help in chasing a whale they had in sight. Commander Farragut, desirous of seeing Ned Land at work, gave him permission to go on board the Monroe. And fate served our Canadian so well that, instead of one whale, he harpooned two with a double blow, striking one straight to the heart, and catching the other after some minutes' pursuit.

Decidedly, if the monster ever had to do with Ned Land's harpoon, I would not bet in its **favor**.

The frigate skirted the south-east coast of America with great rapidity. The 3rd of July we were at the opening of the Straits of Magellan, level with Cape Vierges. But Commander Farragut would not take a **tortuous passage**, but doubled Cape Horn.

The ship's crew agreed with him. And certainly, it was possible that they might meet the narwhal in this narrow pass. Many of the sailors affirmed that the monster could not pass there, "that he was too big for that!"

The 6th of July, about three o'clock in the afternoon, the Abraham Lincoln, at fifteen miles to the south, doubled the **solitary** island, this lost rock at the extremity of the American continent, to which some Dutch sailors gave the name of their native town, Cape Horn. The course was taken towards the north-west, and the next day the screw of the frigate was at last

31 beating the waters of the Pacific.

32 "Keep your eyes open!" called out the sailors.

33 And they were opened widely. Both eyes and glasses, a little
34 **dazzled**, it is true, by the prospect of two thousand dollars, had
35 not an instant's repose.

36 I myself, for whom money had no charms, was not the least
37 **attentive** on board. Giving but few minutes to my meals, but a
38 few hours to sleep, **indifferent** to either rain or sunshine, I did
39 not leave the poop of the vessel. Now leaning on the netting of
40 the forecastle, now on the taffrail[22], I **devoured** with eagerness
41 the soft foam which whitened the sea as far as the eye could
42 reach; and how often have I shared the emotion of the majority
43 of the crew, when some **capricious** whale raised its black back
44 above the waves! The poop of the vessel was crowded on a
45 moment. The cabins poured forth a torrent of sailors and officers,
46 each with heaving chest and troubled eye watching the course of
47 the cetacean. I looked and looked till I was nearly blind, whilst
48 Conseil kept repeating in a calm voice:

49 "If, sir, you would not squint so much, you would see better!"

50 But vain excitement! The Abraham Lincoln checked its speed
51 and made for the animal signaled, a simple whale, or common
52 cachalot, which soon disappeared amidst a storm of abuse.

53 But the weather was good. The voyage was being accomplished
54 under the most favorable auspices. It was then the bad season
55 in Australia, the July of that zone corresponding to our January
56 in Europe, but the sea was beautiful and easily scanned round a
57 vast circumference.

58 The 20th of July, the tropic of Capricorn was cut by 105d of
59 longitude, and the 27th of the same month we crossed the
60 Equator on the 110th meridian. This passed, the frigate took
61 a more decided westerly direction, and scoured the central
62 waters of the Pacific. Commander Farragut thought, and with

22   a rail and ornamentation around a ship's stern (rear)

63 reason, that it was better to remain in deep water, and keep
64 clear of continents or islands, which the beast itself seemed to
65 shun (perhaps because there was not enough water for him!
66 suggested the greater part of the crew). The frigate passed at
67 some distance from the Marquesas and the Sandwich Islands,
68 crossed the tropic of Cancer, and made for the China Seas. We
69 were on the **theatre** of the last **diversions** of the monster: and, to
70 say truth, we no longer LIVED on board. The entire ship's crew
71 were undergoing a nervous excitement, of which I can give no
72 idea: they could not eat, they could not sleep—twenty times a
73 day, a misconception or an optical illusion of some sailor seated
74 on the taffrail, would cause **dreadful perspirations**, and these
75 emotions, twenty times repeated, kept us in a state of excitement
76 so violent that a reaction was **unavoidable**.

77 And truly, reaction soon showed itself. For three months, during
78 which a day seemed an age, the Abraham Lincoln **furrowed** all
79 the waters of the Northern Pacific, running at whales, making
80 sharp **deviations** from her course, **veering** suddenly from
81 one tack to another, stopping suddenly, putting on steam, and
82 backing ever and **anon** at the risk of deranging her machinery,
83 and not one point of the Japanese or American coast was left
84 unexplored.

85 The warmest **partisans** of the **enterprise** now became its most
86 **ardent detractors**. Reaction mounted from the crew to the
87 captain himself, and certainly, had it not been for the resolute
88 determination on the part of Captain Farragut, the frigate would
89 have headed due southward. This useless search could not last
90 much longer. The Abraham Lincoln had nothing to **reproach**
91 herself with, she had done her best to succeed. Never had an
92 American ship's crew shown more **zeal** or patience; its failure
93 could not be placed to their charge—there remained nothing but
94 to return.

95 This was represented to the commander. The sailors could not
96 hide their **discontent**, and the service suffered. I will not say
97 there was a mutiny[23] on board, but after a reasonable period of
   23   An open rebellion among solders especially sailors

98 **obstinacy**, Captain Farragut (as Columbus did) asked for three
99 days' patience. If in three days the monster did not appear, the
100 man at the helm should give three turns of the wheel, and the
101 Abraham Lincoln would make for the European seas.

102 This promise was made on the 2nd of November. It had the
103 effect of rallying the ship's crew. The ocean was watched with
104 renewed attention. Each one wished for a last glance in which
105 to sum up his remembrance. Glasses were used with feverish
106 activity. It was a grand defiance given to the giant narwhal, and
107 he could scarcely fail to answer the summons and "appear."

108 Two days passed, the steam was at half pressure; a thousand
109 **schemes** were tried to attract the attention and stimulate the
110 **apathy** of the animal in case it should be met in those parts.
111 Large quantities of bacon were trailed in the wake of the ship,
112 to the great satisfaction (I must say) of the sharks. Small craft
113 radiated in all directions round the Abraham Lincoln as she lay
114 to, and did not leave a spot of the sea unexplored. But the night
115 of the 4th of November arrived without the unveiling of this
116 submarine mystery.

117 The next day, the 5th of November, at twelve, the delay would
118 (morally speaking) expire; after that time, Commander Farragut,
119 faithful to his promise, was to turn the course to the south-east
120 and abandon for ever the northern regions of the Pacific.

121 The frigate was then in 31° 15' N. lat. and 136° 42' E. long.
122 The coast of Japan still remained less than two hundred miles
123 to leeward. Night was approaching. They had just struck eight
124 bells; large clouds veiled the face of the moon, then in its first
125 quarter. The sea undulated peaceably under the stern of the
126 vessel.

127 At that moment I was leaning forward on the starboard netting.
128 Conseil, standing near me, was looking straight before him.
129 The crew, perched in the ratlines[24], examined the horizon which

---

24   Ratlines (pronounced "rattlins") are lengths of thin line tied
between the shrouds of a sailing ship to form a ladder.

130 contracted and darkened by degrees. Officers with their night
131 glasses scoured the growing darkness: sometimes the ocean
132 sparkled under the rays of the moon, which darted between two
133 clouds, then all trace of light was lost in the darkness.

134 In looking at Conseil, I could see he was undergoing a little of
135 the general influence. At least I thought so. Perhaps for the first
136 time his nerves vibrated to a sentiment of curiosity.

137 "Come, Conseil," said I, "this is the last chance of pocketing the
138 two thousand dollars."

139 "May I be permitted to say, sir," replied Conseil, "that I never
140 reckoned on getting the prize; and, had the government of the
141 Union offered a hundred thousand dollars, it would have been
142 none the poorer."

143 "You are right, Conseil. It is a foolish affair after all, and one
144 upon which we entered too lightly. What time lost, what useless
145 emotions! We should have been back in France six months ago."

146 "In your little room, sir," replied Conseil, "and in your museum,
147 sir; and I should have already classed all your fossils, sir. And
148 the Babiroussa would have been installed in its cage in the
149 Jardin des Plantes, and have drawn all the curious people of the
150 capital!"

151 "As you say, Conseil. I fancy we shall run a fair chance of being
152 laughed at for our pains."

153 "That's tolerably certain," replied Conseil, quietly; "I think they
154 will make fun of you, sir. And, must I say it——?"

155 "Go on, my good friend."

156 "Well, sir, you will only get your deserts."

157 "Indeed!"

158 "When one has the honor of being a ***savant***[25] as you are, sir, one
____
25   a learned person, especially a distinguished scientist

159   should not expose one's self to———"

160   Conseil had not time to finish his compliment. In the midst of
161   general silence a voice had just been heard. It was the voice of
162   Ned Land shouting:

163   "Look out there! The very thing we are looking for—on our
164   weather beam!"

Vocabulary Part 1 chapter 5

dexterity, favor, tortuous, passage, solitary, dazzled, indifferent, devoured, theatre, diversions, dreadful, perspirations, unavoidable, deviations veering, anon, enterprise, ardent, detractors, reproach, zeal, discontent, obstinacy, schemes, apathy apathy

Questions for part 1 chapter 5

1. In line 47, the author states "I looked and looked till I was nearly blind"… The use of the word "blind" is
   a.   Metaphor
   b.   Simile
   c.   Exaggeration,
   d.   Personification

2. Why do you think the word "LIVED" on line 70 is in all caps?

   ____

   ____

3. What happens when the ship goes to the China Sea, and what happens to the nerves of the crew?

   ____

   ____

4. "Hope drawn out causes heart disease" is a *pasuk* found in Mishlai (13:12). How would that idea apply to those hoping to catch a glimpse of the sea monster?

   ____

   ____

5. "In lines 134-136, the author writes: "In looking at Conseil, I could see he was undergoing a little of the general influence. At least I thought so. Perhaps for the first time his nerves vibrated to a sentiment of curiosity." What does it mean that "perhaps for the first time" curiosity had provoked Conseil, and what does it say about Conseil's character? How does his name sort of fit his personality?

   ____

   ____

6. In the last few sentences of this chapter-what do you
    think Conseil was about to tell the professor before he
    was cut off by the sighting of "the beast"?

    ____

    ____

7. Who discovered the "thing" in line 114 and why was it
    appropriate that he was the one to discover it?

    ____

    ____

Chapter 6

AT FULL STEAM

At this cry the whole ship's crew hurried towards the harpooner—commander, officers, masters, sailors, cabin boys; even the engineers left their engines, and the stokers their furnaces.

The order to stop her had been given, and the frigate now simply went on by her own **momentum**. The darkness was then profound, and, however good the Canadian's eyes were, I asked myself how he had managed to see, and what he had been able to see. My heart beat as if it would break. But Ned Land was not mistaken, and we all perceived the object he pointed to. At two cables' length from the Abraham Lincoln, on the starboard[1] quarter, the sea seemed to be illuminated all over. It was not a mere phosphoric phenomenon. The monster emerged some fathoms from the water, and then threw out that very intense but mysterious light mentioned in the report of several captains. This magnificent **irradiation** must have been produced by an agent of great SHINING power. The luminous part traced on the sea an immense **oval**, much **elongated**, the center of which **condensed** a burning heat, whose overpowering brilliancy died out by **successive gradations**.

"It is only a **massing** of phosphoric particles[2]," cried one of the officers.

"No, sir, certainly not," I replied. "That brightness is of an essentially electrical nature. Besides, see, see! it moves; it is moving forwards, backwards; it is darting towards us!"

A general cry arose from the frigate.

---

1   the side of a ship or aircraft that is on the right when one is facing forward. The opposite of port

2   Particles that naturally light up

27 "Silence!" said the captain. "Up with the helm, reverse the
28 engines."

29 The steam was shut off, and the Abraham Lincoln, beating to
30 port, described a semicircle.

31 "Right the helm, go ahead," cried the captain.

32 These orders were executed, and the frigate moved rapidly from
33 the burning light.

34 I was mistaken. She tried to **sheer** off, but the supernatural
35 animal approached with a **velocity** double her own.

36 We gasped for breath. **Stupefaction** more than fear made us
37 dumb and motionless. The animal gained on us, sporting with
38 the waves. It made the round of the frigate, which was then
39 making fourteen knots, and enveloped it with its electric rings
40 like luminous dust.

41 Then it moved away two or three miles, leaving a phosphorescent
42 track, like those volumes of steam that the express trains leave
43 behind. All at once from the dark line of the horizon whither
44 it retired to gain its **momentum**, the monster rushed suddenly
45 towards the Abraham Lincoln with alarming rapidity, stopped
46 suddenly about twenty feet from the hull, and died out—not
47 diving under the water, for its brilliancy did not **abate**—but
48 suddenly, and as if the source of this brilliant **emanation** was
49 exhausted. Then it reappeared on the other side of the vessel,
50 as if it had turned and slid under the hull. Any moment a
51 collision might have occurred which would have been fatal to
52 us. However, I was astonished at the **maneuvers** of the frigate.
53 She fled and did not attack.

54 On the captain's face, generally so impassive, was an expression
55 of **unaccountable** astonishment.

56 "Mr. Aronnax," he said, "I do not know with what formidable
57 being I have to deal, and I will not **imprudently** risk my frigate
58 in the midst of this darkness. Besides, how attack this unknown

59 thing, how defend one's self from it? Wait for daylight, and the
60 scene will change."

61 "You have no further doubt, captain, of the nature of the animal?"

62 "No, sir; it is evidently a gigantic narwhal, and an electric one."

63 "Perhaps," added I, "one can only approach it with a torpedo."

64 "Undoubtedly," replied the captain, "if it possesses such dreadful
65 power, it is the most terrible animal that ever was created. That
66 is why, sir, I must be on my guard."

67 The crew were on their feet all night. No one thought of sleep.
68 The Abraham Lincoln, not being able to struggle with such
69 velocity, had moderated its pace, and sailed at half speed. For its
70 part, the narwhal, imitating the frigate, let the waves rock it at
71 will, and seemed decided not to leave the scene of the struggle.
72 Towards midnight, however, it disappeared, or, to use a more
73 appropriate term, it "died out" like a large glow-worm. Had it
74 fled? One could only fear, not hope it. But at seven minutes to
75 one o'clock in the morning a deafening whistling was heard, like
76 that produced by a body of water rushing with great violence.

77 The captain, Ned Land, and I were then on the poop, eagerly
78 peering through the profound darkness.

79 "Ned Land," asked the commander, "you have often heard the
80 roaring of whales?"

81 "Often, sir; but never such whales the sight of which brought
82 me in two thousand dollars. If I can only approach within four
83 harpoons' length of it!"

84 "But to approach it," said the commander, "I ought to put a
85 whaler at your disposal?"

86 "Certainly, sir."

87 "That will be **trifling** with the lives of my men."

88   "And mine too," simply said the harpooner.

89   Towards two o'clock in the morning, the burning light reappeared,
90   not less intense, about five miles to windward of the Abraham
91   Lincoln. Notwithstanding the distance, and the noise of the wind
92   and sea, one heard distinctly the loud strokes of the animal's tail,
93   and even its panting breath. It seemed that, at the moment that
94   the enormous narwhal had come to take breath at the surface of
95   the water, the air was engulfed in its lungs, like the steam in the
96   vast cylinders of a machine of two thousand horse-power.

97   "Hum!" thought I, "a whale with the strength of a cavalry
98   regiment would be a pretty whale!"

99   We were on the qui vive[3] till daylight, and prepared for the
100 combat. The fishing implements were laid along the hammock
101 nettings. The second lieutenant loaded the blunder busses, which
102 could throw harpoons to the distance of a mile, and long duck-
103 guns, with explosive bullets, which inflicted mortal wounds
104 even to the most terrible animals. Ned Land **contented** himself
105 with sharpening his harpoon—a terrible weapon in his hands.

106 At six o'clock day began to break; and, with the first glimmer
107 of light, the electric light of the narwhal disappeared. At seven
108 o'clock the day was sufficiently advanced, but a very thick sea
109 fog obscured our view, and the best spy glasses could not pierce
110 it. That caused disappointment and anger.

111 I climbed the mizzen-mast. Some officers were already perched
112 on the mast-heads. At eight o'clock the fog lay heavily on the
113 waves, and its thick scrolls rose little by little. The horizon grew
114 wider and clearer at the same time. Suddenly, just as on the day
115 before, Ned Land's voice was heard:

116 "The thing itself on the port quarter!" cried the harpooner.

117 Every eye was turned towards the point indicated. There, a
118 mile and a half from the frigate, a long blackish body emerged
119 a yard above the waves. Its tail, violently agitated, produced

3   On the alert or lookout

120 a considerable eddy[4]. Never did a tail beat the sea with such
121 violence. An immense track, of dazzling whiteness, marked the
122 passage of the animal, and described a long curve.

123 The frigate approached the cetacean. I examined it thoroughly.

124 The reports of the Shannon and of the Helvetia had rather
125 exaggerated its size, and I estimated its length at only two
126 hundred and fifty feet. As to its dimensions, I could only
127 conjecture them to be admirably **proportioned**. While I watched
128 this phenomenon, two jets of steam and water were ejected from
129 its vents, and rose to the height of 120 feet; thus I ascertained its
130 way of breathing. I concluded definitely that it belonged to the
131 vertebrate branch, class mammalia.

132 The crew waited impatiently for their chief's orders. The latter,
133 after having observed the animal attentively, called the engineer.
134 The engineer ran to him.

135 "Sir," said the commander, "you have steam up?"

136 "Yes, sir," answered the engineer.

137 "Well, make up your fires and put on all steam."

138 Three hurrahs greeted this order. The time for the struggle had
139 arrived. Some moments after, the two funnels of the frigate
140 vomited torrents of black smoke, and the bridge quaked under
141 the trembling of the boilers.

142 The Abraham Lincoln, propelled by her wonderful screw, went
143 straight at the animal. The latter allowed it to come within half a
144 cable's length; then, as if disdaining to dive, it took a little turn,
145 and stopped a short distance off.

146 This pursuit lasted nearly three-quarters of an hour, without the
147 frigate gaining two yards on the cetacean. It was quite evident
148 that at that rate we should never come up with it.

149 "Well, Mr. Land," asked the captain, "do you advise me to put

4   A swirling of water

150   the boats out to sea?"

151   "No, sir," replied Ned Land; "because we shall not take that
152   beast easily."

153   "What shall we do then?"

154   "Put on more steam if you can, sir. With your leave, I mean to
155   post myself under the bowsprit, and, if we get within harpooning
156   distance, I shall throw my harpoon."

157   "Go, Ned," said the captain. "Engineer, put on more pressure."

158   Ned Land went to his post. The fires were increased, the screw
159   revolved forty-three times a minute, and the steam poured out of
160   the valves. We heaved the log[5], and calculated that the Abraham
161   Lincoln was going at the rate of 18 1/2 miles an hour.

162   But the accursed animal swam at the same speed.

163   For a whole hour the frigate kept up this pace, without gaining
164   six feet. It was humiliating for one of the swiftest sailers in the
165   American navy. A stubborn anger seized the crew; the sailors
166   abused the monster, who, as before, **disdained** to answer them;
167   the captain no longer contented himself with twisting his beard—
168   he **gnawed** it.

169   The engineer was called again.

170   "You have turned full steam on?"

171   "Yes, sir," replied the engineer.

172   The speed of the Abraham Lincoln increased. Its masts trembled
173   down to their stepping holes, and the clouds of smoke could
174   hardly find way out of the narrow funnels.

175   They heaved the log a second time.

176   "Well?" asked the captain of the man at the wheel.

---

5   To figure out a ship's speed using a device

177   "Nineteen miles and three-tenths, sir."

178   "Clap on more steam."

179   The engineer obeyed. The manometer showed ten degrees. But
180   the cetacean grew warm itself, no doubt; for without straining
181   itself, it made 19 3/10 miles.

182   What a pursuit! No, I cannot describe the emotion that vibrated
183   through me. Ned Land kept his post, harpoon in hand. Several
184   times the animal let us gain upon it.—"We shall catch it! we
185   shall catch it!" cried the Canadian. But just as he was going to
186   strike, the cetacean stole away with a rapidity that could not be
187   estimated at less than thirty miles an hour, and even during our
188   maximum of speed, it **bullied** the frigate, going round and round
189   it. A cry of fury broke from everyone!

190   At noon we were no further advanced than at eight o'clock in
191   the morning.

192   The captain then decided to take more direct means.

193   "Ah!" said he, "that animal goes quicker than the Abraham
194   Lincoln. Very well! we will see whether it will escape these
195   conical bullets. Send your men to the forecastle, sir."

196   The forecastle gun was immediately loaded and **slewed** round.
197   But the shot passed some feet above the cetacean, which was
198   half a mile off.

199   "Another, more to the right," cried the commander, "and five
200   dollars to whoever will hit that **infernal** beast."

201   An old gunner with a grey beard—that I can see now—with
202   steady eye and grave face, went up to the gun and took a long
203   aim. A loud report was heard, with which were mingled the
204   cheers of the crew.

205   The bullet did its work; it hit the animal, and, sliding off the
206   rounded surface, was lost in two miles depth of sea.

207 The chase began again, and the captain, leaning towards me,
208 said:

209 "I will pursue that beast till my frigate bursts up."

210 "Yes," answered I; "and you will be quite right to do it."

211 I wished the beast would exhaust itself, and not be **insensible** to
212 fatigue like a steam engine. But it was of no use. Hours passed,
213 without its showing any signs of exhaustion.

214 However, it must be said in praise of the Abraham Lincoln that
215 she struggled on indefatigably[6]. I cannot reckon the distance
216 she made under three hundred miles during this unlucky day,
217 November the 6th. But night came on, and **overshadowed** the
218 rough ocean.

219 Now I thought our expedition was at an end, and that we should
220 never again see the extraordinary animal. I was mistaken. At ten
221 minutes to eleven in the evening, the electric light reappeared
222 three miles to windward of the frigate, as pure, as intense as
223 during the **preceding** night.

224 The narwhal seemed motionless; perhaps, tired with its day's
225 work, it slept, letting itself float with the undulation of the
226 waves. Now was a chance of which the captain resolved to take
227 advantage.

228 He gave his orders. The Abraham Lincoln kept up half steam,
229 and advanced cautiously so as not to awake its adversary. It is
230 no rare thing to meet in the middle of the ocean whales so sound
231 asleep that they can be successfully attacked, and Ned Land had
232 harpooned more than one during its sleep. The Canadian went to
233 take his place again under the bowsprit.

234 The frigate approached noiselessly, stopped at two cables' lengths
235 from the animal, and following its track. No one breathed; a
236 deep silence reigned on the bridge. We were not a hundred feet
237 from the burning focus, the light of which increased and dazzled
238 our eyes.

---

6   Not tiring

At this moment, leaning on the forecastle bulwark, I saw below me Ned Land grappling the martingale in one hand, brandishing his terrible harpoon in the other, scarcely twenty feet from the motionless animal. Suddenly his arm straightened, and the harpoon was thrown; I heard the sonorous stroke of the weapon, which seemed to have struck a hard body. The electric light went out suddenly, and two enormous waterspouts broke over the bridge of the frigate, rushing like a torrent from stem to stern, overthrowing men, and breaking the lashings of the spars. A fearful shock followed, and, thrown over the rail without having time to stop myself, I fell into the sea.

Vocabulary Part 1 Ch. 6

momentum, irradiation, oval, elongated, condensed, gradations, massing, sheer, velocity, Stupefaction, abate, emanation, maneuvers, unaccountable, trifling, proportioned, disdained, gnawed, bullied, slewed, infernal, insensible, overshadowed, preceding

Questions for part 1 chapter 6

1. In lines 52-55 it states: "However, I was astonished at the maneuvers of the frigate. She fled and did not attack. On the captain's face, generally so impassive, was an expression of unaccountable astonishment." How does the commander seem to lose his nerve, and how does that contrast with the author's description of him in previous chapters?

   ____

2. What is the intent of Ned Land when he says in line 88 "And mine too…"?

   ____

3. In lines 167-168, what does the gnawing of the captain's beard indicate about the captain's state of mind?

   ____

4. What does the Professor still think about "the thing" at the end of the chapter?

   ____

5. What happens to the Professor at the end of this chapter and how do you think it happened?

   ____

Chapter 7

AN UNKNOWN
SPECIES OF WHALE

1 **This unexpected fall** so stunned me that I have no clear
2 recollection of my **sensations** at the time. I was at first drawn
3 down to a depth of about twenty feet. I am a good swimmer
4 (though without pretending to rival Byron or Edgar Poe, who
5 were masters of the art), and in that plunge I did not lose my
6 presence of mind. Two **vigorous** strokes brought me to the
7 surface of the water. My first care was to look for the frigate.
8 Had the crew seen me disappear? Had the Abraham Lincoln
9 **veered** round? Would the captain put out a boat? Might I hope
10 to be saved?

11 The darkness was intense. I caught a glimpse of a black mass
12 disappearing in the east, its **beacon** lights dying out in the
13 distance. It was the frigate! I was lost.

14 "Help, help!" I shouted, swimming towards the Abraham
15 Lincoln in desperation.

16 My clothes **encumbered** me; they seemed glued to my body,
17 and paralyzed my movements.

18 I was sinking! I was suffocating!

19 "Help!"

20 This was my last cry. My mouth filled with water; I struggled
21 against being drawn down the **abyss**. Suddenly my clothes were
22 seized by a strong hand, and I felt myself quickly drawn up
23 to the surface of the sea; and I heard, yes, I heard these words
24 pronounced in my ear:

25 "If master would be so good as to lean on my shoulder, master
26 would swim with much greater ease."

27 I seized with one hand my faithful Conseil's arm.

28 "Is it you?" said I, "you?"

29 "Myself," answered Conseil; "and waiting master's orders."

30 "That shock threw you as well as me into the sea?"

31 "No; but, being in my master's service, I followed him."

32 The worthy fellow thought that was but natural.

33 "And the frigate?" I asked.

34 "The frigate?" replied Conseil, turning on his back; "I think that
35 master had better not count too much on her."

36 "You think so?"

37 "I say that, at the time I threw myself into the sea, I heard the
38 men at the wheel say, 'The screw and the rudder are broken.'

39 "Broken?"

40 "Yes, broken by the monster's teeth. It is the only injury the
41 Abraham Lincoln has sustained. But it is a bad look-out for us—
42 she no longer answers her helm."

43 "Then we are lost!"

44 "Perhaps so," calmly answered Conseil. "However, we have still
45 several hours before us, and one can do a good deal in some
46 hours."

47 Conseil's **imperturbable** coolness set me up again. I swam
48 more vigorously; but, cramped by my clothes, which stuck to
49 me like a **leaden** weight, I felt great difficulty in **bearing** up.
50 Conseil saw this.

51 "Will master let me make a **slit**?" said he; and, slipping an open
52 knife under my clothes, he ripped them up from top to bottom
53 very rapidly. Then he cleverly slipped them off me, while I swam
54 for both of us.

55   Then I did the same for Conseil, and we continued to swim near
56   to each other.

57   Nevertheless, our situation was no less terrible. Perhaps our
58   disappearance had not been noticed; and, if it had been, the
59   frigate could not tack[7], being without its helm. Conseil argued on
60   this **supposition**, and laid his plans accordingly. This quiet boy
61   was perfectly self-possessed. We then decided that, as our only
62   chance of safety was being picked up by the Abraham Lincoln's
63   boats, we ought to manage so as to wait for them as long as
64   possible. I resolved then to **husband** our strength, so that both
65   should not be exhausted at the same time; and this is how we
66   managed: while one of us lay on our back, quite still, with arms
67   crossed, and legs stretched out, the other would swim and push
68   the other on in front. This towing business did not last more than
69   ten minutes each; and **relieving** each other thus, we could swim
70   on for some hours, perhaps till day-break. Poor chance! but hope
71   is so firmly **rooted** in the heart of man! Moreover, there were
72   two of us. Indeed I declare (though it may seem **improbable**) if
73   I sought to destroy all hope—if I wished to despair, I could not.

74   The collision of the frigate with the cetacean had occurred about
75   eleven o'clock in the evening before. I **reckoned** then we should
76   have eight hours to swim before sunrise, an operation quite
77   practicable if we relieved each other. The sea, very calm, was
78   in our favor. Sometimes I tried to pierce the intense darkness
79   that was only dispelled by the phosphorescence caused by our
80   movements. I watched the **luminous** waves that broke over my
81   hand, whose mirror-like surface was spotted with silvery rings.
82   One might have said that we were in a bath of quicksilver.

83   Near one o'clock in the morning, I was seized with dreadful
84   **fatigue**. My limbs stiffened under the strain of violent cramp.
85   Conseil was obliged to keep me up, and our preservation
86   **devolved** on him alone. I heard the poor boy pant; his breathing
87   became short and hurried. I found that he could not keep up
88   much longer.

---

7   Turn around

89 "Leave me! leave me!" I said to him.

90 "Leave my master? Never!" replied he. "I would drown first."

91 Just then the moon appeared through the fringes of a thick cloud
92 that the wind was driving to the east. The surface of the sea
93 glittered with its rays. This kindly light reanimated us. My head
94 got better again. I looked at all points of the horizon. I saw the
95 frigate! She was five miles from us, and looked like a dark mass,
96 hardly **discernible**. But no boats!

97 I would have cried out. But what good would it have been at such
98 a distance! My swollen lips could utter no sounds. Conseil could
99 **articulate** some words, and I heard him repeat at **intervals**,
100 "Help! help!"

101 Our movements were suspended for an instant; we listened. It
102 might be only a singing in the ear, but it seemed to me as if a cry
103 answered the cry from Conseil.

104 "Did you hear?" I murmured.

105 "Yes! Yes!"

106 And Conseil gave one more **despairing** cry.

107 This time there was no mistake! A human voice responded to
108 ours! Was it the voice of another unfortunate creature, abandoned
109 in the middle of the ocean, some other victim of the shock
110 sustained by the vessel? Or rather was it a boat from the frigate,
111 that was hailing us in the darkness?

112 Conseil made a last effort, and, leaning on my shoulder, while I
113 struck out in a desperate effort, he raised himself half out of the
114 water, then fell back exhausted.

115 "What did you see?"

116 "I saw——" murmured he; "I saw—but do not talk—reserve all
117 your strength!"

What had he seen? Then, I know not why, the thought of the monster came into my head for the first time! But that voice! The time is past for Jonahs to take refuge in whales' bellies! However, Conseil was towing me again. He raised his head sometimes, looked before us, and uttered a cry of recognition, which was responded to by a voice that came nearer and nearer. I scarcely heard it. My strength was exhausted; my fingers stiffened; my hand afforded me support no longer; my mouth, **convulsively** opening, filled with salt water. Cold crept over me. I raised my head for the last time, then I sank.

At this moment a hard body struck me. I clung to it: then I felt that I was being drawn up, that I was brought to the surface of the water, that my chest collapsed—I fainted.

It is certain that I soon came to, thanks to the vigorous rubbings that I received. I half opened my eyes.

"Conseil!" I murmured.

"Does master call me?" asked Conseil.

Just then, by the waning light of the moon which was sinking down to the horizon, I saw a face which was not Conseil's and which I immediately recognized.

"Ned!" I cried.

"The same, sir, who is seeking his prize!" replied the Canadian.

"Were you thrown into the sea by the shock to the frigate?"

"Yes, Professor; but more fortunate than you, I was able to find a footing almost directly upon a floating island."

"An island?"

"Or, more correctly speaking, on our gigantic narwhal."

"Explain yourself, Ned!"

146 "Only I soon found out why my harpoon had not entered its skin
147 and was blunted."

148 "Why, Ned, why?"

149 "Because, Professor, that beast is made of sheet iron."

150 The Canadian's last words produced a sudden revolution in my
151 brain. I wriggled myself quickly to the top of the being, or object,
152 half out of the water, which served us for a refuge. I kicked it.
153 It was evidently a hard, impenetrable body, and not the soft
154 substance that forms the bodies of the great marine mammalia.
155 But this hard body might be a bony covering, like that of the
156 antediluvian [8]animals; and I should be free to class this monster
157 among amphibious reptiles, such as tortoises or alligators.

158 Well, no! the blackish back that supported me was smooth,
159 polished, without scales. The blow produced a metallic sound;
160 and, incredible though it may be, it seemed, I might say, as if it
161 was made of riveted plates.

162 There was no doubt about it! This monster, this natural
163 phenomenon that had puzzled the learned world, and over thrown
164 and misled the imagination of seamen of both hemispheres,
165 it must be owned was a still more astonishing phenomenon,
166 **inasmuch** as it was a simply human construction.

167 We had no time to lose, however. We were lying upon the back
168 of a sort of submarine boat, which appeared (as far as I could
169 judge) like a huge fish of steel. Ned Land's mind was made up
170 on this point. Conseil and I could only agree with him.

171 Just then a bubbling began at the back of this strange thing (which
172 was evidently propelled by a screw), and it began to move. We
173 had only just time to seize hold of the upper part, which rose
174 about seven feet out of the water, and happily its speed was not
175 great.

176 "As long as it sails horizontally," muttered Ned Land, "I do not

---

8   Belonging to the period of time prior to the *mabul*

177 mind; but, if it takes a fancy to dive, I would not give two straws
178 for my life."

179 The Canadian might have said still less. It became really
180 necessary to communicate with the beings, whatever they were,
181 shut up inside the machine. I searched all over the outside for an
182 **aperture**, a panel, or a manhole, to use a technical expression;
183 but the lines of the iron rivets, solidly driven into the joints
184 of the iron plates, were clear and uniform. Besides, the moon
185 disappeared then, and left us in total darkness.

186 At last this long night passed. My **indistinct** remembrance
187 prevents my describing all the impressions it made. I can only
188 recall one circumstance. During some lulls of the wind and sea,
189 I fancied I heard several times vague sounds, a sort of fugitive
190 harmony produced by words of command. What was, then,
191 the mystery of this submarine craft, of which the whole world
192 **vainly** sought an explanation? What kind of beings existed in
193 this strange boat? What mechanical agent caused its **prodigious**
194 speed?

195 Daybreak appeared. The morning mists surrounded us, but they
196 soon cleared off. I was about to examine the hull, which formed
197 on deck a kind of horizontal platform, when I felt it gradually
198 sinking.

199 "Oh! **confound** it!" cried Ned Land, kicking the resounding
200 plate. "Open, you **inhospitable** rascals!"

201 Happily the sinking movement ceased. Suddenly a noise, like
202 iron works violently pushed aside, came from the interior of the
203 boat. One iron plate was moved, a man appeared, uttered an odd
204 cry, and disappeared immediately.

205 Some moments after, eight strong men, with masked faces,
206 appeared noiselessly, and drew us down into their **formidable**
207 machine.

Vocabulary part 1 Ch. 7

sensations, vigorous, veered, beacon, encumbered, abyss,
imperturbable, leaden, bearing, husband, relieving, rooted,
improbable, reckoned, luminous, fatigue, devolved, discernible,
articulate, intervals, despairing, convulsively, inasmuch, aperture,
indistinct, vainly, confound, inhospitable, devoured

Questions for part 1 chapter 7

1. In lines 25-26 it states: "If master would be so good
    as to lean on my shoulder, master would swim with
    much greater ease." What do you notice about Conseil's
    manner in which he addresses his master, and what does
    it say about the respect he has for him?

2. In line 120 it states, "The time is past for Jonahs to take
    refuge in whales' bellies!" What is the meaning of this
    statement?

3. Name three other character traits that Conseil shows
    us in this chapter which are admirable to some degree.
    Where do you see it, and are they always admirable
    according to the Torah?

Chapter 8

MOBILIS IN MOBILI

1 **This forcible abduction**[9], so roughly carried out, was
2 accomplished with the **rapidity** of lightning. I shivered all over.
3 Whom had we to deal with? No doubt some new sort of pirates,
4 who explored the sea in their own way. Hardly had the narrow
5 panel closed upon me, when I was enveloped in darkness. My
6 eyes, dazzled with the outer light, could distinguish nothing. I
7 felt my..feet cling to the rungs of an iron ladder. Ned Land and
8 Conseil, firmly seized, followed me. At the bottom of the ladder,
9 a door opened, and shut after us immediately with a bang.

10 We were alone. Where, I could not say, hardly imagine. All was
11 black, and such a dense black that, after some minutes, my eyes
12 had not been able to discern[10] even the faintest glimmer.

13 Meanwhile, Ned Land, furious at these **proceedings**, gave free
14 **vent** to his **indignation**.

15 "**Confound** it!" cried he, "here are people who come up to the
16 Scotch for hospitality. They only just miss being cannibals. I
17 should not be surprised at it, but I declare that they shall not eat
18 me without my protesting."

19 "Calm yourself, friend Ned, calm yourself," replied Conseil,
20 quietly. "Do not cry out before you are hurt. We are not quite
21 done for yet."

22 "Not quite," sharply replied the Canadian, "but pretty near, at
23 all events. Things look black. Happily, my bowie knife I have
24 still, and I can always see well enough to use it. The first of these
25 pirates who lays a hand on me——"

26 "Do not excite yourself, Ned," I said to the harpooner, "and do
27 not **compromise** us by useless violence. Who knows that they
28 <u>will not listen</u> to us? Let us rather try to find out where we are."

9   kidnapping
10   tell

29 I groped about. In five steps I came to an iron wall, made of plates
30 bolted together. Then turning back I struck against a wooden
31 table, near which were ranged several stools. The boards of this
32 prison were concealed under a thick mat, which deadened the
33 noise of the feet. The bare walls revealed no trace of window
34 or door. Conseil, going round the reverse way, met me, and we
35 went back to the middle of the cabin, which measured about
36 twenty feet by ten. As to its height, Ned Land, in spite of his own
37 great height, could not measure it.

38 Half an hour had already passed without our situation being
39 bettered, when the dense darkness suddenly gave way to extreme
40 light. Our prison was suddenly lighted, that is to say, it became
41 filled with a luminous matter, so strong that I could not bear it
42 at first. In its whiteness and intensity I recognized that electric
43 light which played round the submarine boat like a magnificent
44 phenomenon of **phosphorescence**. After shutting my eyes
45 involuntarily, I opened them, and saw that this **luminous** agent
46 came from a half globe, unpolished, placed in the roof of the
47 cabin.

48 "At last one can see," cried Ned Land, who, knife in hand, stood
49 on the defensive.

50 "Yes," said I; "but we are still in the dark about ourselves."

51 "Let master have patience," said the **imperturbable** Conseil.

52 The sudden lighting of the cabin enabled me to examine it
53 minutely. It only contained a table and five stools. The invisible
54 door might be hermetically sealed. No noise was heard. All
55 seemed dead in the interior of this boat. Did it move, did it float
56 on the surface of the ocean, or did it dive into its depths? I could
57 not guess.

58 A noise of bolts was now heard, the door opened, and two men
59 appeared.

60 One was short, very muscular, broad-shouldered, with **robust**
61 limbs, strong head, an abundance of black hair, thick moustache,

62 a quick penetrating look, and the **vivacity** which characterizes
63 the population of Southern France.

64 The second stranger merits a more detailed description. I made
65 out his prevailing qualities directly: self-confidence—because
66 his head was well set on his shoulders, and his black eyes looked
67 around with cold assurance; calmness—for his skin, rather pale,
68 showed his coolness of blood; energy—**evinced** by the rapid
69 contraction of his lofty brows; and courage—because his deep
70 breathing denoted great power of lungs.

71 Whether this person was thirty-five or fifty years of age, I could
72 not say. He was tall, had a large forehead, straight nose, a clearly
73 cut mouth, beautiful teeth, with fine taper hands, indicative of a
74 highly nervous **temperament**. This man was certainly the most
75 admirable specimen I had ever met. One particular feature was
76 his eyes, rather far from each other, and which could take in
77 nearly a quarter of the horizon at once.

78 This faculty—(I verified it later)—gave him a range of vision
79 far superior to Ned Land's. When this stranger fixed upon an
80 object, his eyebrows met, his large eyelids closed around so as to
81 contract the range of his vision, and he looked as if he magnified
82 the objects lessened by distance, as if he pierced those sheets of
83 water so opaque[11] to our eyes, and as if he read the very depths
84 of the seas.

85 The two strangers, with caps made from the fur of the sea otter,
86 and shod[12] with sea boots of seal's skin, were dressed in clothes of
87 a particular texture, which allowed free movement of the limbs.
88 The taller of the two, evidently the chief on board, examined
89 us with great attention, without saying a word; then, turning to
90 his companion, talked with him in an unknown tongue. It was a
91 **sonorous**, harmonious, and flexible dialect, the vowels seeming
92 to admit of very varied **accentuation**.

93 The other replied by a shake of the head, and added two or three

---

11   unclear
12   fit

94   perfectly **incomprehensible** words. Then he seemed to question
95   me by a look.

96   I replied in good French that I did not know his language; but
97   he seemed not to understand me, and my situation became more
98   embarrassing.

99   "If master were to tell our story," said Conseil, "perhaps these
100 gentlemen may understand some words."

101 I began to tell our adventures, **articulating** each syllable clearly,
102 and without omitting one single detail. I announced our names
103 and rank, introducing in person Professor Aronnax, his servant
104 Conseil, and master Ned Land, the harpooner.

105 The man with the soft calm eyes listened to me quietly,
106 even politely, and with extreme attention; but nothing in his
107 **countenance** indicated that he had understood my story. When I
108 finished, he said not a word.

109 There remained one resource, to speak English. Perhaps they
110 would know this almost universal language. I knew it—as well
111 as the German language—well enough to read it fluently, but
112 not to speak it correctly. But, anyhow, we must make ourselves
113 understood.

114 "Go on in your turn," I said to the harpooner; "speak your best
115 Anglo-Saxon, and try to do better than I."

116 Ned did not beg off, and **recommenced** our story.

117 To his great disgust, the harpooner did not seem to have made
118 himself more intelligible than I had. Our visitors did not stir.
119 They evidently understood neither the language of England nor
120 of France.

121 Very much embarrassed, after having vainly[13] exhausted our
122 speaking resources, I knew not what part to take, when Conseil
123 said:

____

13   In vain-no use

124 "If master will permit me, I will relate it in German."

125 But in spite of the elegant terms and good accent of the narrator,
126 the German language had no success. At last, **nonplussed**, I
127 tried to remember my first lessons, and to narrate our adventures
128 in Latin, but with no better success. This last attempt being of
129 no avail[14], the two strangers exchanged some words in their
130 unknown language, and retired.

131 The door shut.

132 "It is an **infamous** shame," cried Ned Land, who broke out for
133 the twentieth time. "We speak to those **rogues** in French, English,
134 German, and Latin, and not one of them has the politeness to
135 answer!"

136 "Calm yourself," I said to the **impetuous** Ned; "anger will do
137 no good."

138 "But do you see, Professor," replied our **irascible** companion,
139 "that we shall absolutely die of hunger in this iron cage?"

140 "Bah!" said Conseil, philosophically; "we can hold out some
141 time yet."

142 "My friends," I said, "we must not despair[15]. We have been worse
143 off than this. Do me the favor to wait a little before forming an
144 opinion upon the commander and crew of this boat."

145 "My opinion is formed," replied Ned Land, sharply. "They are
146 rascals."

147 "Good! and from what country?"

148 "From the land of rogues[16]!"

149 "My brave Ned, that country is not clearly indicated on the map
150 of the world; but I admit that the nationality of the two strangers

---

14   No luck
15   Give up hope
16   thugs

151 is hard to determine. Neither English, French, nor German,
152 that is quite certain. However, I am inclined to think that the
153 commander and his companion were born in low latitudes.
154 There is southern blood in them. But I cannot decide by their
155 appearance whether they are Spaniards, Turks, Arabians, or
156 Indians. As to their language, it is quite incomprehensible."

157 "There is the disadvantage of not knowing all languages,"
158 said Conseil, "or the disadvantage of not having one universal
159 language."

160 As he said these words, the door opened. A steward entered. He
161 brought us clothes, coats and trousers, made of a stuff I did not
162 know. I **hastened** to dress myself, and my companions followed
163 my example. During that time, the steward—dumb, perhaps
164 deaf—had arranged the table, and laid three plates.

165 "This is something like!" said Conseil.

166 "Bah!" said the angry harpooner, "what do you suppose they
167 eat here? Tortoise liver, filleted shark, and beef steaks from
168 seadogs."

169 "We shall see," said Conseil.

170 The dishes, of bell metal, were placed on the table, and we took
171 our places. Undoubtedly we had to do with civilized people, and,
172 had it not been for the electric light which flooded us, I could
173 have fancied I was in the dining-room of the Adelphi Hotel at
174 Liverpool, or at the Grand Hotel in Paris. I must say, however,
175 that there was neither bread nor wine. The water was fresh and
176 clear, but it was water and did not suit Ned Land's taste. Amongst
177 the dishes which were brought to us, I recognized several fish
178 delicately dressed; but of some, although excellent, I could give
179 no opinion, neither could I tell to what kingdom they belonged,
180 whether animal or vegetable. As to the dinner-service, it was
181 elegant, and in perfect taste. Each utensil—spoon, fork, knife,
182 plate—had a letter engraved on it, with a **motto** above it, of
183 which this is an exact **facsimile**:

The letter N was no doubt the initial of the name of the **enigmatical** person who commanded at the bottom of the seas.

Ned and Conseil did not reflect much. They **devoured** the food, and I did likewise. I was, besides, reassured as to our fate; and it seemed evident that our hosts would not let us die of want.

However, everything has an end, everything passes away, even the hunger of people who have not eaten for fifteen hours. Our appetites satisfied, we felt overcome with sleep.

"Faith! I shall sleep well," said Conseil.

"So shall I," replied Ned Land.

My two companions stretched themselves on the cabin carpet, and were soon sound asleep. For my own part, too many thoughts crowded my brain, too many insoluble[17] questions pressed upon me, too many fancies[18] kept my eyes half open. Where were we? What strange power carried us on? I felt—or rather fancied I felt—the machine sinking down to the lowest beds of the sea. Dreadful nightmares beset[19] me; I saw in these mysterious asylums[20] a world of unknown animals, amongst which this submarine boat seemed to be of the same kind, living, moving, and formidable[21] as they. Then my brain grew calmer, my imagination wandered into vague unconsciousness, and I soon fell into a deep sleep.

---

17   Not able to blend into a solution-i.e. not answerable
18   Imaginative thoughts
19   Came upon
20   Shelter, refuge
21   Inspiring fear

Vocabulary part 1 chapter 8

vent, indignation, compromise, phosphorescence, robust, evinced, sonorous, accentuation, incomprehensible, articulating, countenance, recommenced, nonplussed, infamous, rouges, impetuous, irascible, hastened, facsimile, enigmatical,

Questions for part 1 chapter 8

1. In lines 48-50 the author writes: At last one can see," cried Ned Land, who, knife in hand, stood on the defensive. "Yes," said I; "but we are still in the dark about ourselves ." How is darkness a metaphor for their situation, and how is this a play on words?

    ____

    ____

2. In lines 71-75, the author writes: "Whether this person was thirty-five or fifty years of age, I could not say. He was tall, had a large forehead, straight nose, a clearly cut mouth, beautiful teeth, with fine taper hands, indicative of a highly nervous temperament. This man was certainly the most admirable specimen I had ever met." How does describing another human being as a "specimen" indicate how the professor views everything?

    ____

    ____

    ____

3. In lines 136-137, Conseil advises Ned Land saying, "Calm yourself," I said to the **impetuous** Ned; "anger will do no good.". How does this advice reflect a Torah position? _______________________

    ____

4. In lines 145-150 it states; My opinion is formed,"
    replied Ned Land, sharply. "They are rascals." "Good!
    and from what country?" "From the land of rogues!"
    "My brave Ned, that country is not clearly indicated on
    the map of the world…" What does Ned Land mean by
    saying they are "from the land of rouges"?

____

____

Chapter 9
NED LAND'S TEMPERS

How long we slept I do not know; but our sleep must have lasted long, for it rested us completely from our **fatigues**. I woke first. My companions had not moved, and were still stretched in their corner.

Hardly roused from my somewhat hard couch, I felt my brain freed, my mind clear. I then began an **attentive** examination of our cell. Nothing was changed inside. The prison was still a prison—the prisoners, prisoners. However, the steward, during our sleep, had cleared the table. I breathed with difficulty. The heavy air seemed to oppress my lungs. Although the cell was large, we had evidently consumed a great part of the oxygen that it contained. Indeed, each man consumes, in one hour, the oxygen contained in more than 176 pints of air, and this air, charged (as then) with a nearly equal quantity of carbonic acid, becomes unbreathable.

It became necessary to renew the atmosphere of our prison, and no doubt the whole in the submarine boat. That gave rise to a question in my mind. How would the commander of this floating dwelling-place proceed? Would he obtain air by chemical means, in getting by heat the oxygen contained in chlorate of potash, and in absorbing carbonic acid by caustic potash? Or—a more convenient, economical, and consequently more probable alternative—would he be satisfied to rise and take breath at the surface of the water, like a whale, and so renew for twenty-four hours the **atmospheric provision**?

In fact, I was already obliged to increase my **respirations** to eke out of this cell the little oxygen it contained, when suddenly I was refreshed by a current of pure air, and perfumed with **saline emanations**. It was an **invigorating** sea breeze, charged with iodine. I opened my mouth wide, and my lungs **saturated**

31 themselves with fresh particles[22].

32 At the same time I felt the boat rolling. The iron-plated monster
33 had evidently just risen to the surface of the ocean to breathe,
34 after the fashion of whales. I found out from that the mode of
35 **ventilating** the boat.

36 When I had inhaled this air freely, I sought the **conduit** pipe,
37 which conveyed to us the beneficial[23] whiff, and I was not long
38 in finding it. Above the door was a ventilator, through which
39 volumes of fresh air renewed the **impoverished** atmosphere of
40 the cell.

41 I was making my observations, when Ned and Conseil awoke
42 almost at the same time, under the influence of this reviving air.
43 They rubbed their eyes, stretched themselves, and were on their
44 feet in an instant.

45 "Did master sleep well?" asked Conseil, with his usual politeness.

46 "Very well, my brave boy. And you, Mr. Land?"

47 "Soundly, Professor. But, I don't know if I am right or not, there
48 seems to be a sea breeze!"

49 A seaman could not be mistaken, and I told the Canadian all that
50 had passed during his sleep.

51 "Good!" said he. "That accounts for those roarings we heard,
52 when the supposed narwhal sighted the Abraham Lincoln."

53 "Quite so, Master Land; it was taking breath."

54 "Only, Mr. Aronnax, I have no idea what o'clock it is, unless it
55 is dinner-time."

56 "Dinner-time! my good fellow? Say rather breakfast-time, for
57 we certainly have begun another day."

---

22   Parts of something-i.e. air, oxygen
23   good

58 "So," said Conseil, "we have slept twenty-four hours?"

59 "That is my opinion."

60 "I will not contradict you," replied Ned Land. "But, dinner or
61 breakfast, the steward will be welcome, whichever he brings."

62 "Master Land, we must conform to the rules on board, and I
63 suppose our appetites are in advance of the dinner hour."

64 "That is just like you, friend Conseil," said Ned, impatiently.
65 "You are never out of temper, always calm; you would return
66 thanks before grace[24], and die of hunger rather than complain!"

67 Time was getting on, and we were fearfully hungry; and this
68 time the steward did not appear. It was rather too long to leave
69 us, if they really had good intentions towards us. Ned Land,
70 tormented by the cravings of hunger, got still more angry; and,
71 **notwithstanding** his promise, I dreaded an explosion when he
72 found himself with one of the crew.

73 For two hours more Ned Land's temper increased; he cried, he
74 shouted, but in vain. The walls were deaf. There was no sound
75 to be heard in the boat; all was still as death. It did not move,
76 for I should have felt the trembling motion of the hull under
77 the influence of the screw. Plunged in the depths of the waters,
78 it belonged no longer to earth: this silence was dreadful. I felt
79 terrified, Conseil was calm, Ned Land roared.

80 Just then a noise was heard outside. Steps sounded on the metal
81 flags. The locks were turned, the door opened, and the steward
82 appeared.

83 Before I could rush forward to stop him, the Canadian had
84 thrown him down, and held him by the throat. The steward was
85 choking under the grip of his powerful hand.

86 Conseil was already trying to unclasp the harpooner's hand
87 from his half-suffocated victim, and I was going to fly to the

24   Maybe: you would offer thanks before ever been granted anything
yet

88   rescue, when suddenly I was nailed to the spot by hearing these
89   words in French: "Be quiet, Master Land; and you, Professor,
90   will you be so good as to listen to me?"

Vocabulary part 1 chapter 9

fatigues, atmospheric, provision, respirations, saline, invigorating, saturated, ventilating, conduit, impoverished, notwithstanding, unclasp

Questions: for part 1 chapter 9

1. In lines 47-50 it reads: "Soundly, Professor. But, I don't know if I am right or not, there seems to be a sea breeze!" A seaman could not be mistaken, and I told the Canadian all that had passed during his sleep" What does it matter that Ned Land is a seaman?

    ____

    ____

    ____

2. In lines 62-65 it says: "Master Land, we must conform to the rules on board, and I suppose our appetites are in advance of the dinner hour." "That is just like you, friend Conseil," said Ned, impatiently. "You are never out of temper, always calm;…" How does Conseil annoy Ned land, and why does this annoyance come about because of Ned Lands temperament? Which two *middos* are displayed here, and which is a more refined *middah*? Why do you think the author put these two very different personalities together?

    ____

    ____

    ____

    ____

    ____

3. In lines 74-79 it states: "There was no sound to be heard in the boat; all was still as death. It did not move, for I should have felt the trembling motion of the hull under the influence of the screw. Plunged in the depths of the waters, it belonged no longer to earth: this silence was dreadful. " What frightens the Professor the most? What spiritual support could a frum Jew draw from in such a situation?

____

____

____

4. In the end, why do you think the crew keeps the three imprisoned for so long?

____

____

____

____

Chapter 10a
THE MAN OF THE SEAS

1 **It was the** commander of the vessel who thus spoke.

2 At these words, Ned Land rose suddenly. The steward, nearly
3 strangled, **tottered** out on a sign from his master. But such
4 was the power of the commander on board, that not a gesture
5 betrayed the **resentment** which this man must have felt towards
6 the Canadian. Conseil interested in spite of himself, I **stupefied**,
7 awaited in silence the result of this scene.

8 The commander, leaning against the corner of a table with his
9 arms folded, scanned us with **profound** attention. Did he hesitate
10 to speak? Did he regret the words which he had just spoken in
11 French? One might almost think so.

12 After some moments of silence, which not one of us dreamed
13 of breaking, "Gentlemen," said he, in a calm and penetrating
14 voice, "I speak French, English, German, and Latin equally
15 well. I could, therefore, have answered you at our first interview,
16 but I wished to know you first, then to reflect. The story told by
17 each one, entirely agreeing in the main points, convinced me of
18 your identity. I know now that chance has brought before me
19 M. Pierre Aronnax, Professor of Natural History at the Museum
20 of Paris, entrusted with a scientific mission abroad, Conseil, his
21 servant, and Ned Land, of Canadian origin, harpooner on board
22 the frigate Abraham Lincoln of the navy of the United States of
23 America."

24 I bowed **assent**. It was not a question that the commander put
25 to me. Therefore there was no answer to be made. This man
26 expressed himself with perfect ease, without any accent. His
27 sentences were well turned, his words clear, and his fluency of
28 speech remarkable. Yet, I did not recognize in him a fellow-
29 countryman.

30 He continued the conversation in these terms:

"You have doubtless thought, sir, that I have delayed long in paying you this second visit. The reason is that, your identity recognized, I wished to weigh maturely what part to act towards you. I have hesitated much. Most annoying circumstances have brought you into the presence of a man who has broken all the ties of humanity. You have come to trouble my existence."

"**Unintentionally**!" said I.

"Unintentionally?" replied the stranger, raising his voice a little. "Was it unintentionally that the Abraham Lincoln pursued me all over the seas? Was it unintentionally that you took passage in this frigate? Was it unintentionally that your cannon-balls **rebounded** off the plating of my vessel? Was it unintentionally that Mr. Ned Land struck me with his harpoon?"

I detected a restrained irritation in these words. But to these **recriminations** I had a very natural answer to make, and I made it.

"Sir," said I, "no doubt you are ignorant of the discussions which have taken place concerning you in America and Europe. You do not know that divers accidents, caused by collisions with your submarine machine, have excited public feeling in the two continents. I omit the theories without number by which it was sought to explain that of which you alone possess the secret. But you must understand that, in pursuing you over the high seas of the Pacific, the Abraham Lincoln believed itself to be chasing some powerful sea-monster, of which it was necessary to rid the ocean at any price."

A half-smile curled the lips of the commander: then, in a calmer tone:

"M. Aronnax," he replied, "dare you **affirm** that your frigate would not as soon have pursued and **cannonaded** a submarine boat as a monster?"

This question embarrassed me, for certainly Captain Farragut might not have hesitated. He might have thought it his duty

64 to destroy a **contrivance** of this kind, as he would a gigantic
65 narwhal.

66 "You understand then, sir," continued the stranger, "that I have
67 the right to treat you as enemies?"

68 I answered nothing, purposely. For what good would it be to
69 discuss such a **proposition**, when force could destroy the best
70 arguments?

71 "I have hesitated some time," continued the commander; "nothing
72 **obliged** me to show you hospitality. If I chose to separate myself
73 from you, I should have no interest in seeing you again; I could
74 place you upon the deck of this vessel which has served you as a
75 refuge, I could sink beneath the waters, and forget that you had
76 ever existed. Would not that be my right?"

77 "It might be the right of a savage," I answered, "but not that of
78 a civilized man."

79 "Professor," replied the commander, quickly, "I am not what
80 you call a civilized man! I have done with society entirely, for
81 reasons which I alone have the right of appreciating. I do not,
82 therefore, obey its laws, and I desire you never to allude to them
83 before me again!"

84 This was said plainly. A flash of anger and **disdain** kindled in the
85 eyes of the Unknown, and I had a glimpse of a terrible past in the
86 life of this man. Not only had he put himself beyond the pale of
87 human laws, but he had made himself independent of them, free
88 in the strictest acceptation of the word, quite beyond their reach!
89 Who then would dare to pursue him at the bottom of the sea,
90 when, on its surface, he defied all attempts made against him?

91 What vessel could resist the shock of his submarine monitor?
92 What **cuirass**, however thick, could withstand the blows of his
93 spur? No man could demand from him an account of his actions;
94 God, if he believed in one—his conscience, if he had one—were
95 the sole judges to whom he was answerable.

96   These reflections crossed my mind rapidly, whilst the stranger
97   **personage** was silent, absorbed, and as if wrapped up in himself.
98   I regarded him with fear mingled with interest, as, doubtless,
99   Oedipus regarded the Sphinx[25].

100   After rather a long silence, the commander resumed the
101   conversation.

102   "I have hesitated," said he, "but I have thought that my interest
103   might be **reconciled** with that pity to which every human being
104   has a right. You will remain on board my vessel, since **fate** has
105   cast you there. You will be free; and, in exchange for this liberty,
106   I shall only impose one single condition. Your word of honor to
107   submit to it will suffice."

108   "Speak, sir," I answered. "I suppose this condition is one which
109   a man of honor may accept?"

110   "Yes, sir; it is this: It is possible that certain events, unforeseen,
111   may oblige me to consign you to your cabins for some hours or
112   some days, as the case may be. As I desire never to use violence,
113   I expect from you, more than all the others, a passive **obedience**.
114   In thus acting, I take all the responsibility: I **acquit** you entirely,
115   for I make it an impossibility for you to see what ought not to be
116   seen. Do you accept this condition?"

117   Then things took place on board which, to say the least, were
118   singular, and which ought not to be seen by people who were
119   not placed beyond the pale of social laws. Amongst the surprises
120   which the future was preparing for me, this might not be the
121   least.

122   "We accept," I answered; "only I will ask your permission, sir,
123   to address one question to you—one only."

---

25   This is a reference to a Greek story where Oedipus the King must
answer a Sphinx's riddle in order to save himself and his nation-Thebes.
In Greek tradition, the sphinx is a merciless creature who has the head of
a woman, the haunches of a lion, and the wings of a bird and kills anyone
who can't answer its riddles.

124 "Speak, sir."

125 "You said that we should be free on board."

126 "Entirely."

127 "I ask you, then, what you mean by this liberty?"

128 "Just the liberty to go, to come, to see, to observe even all that
129 passes here save under rare circumstances—the liberty, in short,
130 which we enjoy ourselves, my companions and I."

131 It was evident that we did not understand one another.

132 "Pardon me, sir," I resumed, "but this liberty is only what every
133 prisoner has of pacing his prison. It cannot suffice us[26]."

134 "It must suffice you, however."

135 "What! we must renounce[27] for ever seeing our country, our
136 friends, our relations again?"

137 "Yes, sir. But to renounce that **unendurable** worldly yoke which
138 men believe to be liberty is not perhaps so painful as you think."

139 "Well," exclaimed Ned Land, "never will I give my word of
140 honor not to try to escape."

141 "I did not ask you for your word of honor, Master Land,"
142 answered the commander, coldly.

143 "Sir," I replied, beginning to get angry in spite of myself, "you
144 abuse your situation towards us; it is cruelty."

145 "No, sir, it is **clemency**. You are my prisoners of war. I keep
146 you, when I could, by a word, plunge you into the depths of the
147 ocean. You attacked me. You came to surprise a secret which
148 no man in the world must penetrate—the secret of my whole
149 existence. And you think that I am going to send you back to that
150 world which must know me no more? Never! In **retaining** you,

26   Be enough for us
27   Give up

151 it is not you whom I guard—it is myself.”

152 These words indicated a resolution taken on the part of the
153 commander, against which no arguments would prevail.

154 “So, sir,” I rejoined, “you give us simply the choice between life
155 and death?”

156 “Simply.”

157 “My friends,” said I, “to a question thus put, there is nothing
158 to answer. But no word of honor binds us to the master of this
159 vessel.”

160 “None, sir,” answered the Unknown.

161 Then, in a gentler tone, he continued:

162 “Now, permit me to finish what I have to say to you. I know you,
163 M. Aronnax. You and your companions will not, perhaps, have
164 so much to complain of in the chance which has bound you to
165 my fate. You will find amongst the books which are my favorite
166 study the work which you have published on `the depths of the
167 sea.’ I have often read it. You have carried out your work as
168 far as terrestrial science permitted you. But you do not know
169 all—you have not seen all. Let me tell you then, Professor, that
170 you will not regret the time passed on board my vessel. You are
171 going to visit the land of marvels.”

172 These words of the commander had a great effect upon me. I
173 cannot deny it. My weak point was touched; and I forgot, for a
174 moment, that the contemplation of these sublime subjects was
175 not worth the loss of liberty. Besides, I trusted to the future to
176 decide this grave question. So I contented myself with saying:

177 “By what name ought I to address you?”

Vocabulary part 1 chapter 10a

tottered, stupefied, profound, unintentionally, rebounded, restrained, recriminations, affirm, cannonaded, contrivance, proposition, disdain, cuirass, personage, reconciled, fate, obedience, acquit, unendurable, clemency, retaining

Questions for part 1 chapter 10a

In lines 2-3 it says: "At these words, Ned Land rose suddenly. The steward, nearly strangled, tottered out on a sign from his master. But such was the power of the commander on board, that not a gesture betrayed the resentment which this man must have felt towards the Canadian."

1. What "power" impresses the Professor so much? What virtue is being highlighted?

____

____

____

____

In lines 8-11 it states: "The commander, leaning against the corner of a table with his arms folded, scanned us with **profound** attention. Did he hesitate to speak? Did he regret the words which he had just spoken in French? One might almost think so."

2. What kind of regret do you think he is referring to here?

____

____

____

____

In lines 18-23 it states: "I know now that chance has brought before me M. Pierre Aronnax, Professor of Natural History at the Museum of Paris, entrusted with a scientific mission abroad, Conseil, his servant, and Ned Land, of Canadian origin, harpooner on board the frigate Abraham Lincoln of the navy of the United States of America."

   3.   If the commander believed in Divine Providence (*Hashgacha Pratis*) what words(s) would be different in this sentence?

____

____

____

____

In lines 59-70 the Captain says: "M. Aronnax," he replied, "dare you affirm that your frigate would not as soon have pursued and cannonaded a submarine boat as a monster?" This question embarrassed me, for certainly Captain Farragut might not have hesitated. He might have thought it his duty to destroy a contrivance of this kind, as he would a gigantic narwhal. "You understand then, sir," continued the stranger, "that I have the right to treat you as enemies?" What is the logic behind the commander's arguments? __________________________

____

"I answered nothing, purposely. For what good would it be to discuss such a **proposition**, when force could destroy the best arguments?"

   4.   What does he mean that force can destroy the best arguments? What argument could the Professor put forth that would refute the commander's argument? Is it fair that this is the case? Why or why not?

____

____

____

____

In lines 71-80 the author writes: "I have hesitated some time," continued the commander; "nothing **obliged** me to show you hospitality. If I chose to separate myself from you, I should have no interest in seeing you again; I could place you upon the deck of this vessel which has served you as a refuge, I could sink beneath the waters, and forget that you had ever existed. Would not that be my right?"

"It might be the right of a savage," I answered, "but not that of a civilized man."

5. What is the argument the Professor makes to the Captain?

____

____

____

____

In lines 84-90 the protagonist says: "This was said plainly. A flash of anger and **disdain** kindled in the eyes of the Unknown, and I had a glimpse of a terrible past in the life of this man. Not only had he put himself beyond the pale of human laws, but he had made himself independent of them, free in the strictest acceptation of the word, quite beyond their reach! Who then would dare to pursue him at the bottom of the sea, when, on its surface, he defied all attempts made against him?"

6. In Torah thought, is this Captain free? Bring proof to your opinion.

____

____

____

____

In lines 91-95 the protagonist thinks: "What vessel could resist the shock of his submarine monitor? What cuirass, however thick, could withstand the blows of his spur? No man could demand from him an account of his actions; God, if he believed in one—his conscience, if he had one—were the sole judges to whom he was answerable".

7. How would you like to be someone who had to answer to no society or to anyone? Is this a Jewish ideal? Why or why not?

———————————————————————————
———————————————————————————
———————————————————————————

In lines 96-99 it says: "These reflections crossed my mind rapidly, whilst the stranger personage was silent, absorbed, and as if wrapped up in himself. I regarded him with fear mingled with interest, as, doubtless, Oedipus regarded the Sphinx".

8. What does he mean when he says "I regarded him with fear mingled with interest?

———————————————————————————
———————————————————————————
———————————————————————————

In lines 92-97 the Professor says: "Pardon me, sir," I resumed, "but this liberty is only what every prisoner has of pacing his prison. It cannot suffice us." "It must suffice you, however." "What! we must renounce for ever seeing our country, our friends, our relations again?" "Yes, sir. But to renounce that unendurable worldly yoke which men believe to be liberty is not perhaps so painful as you think."

9. What do you think the commander means? What does he seem to express about the fundamental idea and right of liberty of movement? How does the Torah look at this liberty, is it a fundamental right or not (hint see Rosh Hashana 11b)?

———————————————————————————
———————————————————————————
———————————————————————————

In lines 102-107 After rather a long silence, the commander resumed the conversation. "I have hesitated," said he, "but I have thought that my interest might be reconciled with that pity to which every human being has a right. You will remain on board my vessel, since fate has cast you there. You will be free; and, in exchange for this liberty, I shall only impose one single condition. Your word of honor to submit to it will suffice."

10. What *middah* makes the Captain change his mind?

____

____

____

____

In lines 145-151 the antagonist states: "No, sir, it is clemency. You are my prisoners of war. I keep you, when I could, by a word, plunge you into the depths of the ocean. You attacked me. You came to surprise a secret which no man in the world must penetrate—the secret of my whole existence. And you think that I am going to send you back to that world which must know me no more? Never! In retaining you, it is not you whom I guard—it is myself."

11. Summarize the commander's justification for keeping the people prisoners, and what do you think of his rationale? Is there some justification to his demand?

____

____

____

____

In lines 157-160 the author writes: "My friends," said I, "to a question thus put, there is nothing to answer. But no word of honor binds us to the master of this vessel." "None, sir," answered the Unknown.

12. Why is the word "unknown" written in uppercase? What does the fact that no "word of honor" was offered which would allow them to leave if the opportunity arose say about the values these people put on truth saying?

____

____

____

____

In lines 172-176 the protagonist admits: "These words of the commander had a great effect upon me. I cannot deny it. My weak point was touched; and I forgot, **for a moment, that the contemplation of these sublime subjects was not worth the loss of liberty**. Besides, I trusted to the future to decide this grave question.

13. What fundamental concept is being expressed in these sentences?

____

____

____

____

1 "**Sir**," **replied the** commander, "I am nothing to you but
2 Captain Nemo; and you and your **companions** are nothing to
3 me but the passengers of the Nautilus."

4 Captain Nemo called. A steward appeared. The captain gave him
5 his orders in that strange language which I did not understand.
6 Then, turning towards the Canadian and Conseil:

7 "A **repast** awaits you in your cabin," said he. "Be so good as to
8 follow this man.

9 "And now, M. Aronnax, our breakfast is ready. Permit me to
10 lead the way."

11 "I am at your service, Captain."

12 I followed Captain Nemo; and as soon as I had passed through the
13 door, I found myself in a kind of passage lighted by electricity,
14 similar to the waist of a ship. After we had proceeded a dozen
15 yards, a second door opened before me.

16 I then entered a dining-room, decorated and furnished in **severe**
17 taste. High oaken sideboards, inlaid[28] with ebony, stood at the
18 two extremities of the room, and upon their shelves glittered
19 china, porcelain, and glass of **inestimable** value. The plate on
20 the table sparkled in the rays which the **luminous** ceiling shed
21 around, while the light was **tempered** and softened by **exquisite**
22 paintings.

23 In the center of the room was a table richly laid out. Captain
24 Nemo indicated the place I was to occupy.

25 The breakfast consisted of a certain number of dishes, the
26 contents of which were furnished by the sea alone; and I was
27 ignorant of the nature and mode of preparation of some of them.
28 I acknowledged that they were good, but they had a peculiar
29 flavor, which I easily became accustomed to. These different

---

28   decorated

30 **aliments** appeared to me to be rich in phosphorus, and I thought
31 they must have a marine origin.

32 Captain Nemo looked at me. I asked him no questions, but
33 he guessed my thoughts, and answered of his own accord the
34 questions which I was burning to address to him.

35 "The greater part of these dishes are unknown to you," he said to
36 me. "However, you may partake of them without fear. They are
37 wholesome and nourishing. For a long time I have renounced
38 the food of the earth, and I am never ill now. My crew, who are
39 healthy, are fed on the same food."

40 "So," said I, "all these eatables are the produce of the sea?"

41 "Yes, Professor, the sea supplies all my wants. Sometimes I cast
42 my nets in tow, and I draw them in ready to break. Sometimes I
43 hunt in the midst of this element, which appears to be inaccessible
44 to man, and **quarry** the game which dwells in my submarine
45 forests. My flocks, like those of old shepherds, graze fearlessly
46 in the immense prairies of the ocean. I have a vast property there,
47 which I cultivate myself, and which is always sown by the hand
48 of the Creator of all things."

49 "I can understand perfectly, sir, that your nets furnish excellent
50 fish for your table; I can understand also that you hunt aquatic[29]
51 game in your submarine forests; but I cannot understand at all
52 how a particle of meat, no matter how small, can figure in your
53 bill of fare[30]."

54 "This, which you believe to be meat, Professor, is nothing else
55 than fillet of turtle. Here are also some dolphins' livers, which
56 you take to be ragout of pork. My cook is a clever fellow, who
57 excels in dressing these various products of the ocean. Taste all
58 these dishes. Here is a preserve of sea-cucumber, which a Malay
59 would declare to be unrivalled in the world; here is a cream, of
60 which the milk has been furnished by the Cetacea, and the sugar
61 by the great fucus of the North Sea; and, lastly, permit me to

29   Having to do with water
30   diet

62 offer you some preserve of anemones, which is equal to that of
63 the most delicious fruits."

64 I tasted, more from curiosity than as a connoisseur[31], whilst
65 Captain Nemo enchanted[32] me with his extraordinary stories.

66 "You like the sea, Captain?"

67 "Yes; I love it! The sea is everything. It covers seven tenths of the
68 terrestrial globe. Its breath is pure and healthy. It is an immense
69 desert, where man is never lonely, for he feels life stirring on all
70 sides. The sea is only the embodiment[33] of a supernatural and
71 wonderful existence. It is nothing but love and emotion; it is the
72 'Living Infinite,' as one of your poets has said. In fact, Professor,
73 Nature manifests herself in it by her three kingdoms—mineral,
74 vegetable, and animal. The sea is the vast reservoir of Nature.
75 The globe began with sea, so to speak; and who knows if it will
76 not end with it? In it is supreme tranquility[34]. The sea does not
77 belong to despots[35]. Upon its surface men can still exercise unjust
78 laws, fight, tear one another to pieces, and be carried away with
79 terrestrial horrors. But at thirty feet below its level, their reign
80 ceases, their influence is quenched[36], and their power disappears.
81 Ah! sir, live—live in the bosom[37] of the waters! There only is
82 independence! There I recognize no masters! There I am free!"

83 Captain Nemo suddenly became silent in the midst of this
84 enthusiasm, by which he was quite carried away. For a few
85 moments he paced up and down, much agitated[38]. Then he became
86 more calm, regained his accustomed coldness of expression, and
87 turning towards me:

88 "Now, Professor," said he, "if you wish to go over the Nautilus,

---

31   specialist
32   Pleasurably absorbed
33   the fulfillment, the essence
34   peaceful
35   An all-encompassing ruler
36   satisfied
37   Middle
38   Excited, distressed

89   I am at your service."

90   Captain Nemo rose. I followed him. A double door, **contrived** at
91   the back of the dining-room, opened, and I entered a room equal
92   in dimensions to that which I had just quitted.

93   It was a library. High pieces of furniture, of black violet ebony
94   inlaid with brass, supported upon their wide shelves a great
95   number of books uniformly bound. They followed the shape of
96   the room, terminating[39] at the lower part in huge **divans**, covered
97   with brown leather, which were curved, to afford the greatest
98   comfort. Light movable desks, made to slide in and out at will,
99   allowed one to rest one's book while reading. In the center stood
100   an immense table, covered with pamphlets, amongst which were
101   some newspapers, already of old date. The electric light flooded
102   everything; it was shed from four unpolished globes half sunk in
103   the **volutes** of the ceiling. I looked with real admiration at this
104   room, so ingeniously[40] fitted up, and I could scarcely believe my
105   eyes.

106   "Captain Nemo," said I to my host, who had just thrown himself
107   on one of the divans, "this is a library which would do honor to
108   more than one of the continental palaces, and I am absolutely
109   astounded when I consider that it can follow you to the bottom
110   of the seas."

111   "Where could one find greater solitude or silence, Professor?"
112   replied Captain Nemo. "Did your study in the Museum afford
113   you such perfect quiet?"

114   "No, sir; and I must confess that it is a very poor one after yours.
115   You must have six or seven thousand volumes here."

116   "Twelve thousand, M. Aronnax. These are the only ties which
117   bind me to the earth. But I had done with the world on the
118   day when my Nautilus plunged for the first time beneath the
119   waters. That day I bought my last volumes, my last pamphlets,
120   my last papers, and from that time I wish to think that men no

39   ending
40   Brilliantly

121 longer think or write. These books, Professor, are at your service
122 besides, and you can make use of them freely."

123 I thanked Captain Nemo, and went up to the shelves of the library.
124 Works on science, morals, and literature abounded in every
125 language; but I did not see one single work on political economy;
126 that subject appeared to be strictly **proscribed**. Strange to say,
127 all these books were irregularly arranged, in whatever language
128 they were written; and this **medley** proved that the Captain of
129 the Nautilus must have read indiscriminately[41] the books which
130 he took up by chance.

131 "Sir," said I to the Captain, "I thank you for having placed this
132 library at my disposal. It contains treasures of science, and I
133 shall profit by them."

134 "This room is not only a library," said Captain Nemo, "it is also
135 a smoking-room."

136 "A smoking-room!" I cried. "Then one may smoke on board?"

137 "Certainly."

138 "Then, sir, I am forced to believe that you have kept up a
139 communication with Havannah[42]."

140 "Not any," answered the Captain. "Accept this cigar, M.
141 Aronnax; and, though it does not come from Havannah, you will
142 be pleased with it, if you are a connoisseur."

143 I took the cigar which was offered me; its shape recalled the
144 London ones, but it seemed to be made of leaves of gold.
145 I lighted it at a little brazier[43], which was supported upon an
146 elegant bronze stem, and drew the first whiffs with the delight of
147 a lover of smoking who has not smoked for two days.

148 "It is excellent, but it is not tobacco."

---

41   With no order or reason
42   The capital of Cuba known for its good cigars
43   Open fire

149 "No!" answered the Captain, "this tobacco comes neither from
150 Havannah nor from the East. It is a kind of sea-weed, rich
151 in nicotine, with which the sea provides me, but somewhat
152 sparingly."

153 At that moment Captain Nemo opened a door which stood
154 opposite to that by which I had entered the library, and I passed
155 into an immense drawing-room splendidly lighted.

156 It was a vast, four-sided room, thirty feet long, eighteen wide, and
157 fifteen high. A luminous ceiling, decorated with light arabesques,
158 shed a soft clear light over all the marvels accumulated in this
159 museum. For it was in fact a museum, in which an intelligent
160 and prodigal[44] hand had gathered all the treasures of nature and
161 art, with the artistic confusion which distinguishes a painter's
162 studio.

163 Thirty first-rate pictures, uniformly framed, separated by bright
164 drapery, ornamented the walls, which were hung with tapestry
165 of severe design. I saw works of great value, the greater part of
166 which I had admired in the special collections of Europe, and in
167 the exhibitions of paintings… Amazement, as the Captain of the
168 Nautilus had predicted, had already begun to take possession of
169 me.

170 "Professor," said this strange man, "you must excuse the
171 **unceremonious** way in which I receive you, and the disorder of
172 this room."

173 "Sir," I answered, "without seeking to know who you are, I
174 recognize in you an artist."

175 "An amateur, nothing more, sir. Formerly I loved to collect
176 these beautiful works created by the hand of man. I sought
177 them greedily, and **ferreted** them out **indefatigably**, and I have
178 been able to bring together some objects of great value. These
179 are my last souvenirs of that world which is dead to me. In my
180 eyes, your modern artists are already old; they have two or three

---

44   Someone who spends with no care

181   thousand years of existence; I confound them in my own mind.
182   Masters have no age."

183   "And these musicians?" said I, pointing out some works of
184   Weber, Rossini, Mozart, Beethoven, Haydn, Meyerbeer, Herold,
185   Wagner, Auber, Gounod, and a number of others, scattered over
186   a large model piano-organ which occupied one of the panels of
187   the drawing-room.

188   "These musicians," replied Captain Nemo, "are the
189   contemporaries of Orpheus[45]; for in the memory of the dead all
190   chronological differences are effaced[46]; and I am dead, Professor;
191   as much dead as those of your friends who are sleeping six feet
192   under the earth!"

193   Captain Nemo was silent, and seemed lost in a profound
194   reverie[47]. I **contemplated** him with deep interest, analyzing in
195   silence the strange expression of his **countenance**. Leaning on
196   his elbow against an angle of a costly mosaic table, he no longer
197   saw me,—he had forgotten my presence.

198   I did not disturb this reverie, and continued my observation of
199   the curiosities which enriched this drawing-room.

200   Under elegant glass cases, fixed by copper rivets, were classed
201   and labelled the most precious productions of the sea which had
202   ever been presented to the eye of a naturalist. My delight as a
203   Professor may be conceived[48].

204   The division containing the zoophytes presented the most curious
205   specimens of the two groups of polypi and echinodermes.

206   Apart, in separate compartments, were spread out chaplets of
207   pearls of the greatest beauty, which reflected the electric light
208   in little sparks of fire; pink pearls, torn from the pinna-marina
209   of the Red Sea; green pearls of the haliotyde iris; yellow, blue

---

45   Legendary musician in ancient Greece
46   erased
47   Trance, daydream
48   imagined

210 and black pearls, the curious productions of the divers molluscs
211 of every ocean, and certain mussels of the water-courses of the
212 North; lastly, several specimens of inestimable value which had
213 been gathered from the rarest pintadines. Some of these pearls
214 were larger than a pigeon's egg, and were worth as much, and
215 more than that which the traveler Tavernier sold to the Shah of
216 Persia for three millions, and **surpassed** the one in the possession
217 of the Imaum of Muscat, which I had believed to be **unrivalled**
218 in the world.

219 Therefore, to estimate the value of this collection was simply
220 impossible. Captain Nemo must have expended millions in the
221 acquirement of these various specimens, and I was thinking
222 what source he could have drawn from, to have been able thus
223 to gratify[49] his fancy for collecting, when I was interrupted by
224 these words:

225 "You are examining my shells, Professor? Unquestionably they
226 must be interesting to a naturalist; but for me they have a far
227 greater charm, for I have collected them all with my own hand,
228 and there is not a sea on the face of the globe which has escaped
229 my researches."

230 "I can understand, Captain, the delight of wandering about in the
231 midst of such riches. You are one of those who have collected
232 their treasures themselves. No museum in Europe possesses
233 such a collection of the produce of the ocean. But if I exhaust
234 all my admiration upon it, I shall have none left for the vessel
235 which carries it. I do not wish to pry into your secrets: but I
236 must confess that this Nautilus, with the motive[50] power which
237 is confined in it, the **contrivances** which enable it to be worked,
238 the powerful agent which propels it, all excite my curiosity to
239 the highest pitch. I see suspended on the walls of this room
240 instruments of whose use I am ignorant."

241 "You will find these same instruments in my own room, Professor,
242 where I shall have much pleasure in explaining their use to you.

---

49   satisfy
50   moving

243 But first come and inspect the cabin which is set apart for your
244 own use. You must see how you will be accommodated on board
245 the Nautilus."

246 I followed Captain Nemo who, by one of the doors opening
247 from each panel of the drawing-room, regained the waist. He
248 conducted me towards the bow, and there I found, not a cabin,
249 but an elegant room, with a bed, dressing-table, and several other
250 pieces of excellent furniture.

251 I could only thank my host.

252 "Your room adjoins mine," said he, opening a door, "and mine
253 opens into the drawing-room that we have just quitted."

254 I entered the Captain's room: it had a severe, almost a monkish
255 aspect. A small iron bedstead, a table, some articles for the
256 toilet; the whole lighted by a skylight. No comforts, the strictest
257 necessaries only.

258 Captain Nemo pointed to a seat.

259 "Be so good as to sit down," he said. I seated myself, and he
260 began thus:

Vocabulary part 1 chapter 10b

companions, repast, severe, inestimable, tempered, exquisite, aliments, quarry, contrived, divans, volutes, proscribed, medley, unceremonious, ferreted, indefatigably, contemplated, surpassed, unrivalled

Questions for part 1 chapter 10b

1. What evidence in lines 46-48 can be drawn to show that the Captain believes in a higher being that created the world?

   ____

   ____

   ____

2. How does the Captain get his food?

   ____

   ____

3. In line 68-70, Captain Nemo states regarding the oceans: "It is an immense desert, where man is never lonely, for he feels life stirring on all sides." What is confusing about this sentence?

   ____

   ____

4. Captain Nemo says in lines 75-76: "The globe began with sea, so to speak; and who knows if it will not end with it?" What do you think he means that the globe began with the sea? (Hint it's found in the Torah)

   ____

   ____

5. In lines 67-82, Captain Nemo informs us of some of the reasons why he lives where he does. Explain what may be motivating Captain Nemo to live in the oceans and seas of the world.

   ____

   ____

   ____

6. In lines 190-192, Captain Nemo states: "and I am dead,
   Professor; as much dead as those of your friends who
   are sleeping six feet under the earth!". What do you
   think he means by this?

____

____

____

Chapter 11

ALL BY ELECTRICITY

"**Sir,**" **said Captain** Nemo, showing me the instruments hanging on the walls of his room, "here are the **contrivances** required for the navigation of the Nautilus. Here, as in the drawing-room, I have them always under my eyes, and they indicate my position and exact direction in the middle of the ocean. Some are known to you, such as the thermometer, which gives the internal temperature of the Nautilus; the barometer, which indicates the weight of the air and foretells the changes of the weather; the hygrometer, which marks the dryness of the atmosphere; the storm-glass, the contents of which, by decomposing, announce the approach of **tempests**; the compass, which guides my course; the sextant, which shows the latitude by the altitude of the sun; chronometers, by which I calculate the longitude; and glasses for day and night, which I use to examine the points of the horizon, when the Nautilus rises to the surface of the waves."

"These are the usual nautical instruments," I replied, "and I know the use of them. But these others, no doubt, answer to the particular requirements of the Nautilus. This dial with movable needle is a manometer, is it not?"

"It is actually a manometer. But by communication with the water, whose external pressure it indicates, it gives our depth at the same time."

"And these other instruments, the use of which I cannot guess?"

"Here, Professor, I ought to give you some explanations. Will you be kind enough to listen to me?"

He was silent for a few moments, then he said:

"There is a powerful agent, obedient[51], rapid, easy, which

---

51   Follows instructions

29 conforms to every use, and reigns supreme[52] on board my vessel.
30 Everything is done by means of it. It lights, warms it, and is the
31 soul of my mechanical apparatus[53]. This agent is electricity."

32 "Electricity?" I cried in surprise.

33 "Yes, sir."

34 "Nevertheless, Captain, you possess an extreme rapidity of
35 movement, which does not agree well with the power of
36 electricity. Until now, its dynamic force has remained under
37 restraint, and has only been able to produce a small amount of
38 power."

39 "Professor," said Captain Nemo, "my electricity is not
40 everybody's. You know what sea-water is composed of. In
41 a thousand grammes are found 96 1/2 per cent. of water, and
42 about 2 2/3 per cent. of chloride of sodium; then, in a smaller
43 quantity, chlorides of magnesium and of potassium, bromide
44 of magnesium, sulphate of magnesia, sulphate and carbonate
45 of lime. You see, then, that chloride of sodium forms a large
46 part of it. So it is this sodium that I extract from the sea-water,
47 and of which I compose my ingredients. I owe all to the ocean;
48 it produces electricity, and electricity gives heat, light, motion,
49 and, in a word, life to the Nautilus."

50 "But not the air you breathe?"

51 "Oh! I could manufacture the air necessary for my consumption,
52 but it is useless, because I go up to the surface of the water when
53 I please. However, if electricity does not furnish me with air to
54 breathe, it works at least the powerful pumps that are stored in
55 spacious reservoirs, and which enable me to prolong at need,
56 and as long as I will, my stay in the depths of the sea. It gives a
57 uniform and unintermittent[54] light, which the sun does not. Now
58 look at this clock; it is electrical, and goes with a regularity that

------

52   Is the boss over all things
53   device
54   Something that doesn't stop

59 defies[55] the best chronometers[56]. I have divided it into twenty-
60 four hours, like the Italian clocks, because for me there is neither
61 night nor day, sun nor moon, but only that **factitious** light that
62 I take with me to the bottom of the sea. Look! just now, it is ten
63 o'clock in the morning."

64 "Exactly."

65 "Another application of electricity. This dial hanging in front of
66 us indicates the speed of the Nautilus. An electric thread puts it
67 in communication with the screw, and the needle indicates the
68 real speed. Look! now we are spinning along with a uniform
69 speed of fifteen miles an hour."

70 "It is marvelous! And I see, Captain, you were right to make use
71 of this agent that takes the place of wind, water, and steam."

72 "We have not finished, M. Aronnax," said Captain Nemo,
73 rising. "If you will allow me, we will examine the stern of the
74 Nautilus."…

75 I followed Captain Nemo through the waist, and arrived at the
76 center of the boat. There was a sort of well that opened between
77 two partitions. An iron ladder, fastened with an iron hook to
78 the partition, led to the upper end. I asked the Captain what the
79 ladder was used for.

80 "It leads to the small boat," he said.

81 "What! have you a boat?" I exclaimed, in surprise.

82 "Of course; an excellent vessel, light and insubmersible[57], that
83 serves either as a fishing or as a pleasure boat."

84 "But then, when you wish to embark, you are obliged to come to
85 the surface of the water?"

86 "Not at all. This boat is attached to the upper part of the hull of the

---

55   beats
56   Time pieces
57   Unsinkable

87 Nautilus, and occupies a cavity[58] made for it. It is decked, quite
88 water-tight, and held together by solid bolts. This ladder leads
89 to a man-hole made in the hull of the Nautilus, that corresponds
90 with a similar hole made in the side of the boat. By this double
91 opening I get into the small vessel. They shut the one belonging
92 to the Nautilus; I shut the other by means of screw pressure. I
93 undo the bolts, and the little boat goes up to the surface of the sea
94 with prodigious rapidity[59]. I then open the panel of the bridge,
95 carefully shut till then; I mast it, hoist my sail, take my oars, and
96 I'm off."

97 "But how do you get back on board?"

98 "I do not come back, M. Aronnax; the Nautilus comes to me."

99 "By your orders?"

100 "By my orders. An electric thread connects us. I telegraph to it,
101 and that is enough."

102 "Really," I said, astonished at these marvels, "nothing can be
103 more simple."

104 After having passed by the cage of the staircase that led to the
105 platform, I saw a cabin six feet long, in which Conseil and
106 Ned Land, enchanted with their **repast**, were devouring it with
107 **avidity**. Then a door opened into a kitchen nine feet long, situated
108 between the large store-rooms. There electricity, better than gas
109 itself, did all the cooking. The streams under the furnaces gave
110 out to the sponges of platina a heat which was regularly kept up
111 and distributed. They also heated a **distilling** apparatus, which,
112 by evaporation, furnished excellent drinkable water. Near this
113 kitchen was a bathroom comfortably furnished, with hot and
114 cold water taps.

115 Next to the kitchen was the berth-room of the vessel, sixteen feet
116 long. But the door was shut, and I could not see the management
117 of it, which might have given me an idea of the number of men

58   Hollowed out space
59   Great speed

118 employed on board the Nautilus.

119 At the bottom was a fourth partition that separated this office
120 from the engine-room. A door opened, and I found myself in
121 the compartment where Captain Nemo—certainly an engineer
122 of a very high order—had arranged his locomotive machinery.
123 This engine-room, clearly lighted, did not measure less than
124 sixty-five feet in length. It was divided into two parts; the first
125 contained the materials for producing electricity, and the second
126 the machinery that connected it with the screw. I examined it
127 with great interest, in order to understand the machinery of the
128 Nautilus.

129 "You see," said the Captain, "I use Bunsen's contrivances, not
130 Ruhmkorff's. Those would not have been powerful enough.
131 Bunsen's are fewer in number, but strong and large, which
132 experience proves to be the best. The electricity produced passes
133 forward, where it works, by electro-magnets of great size, on
134 a system of levers and cog-wheels that transmit the movement
135 to the axle of the screw. This one, the diameter of which is
136 nineteen feet, and the thread twenty-three feet, performs about
137 120 revolutions in a second."

138 "And you get then?"

139 "A speed of fifty miles an hour."

140 "I have seen the Nautilus maneuver before the Abraham
141 Lincoln, and I have my own ideas as to its speed. But this is not
142 enough. We must see where we go. We must be able to direct
143 it to the right, to the left, above, below. How do you get to the
144 great depths, where you find an increasing resistance, which is
145 rated by hundreds of atmospheres? How do you return to the
146 surface of the ocean? And how do you maintain yourselves in
147 the **requisite medium**? Am I asking too much?"

148 "Not at all, Professor," replied the Captain, with some hesitation;
149 "since you may never leave this submarine boat. Come into the
150 saloon, it is our usual study, and there you will learn all you want

151   to know about the Nautilus."

Vocabulary part 1 chapter 11

tempests, factitious, avidity, distilling, requisite, medium

Questions for part 1 chapter 11

1. What metaphor does Captain Nemo use to describe electricity in line 28, and how is that a good metaphor for electricity?

2. Why doesn't the Captain produce his own air through electricity?

3. Is the Captain eager to explain his ships inner workings? How is this known?

4. How does the Captain acquire his electricity?

5. How big is the Nautilus and why do you think it's important for the story?

Chapter 12

SOME FIGURES

1 𝔄 **moment after** we were seated on a divan in the saloon
2 smoking. The Captain showed me a sketch that gave the plan,
3 section, and elevation of the Nautilus. Then he began his
4 description in these words:

5 "Here, M. Aronnax, are the several dimensions of the boat you
6 are in. It is an elongated cylinder with **conical** ends. It is very like
7 a cigar in shape, a shape already adopted in London in several
8 constructions of the same sort. The length of this cylinder, from
9 stem to stern, is exactly 232 feet, and its maximum breadth is
10 twenty-six feet....

11 "The Nautilus is composed of two **hulls**, one inside, the other
12 outside, joined by T-shaped irons, which **render** it very strong.
13 Indeed, owing to this **cellular** arrangement it resists like
14 a block, as if it were solid. Its sides cannot yield; it **coheres**
15 **spontaneously**, and not by the closeness of its rivets; and its
16 perfect union of the materials enables it to defy the roughest
17 seas.

18 "Well, Captain, but now we come to the real difficulty. I can
19 understand your rising to the surface; but, diving below the
20 surface, does not your submarine contrivance[60] encounter a
21 pressure, and consequently undergo an upward thrust[61] of one
22 atmosphere for every thirty feet of water, just about fifteen
23 pounds per square inch?"

24 "Just so, sir."

25 "Then, unless you quite fill the Nautilus, I do not see how you
26 can draw it down to those depths."

27 "Professor, you must not **confound** statics with dynamics or

---

28 60   something invented
29 61   push forward

30 you will be exposed to grave errors. There is very little labor
31 spent in attaining the lower regions of the ocean, for all bodies
32 have a tendency to sink. When I wanted to find out the necessary
33 increase of weight required to sink the Nautilus, I had only
34 to calculate the reduction of volume that sea-water acquires
35 according to the depth."

36 "That is evident."

37 "Now, if water is not absolutely incompressible, it is at least
38 capable of very slight compression. Indeed, after the most recent
39 calculations this reduction is only .000436 of an atmosphere for
40 each thirty feet of depth. If we want to sink 3,000 feet, I should
41 keep account of the reduction of bulk under a pressure equal to
42 that of a column of water of a thousand feet. The calculation is
43 easily verified. Now, I have supplementary reservoirs capable of
44 holding a hundred tons. Therefore I can sink to a considerable
45 depth. When I wish to rise to the level of the sea, I only let off
46 the water, and empty all the reservoirs if I want the Nautilus to
47 emerge from the tenth part of her total capacity."

48 I had nothing to object to these reasonings.

49 "I admit your calculations, Captain," I replied; "I should be
50 wrong to dispute them since daily experience confirms them;
51 but I foresee a real difficulty in the way."

52 "What, sir?"

53 "When you are about 1,000 feet deep, the walls of the Nautilus
54 bear a pressure of 100 atmospheres. If, then, just now you were
55 to empty the supplementary reservoirs, to lighten the vessel, and
56 to go up to the surface, the pumps must overcome the pressure
57 of 100 atmospheres, which is 1,500 lbs. per square inch. From
58 that a power——"

59 "That electricity alone can give," said the Captain, hastily. "I
60 repeat, sir, that the dynamic power of my engines is almost
61 infinite. The pumps of the Nautilus have an enormous power,
62 as you must have observed when their jets of water burst like

63 a torrent upon the Abraham Lincoln. Besides, I use subsidiary
64 reservoirs only to attain a mean depth of 750 to 1,000 fathoms,
65 and that with a view of managing my machines. Also, when I
66 have a mind to visit the depths of the ocean five or six mlles
67 below the surface, I make use of slower but not less infallible
68 means."

69 "What are they, Captain?"

70 "That involves my telling you how the Nautilus is worked."

71 "I am impatient to learn."

72 "To steer this boat to starboard or port, to turn, in a word,
73 following a horizontal plan, I use an ordinary rudder fixed on the
74 back of the stern-post, and with one wheel and some tackle to
75 steer by. But I can also make the Nautilus rise and sink, and sink
76 and rise, by a vertical movement by means of two inclined planes
77 fastened to its sides, opposite the center of flotation, planes that
78 move in every direction, and that are worked by powerful levers
79 from the interior. If the planes are kept parallel with the boat, it
80 moves horizontally. If slanted, the Nautilus, according to this
81 inclination, and under the influence of the screw, either sinks
82 diagonally or rises diagonally as it suits me. And even if I wish
83 to rise more quickly to the surface, I ship the screw, and the
84 pressure of the water causes the Nautilus to rise vertically like a
85 balloon filled with hydrogen."

86 "Bravo, Captain! But how can the steersman follow the route in
87 the middle of the waters?"

88 "The steersman is placed in a glazed box, that is raised about the
89 hull of the Nautilus, and furnished with lenses."

90 "Are these lenses capable of resisting such pressure?"

91 "Perfectly. Glass, which breaks at a blow, is, nevertheless,
92 capable of offering considerable resistance. During some
93 experiments of fishing by electric light in 1864 in the Northern
94 Seas, we saw plates less than a third of an inch thick resist a

95 pressure of sixteen atmospheres. Now, the glass that I use is not
96 less than thirty times thicker.”

97 “Granted. But, after all, in order to see, the light must exceed the
98 darkness, and in the midst of the darkness in the water, how can
99 you see?”

100 “Behind the steersman’s cage is placed a powerful electric
101 reflector, the rays from which light up the sea for half a mile in
102 front.”

103 “Ah! bravo, bravo, Captain! Now I can account for this
104 **phosphorescence** in the supposed narwhal that puzzled us so.
105 I now ask you if the boarding of the Nautilus and of the Scotia,
106 that has made such a noise, has been the result of a chance
107 rencontre?”

108 “Quite accidental, sir. I was sailing only one fathom below the
109 surface of the water when the shock came. It had no bad result.”

110 “None, sir. But now, about your **rencontre** with the Abraham
111 Lincoln?”

112 “Professor, I am sorry for one of the best vessels in the American
113 navy; but they attacked me, and I was bound to defend myself.
114 I contented myself, however, with putting the frigate hors de
115 combat; she will not have any difficulty in getting repaired at the
116 next port.”

117 “Ah, Commander! your Nautilus is certainly a marvelous boat.”

118 “Yes, Professor; and I love it as if it were part of myself. If danger
119 threatens one of your vessels on the ocean, the first impression is
120 the feeling of an **abyss** above and below. On the Nautilus men’s
121 hearts never fail them. No defects to be afraid of, for the double
122 shell is as firm as iron; no rigging to attend to; no sails for the
123 wind to carry away; no boilers to burst; no fire to fear, for the
124 vessel is made of iron, not of wood; no coal to run short, for
125 electricity is the only mechanical agent; no collision to fear, for
126 it alone swims in deep water; no tempest to brave, for when

127 it dives below the water it reaches absolute **tranquility**. There,
128 sir! that is the perfection of vessels! And if it is true that the
129 engineer has more confidence in the vessel than the builder, and
130 the builder than the captain himself, you understand the trust I
131 **repose** in my Nautilus; for I am at once Captain, builder, and
132 engineer."

133 "But how could you construct this wonderful Nautilus in secret?"

134 "Each separate portion, M. Aronnax, was brought from different
135 parts of the globe."

136 "But these parts had to be put together and arranged?"

137 "Professor, I had set up my workshops upon a desert island in
138 the ocean. There my workmen, that is to say, the brave men
139 that I instructed and educated, and myself have put together our
140 Nautilus. Then, when the work was finished, fire destroyed all
141 trace of our proceedings on this island, that I could have jumped
142 over if I had liked."

143 "Then the cost of this vessel is great?"

144 "M. Aronnax, an iron vessel costs L145 per ton. Now the Nautilus
145 weighed 1,500. It came therefore to L67,500, and L80,000 more
146 for fitting it up, and about L200,000, with the works of art and
147 the collections it contains."

148 "One last question, Captain Nemo."

149 "Ask it, Professor."

150 "You are rich?"

151 "Immensely rich, sir; and I could, without missing it, pay the
152 national debt of France."

153 I stared at the **singular** person who spoke thus. Was he playing
154 upon my **credulity**? The future would decide that.

Vocabulary part 1 chapter 12

conical, hulls, cellular, coheres, spontaneously, tranquility, credulity, singular

Questions for part 1 chapter 12

1. Was the Professor right in his assessment of the length of the submarine from the outset?

2. What is bothering the Professor in lines 18-26?

3. Without getting into too much detail, what does the Captain answer to question 2?

4. In lines 59-62, what power does the Captain say is capable of driving out the water from the tanks when under much pressure?

5. What move does the Captain employ to get the submarine down to the lowest regions of the oceans?

6. How does the submarine know where to navigate under the sea if it is so dark deep in the ocean?

7. How does the pilot see where he is going underneath the ocean?

8. What are five things that the Captain says in lines
    120-128 that makes the Nautilus stand out from among
    other sea going vessels?

    ____

    ____

    ____

9. Do you think the Captain is a show off? A baal gaava?
    If yes, prove it?

    ____

    ____

    ____

Chapter 13
THE BLACK RIVER

1 **The portion of** the **terrestrial** globe which is covered by water
2 is estimated at upwards of eighty millions of acres. This fluid
3 mass comprises two billions two hundred and fifty millions of
4 cubic miles, forming a spherical body of a diameter of sixty
5 leagues, the weight of which would be three quintillions of tons.
6 To comprehend the meaning of these figures, it is necessary to
7 observe that a quintillion is to a billion as a billion is to unity; in
8 other words, there are as many billions in a quintillion as there
9 are units in a billion. …

10 The Pacific Ocean extends from north to south between the two
11 Polar Circles, and from east to west between Asia and America,
12 over an extent of 145 degrees of longitude. It is the quietest of
13 seas; its currents are broad and slow, it has medium tides, and
14 abundant rain. Such was the ocean that my fate destined me first
15 to travel over under these strange conditions.

16 "Sir," said Captain Nemo, "we will, if you please, take our
17 **bearings** and fix the starting-point of this voyage. It is a quarter
18 to twelve; I will go up again to the surface."

19 The Captain pressed an electric clock three times. The pumps
20 began to drive the water from the tanks; the needle of the
21 manometer marked by a different pressure the **ascent** of the
22 Nautilus, then it stopped.

23 "We have arrived," said the Captain.

24 I went to the central staircase which opened on to the platform,
25 **clambered** up the iron steps, and found myself on the upper part
26 of the Nautilus.

27 The platform was only three feet out of water. The front and
28 back of the Nautilus was of that spindle-shape which caused it
29 justly to be compared to a cigar. I noticed that its iron plates,

30 slightly overlaying each other, resembled the shell which clothes
31 the bodies of our large terrestrial reptiles. It explained to me how
32 natural it was, in spite of all glasses, that this boat should have
33 been taken for a marine animal.

34 Toward the middle of the platform the longboat, half buried in
35 the hull of the vessel, formed a slight excrescence. Fore and aft
36 rose two cages of medium height with inclined sides, and partly
37 closed by thick lenticular glasses; one destined for the steersman
38 who directed the Nautilus, the other containing a brilliant lantern
39 to give light on the road.

40 The sea was beautiful, the sky pure. Scarcely could the long
41 vehicle feel the broad undulations of the ocean. A light breeze
42 from the east rippled the surface of the waters. The horizon, free
43 from fog, made observation easy. Nothing was in sight. Not a
44 quicksand, not an island. A vast desert.

45 Captain Nemo, by the help of his sextant, took the altitude of
46 the sun, which ought also to give the latitude. He waited for
47 some moments till its disc touched the horizon. Whilst taking
48 observations not a muscle moved, the instrument could not have
49 been more motionless in a hand of marble.

50 "Twelve o'clock, sir," said he. "When you like——"

51 I cast a last look upon the sea, slightly yellowed by the Japanese
52 coast, and descended to the saloon.

53 "And now, sir, I leave you to your studies," added the Captain;
54 "our course is E.N.E., our depth is twenty-six fathoms. Here are
55 maps on a large scale by which you may follow it. The saloon
56 is at your disposal, and, with your permission, I will retire."
57 Captain Nemo bowed, and I remained alone, lost in thoughts all
58 bearing on the commander of the Nautilus.

59 For a whole hour was I deep in these reflections, seeking to pierce
60 this mystery so interesting to me. Then my eyes fell upon the
61 vast planisphere spread upon the table, and I placed my finger
62 on the very spot where the given latitude and longitude crossed.

The sea has its large rivers like the continents. They are special currents known by their temperature and their color. The most remarkable of these is known by the name of the Gulf Stream. Science has decided on the globe the direction of five principal currents: one in the North Atlantic, a second in the South, a third in the North Pacific, a fourth in the South, and a fifth in the Southern Indian Ocean. It is even probable that a sixth current existed at one time or another in the Northern Indian Ocean, when the Caspian and Aral Seas formed but one vast sheet of water.

At this point indicated on the planisphere one of these currents was rolling, the Kuro-Scivo of the Japanese, the Black River, which, leaving the Gulf of Bengal, where it is warmed by the perpendicular rays of a tropical sun, crosses the Straits of Malacca along the coast of Asia, turns into the North Pacific to the Aleutian Islands, carrying with it trunks of camphor-trees and other **indigenous** productions, and edging the waves of the ocean with the pure **indigo** of its warm water. It was this current that the Nautilus was to follow. I followed it with my eye; saw it lose itself in the vastness of the Pacific, and felt myself drawn with it, when Ned Land and Conseil appeared at the door of the saloon.

My two brave companions remained petrified at the sight of the wonders spread before them.

"Where are we, where are we?" exclaimed the Canadian. "In the museum at Quebec?"

"My friends," I answered, making a sign for them to enter, "you are not in Canada, but on board the Nautilus, fifty yards below the level of the sea."

"But, M. Aronnax," said Ned Land, "can you tell me how many men there are on board? Ten, twenty, fifty, a hundred?"

"I cannot answer you, Mr. Land; it is better to abandon for a time all idea of seizing the Nautilus or escaping from it. This ship

96 is a masterpiece of modern industry, and I should be sorry not
97 to have seen it. Many people would accept the situation forced
98 upon us, if only to move amongst such wonders. So be quiet and
99 let us try and see what passes around us."

100 "See!" exclaimed the harpooner, "but we can see nothing in this
101 iron prison! We are walking—we are sailing—blindly."

102 Ned Land had scarcely pronounced these words when all was
103 suddenly darkness. The luminous ceiling was gone, and so
104 rapidly that my eyes received a painful impression.

105 We remained mute, not stirring, and not knowing what surprise
106 awaited us, whether agreeable or disagreeable. A sliding noise
107 was heard: one would have said that panels were working at the
108 sides of the Nautilus.

109 "It is the end of the end!" said Ned Land.

110 Suddenly light broke at each side of the saloon, through two
111 oblong openings. The liquid mass appeared vividly lit up by the
112 electric gleam. Two crystal plates separated us from the sea. At
113 first I trembled at the thought that this frail partition might break,
114 but strong bands of copper bound them, giving an almost infinite
115 power of resistance.

116 The sea was distinctly visible for a mile all round the Nautilus.
117 What a spectacle! What pen can describe it? Who could paint the
118 effects of the light through those transparent sheets of water, and
119 the softness of the **successive gradations** from the lower to the
120 **superior strata** of the ocean?

121 We know the transparency of the sea and that its clearness is far
122 beyond that of rock-water. The mineral and organic substances
123 which it holds in suspension heightens its transparency. In certain
124 parts of the ocean at the Antilles, under seventy-five fathoms of
125 water, can be seen with surprising clearness a bed of sand. The
126 penetrating power of the solar rays does not seem to cease for
127 a depth of one hundred and fifty fathoms. But in this middle
128 fluid travelled over by the Nautilus, the electric brightness was

129 produced even in the bosom of the waves. It was no longer
130 luminous water, but liquid light.

131 On each side a window opened into this unexplored abyss. The
132 obscurity of the saloon showed to advantage the brightness
133 outside, and we looked out as if this pure crystal had been the
134 glass of an immense aquarium.

135 "You wished to see, friend Ned; well, you see now."

136 "Curious! curious!" muttered the Canadian, who, forgetting his
137 ill-temper, seemed to submit to some irresistible attraction; "and
138 one would come further than this to admire such a sight!"

139 "Ah!" thought I to myself, "I understand the life of this man; he
140 has made a world apart for himself, in which he treasures all his
141 greatest wonders."

142 For two whole hours an aquatic army escorted the Nautilus.
143 During their games, their bounds, while rivalling each other
144 in beauty, brightness, and velocity, I distinguished the green
145 labre…, serpents six feet long, with eyes small and lively, and a
146 huge mouth bristling with teeth; with many other species.

147 Our imagination was kept at its height, interjections followed
148 quickly on each other. Ned named the fish, and Conseil classed
149 them. I was in **ecstasies** with the **vivacity** of their movements
150 and the beauty of their forms. Never had it been given to me
151 to surprise these animals, alive and at liberty, in their natural
152 element. I will not mention all the varieties which passed before
153 my dazzled eyes, all the collection of the seas of China and
154 Japan. These fish, more numerous than the birds of the air, came,
155 attracted, no doubt, by the brilliant focus of the electric light.

156 Suddenly there was daylight in the saloon, the iron panels closed
157 again, and the enchanting vision disappeared. But for a long time
158 I dreamt on, till my eyes fell on the instruments hanging on the
159 partition. The compass still showed the course to be E.N.E., the
160 manometer indicated a pressure of five atmospheres, equivalent
161 to a depth of twenty five fathoms, and the electric log gave a

162 speed of fifteen miles an hour. I expected Captain Nemo, but he
163 did not appear. The clock marked the hour of five.

164 Ned Land and Conseil returned to their cabin, and I retired to my
165 chamber. My dinner was ready. It was composed of turtle soup
166 made of the most delicate hawks bills, of a surmullet served
167 with puff paste (the liver of which, prepared by itself, was most
168 delicious), and fillets of the emperor-holocanthus, the savor of
169 which seemed to me superior even to salmon.

170 I passed the evening reading, writing, and thinking. Then sleep
171 overpowered me, and I stretched myself on my couch of zostera,
172 and slept profoundly, whilst the Nautilus was gliding rapidly

173 through the current of the Black River.

Vocabulary part 1 chapter 13

terrestrial, ascent, clambered, indigenous, indigo, successive, superior, transparency, ecstasies, vivacity, enchanting,

Questions for part 1 chapter 13

1. What does the author say a *quintillion* is in line 7?

2. What are currents in the ocean mentioned in lines 63-70? Name three and where do they travel.

3. What is the argument of the Professor to Ned Land in lines 94-101?

4. What helps ease the tension that Ned Land feels about being imprisoned on this submarine?

A NOTE OF INVITATION

The next day was the 9th of November. I awoke after a long sleep of twelve hours. Conseil came, according to custom, to know "how I passed the night," and to offer his services. He had left his friend the Canadian sleeping like a man who had never done anything else all his life. I let the worthy fellow **chatter** as he pleased, without caring to answer him. I was preoccupied by the absence of the Captain during our sitting of the day before, and hoping to see him to-day.

As soon as I was dressed I went into the saloon. It was deserted. I plunged into the study of the shell treasures hidden behind the glasses.

The whole day passed without my being honored by a visit from Captain Nemo. The panels of the saloon did not open. Perhaps they did not wish us to tire of these beautiful things.

The course of the Nautilus was E.N.E., her speed twelve knots, the depth below the surface between twenty-five and thirty **fathoms**.

The next day, 10th of November, the same desertion, the same solitude. I did not see one of the ship's crew: Ned and Conseil spent the greater part of the day with me. They were astonished at the puzzling absence of the Captain. Was this singular man ill?—had he altered his intentions with regard to us?

After all, as Conseil said, we enjoyed perfect liberty, we were delicately and abundantly fed. Our host kept to his terms of the **treaty**. We could not complain, and, indeed, the **singularity** of our fate reserved such wonderful **compensation** for us that we had no right to accuse it as yet.

That day I **commenced** the journal of these adventures which has enabled me to relate them with more **scrupulous exactitude**

30   and minute detail.

31   11th November, early in the morning. The fresh air spreading
32   over the interior of the Nautilus told me that we had come to the
33   surface of the ocean to renew our supply of oxygen. I directed
34   my steps to the central staircase, and mounted the platform.

35   It was six o'clock, the weather was cloudy, the sea grey, but
36   calm. Scarcely a billow. Captain Nemo, whom I hoped to meet,
37   would he be there? I saw no one but the steersman imprisoned in
38   his glass cage. Seated upon the projection formed by the hull of
39   the pinnace, I inhaled the salt breeze with delight.

40   By degrees the fog disappeared under the action of the sun's
41   rays, the radiant orb rose from behind the eastern horizon.
42   The sea flamed under its glance like a train of gunpowder. The
43   clouds scattered in the heights were coloured with lively tints of
44   beautiful shades, and numerous "mare's tails," which **betokened**
45   wind for that day. But what was wind to this Nautilus, which
46   tempests could not frighten!

47   I was admiring this joyous rising of the sun, so gay, and so
48   life-giving, when I heard steps approaching the platform. I was
49   prepared to salute Captain Nemo, but it was his second (whom
50   I had already seen on the Captain's first visit) who appeared.
51   He advanced on the platform, not seeming to see me. With his
52   powerful glass to his eye, he scanned every point of the horizon
53   with great attention. This examination over, he approached the
54   panel and pronounced a sentence in exactly these terms. I have
55   remembered it, for every morning it was repeated under exactly
56   the same conditions. It was thus worded:

57   "Nautron respoc lorni virch."

58   What it meant I could not say.

59   These words pronounced, the second descended. I thought that
60   the Nautilus was about to return to its submarine navigation. I
61   regained the panel and returned to my chamber.

Five days sped thus, without any change in our situation. Every morning I mounted the platform. The same phrase was pronounced by the same individual. But Captain Nemo did not appear.

I had made up my mind that I should never see him again, when, on the 16th November, on returning to my room with Ned and Conseil, I found upon my table a note addressed to me. I opened it impatiently. It was written in a bold, clear hand, the characters rather pointed, recalling the German type. The note was worded as follows:

TO PROFESSOR ARONNAX, On board the Nautilus. 16th of November, 1867.

Captain Nemo invites Professor Aronnax to a hunting-party, which will take place to-morrow morning in the forests of the Island of Crespo. He hopes that nothing will prevent the Professor from being present, and he will with pleasure see him joined by his companions.

CAPTAIN NEMO, Commander of the Nautilus.

"A hunt!" exclaimed Ned.

"And in the forests of the Island of Crespo!" added Conseil.

"Oh! then the gentleman is going on **terra firma**?" replied Ned Land.

"That seems to me to be clearly indicated," said I, reading the letter once more.

"Well, we must accept," said the Canadian. "But once more on dry ground, we shall know what to do. Indeed, I shall not be sorry to eat a piece of fresh **venison**."

Without seeking to **reconcile** what was contradictory between

92 Captain Nemo's manifest aversion to islands and continents,
93 and his invitation to hunt in a forest, I contented myself with
94 replying:

95 "Let us first see where the Island of Crespo is."

96 I consulted the planisphere, and in 32° 40' N. lat. and 157° 50'
97 W. long., I found a small island, recognized in 1801 by Captain
98 Crespo, and marked in the ancient Spanish maps as Rocca de la
99 Plata, the meaning of which is The Silver Rock. We were then
100 about eighteen hundred miles from our starting-point, and the
101 course of the Nautilus, a little changed, was bringing it back
102 towards the southeast.

103 I showed this little rock, lost in the midst of the North Pacific, to
104 my companions.

105 "If Captain Nemo does sometimes go on dry ground," said I, "he
106 at least chooses desert islands."

107 Ned Land shrugged his shoulders without speaking, and Conseil
108 and he left me.

109 After supper, which was served by the steward, mute and
110 impassive, I went to bed, not without some anxiety.

111 The next morning, the 17th of November, on awakening, I
112 felt that the Nautilus was perfectly still. I dressed quickly and
113 entered the saloon.

114 Captain Nemo was there, waiting for me. He rose, bowed, and
115 asked me if it was convenient for me to accompany him. As he
116 made no **allusion** to his absence during the last eight days, I did
117 not mention it, and simply answered that my companions and
118 myself were ready to follow him.

119 We entered the dining-room, where breakfast was served.

120 "M. Aronnax," said the Captain, "pray, share my breakfast
121 without ceremony; we will chat as we eat. For, though I promised

122 you a walk in the forest, I did not undertake to find hotels there.
123 So breakfast as a man who will most likely not have his dinner
124 till very late."

125 I did honor to the repast. It was composed of several kinds of
126 fish, and slices of sea-cucumber, and different sorts of seaweed.
127 Our drink consisted of pure water, to which the Captain added
128 some drops of a fermented liquor, extracted by the Kamschatcha
129 method from a seaweed known under the name of Rhodomenia
130 palmata. Captain Nemo ate at first without saying a word. Then
131 he began:

132 "Sir, when I proposed to you to hunt in my submarine forest of
133 Crespo, you evidently thought me mad. Sir, you should never
134 judge lightly of any man."

135 "But Captain, believe me——"

136 "Be kind enough to listen, and you will then see whether you
137 have any cause to accuse me of **folly** and contradiction."

138 "I listen."

139 "You know as well as I do, Professor, that man can live under
140 water, providing he carries with him a sufficient supply of
141 breathable air. In submarine works, the workman, clad in an
142 **impervious** dress, with his head in a metal helmet, receives air
143 from above by means of forcing pumps and regulators."

144 "That is a diving apparatus," said I.

145 "Just so, but under these conditions the man is not at liberty;
146 he is attached to the pump which sends him air through an
147 india-rubber tube, and if we were obliged to be thus held to the
148 Nautilus, we could not go far."

149 "And the means of getting free?" I asked.

150 "It is to use the Rouquayrol apparatus, invented by two of
151 your own countrymen, which I have brought to perfection for

152 my own use, and which will allow you to risk yourself under
153 these new physiological conditions without any organ whatever
154 suffering…

155 "Perfectly, Captain Nemo; but the air that you carry with you
156 must soon be used; when it only contains fifteen per cent. of
157 oxygen it is no longer fit to breathe."

158 "Right! But I told you, M. Aronnax, that the pumps of the
159 Nautilus allow me to store the air under considerable pressure,
160 and on those conditions the reservoir of the apparatus can furnish
161 breathable air for nine or ten hours."

162 "I have no further objections to make," I answered. "I will only
163 ask you one thing, Captain—how can you light your road at the
164 bottom of the sea?"

165 "With the Ruhmkorff apparatus, M. Aronnax; one is carried on
166 the back, the other is fastened to the waist. …When the apparatus
167 is at work this gas becomes luminous, giving out a white and
168 continuous light. Thus provided, I can breathe and I can see."

169 "Captain Nemo, to all my objections you make such crushing
170 answers that I dare no longer doubt. But, if I am forced to admit
171 the Rouquayrol and Ruhmkorff apparatus, I must be allowed
172 some reservations with regard to the gun I am to carry."

173 "But it is not a gun for powder," answered the Captain.

174 "Then it is an air-gun."

175 "Doubtless! How would you have me manufacture gun powder
176 on board, without either saltpetre, sulphur, or charcoal?"

177 "Besides," I added, "to fire under water in a medium eight
178 hundred and fifty-five times denser than the air, we must conquer
179 very considerable resistance."

180 "That would be no difficulty. There exist guns, according to
181 Fulton, perfected in England by Philip Coles and Burley, in

182 France by Furcy, and in Italy by Landi, which are furnished
183 with a peculiar system of closing, which can fire under these
184 conditions. But I repeat, having no powder, I use air under great
185 pressure, which the pumps of the Nautilus furnish abundantly."

186 "But this air must be rapidly used?"

187 "Well, have I not my Rouquayrol reservoir, which can furnish it
188 at need? A tap is all that is required. Besides M. Aronnax, you
189 must see yourself that, during our submarine hunt, we can spend
190 but little air and but few balls."

191 "But it seems to me that in this twilight, and in the midst of this
192 fluid, which is very dense compared with the atmosphere, shots
193 could not go far, nor easily prove mortal."

194 "Sir, on the contrary, with this gun every blow is mortal; and,
195 however lightly the animal is touched, it falls as if struck by a
196 thunderbolt."

197 "Why?"

198 "Because the balls sent by this gun are not ordinary balls, but
199 little cases of glass. These glass cases are covered with a case of
200 steel, and weighted with a pellet of lead; they are real Leyden
201 bottles, into which the electricity is forced to a very high tension.
202 With the slightest shock they are discharged, and the animal,
203 however strong it may be, falls dead. I must tell you that these
204 cases are size number four, and that the charge for an ordinary
205 gun would be ten."

206 "I will argue no longer," I replied, rising from the table. "I have
207 nothing left me but to take my gun. At all events, I will go where
208 you go." Captain Nemo then led me aft; and in passing before
209 Ned's and Conseil's cabin, I called my two companions, who
210 followed **promptly**. We then came to a cell near the machinery-
211 room, in which we put on our walking-dress.

For vocabulary on Chapter 14, see the end of Chapter 15.
For questions on Chapter 14 - please see the end of Chapter 16.

Chapter 15

A WALK ON THE BOTTOM OF THE SEA

This cell was, to speak correctly, the arsenal and wardrobe of the Nautilus. A dozen diving apparatuses hung from the partition waiting our use.

Ned Land, on seeing them, showed evident repugnance to dress himself in one.

"But, my worthy Ned, the forests of the Island of Crespo are nothing but submarine forests."

"Good!" said the disappointed harpooner, who saw his dreams of fresh meat fade away. "And you, M. Aronnax, are you going to dress yourself in those clothes?"

"There is no alternative, Master Ned."

"As you please, sir," replied the harpooner, shrugging his shoulders; "but, as for me, unless I am forced, I will never get into one."

"No one will force you, Master Ned," said Captain Nemo.

"Is Conseil going to risk it?" asked Ned.

"I follow my master wherever he goes," replied Conseil.

….Captain Nemo and one of his companions (a sort of Hercules, who must have possessed great strength), Conseil and myself were soon enveloped in the dresses. There remained nothing more to be done but to enclose our heads in the metal box. But, before proceeding to this operation, I asked the Captain's permission to examine the guns.

One of the Nautilus men gave me a simple gun, the butt end of which, made of steel, hollow in the centre, was rather large. It

26 served as a reservoir for compressed air, which a valve, worked
27 by a spring, allowed to escape into a metal tube. A box of
28 projectiles in a groove in the thickness of the butt end contained
29 about twenty of these electric balls, which, by means of a spring,
30 were forced into the barrel of the gun. As soon as one shot was
31 fired, another was ready.

32 "Captain Nemo," said I, "this arm is perfect, and easily handled:
33 I only ask to be allowed to try it. But how shall we gain the
34 bottom of the sea?"

35 "At this moment, Professor, the Nautilus is stranded in five
36 fathoms, and we have nothing to do but to start."

37 "But how shall we get off?"

38 "You shall see."

39 Captain Nemo thrust his head into the helmet, Conseil and I did
40 the same, not without hearing an ironical "Good sport!" from
41 the Canadian. The upper part of our dress terminated in a copper
42 collar upon which was screwed the metal helmet. Three holes,
43 protected by thick glass, allowed us to see in all directions, by
44 simply turning our head in the interior of the head-dress. As soon
45 as it was in position, the Rouquayrol apparatus on our backs
46 began to act; and, for my part, I could breathe with ease.

47 With the Ruhmkorff lamp hanging from my belt, and the gun
48 in my hand, I was ready to set out. But to speak the truth,
49 imprisoned in these heavy garments, and glued to the deck by
50 my leaden soles, it was impossible for me to take a step.

51 But this state of things was provided for. I felt myself being
52 pushed into a little room contiguous to the wardrobe room. My
53 companions followed, towed along in the same way. I heard a
54 water-tight door, furnished with stopper plates, close upon us,
55 and we were wrapped in profound darkness.

56 After some minutes, a loud hissing was heard. I felt the cold
57 mount from my feet to my chest. Evidently from some part of

58 the vessel they had, by means of a tap, given entrance to the
59 water, which was invading us, and with which the room was
60 soon filled. A second door cut in the side of the Nautilus then
61 opened. We saw a faint light. In another instant our feet trod the
62 bottom of the sea.

63 And now, how can I retrace the impression left upon me by
64 that walk under the waters? Words are impotent to relate
65 such wonders! Captain Nemo walked in front, his companion
66 followed some steps behind. Conseil and I remained near each
67 other, as if an exchange of words had been possible through our
68 metallic cases. I no longer felt the weight of my clothing, or of
69 my shoes, of my reservoir of air, or my thick helmet, in the midst
70 of which my head rattled like an almond in its shell.

71 The light, which lit the soil thirty feet below the surface of
72 the ocean, astonished me by its power. The solar rays shone
73 through the watery mass easily, and **dissipated** all color, and
74 I clearly distinguished objects at a distance of a hundred and
75 fifty yards. Beyond that the tints darkened into fine gradations
76 of ultramarine, and faded into vague obscurity. Truly this water
77 which surrounded me was but another air denser than the
78 terrestrial atmosphere, but almost as transparent. Above me was
79 the calm surface of the sea. We were walking on fine, even sand,
80 not wrinkled, as on a flat shore, which retains the impression of
81 the **billows**. This dazzling carpet, really a reflector, **repelled** the
82 rays of the sun with wonderful intensity, which accounted for
83 the vibration which penetrated every atom of liquid. Shall I be
84 believed when I say that, at the depth of thirty feet, I could see
85 as if I was in broad daylight?

86 For a quarter of an hour I trod on this sand, sown with the
87 **impalpable** dust of shells. The hull of the Nautilus, resembling
88 a long shoal, disappeared by degrees; but its lantern, when
89 darkness should overtake us in the waters, would help to guide
90 us on board by its distinct rays.

91 Soon forms of objects outlined in the distance were discernible. I
92 recognised magnificent rocks, hung with a tapestry of zoophytes

93   of the most beautiful kind, and I was at first struck by the peculiar
94   effect of this medium.

95   It was then ten in the morning; the rays of the sun struck the
96   surface of the waves at rather an **oblique** angle, and at the touch
97   of their light, decomposed by refraction as through a prism,
98   flowers, rocks, plants, shells, and polypi were shaded at the
99   edges by the seven solar colors. It was marvelous, a feast for the
100 eyes, this complication of colored tints, a perfect **kaleidoscope**
101 of green, yellow, orange, violet, indigo, and blue; in one word,
102 the whole **palette** of an enthusiastic **colorist**! Why could I
103 not communicate to Conseil the lively sensations which were
104 mounting to my brain, and rival him in expressions of admiration?
105 For **aught** I knew, Captain Nemo and his companion might be
106 able to exchange thoughts by means of signs previously agreed
107 upon. So, for want of better, I talked to myself; I **declaimed** in
108 the copper box which covered my head, thereby expending more
109 air in vain words than was perhaps wise.

110 Various kinds of isis, clusters of pure tuft-coral, prickly fungi,
111 and anemones formed a brilliant garden of flowers, decked with
112 their collarettes of blue tentacles, sea-stars studding the sandy
113 bottom. ...

114 We had quitted the Nautilus about an hour and a half. It was near
115 noon; I knew by the **perpendicularity** of the sun's rays, which
116 were no longer refracted. The magical colors disappeared by
117 degrees, and the shades of emerald and sapphire were **effaced**.
118 We walked with a regular step, which rang upon the ground with
119 astonishing intensity; the slightest noise was transmitted with a
120 quickness to which the ear is unaccustomed on the earth; indeed,
121 water is a better conductor of sound than air, in the ratio of four
122 to one. At this period the earth sloped downwards; the light took
123 a uniform tint. We were at a depth of a hundred and five yards
124 and twenty inches, undergoing a pressure of six atmospheres.

125 At this depth I could still see the rays of the sun, though **feebly**;
126 to their intense brilliancy had succeeded a reddish twilight, the
127 lowest state between day and night; but we could still see well

128 enough; it was not necessary to resort to the Ruhmkorff apparatus
129 as yet. At this moment Captain Nemo stopped; he waited till I
130 joined him, and then pointed to an obscure mass, looming in the
131 shadow, at a short distance.

132 "It is the forest of the Island of Crespo," thought I; and I was not
133 mistaken.

Vocabulary for part 1 chapter 14

chatter, fathoms, treaty, singularity, terra-firma, venison, reconcile, allusion, folly, impervious, promptly,

For questions on chapter 14-see the end of chapter 16

Vocabulary for part 1 Chapter 15

dissipated, billows, repelled, impalpable, oblique, kaleidoscope, palette, colorist, aught, declaimed, perpendicularity, effaced, feebly,

For questions on chapter 15-see the end of chapter 16

Chapter 16

A SUBMARINE FOREST

We had at last arrived on the borders of this forest, doubtless one of the finest of Captain Nemo's **immense domains**. He looked upon it as his own, and considered he had the same right over it that the first men had in the first days of the world. And, indeed, who would have disputed with him the possession of this submarine property? What other hardier pioneer would come, hatchet in hand, to cut down the dark copses?

This forest was composed of large tree-plants; and the moment we penetrated under its vast arcades, I was struck by the singular position of their branches—a position I had not yet observed.

Not an herb which carpeted the ground, not a branch which clothed the trees, was either broken or bent, nor did they extend horizontally; all stretched up to the surface of the ocean. Not a **filament**, not a ribbon, however thin they might be, but kept as straight as a rod of iron. The fuci and llianas grew in rigid perpendicular lines, due to the density of the element which had produced them. Motionless yet, when bent to one side by the hand, they directly resumed their former position. Truly it was the region of perpendicularity!

I soon accustomed myself to this fantastic position, as well as to the comparative darkness which surrounded us. The soil of the forest seemed covered with sharp blocks, difficult to avoid. The submarine flora struck me as being very perfect, and richer even than it would have been in the arctic or tropical zones, where these productions are not so plentiful. But for some minutes I involuntarily **confounded** the genera, taking animals for plants; and who would not have been mistaken? The **fauna** and the **flora** are too closely allied in this submarine world.

These plants are self-**propagated**, and the principle of their existence is in the water, which upholds and nourishes them. The greater number, instead of leaves, shoot forth blades of

32 capricious shapes, comprised within a scale of colours pink,
33 carmine, green, olive, fawn, and brown.

34 "Curious anomaly, fantastic element!" said an ingenious
35 naturalist, "in which the animal kingdom blossoms, and the
36 vegetable does not!"

37 In about an hour Captain Nemo gave the signal to halt; I, for my
38 part, was not sorry, and we stretched ourselves under an arbour
39 of alariae, the long thin blades of which stood up like arrows.

40 This short rest seemed delicious to me; there was nothing
41 wanting but the charm of conversation; but, impossible to
42 speak, impossible to answer, I only put my great copper head to
43 Conseil's. I saw the worthy fellow's eyes glistening with delight,
44 and, to show his satisfaction, he shook himself in his breastplate
45 of air, in the most comical way in the world.

46 After four hours of this walking, I was surprised not to find
47 myself dreadfully hungry. How to account for this state of the
48 stomach I could not tell. But instead I felt an **insurmountable**
49 desire to sleep, which happens to all divers. And my eyes soon
50 closed behind the thick glasses, and I fell into a heavy slumber,
51 which the movement alone had prevented before. Captain Nemo
52 and his robust companion, stretched in the clear crystal, set us
53 the example.

54 How long I remained buried in this drowsiness I cannot judge,
55 but, when I woke, the sun seemed sinking towards the horizon.
56 Captain Nemo had already risen, and I was beginning to stretch
57 my limbs, when an unexpected **apparition** brought me briskly
58 to my feet.

59 A few steps off, a monstrous sea-spider, about thirty-eight inches
60 high, was watching me with squinting eyes, ready to spring upon
61 me. Though my diver's dress was thick enough to defend me from
62 the bite of this animal, I could not help shuddering with horror.
63 Conseil and the sailor of the Nautilus awoke at this moment.
64 Captain Nemo pointed out the hideous crustacean, which a

65 blow from the butt end of the gun knocked over, and I saw the
66 horrible claws of the monster **writhe** in terrible convulsions.
67 This incident reminded me that other animals more to be feared
68 might haunt these obscure depths, against whose attacks my
69 diving-dress would not protect me. I had never thought of
70 it before, but I now resolved to be upon my guard. Indeed, I
71 thought that this halt would mark the termination of our walk;
72 but I was mistaken, for, instead of returning to the Nautilus,
73 Captain Nemo continued his bold excursion. The ground was
74 still on the incline, its **declivity** seemed to be getting greater,
75 and to be leading us to greater depths. It must have been about
76 three o'clock when we reached a narrow valley, between high
77 perpendicular walls, situated about seventy-five fathoms deep.
78 Thanks to the perfection of our apparatus, we were forty-five
79 fathoms below the limit which nature seems to have imposed on
80 man as to his submarine excursions.

81 I say seventy-five fathoms, though I had no instrument by which
82 to judge the distance. But I knew that even in the clearest waters
83 the solar rays could not penetrate further. And accordingly the
84 darkness deepened. At ten paces not an object was visible.
85 I was groping my way, when I suddenly saw a brilliant white
86 light. Captain Nemo had just put his electric apparatus into use;
87 his companion did the same, and Conseil and I followed their
88 example. By turning a screw I established a communication
89 between the wire and the spiral glass, and the sea, lit by our four
90 lanterns, was illuminated for a circle of thirty-six yards.

91 As we walked I thought the light of our Ruhmkorff apparatus
92 could not fail to draw some inhabitant from its dark couch. But
93 if they did approach us, they at least kept at a respectful distance
94 from the hunters. Several times I saw Captain Nemo stop, put his
95 gun to his shoulder, and after some moments drop it and walk on.
96 At last, after about four hours, this marvellous excursion came to
97 an end. A wall of superb rocks, in an imposing mass, rose before
98 us, a heap of gigantic blocks, an enormous, steep granite shore,
99 forming dark grottos, but which presented no practicable slope;
100 it was the prop of the Island of Crespo. It was the earth! Captain

101 Nemo stopped suddenly. A gesture of his brought us all to a halt;
102 and, however desirous I might be to scale the wall, I was obliged
103 to stop. Here ended Captain Nemo's domains. And he would not
104 go beyond them. Further on was a portion of the globe he might
105 not trample upon.

106 The return began. Captain Nemo had returned to the head of his
107 little band, directing their course without hesitation. I thought
108 we were not following the same road to return to the Nautilus.
109 The new road was very steep, and consequently very painful. We
110 approached the surface of the sea rapidly. But this return to the
111 upper strata was not so sudden as to cause relief from the pressure
112 too rapidly, which might have produced serious disorder in our
113 organisation, and brought on internal lesions, so fatal to divers.
114 Very soon light reappeared and grew, and, the sun being low
115 on the horizon, the refraction edged the different objects with a
116 spectral ring. At ten yards and a half deep, we walked amidst a
117 shoal of little fishes of all kinds, more numerous than the birds
118 of the air, and also more agile; but no aquatic game worthy of
119 a shot had as yet met our gaze, when at that moment I saw the
120 Captain shoulder his gun quickly, and follow a moving object
121 into the shrubs. He fired; I heard a slight hissing, and a creature
122 fell stunned at some distance from us. It was a magnificent sea-
123 otter, an enhydrus, the only exclusively marine quadruped. This
124 otter was five feet long, and must have been very valuable. Its
125 skin, chestnut-brown above and silvery underneath, would have
126 made one of those beautiful furs so sought after in the Russian
127 and Chinese markets: the fineness and the lustre of its coat
128 would certainly fetch L80. I admired this curious mammal, with
129 its rounded head ornamented with short ears, its round eyes, and
130 white whiskers like those of a cat, with webbed feet and nails,
131 and tufted tail. This precious animal, hunted and tracked by
132 fishermen, has now become very rare, and taken refuge chiefly
133 in the northern parts of the Pacific, or probably its race would
134 soon become extinct.

135 Captain Nemo's companion took the beast, threw it over his
136 shoulder, and we continued our journey. For one hour a plain

137 of sand lay stretched before us. Sometimes it rose to within two
138 yards and some inches of the surface of the water. I then saw our
139 image clearly reflected, drawn inversely, and above us appeared
140 an identical group reflecting our movements and our actions; in
141 a word, like us in every point, except that they walked with their
142 heads downward and their feet in the air.

143 Another effect I noticed, which was the passage of thick
144 clouds which formed and vanished rapidly; but on reflection I
145 understood that these seeming clouds were due to the varying
146 thickness of the reeds at the bottom, and I could even see the
147 fleecy foam which their broken tops multiplied on the water, and
148 the shadows of large birds passing above our heads, whose rapid
149 flight I could discern on the surface of the sea.

150 On this occasion I was witness to one of the finest gun shots
151 which ever made the nerves of a hunter thrill. A large bird of
152 great breadth of wing, clearly visible, approached, hovering over
153 us. Captain Nemo's companion shouldered his gun and fired,
154 when it was only a few yards above the waves. The creature fell
155 stunned, and the force of its fall brought it within the reach of
156 dexterous hunter's grasp. It was an albatross of the finest kind.

157 Our march had not been interrupted by this incident. For two
158 hours we followed these sandy plains, then fields of algae very
159 disagreeable to cross. Candidly, I could do no more when I saw
160 a glimmer of light, which, for a half mile, broke the darkness
161 of the waters. It was the lantern of the Nautilus. Before twenty
162 minutes were over we should be on board, and I should be able
163 to breathe with ease, for it seemed that my reservoir supplied air
164 very **deficient** in oxygen. But I did not reckon on an accidental
165 meeting which delayed our arrival for some time.

166 I had remained some steps behind, when I presently saw Captain
167 Nemo coming hurriedly towards me. With his strong hand he
168 bent me to the ground, his companion doing the same to Conseil.
169 At first I knew not what to think of this sudden attack, but I was
170 soon reassured by seeing the Captain lie down beside me, and
171 remain immovable.

172 I was stretched on the ground, just under the shelter of a bush
173 of algae, when, raising my head, I saw some enormous mass,
174 casting phosphorescent gleams, pass **blusteringly** by.

175 My blood froze in my veins as I recognized two formidable
176 sharks which threatened us. It was a couple of tintoreas, terrible
177 creatures, with enormous tails and a dull glassy stare, the
178 phosphorescent matter ejected from holes pierced around the
179 muzzle. Monstrous brutes! which would crush a whole man
180 in their iron jaws. I did not know whether Conseil stopped to
181 classify them; for my part, I noticed their silver bellies, and their
182 huge mouths bristling with teeth, from a very unscientific point
183 of view, and more as a possible victim than as a naturalist.

184 Happily the **voracious** creatures do not see well. They passed
185 without seeing us, brushing us with their brownish fins, and
186 we escaped by a miracle from a danger certainly greater than
187 meeting a tiger full-face in the forest. Half an hour after, guided
188 by the electric light we reached the Nautilus. The outside door
189 had been left open, and Captain Nemo closed it as soon as we
190 had entered the first cell. He then pressed a knob. I heard the
191 pumps working in the midst of the vessel, I felt the water sinking
192 from around me, and in a few moments the cell was entirely
193 empty. The inside door then opened, and we entered the **vestry**.

194 There our diving-dress was taken off, not without some trouble,
195 and, fairly worn out from want of food and sleep, I returned
196 to my room, in great wonder at this surprising excursion at the
197 bottom of the sea.

Vocabulary part 1 chapter 16

immense, domains, arcades, filament, fauna, flora, self-propagated, insurmountable, writhe, declivity, deficient, blusteringly, voracious, vestry,

Questions for part 1 chapter 14-16

1. What 3 devices made the trip to the underwater forest possible?

   ____

   ____

2. What was strange about the trees in the forest?

   ____

3. What was Ned Lands thought when he heard about a hunting excursion and what did it turn out to be?

   ____

   ____

4. Where did Captain Nemo stop when going on the excursion in the forest and why? Why do you think he has such a hate/fear/revulsion of land?

   ____

   ____

   ____

   ____

Chapter 17

FOUR THOUSAND LEAGUES UNDER THE PACIFIC

The next morning, the 18th of November, I had quite recovered from my fatigues of the day before, and I went up on to the platform, just as the second lieutenant was uttering his daily phrase.

I was admiring the magnificent aspect of the ocean when Captain Nemo appeared. He did not seem to be aware of my presence, and began a series of astronomical observations. Then, when he had finished, he went and leant on the cage of the watch-light, and gazed **abstractedly** on the ocean. In the meantime, a number of the sailors of the Nautilus, all strong and healthy men, had come up onto the platform. They came to draw up the nets that had been laid all night. These sailors were evidently of different nations, although the European type was visible in all of them. I recognized some unmistakable Irishmen, Frenchmen, some Sclaves, and a Greek, or a Candiote. They were civil, and only used that odd language among themselves, the origin of which I could not guess, neither could I question them.

The nets were hauled in. They were a large kind of "chaluts," like those on the Normandy coasts, great pockets that the waves and a chain fixed in the smaller meshes kept open. These pockets, drawn by iron poles, swept through the water, and gathered in everything in their way. That day they brought up curious specimens from those productive coasts.

I reckoned that the haul had brought in more than nine hundredweight of fish. It was a fine haul, but not to be wondered at. Indeed, the nets are let down for several hours, and enclose in their meshes an infinite variety. We had no lack of excellent food, and the rapidity of the Nautilus and the attraction of the electric light could always renew our supply. These several productions of the sea were immediately lowered through the panel to the

31 steward's room, some to be eaten fresh, and others pickled.

32 The fishing ended, the provision of air renewed, I thought that
33 the Nautilus was about to continue its submarine excursion,
34 and was preparing to return to my room, when, without further
35 preamble, the Captain turned to me, saying:

36 "Professor, is not this ocean gifted with real life? It has its tempers
37 and its gentle moods. Yesterday it slept as we did, and now it has
38 woke after a quiet night. Look!" he continued, "it wakes under
39 the caresses of the sun. It is going to renew its **diurnal** existence.
40 It is an interesting study to watch the play of its organization. It
41 has a pulse, arteries, spasms; and I agree with the learned Maury,
42 who discovered in it a circulation as real as the circulation of
43 blood in animals.

44 "Yes, the ocean has indeed circulation, and to promote it, the
45 Creator has caused things to multiply in it—caloric, salt, and
46 animalculae."

47 When Captain Nemo spoke thus, he seemed altogether changed,
48 and aroused an extraordinary emotion in me.

49 "Also," he added, "true existence is there; and I can imagine
50 the foundations of nautical towns, clusters of submarine houses,
51 which, like the Nautilus, would ascend every morning to breathe
52 at the surface of the water, free towns, independent cities. Yet
53 who knows whether some despot——"

54 Captain Nemo finished his sentence with a violent gesture. Then,
55 addressing me as if to chase away some sorrowful thought:

56 "M. Aronnax," he asked, "do you know the depth of the ocean?"

57 "I only know, Captain, what the principal soundings have taught
58 us."

59 "Could you tell me them, so that I can suit them to my purpose?"

60 "These are some," I replied, "that I remember. If I am not

61 mistaken, a depth of 8,000 yards has been found in the North
62 Atlantic, and 2,500 yards in the Mediterranean. The most
63 remarkable soundings have been made in the South Atlantic,
64 near the thirty-fifth parallel, and they gave 12,000 yards, 14,000
65 yards, and 15,000 yards. To sum up all, it is reckoned that if the
66 bottom of the sea were levelled, its mean depth would be about
67 one and three-quarter leagues."

68 "Well, Professor," replied the Captain, "we shall show you better
69 than that I hope. As to the mean depth of this part of the Pacific,
70 I tell you it is only 4,000 yards."

71 Having said this, Captain Nemo went towards the panel, and
72 disappeared down the ladder. I followed him, and went into the
73 large drawing-room. The screw was immediately put in motion,
74 and the log gave twenty miles an hour.

75 During the days and weeks that passed, Captain Nemo was very
76 sparing of his visits. I seldom saw him. The lieutenant pricked
77 the ship's course regularly on the chart, so I could always tell
78 exactly the route of the Nautilus.

79 Nearly every day, for some time, the panels of the drawing-
80 room were opened, and we were never tired of penetrating the
81 mysteries of the submarine world.

82 The general direction of the Nautilus was south-east, and it kept
83 between 100 and 150 yards of depth. One day, however, I do
84 not know why, being drawn diagonally by means of the inclined
85 planes, it touched the bed of the sea. The thermometer indicated
86 a temperature of 4.25 (cent.): a temperature that at this depth
87 seemed common to all latitudes.

88 At three o'clock in the morning of the 26th of November the
89 Nautilus crossed the tropic of Cancer at 172° long. On 27th
90 instant it sighted the Sandwich Islands, where Cook died,
91 February 14, 1779. We had then gone 4,860 leagues from our
92 starting-point. In the morning, when I went on the platform, I
93 saw two miles to windward, Hawaii, the largest of the seven

94 islands that form the group. I saw clearly the cultivated ranges,
95 and the several mountain-chains that run parallel with the side,
96 and the volcanoes that overtop Mouna-Rea, which rise 5,000
97 yards above the level of the sea. Besides other things the nets
98 brought up, were several flabellariae and graceful polypi, that are
99 **peculiar** to that part of the ocean. The direction of the Nautilus
100 was still to the south-east. It crossed the equator December 1,
101 in 142° long.; and on the 4th of the same month, after crossing
102 rapidly and without anything in particular occurring, we sighted
103 the Marquesas group. I saw, three miles off, Martin's peak in
104 Nouka-Hiva, the largest of the group that belongs to France.
105 I only saw the woody mountains against the horizon, because
106 Captain Nemo did not wish to bring the ship to the wind. There
107 the nets brought up beautiful specimens of fish: some with
108 azure fins and tails like gold, the flesh of which is unrivalled;
109 some nearly destitute of scales, but of exquisite flavour; others,
110 with bony jaws, and yellow-tinged gills, as good as bonitos; all
111 fish that would be of use to us. After leaving these charming
112 islands protected by the French flag, from the 4th to the 11th of
113 December the Nautilus sailed over about 2,000 miles.

114 During the daytime of the 11th of December I was busy reading
115 in the large drawing-room. Ned Land and Conseil watched the
116 luminous water through the half-open panels. The Nautilus was
117 immovable. While its reservoirs were filled, it kept at a depth of
118 1,000 yards, a region rarely visited in the ocean, and in which
119 large fish were seldom seen.

120 I was then reading a charming book by Jean Mace, The Slaves
121 of the Stomach, and I was learning some valuable lessons from
122 it, when Conseil interrupted me.

123 "Will master come here a moment?" he said, in a curious voice.

124 "What is the matter, Conseil?"

125 "I want master to look."

126 I rose, went, and leaned on my elbows before the panes and

127   watched.

128   In a full electric light, an enormous black mass, quite immovable,
129   was suspended in the midst of the waters. I watched it attentively,
130   seeking to find out the nature of this gigantic cetacean. But a
131   sudden thought crossed my mind. "A vessel!" I said, half aloud.

132   "Yes," replied the Canadian, "a disabled ship that has sunk
133   perpendicularly."

134   Ned Land was right; we were close to a vessel of which the
135   tattered shrouds still hung from their chains. The keel seemed
136   to be in good order, and it had been wrecked at most some few
137   hours. Three stumps of masts, broken off about two feet above
138   the bridge, showed that the vessel had had to sacrifice its masts.
139   But, lying on its side, it had filled, and it was heeling over to
140   port. This skeleton of what it had once been was a sad spectacle
141   as it lay lost under the waves, but sadder still was the sight of the
142   bridge, where some corpses, bound with ropes, were still lying.
143   I counted five—four men, one of whom was standing at the
144   helm, and a woman standing by the poop, holding an infant in
145   her arms. She was quite young. I could distinguish her features,
146   which the water had not **decomposed**, by the brilliant light from
147   the Nautilus. In one **despairing** effort, she had raised her infant
148   above her head—poor little thing!—whose arms encircled its
149   mother's neck. The attitude of the four sailors was frightful,
150   **distorted** as they were by their convulsive movements, whilst
151   making a last effort to free themselves from the cords that bound
152   them to the vessel. The steersman alone, calm, with a grave, clear
153   face, his grey hair glued to his forehead, and his hand clutching
154   the wheel of the helm, seemed even then to be guiding the three
155   broken masts through the depths of the ocean.

156   What a scene! We were dumb; our hearts beat fast before this
157   shipwreck, taken as it were from life and photographed in its
158   last moments. And I saw already, coming towards it with hungry
159   eyes, enormous sharks, attracted by the human flesh.

160   However, the Nautilus, turning, went round the submerged

161 vessel, and in one instant I read on the stern—"The Florida,
162 Sunderland."

𝔉or questions on Chapter 17 - see the end of Chapter 18.

Chapter 18

VANIKORO

This terrible spectacle was the forerunner of the series of maritime catastrophes that the Nautilus was destined to meet with in its route. As long as it went through more frequented waters, we often saw the hulls of shipwrecked vessels that were rotting in the depths, and deeper down cannons, bullets, anchors, chains, and a thousand other iron materials eaten up by rust. However, on the 11th of December we sighted the Pomotou Islands, the old "dangerous group" of Bougainville, that extend over a space of 500 leagues at E.S.E. to W.N.W., from the Island Ducie to that of Lazareff. This group covers an area of 370 square leagues, and it is formed of sixty groups of islands, among which the Gambier group is remarkable, over which France exercises sway. These are coral islands, slowly raised, but continuous, created by the daily work of polypi. Then this new island will be joined later on to the neighboring groups, and a fifth continent will stretch from New Zealand and New Caledonia, and from thence to the Marquesas.

One day, when I was suggesting this theory to Captain Nemo, he replied coldly:

"The earth does not want new continents, but new men."

Towards evening Clermont-Tonnerre was lost in the distance, and the route of the Nautilus was sensibly changed. After having crossed the tropic of Capricorn in 135° longitude, it sailed W.N.W., making again for the tropical zone. Although the summer sun was very strong, we did not suffer from heat, for at fifteen or twenty fathoms below the surface, the temperature did not rise above from ten to twelve degrees.

On 15th of December, we left to the east the bewitching group of the Societies and the graceful Tahiti, queen of the Pacific. I saw in the morning, some miles to the windward, the elevated summits of the island. These waters furnished our table with

32 excellent fish, mackerel, bonitos, and some varieties of a sea-
33 serpent.

34 I had not seen Captain Nemo for a week, when, on the morning of
35 the 27th, he came into the large drawing-room, always seeming
36 as if he had seen you five minutes before. I was busily tracing
37 the route of the Nautilus on the planisphere. The Captain came
38 up to me, put his finger on one spot on the chart, and said this
39 single word.

40 "Vanikoro."

41 The effect was magical! It was the name of the islands on which
42 La Perouse had been lost! I rose suddenly.

43 "The Nautilus has brought us to Vanikoro?" I asked.

44 "Yes, Professor," said the Captain.

45 "And I can visit the celebrated islands where the Boussole and
46 the Astrolabe struck?"

47 "If you like, Professor."

48 "When shall we be there?"

49 "We are there now."

50 Followed by Captain Nemo, I went up on to the platform, and
51 greedily scanned the horizon.

52 To the N.E. two volcanic islands emerged of unequal size,
53 surrounded by a coral reef that measured forty miles in
54 circumference. We were close to Vanikoro, really the one to
55 which Dumont d'Urville gave the name of Isle de la Recherche,
56 and exactly facing the little harbor of Vanou, situated in 16° 4'
57 S. lat., and 164° 32' E. long. The earth seemed covered with
58 verdure from the shore to the summits in the interior, that were
59 crowned by Mount Kapogo, 476 feet high. The Nautilus, having
60 passed the outer belt of rocks by a narrow strait, found itself
61 among breakers where the sea was from thirty to forty fathoms

62 deep. Under the **verdant** shade of some mangroves I perceived
63 some savages, who appeared greatly surprised at our approach.
64 In the long black body, moving between wind and water, did
65 they not see some **formidable** cetacean that they regarded with
66 suspicion?

67 Just then Captain Nemo asked me what I knew about the wreck
68 of La Perouse.

69 "Only what everyone knows, Captain," I replied.

70 "And could you tell me what everyone knows about it?" he
71 inquired, **ironically**.

72 "Easily."

73 I related to him all that the last works of Dumont d'Urville
74 had made known—works from which the following is a brief
75 account.

76 La Perouse, and his second, Captain de Langle, were sent by
77 Louis XVI, in 1785, on a voyage of circumnavigation. They
78 embarked in the corvettes Boussole and the Astrolabe, neither
79 of which were again heard of. In 1791, the French Government,
80 justly uneasy as to the fate of these two sloops, manned two
81 large merchantmen, the Recherche and the Esperance, which
82 left Brest the 28th of September under the command of Bruni
83 d'Entrecasteaux.

84 Two months after, they learned from Bowen, commander of the
85 Albemarle, that the debris of shipwrecked vessels had been seen
86 on the coasts of New Georgia. But D'Entrecasteaux, ignoring
87 this communication—rather uncertain, besides—directed his
88 course towards the Admiralty Islands, mentioned in a report
89 of Captain Hunter's as being the place where La Perouse was
90 wrecked.

91 They sought in vain. The Esperance and the Recherche passed
92 before Vanikoro without stopping there, and, in fact, this voyage
93 was most disastrous, as it cost D'Entrecasteaux his life, and

94 those of two of his lieutenants, besides several of his crew.

95 Captain Dillon, a shrewd old Pacific sailor, was the first to find
96 unmistakable traces of the wrecks. On the 15th of May, 1824, his
97 vessel, the St. Patrick, passed close to Tikopia, one of the New
98 Hebrides. There a Lascar came alongside in a canoe, sold him
99 the handle of a sword in silver that bore the print of characters
100 engraved on the hilt. The Lascar pretended that six years before,
101 during a stay at Vanikoro, he had seen two Europeans that
102 belonged to some vessels that had run aground on the reefs some
103 years ago.

104 Dillon guessed that he meant La Perouse, whose disappearance
105 had troubled the whole world. He tried to get on to Vanikoro,
106 where, according to the Lascar, he would find numerous debris
107 of the wreck, but winds and tides prevented him.

108 Dillon returned to Calcutta. There he interested the Asiatic
109 Society and the Indian Company in his discovery. A vessel,
110 to which was given the name of the Recherche, was put at his
111 disposal, and he set out, 23rd January, 1827, accompanied by a
112 French agent.

113 The Recherche, after touching at several points in the Pacific,
114 cast anchor before Vanikoro, 7th July, 1827, in that same harbour
115 of Vanou where the Nautilus was at this time.

116 There it collected numerous relics of the wreck—iron utensils,
117 anchors, pulley-strops, swivel-guns, an 18 lb. shot, fragments of
118 astronomical instruments, a piece of crown work, and a bronze
119 clock, bearing this inscription—"Bazin m'a fait," the mark of
120 the foundry of the arsenal at Brest about 1785. There could be
121 no further doubt.

122 Dillon, having made all inquiries, stayed in the unlucky place
123 till October. Then he quitted Vanikoro, and directed his course
124 towards New Zealand; put into Calcutta, 7th April, 1828,
125 and returned to France, where he was warmly welcomed by
126 Charles X.

127 But at the same time, without knowing Dillon's movements,
128 Dumont d'Urville had already set out to find the scene of the
129 wreck. And they had learned from a whaler that some medals
130 and a cross of St. Louis had been found in the hands of some
131 savages of Louisiade and New Caledonia. Dumont d'Urville,
132 commander of the Astrolabe, had then sailed, and two months
133 after Dillon had left Vanikoro he put into Hobart Town. There he
134 learned the results of Dillon's inquiries, and found that a certain
135 James Hobbs, second lieutenant of the Union of Calcutta, after
136 landing on an island situated 8° 18' S. lat., and 156° 30' E. long.,
137 had seen some iron bars and red stuffs used by the natives of
138 these parts. Dumont d'Urville, much perplexed, and not knowing
139 how to credit the reports of low-class journals, decided to follow
140 Dillon's track.

141 On the 10th of February, 1828, the Astrolabe appeared off
142 Tikopia, and took as guide and interpreter a deserter found on
143 the island; made his way to Vanikoro, sighted it on the 12th inst.,
144 lay among the reefs until the 14th, and not until the 20th did he
145 cast anchor within the barrier in the harbour of Vanou.

146 On the 23rd, several officers went round the island and brought
147 back some unimportant trifles. The natives, adopting a system
148 of denials and evasions, refused to take them to the unlucky
149 place. This ambiguous conduct led them to believe that the
150 natives had ill-treated the castaways, and indeed they seemed
151
152 to fear that Dumont d'Urville had come to avenge La Perouse
153 and his unfortunate crew.

154 However, on the 26th, appeased by some presents, and
155 understanding that they had no reprisals to fear, they led M.
156 Jacquireot to the scene of the wreck.

157 There, in three or four fathoms of water, between the reefs of
158 Pacou and Vanou, lay anchors, cannons, pigs of lead and iron,
159 embedded in the limy concretions. The large boat and the
160 whaler belonging to the Astrolabe were sent to this place, and,
161 not without some difficulty, their crews hauled up an anchor

162 weighing 1,800 lbs., a brass gun, some pigs of iron, and two
163 copper swivel-guns.

164 Dumont d'Urville, questioning the natives, learned too that La
165 Perouse, after losing both his vessels on the reefs of this island,
166 had constructed a smaller boat, only to be lost a second time.
167 Where, no one knew.

168 But the French Government, fearing that Dumont d'Urville was
169 not acquainted with Dillon's movements, had sent the sloop
170 Bayonnaise, commanded by Legoarant de Tromelin, to Vanikoro,
171 which had been stationed on the west coast of America. The
172 Bayonnaise cast her anchor before Vanikoro some months after
173 the departure of the Astrolabe, but found no new document;
174 but stated that the savages had respected the monument to La
175 Perouse. That is the substance of what I told Captain Nemo.

176 "So," he said, "no one knows now where the third vessel
177 perished that was constructed by the castaways on the island of
178 Vanikoro?"

179 "No one knows."

180 Captain Nemo said nothing, but signed to me to follow him
181 into the large saloon. The Nautilus sank several yards below the
182 waves, and the panels were opened.

183 I hastened to the aperture, and under the crustations of coral,
184 covered with fungi, syphonules, alcyons, madrepores, through
185 myriads of charming fish—girelles, glyphisidri, pompherides,
186 diacopes, and holocentres—I recognized certain debris that
187 the drags had not been able to tear up—iron stirrups, anchors,
188 cannons, bullets, capstan fittings, the stem of a ship, all objects
189 clearly proving the wreck of some vessel, and now carpeted
190 with living flowers. While I was looking on this desolate scene,
191 Captain Nemo said, in a sad voice:

192 "Commander La Perouse set out 7th December, 1785, with his
193 vessels La Boussole and the Astrolabe. He first cast anchor at
194 Botany Bay, visited the Friendly Isles, New Caledonia, then

directed his course towards Santa Cruz, and put into Namouka, one of the Hapai group. Then his vessels struck on the unknown reefs of Vanikoro. The Boussole, which went first, ran aground on the southerly coast. The Astrolabe went to its help, and ran aground too. The first vessel was destroyed almost immediately. The second, stranded under the wind, resisted some days. The natives made the castaways welcome. They installed themselves in the island, and constructed a smaller boat with the debris of the two large ones. Some sailors stayed willingly at Vanikoro; the others, weak and ill, set out with La Perouse. They directed their course towards the Solomon Islands, and there perished, with everything, on the westerly coast of the chief island of the group, between Capes Deception and Satisfaction."

"How do you know that?"

"By this, that I found on the spot where was the last wreck."

Captain Nemo showed me a tin-plate box, stamped with the French arms, and corroded by the salt water. He opened it, and I saw a bundle of papers, yellow but still readable.

They were the instructions of the naval minister to Commander La Perouse, annotated in the margin in Louis XVI's handwriting.

"Ah! it is a fine death for a sailor!" said Captain Nemo, at last. "A coral tomb makes a quiet grave; and I trust that I and my comrades will find no other."

Vocabulary part 1 chapters 17 and 18

abstractedly, diurnal, distorted decomposed, verdant, ironically, circumnavigation

Questions for part 1 chapters 17-18

1. What does Captain Nemo mean when he says that the ocean is "gifted with real life" in ch. 17 line 36?

2. What does Captain Nemo wish could be made in the sea and what thought dashes that hope?

3. The Captain in chapter 18 line 20 says "The earth does not want new continents, but new men". What does this line tell us about Captain Nemo's disposition towards other people?

4. Why does Captain Nemo want the Professor to tell him all about the wreck of La Perouse?

5. What did Louis XVI want La Perouse to do? Why do you think Captain Nemo has interest in this sort of thing?

6. In chapter 18 line 191, Captain Nemo is said to be sad as he recounts what he had learned about La Perouse. Why do you think Captain Nemo is sad?

7. Where does Captain Nemo say he wants to be buried?
    Why do you think he wants to be buried there?

____

____

____

Chapter 19
TORRES STRAITS

During the night of the 27th or 28th of December, the Nautilus left the shores of Vanikoro with great speed. Her course was south-westerly, and in three days she had gone over the 750 leagues that separated it from La Perouse's group and the south-east point of Papua.

Early on the 1st of January, 1863, Conseil joined me on the platform.

"Master, will you permit me to wish you a happy New Year?"

"What! Conseil; exactly as if I was at Paris in my study at the Jardin des Plantes? Well, I accept your good wishes, and thank you for them. Only, I will ask you what you mean by a `Happy New Year' under our circumstances? Do you mean the year that will bring us to the end of our imprisonment, or the year that sees us continue this strange voyage?"

"Really, I do not know how to answer, master. We are sure to see curious things, and for the last two months we have not had time for dullness. The last marvel is always the most astonishing; and, if we continue this progression, I do not know how it will end. It is my opinion that we shall never again see the like. I think then, with no offence to master, that a happy year would be one in which we could see everything."

On 2nd January we had made 11,340 miles, or 5,250 French leagues, since our starting-point in the Japan Seas. Before the ship's head stretched the dangerous shores of the coral sea, on the north-east coast of Australia. Our boat lay along some miles from the redoubtable bank on which Cook's vessel was lost, 10th June, 1770. The boat in which Cook was struck on a rock, and, if it did not sink, it was owing to a piece of coral that was broken by the shock, and fixed itself in the broken keel.

30 I had wished to visit the reef, 360 leagues long, against which
31 the sea, always rough, broke with great violence, with a noise
32 like thunder. But just then the inclined planes drew the Nautilus
33 down to a great depth, and I could see nothing of the high coral
34 walls. I had to content myself with the different specimens of
35 fish brought up by the nets. I remarked, among others, some
36 germons, a species of mackerel as large as a tunny, with bluish
37 sides, and striped with transverse bands, that disappear with the
38 animal's life.

39 These fish followed us in shoals, and furnished us with very
40 delicate food. We took also a large number of gilt-heads, about
41 one and a half inches long, tasting like dorys; and flying pyrapeds
42 like submarine swallows, which, in dark nights, light alternately
43 the air and water with their phosphorescent light. Among the
44 molluscs and zoophytes, I found in the meshes of the net several
45 species of alcyonarians, echini, hammers, spurs, dials, cerites,
46 and hyalleae. The flora was represented by beautiful floating
47 seaweeds, laminariae, and macrocystes, impregnated with the
48 mucilage that transudes through their pores; and among which I
49 gathered an admirable Nemastoma Geliniarois, that was classed
50 among the natural curiosities of the museum.

51 Two days after crossing the coral sea, 4th January, we sighted
52 the Papuan coasts. On this occasion, Captain Nemo informed
53 me that his intention was to get into the Indian Ocean by the
54 Strait of Torres. His communication ended there.

55 The Torres Straits are nearly thirty-four leagues wide; but they are
56 obstructed by an innumerable quantity of islands, islets, breakers,
57 and rocks, that make its navigation almost impracticable; so that
58 Captain Nemo took all needful precautions to cross them. The
59 Nautilus, floating betwixt wind and water, went at a moderate
60 pace. Her screw, like a cetacean's tail, beat the waves slowly.

61 Profiting by this, I and my two companions went up on to the
62 deserted platform. Before us was the steersman's cage, and I
63 expected that Captain Nemo was there directing the course of
64 the Nautilus. I had before me the excellent charts of the Straits of

Torres, and I consulted them attentively. Round the Nautilus the sea dashed furiously. The course of the waves, that went from south-east to north-west at the rate of two and a half miles, broke on the coral that showed itself here and there.

"This is a bad sea!" remarked Ned Land.

"Detestable indeed, and one that does not suit a boat like the Nautilus."

"The Captain must be very sure of his route, for I see there pieces of coral that would do for its keel if it only touched them slightly."

Indeed the situation was dangerous, but the Nautilus seemed to slide like magic off these rocks. It did not follow the routes of the Astrolabe and the Zelee exactly, for they proved fatal to Dumont d'Urville. It bore more northwards, coasted the Islands of Murray, and came back to the south-west towards Cumberland Passage. I thought it was going to pass it by, when, going back to north-west, it went through a large quantity of islands and islets little known, towards the Island Sound and Canal Mauvais.

I wondered if Captain Nemo, foolishly imprudent, would steer his vessel into that pass where Dumont d'Urville's two corvettes touched; when, swerving again, and cutting straight through to the west, he steered for the Island of Gilboa.

It was then three in the afternoon. The tide began to recede, being quite full. The Nautilus approached the island, that I still saw, with its remarkable border of screw-pines. He stood off it at about two miles distant. Suddenly a shock overthrew me. The Nautilus just touched a rock, and stayed immovable, laying lightly to port side.

When I rose, I perceived Captain Nemo and his lieutenant on the platform. They were examining the situation of the vessel, and exchanging words in their incomprehensible dialect.

She was situated thus: Two miles, on the starboard side, appeared

97 Gilboa, stretching from north to west like an immense arm.
98 Towards the south and east some coral showed itself, left by
99 the ebb. We had run aground, and in one of those seas where
100 the tides are middling—a sorry matter for the floating of the
101 Nautilus. However, the vessel had not suffered, for her keel was
102 solidly joined. But, if she could neither glide off nor move, she
103 ran the risk of being for ever fastened to these rocks, and then
104 Captain Nemo's submarine vessel would be done for.

105 I was reflecting thus, when the Captain, cool and calm, always
106 master of himself, approached me.

107 "An accident?" I asked.

108 "No; an incident."

109 "But an incident that will oblige you perhaps to become an
110 inhabitant of this land from which you flee?"

111 Captain Nemo looked at me curiously, and made a negative
112 gesture, as much as to say that nothing would force him to set
113 foot on terra firma again. Then he said:

114 "Besides, M. Aronnax, the Nautilus is not lost; it will carry you
115 yet into the midst of the marvels of the ocean. Our voyage is
116 only begun, and I do not wish to be deprived so soon of the
117 honour of your company."

118 "However, Captain Nemo," I replied, without noticing the
119 ironical turn of his phrase, "the Nautilus ran aground in open sea.
120 Now the tides are not strong in the Pacific; and, if you cannot
121 lighten the Nautilus, I do not see how it will be reinflated."

122 "The tides are not strong in the Pacific: you are right there,
123 Professor; but in Torres Straits one finds still a difference of a
124 yard and a half between the level of high and low seas. To-day
125 is 4th January, and in five days the moon will be full. Now, I
126 shall be very much astonished if that satellite does not raise
127 these masses of water sufficiently, and render me a service that I
128 should be indebted to her for."

129 Having said this, Captain Nemo, followed by his lieutenant,
130 redescended to the interior of the Nautilus. As to the vessel, it
131 moved not, and was immovable, as if the coralline polypi had
132 already walled it up with their in destructible cement.

133 "Well, sir?" said Ned Land, who came up to me after the
134 departure of the Captain.

135 "Well, friend Ned, we will wait patiently for the tide on the 9th
136 instant; for it appears that the moon will have the goodness to
137 put it off again."

138 "Really?"

139 "Really."

140 "And this Captain is not going to cast anchor at all since the tide
141 will suffice?" said Conseil, simply.

142 The Canadian looked at Conseil, then shrugged his shoulders.

143 "Sir, you may believe me when I tell you that this piece of iron
144 will navigate neither on nor under the sea again; it is only fit to
145 be sold for its weight. I think, therefore, that the time has come
146 to part company with Captain Nemo."

147 "Friend Ned, I do not despair of this stout Nautilus, as you do;
148 and in four days we shall know what to hold to on the Pacific
149 tides. Besides, flight might be possible if we were in sight
150 of the English or Provencal coast; but on the Papuan shores,
151 it is another thing; and it will be time enough to come to that
152 extremity if the Nautilus does not recover itself again, which I
153 look upon as a grave event."

154 "But do they know, at least, how to act circumspectly? There
155 is an island; on that island there are trees; under those trees,
156 terrestrial animals, bearers of cutlets and roast beef, to which I
157 would willingly give a trial."

158 "In this, friend Ned is right," said Conseil, "and I agree with

159 him. Could not master obtain permission from his friend Captain
160 Nemo to put us on land, if only so as not to lose the habit of
161 treading on the solid parts of our planet?"

162 "I can ask him, but he will refuse."

163 "Will master risk it?" asked Conseil, "and we shall know how to
164 rely upon the Captain's amiability."

165 To my great surprise, Captain Nemo gave me the permission I
166 asked for, and he gave it very agreeably, without even exacting
167 from me a promise to return to the vessel; but flight across New
168 Guinea might be very perilous, and I should not have counselled
169 Ned Land to attempt it. Better to be a prisoner on board the
170 Nautilus than to fall into the hands of the natives.

171 At eight o'clock, armed with guns and hatchets, we got off the
172 Nautilus. The sea was pretty calm; a slight breeze blew on land.
173 Conseil and I rowing, we sped along quickly, and Ned steered
174 in the straight passage that the breakers left between them. The
175 boat was well handled, and moved rapidly.

176 Ned Land could not restrain his joy. He was like a prisoner that
177 had escaped from prison, and knew not that it was necessary to
178 re-enter it.

179 "Meat! We are going to eat some meat; and what meat!" he
180 replied. "Real game! no, bread, indeed."

181 "I do not say that fish is not good; we must not abuse it; but a
182 piece of fresh venison, grilled on live coals, will agreeably vary
183 our ordinary course."

184 "Glutton!" said Conseil, "he makes my mouth water."

185 "It remains to be seen," I said, "if these forests are full of game,
186 and if the game is not such as will hunt the hunter himself."

187 "Well said, M. Aronnax," replied the Canadian, whose teeth
188 seemed sharpened like the edge of a hatchet; "but I will eat

189 tiger—loin of tiger—if there is no other quadruped on this
190 island.”

191 “Friend Ned is uneasy about it,” said Conseil.

192 “Whatever it may be,” continued Ned Land, “every animal with
193 four paws without feathers, or with two paws without feathers,
194 will be saluted by my first shot.”

195 “Very well! Master Land’s imprudences are beginning.”

196 “Never fear, M. Aronnax,” replied the Canadian; “I do not want
197 twenty-five minutes to offer you a dish, of my sort.”

198 At half-past eight the Nautilus boat ran softly aground on a heavy
199 sand, after having happily passed the coral reef that surrounds
200 the Island of Gilboa.

Questions for chapter 19

In lines 8-21, Conseil and the Professor discuss the voyage and the meaning of happiness.

Do Now: in full sentences, summarize this brief exchange, and in your review, state;

    a.   What is bothering the Professor about the wishes for a new year?

    b.   What is Conseil's response?

    c.   What does Conseil's response say about the nature of happiness

    d.   In accordance with Conseil's outlook, do you think one can be happy even when things are not perfect? Explain.

    e.   If you were in such a predicament, would you agree with Conseil? Why or why not?

Chapter 20

A FEW DAYS ON LAND

I was much impressed on touching land. Ned Land tried the soil with his feet, as if to take possession of it. However, it was only two months before that we had become, according to Captain Nemo, "passengers on board the Nautilus," but, in reality, prisoners of its commander.

In a few minutes we were within musket-shot of the coast. The whole horizon was hidden behind a beautiful curtain of forests. Enormous trees, the trunks of which attained a height of 200 feet, were tied to each other by garlands of bindweed, real natural hammocks, which a light breeze rocked. They were mimosas, figs, hibisci, and palm trees, mingled together in profusion; and under the shelter of their verdant vault grew orchids, leguminous plants, and ferns.

But, without noticing all these beautiful specimens of Papuan flora, the Canadian abandoned the agreeable for the useful. He discovered a coco-tree, beat down some of the fruit, broke them, and we drunk the milk and ate the nut with a satisfaction that protested against the ordinary food on the Nautilus.

"Excellent!" said Ned Land.

"**Exquisite!**" replied Conseil.

"And I do not think," said the Canadian, "that he would object to our introducing a cargo of coco-nuts on board."

"I do not think he would, but he would not taste them."

"So much the worse for him," said Conseil.

"And so much the better for us," replied Ned Land. "There will be more for us."

"One word only, Master Land," I said to the harpooner, who

was beginning to ravage another coco-nut tree. "Coco-nuts are good things, but before filling the canoe with them it would be wise to **reconnoiter** and see if the island does not produce some substance not less useful. Fresh vegetables would be welcome on board the Nautilus."

"Master is right," replied Conseil; "and I propose to reserve three places in our vessel, one for fruits, the other for vegetables, and the third for the **venison**, of which I have not yet seen the smallest specimen."

"Conseil, we must not despair," said the Canadian.

"Let us continue," I returned, "and lie in wait. Although the island seems uninhabited, it might still contain some individuals that would be less hard than we on the nature of game."

"Ho! ho!" said Ned Land, moving his jaws significantly.

"Well, Ned!" said Conseil.

"My word!" returned the Canadian, "I begin to understand the charms of **anthropophagy**."

"Ned! Ned! what are you saying? You, a man-eater? I should not feel safe with you, especially as I share your cabin. I might perhaps wake one day to find myself half devoured."

"Friend Conseil, I like you much, but not enough to eat you unnecessarily."

"I would not trust you," replied Conseil. "But enough. We must absolutely bring down some game to satisfy this cannibal, or else one of these fine mornings, master will find only pieces of his servant to serve him."

While we were talking thus, we were penetrating the somber arches of the forest, and for two hours we surveyed it in all directions.

Chance rewarded our search for eatable vegetables, and one

58 of the most useful products of the tropical zones furnished us
59 with precious food that we missed on board. I would speak of
60 the bread-fruit tree, very abundant in the island of Gilboa; and
61 I remarked chiefly the variety destitute of seeds, which bears in
62 Malaya the name of "rima."

63 Ned Land knew these fruits well. He had already eaten many
64 during his numerous voyages, and he knew how to prepare the
65 eatable substance. Moreover, the sight of them excited him, and
66 he could contain himself no longer.

67 "Master," he said, "I shall die if I do not taste a little of this
68 bread-fruit pie."

69 "Taste it, friend Ned—taste it as you want. We are here to make
70 experiments—make them."

71 "It won't take long," said the Canadian.

72 And, provided with a lentil, he lighted a fire of dead wood that
73 crackled joyously. During this time, Conseil and I chose the best
74 fruits of the bread-fruit. Some had not then attained a sufficient
75 degree of maturity; and their thick skin covered a white but rather
76 fibrous pulp. Others, the greater number yellow and gelatinous,
77 waited only to be picked.

78 These fruits enclosed no kernel. Conseil brought a dozen to Ned
79 Land, who placed them on a coal fire, after having cut them in
80 thick slices, and while doing this repeating:

81 "You will see, master, how good this bread is. More so when one
82 has been deprived of it so long. It is not even bread," added he,
83 "but a delicate pastry. You have eaten none, master?"

84 "No, Ned."

85 "Very well, prepare yourself for a juicy thing. If you do not come
86 for more, I am no longer the king of harpooners."

87 After some minutes, the part of the fruits that was exposed to

88 the fire was completely roasted. The interior looked like a white
89 pasty, a sort of soft crumb, the flavour of which was like that of
90 an artichoke.

91 It must be confessed this bread was excellent, and I ate of it with
92 great relish.

93 "What time is it now?" asked the Canadian.

94 "Two o'clock at least," replied Conseil.

95 "How time flies on firm ground!" sighed Ned Land.

96 "Let us be off," replied Conseil.

97 We returned through the forest, and completed our collection by
98 a raid upon the cabbage-palms, that we gathered from the tops
99 of the trees, little beans that I recognized as the "abrou" of the
100 Malays, and yams of a superior quality.

101 We were loaded when we reached the boat. But Ned Land did
102 not find his provisions sufficient. Fate, however, favored us. Just
103 as we were pushing off, he perceived several trees, from twenty-
104 five to thirty feet high, a species of palm-tree.

105 At last, at five o'clock in the evening, loaded with our riches, we
106 quitted the shore, and half an hour after we hailed the Nautilus. No
107 one appeared on our arrival. The enormous iron-plated cylinder
108 seemed deserted. The provisions embarked, I descended to my
109 chamber, and after supper slept soundly.

110 The next day, 6th January, nothing new on board. Not a sound
111 inside, not a sign of life. The boat rested along the edge, in the
112 same place in which we had left it. We resolved to return to the
113 island. Ned Land hoped to be more fortunate than on the day
114 before with regard to the hunt, and wished to visit another part
115 of the forest.

116 At dawn we set off. The boat, carried on by the waves that flowed
117 to shore, reached the island in a few minutes.

118 We landed, and, thinking that it was better to give in to the
119 Canadian, we followed Ned Land, whose long limbs threatened
120 to distance us. He wound up the coast towards the west: then,
121 fording some torrents, he gained the high plain that was bordered
122 with admirable forests. Some kingfishers were rambling along the
123 water-courses, but they would not let themselves be approached.
124 Their **circumspection** proved to me that these birds knew what
125 to expect from bipeds of our species, and I concluded that, if
126 the island was not inhabited, at least human beings occasionally
127 frequented it.

128 After crossing a rather large prairie, we arrived at the skirts of a
129 little wood that was enlivened by the songs and flight of a large
130 number of birds.

131 "There are only birds," said Conseil.

132 "But they are eatable," replied the harpooner.

133 "I do not agree with you, friend Ned, for I see only parrots there."

134 "Friend Conseil," said Ned, gravely, "the parrot is like pheasant
135 to those who have nothing else."

136 "And," I added, "this bird, suitably prepared, is worth knife and
137 fork."

138 Indeed, under the thick foliage of this wood, a world of parrots
139 were flying from branch to branch, only needing a careful
140 education to speak the human language. For the moment, they
141 were chattering with parrots of all colors, and grave cockatoos,
142 who seemed to meditate upon some philosophical problem,
143 whilst brilliant red lories passed like a piece of bunting carried
144 away by the breeze, papuans, with the finest azure colors, and in
145 all a variety of winged things most charming to behold, but few
146 eatable.

147 However, a bird peculiar to these lands, and which has never
148 passed the limits of the Arrow and Papuan islands, was wanting
149 in this collection. But fortune reserved it for me before long.

150 After passing through a moderately thick copse, we found a plain
151 obstructed with bushes. I saw then those magnificent birds, the
152 **disposition** of whose long feathers obliges them to fly against
153 the wind. Their undulating flight, graceful **aerial** curves, and the
154 shading of their colors, attracted and charmed one's looks. I had
155 no trouble in recognizing them.

156 "Birds of paradise!" I exclaimed.

157 The Malays, who carry on a great trade in these birds with the
158 Chinese, have several means that we could not employ for taking
159 them. Sometimes they put snares on the top of high trees that the
160 birds of paradise prefer to frequent. Sometimes they catch them
161 with a viscous birdlime that paralyses their movements. They
162 even go so far as to poison the fountains that the birds generally
163 drink from. But we were obliged to fire at them during flight,
164 which gave us few chances to bring them down; and, indeed, we
165 vainly exhausted one half our ammunition.

166 About eleven o'clock in the morning, the first range of mountains
167 that form the centre of the island was traversed, and we had
168 killed nothing. Hunger drove us on. The hunters had relied on the
169 products of the chase, and they were wrong. Happily Conseil, to
170 his great surprise, made a double shot and secured breakfast. He
171 brought down a white pigeon and a wood-pigeon, which, cleverly
172 plucked and suspended from a skewer, was roasted before a red
173 fire of dead wood. While these interesting birds were cooking,
174 Ned prepared the fruit of the bread-tree. Then the wood-pigeons
175 were devoured to the bones, and declared excellent. The nutmeg,
176 with which they are in the habit of stuffing their crops, flavors
177 their flesh and renders it delicious eating.

178 "Now, Ned, what do you miss now?"

179 "Some four-footed game, M. Aronnax. All these pigeons are
180 only side-dishes and **trifles**; and until I have killed an animal
181 with cutlets I shall not be content."

182 "Nor I, Ned, if I do not catch a bird of paradise."

183 "Let us continue hunting," replied Conseil. "Let us go towards
184 the sea. We have arrived at the first **declivities** of the mountains,
185 and I think we had better regain the region of forests."

186 That was sensible advice, and was followed out. After walking
187 for one hour we had attained a forest of sago-trees. Some
188 inoffensive serpents glided away from us. The birds of paradise
189 fled at our approach, and truly I despaired of getting near
190 one when Conseil, who was walking in front, suddenly bent
191 down, uttered a triumphal cry, and came back to me bringing a
192 magnificent specimen.

193 "Ah! bravo, Conseil!"

194 "Master is very good."

195 "No, my boy; you have made an excellent stroke. Take one of
196 these living birds, and carry it in your hand."

197 "If master will examine it, he will see that I have not deserved
198 great merit."

199 "Why, Conseil?"

200 "Because this bird is as drunk as a quail."

201 "Drunk!"

202 "Yes, sir; drunk with the nutmegs that it devoured under the
203 nutmeg-tree, under which I found it. See, friend Ned, see the
204 monstrous effects of **intemperance**!"

205 "By!" exclaimed the Canadian, "because I have drunk gin for
206 two months, you must needs reproach me!"

207 However, I examined the curious bird. Conseil was right. The
208 bird, drunk with the juice, was quite powerless. It could not fly;
209 it could hardly walk.

210 This bird belonged to the most beautiful of the eight species that
211 are found in Papua and in the neighboring islands. It was the

"large emerald bird, the most rare kind… Two horned, downy nets rose from below the tail, that prolonged the long light feathers of admirable fineness, and they completed the whole of this marvelous bird, that the natives have poetically named the "bird of the sun."

But if my wishes were satisfied by the possession of the bird of paradise, the Canadian's were not yet. Happily, about two o'clock, Ned Land brought down a magnificent hog; from the brood of those the natives call "bari-outang." The animal came in time for us to procure real quadruped meat, and he was well received. Ned Land was very proud of his shot. The hog, hit by the electric ball, fell stone dead. The Canadian skinned and cleaned it properly, after having taken half a dozen cutlets, destined to furnish us with a grilled repast in the evening. Then the hunt was resumed, which was still more marked by Ned and Conseil's exploits.

Indeed, the two friends, beating the bushes, roused a herd of kangaroos that fled and bounded along on their elastic paws. But these animals did not take to flight so rapidly but what the electric capsule could stop their course.

"Ah, Professor!" cried Ned Land, who was carried away by the delights of the chase, "what excellent game, and stewed, too! What a supply for the Nautilus! Two! three! five down! And to think that we shall eat that flesh, and that the idiots on board shall not have a crumb!"

I think that, in the excess of his joy, the Canadian, if he had not talked so much, would have killed them all. But he contented himself with a single dozen of these interesting marsupians. These animals were small. They were a species of those "kangaroo rabbits" that live habitually in the hollows of trees, and whose speed is extreme; but they are moderately fat, and furnish, at least, estimable food. We were very satisfied with the results of the hunt. Happy Ned proposed to return to this enchanting island the next day, for he wished to **depopulate** it of all the eatable quadrupeds. But he had reckoned without his host.

At six o'clock in the evening we had regained the shore; our boat was **moored** to the usual place. The Nautilus, like a long rock, emerged from the waves two miles from the beach. Ned Land, without waiting, occupied himself about the important dinner business. He understood all about cooking well. The "bari-outang," grilled on the coals, soon scented the air with a delicious odor.

Indeed, the dinner was excellent. Two wood-pigeons completed this extraordinary menu. The sago pasty, the artocarpus bread, some mangoes, half a dozen pineapples, and the liquor fermented from some coco-nuts, overjoyed us. I even think that my worthy companions' ideas had not all the plainness desirable.

"Suppose we do not return to the Nautilus this evening?" said Conseil.

"Suppose we never return?" added Ned Land.

Just then a stone fell at our feet and cut short the harpooner's proposition.

𝔉or questions and vocabulary connected with Chapter 20 - see the end of Chapter 21.

Chapter 21

CAPTAIN NEMO'S THUNDERBOLT

We looked at the edge of the forest without rising, my hand stopping in the action of putting it to my mouth, Ned Land's completing its office.

"Stones do not fall from the sky," remarked Conseil, "or they would merit the name aerolites."

A second stone, carefully aimed, that made a savoury pigeon's leg fall from Conseil's hand, gave still more weight to his observation. We all three arose, shouldered our guns, and were ready to reply to any attack.

"Are they apes?" cried Ned Land.

"Very nearly—they are savages."

"To the boat!" I said, hurrying to the sea.

It was indeed necessary to beat a retreat, for about twenty natives armed with bows and slings appeared on the skirts of a copse that masked the horizon to the right, hardly a hundred steps from us.

Our boat was moored about sixty feet from us. The savages approached us, not running, but making hostile demonstrations. Stones and arrows fell thickly.

Ned Land had not wished to leave his provisions; and, in spite of his imminent danger, his pig on one side and kangaroos on the other, he went tolerably fast. In two minutes we were on the shore. To load the boat with provisions and arms, to push it out to sea, and ship the oars, was the work of an instant. We had not gone two cable-lengths, when a hundred savages, howling and **gesticulating**, entered the water up to their waists. I watched to see if their **apparition** would attract some men from the Nautilus on to the platform. But no. The enormous machine, lying off,

28 was absolutely deserted.

29 Twenty minutes later we were on board. The panels were open.
30 After making the boat fast, we entered into the interior of the
31 Nautilus.

32 I descended to the drawing-room, from whence I heard some
33 chords. Captain Nemo was there, bending over his organ, and
34 plunged in a musical ecstasy.

35 "Captain!"

36 He did not hear me.

37 "Captain!" I said, touching his hand.

38 He shuddered, and, turning round, said, "Ah! it is you,
39 Professor? Well, have you had a good hunt, have you botanized
40 successfully?"

41 "Yes Captain; but we have unfortunately brought a troop of
42 bipeds, whose vicinity troubles me."

43 "What bipeds?"

44 "Savages."

45 "Savages!" he echoed, ironically. "So you are astonished, Professor,
46 at having set foot on a strange land and finding savages? Savages!
47 where are there not any? Besides, are they worse than others,
48 these whom you call savages?"

49 "But Captain——"

50 "How many have you counted?"

51 "A hundred at least."

52 "M. Aronnax," replied Captain Nemo, placing his fingers on the
53 organ stops, "when all the natives of Papua are assembled on this
54 shore, the Nautilus will have nothing to fear from their attacks."

55 The Captain's fingers were then running over the keys of the

56 instrument, and I remarked that he touched only the black keys,
57 which gave his melodies an essentially Scotch character. Soon he
58 had forgotten my presence, and had plunged into a reverie that
59 I did not disturb. I went up again on to the platform: night had
60 already fallen; for, in this low latitude, the sun sets rapidly and
61 without twilight. I could only see the island indistinctly; but the
62 numerous fires, lighted on the beach, showed that the natives did
63 not think of leaving it. I was alone for several hours, sometimes
64 thinking of the natives—but without any dread of them, for
65 the **imperturbable** confidence of the Captain was catching—
66 sometimes forgetting them to admire the splendors of the night
67 in the tropics. My remembrances went to France in the train of
68 those zodiacal stars that would shine in some hours' time. The
69 moon shone in the midst of the constellations of the zenith.

70 The night slipped away without any mischance, the islanders
71 frightened no doubt at the sight of a monster aground in the bay.
72 The panels were open, and would have offered an easy access to
73 the interior of the Nautilus.

74 At six o'clock in the morning of the 8th January I went up on to the
75 platform. The dawn was breaking. The island soon showed itself
76 through the dissipating fogs, first the shore, then the summits.

77 The natives were there, more numerous than on the day before—
78 five or six hundred perhaps—some of them, profiting by the low
79 water, had come on to the coral, at less than two cable-lengths
80 from the Nautilus. I distinguished them easily; they were true
81 Papuans, with athletic figures, men of good race, large high
82 foreheads, large, but not broad and flat, and white teeth. Their
83 woolly hair, with a reddish tinge, showed off on their black
84 shining bodies like those of the Nubians. From the lobes of their
85 ears, cut and distended, hung chaplets of bones.. Some chiefs
86 had ornamented their necks with a crescent and collars of glass
87 beads, red and white; nearly all were armed with bows, arrows,
88 and shields and carried on their shoulders a sort of net containing
89 those round stones which they cast from their slings with great
90 skill. One of these chiefs, rather near to the Nautilus, examined
91 it attentively. He was, perhaps, a "mado" of high rank, for he was

92 draped in a mat of banana-leaves, notched round the edges, and
93 set off with brilliant colours.

94 I could easily have knocked down this native, who was within
95 a short length; but I thought that it was better to wait for real
96 hostile demonstrations. Between Europeans and savages, it is
97 proper for the Europeans to **parry** sharply, not to attack.

98 During low water the natives roamed about near the Nautilus,
99 but were not troublesome; I heard them frequently repeat the
100 word "Assai," and by their gestures I understood that they invited
101 me to go on land, an invitation that I declined.

102 So that, on that day, the boat did not push off, to the great
103 displeasure of Master Land, who could not complete his
104 provisions.

105 This adroit Canadian employed his time in preparing the **viands**
106 and meat that he had brought off the island. As for the savages,
107 they returned to the shore about eleven o'clock in the morning,
108 as soon as the coral tops began to disappear under the rising
109 tide; but I saw their numbers had increased considerably on
110 the shore. Probably they came from the neighboring islands, or
111 very likely from Papua. However, I had not seen a single native
112 canoe. Having nothing better to do, I thought of dragging these
113 beautiful limpid waters, under which I saw a profusion of shells,
114 zoophytes, and marine plants. Moreover, it was the last day that
115 the Nautilus would pass in these parts, if it float in open sea the
116 next day, according to Captain Nemo's promise.

117 I therefore called Conseil, who brought me a little light drag,
118 very like those for the oyster fishery. Now to work! For two hours
119 we fished unceasingly, but without bringing up any rarities. The
120 drag was filled with midas-ears, harps, melames, and particularly
121 the most beautiful hammers I have ever seen. We also brought
122 up some sea-slugs, pearl-oysters, and a dozen little turtles that
123 were reserved for the pantry on board.

124 But just when I expected it least, I put my hand on a wonder, I
125 might say a natural deformity, very rarely met with. Conseil was

126 just dragging, and his net came up filled with divers ordinary
127 shells, when, all at once, he saw me plunge my arm quickly into
128 the net, to draw out a shell, and heard me utter a cry.

129 "What is the matter, sir?" he asked in surprise. "Has master been
130 bitten?"

131 "No, my boy; but I would willingly have given a finger for my
132 discovery."

133 "What discovery?"

134 "This shell," I said, holding up the object of my triumph.

135 "It is simply an olive porphyry, genus olive, order of the
136 pectinibranchidae, class of gasteropods, sub-class mollusca."

137 "Yes, Conseil; but, instead of being rolled from right to left, this
138 olive turns from left to right."

139 "Is it possible?"

140 "Yes, my boy; it is a left shell."

141 Shells are all right-handed, with rare exceptions; and, when by
142 chance their spiral is left, amateurs are ready to pay their weight
143 in gold.

144 Conseil and I were absorbed in the contemplation of our
145 treasure, and I was promising myself to enrich the museum with
146 it, when a stone unfortunately thrown by a native struck against,
147 and broke, the precious object in Conseil's hand. I uttered a cry
148 of despair! Conseil took up his gun, and aimed at a savage who
149 was poising his sling at ten yards from him. I would have stopped
150 him, but his blow took effect and broke the bracelet of amulets
151 which encircled the arm of the savage.

152 "Conseil!" cried I. "Conseil!"

153 "Well, sir! do you not see that the cannibal has commenced the
154 attack?"

155 "A shell is not worth the life of a man," said I.

156 "Ah! the scoundrel!" cried Conseil; "I would rather he had broken
157 my shoulder!"

158 However, the situation had changed some minutes before, and
159 we had not perceived. A score of canoes surrounded the Nautilus.
160 These canoes, scooped out of the trunk of a tree, long, narrow,
161 well adapted for speed, were balanced by means of a long bamboo
162 pole, which floated on the water. They were managed by skilful,
163 half-naked paddlers, and I watched their advance with some
164 uneasiness. It was evident that these Papuans had already had
165 dealings with the Europeans and knew their ships. But this long
166 iron cylinder anchored in the bay, without masts or chimneys,
167 what could they think of it? Nothing good, for at first they kept at
168 a respectful distance. However, seeing it motionless, by degrees
169 they took courage, and sought to familiarize themselves with it.
170 Now this familiarity was precisely what it was necessary to avoid.
171 Our arms, which were noiseless, could only produce a moderate
172 effect on the savages, who have little respect for aught but
173 blustering things. The thunderbolt without the reverberations of
174 thunder would frighten man but little, though the danger lies in
175 the lightning, not in the noise.

176 At this moment the canoes approached the Nautilus, and a
177 shower of arrows alighted on her.

178 I went down to the saloon, but found no one there. I ventured to
179 knock at the door that opened into the Captain's room. "Come
180 in," was the answer.

181 I entered, and found Captain Nemo deep in algebraical
182 calculations of x and other quantities.

183 "I am disturbing you," said I, for courtesy's sake.

184 "That is true, M. Aronnax," replied the Captain; "but I think you
185 have serious reasons for wishing to see me?"

186 "Very grave ones; the natives are surrounding us in their canoes,

187 and in a few minutes we shall certainly be attacked by many
188 hundreds of savages."

189 "Ah!" said Captain Nemo quietly, "they are come with their
190 canoes?"

191 "Yes, sir."

192 "Well, sir, we must close the hatches."

193 "Exactly, and I came to say to you——"

194 "Nothing can be more simple," said Captain Nemo. And, pressing
195 an electric button, he transmitted an order to the ship's crew.

196 "It is all done, sir," said he, after some moments. "The pinnace is
197 ready, and the hatches are closed. You do not fear, I imagine, that
198 these gentlemen could stave in walls on which the balls of your
199 frigate have had no effect?"

200 "No, Captain; but a danger still exists."

201 "What is that, sir?"

202 "It is that to-morrow, at about this hour, we must open the
203 hatches to renew the air of the Nautilus. Now, if, at this moment,
204 the Papuans should occupy the platform, I do not see how you
205 could prevent them from entering."

206 "Then, sir, you suppose that they will board us?"

207 "I am certain of it."

208 "Well, sir, let them come. I see no reason for hindering them.
209 After all, these Papuans are poor creatures, and I am unwilling
210 that my visit to the island should cost the life of a single one of
211 these wretches."

212 Upon that I was going away; But Captain Nemo detained me,
213 and asked me to sit down by him. He questioned me with interest
214 about our excursions on shore, and our hunting; and seemed not
215 to understand the craving for meat that possessed the Canadian.

216 Then the conversation turned on various subjects, and, without
217 being more communicative, Captain Nemo showed himself
218 more **amiable**.

219 Amongst other things, we happened to speak of the situation of
220 the Nautilus, run aground in exactly the same spot in this strait
221 where Dumont d'Urville was nearly lost. Apropos of this:

222 "This D'Urville was one of your great sailors," said the Captain
223 to me, "one of your most intelligent navigators. He is the Captain
224 Cook of you Frenchmen. Unfortunate man of science, after
225 having braved the icebergs of the South Pole, the coral reefs of
226 Oceania, the cannibals of the Pacific, to perish miserably in a
227 railway train! If this energetic man could have reflected during
228 the last moments of his life, what must have been uppermost in
229 his last thoughts, do you suppose?"

230 So speaking, Captain Nemo seemed moved, and his emotion gave
231 me a better opinion of him. Then, chart in hand, we reviewed the
232 travels of the French navigator, his voyages of circumnavigation,
233 his double detention at the South Pole, which led to the discovery
234 of Adelaide and Louis Philippe, and fixing the hydrographical
235 bearings of the principal islands of Oceania.

236 "That which your D'Urville has done on the surface of the seas,"
237 said Captain Nemo, "that have I done under them, and more
238 easily, more completely than he. The Astrolabe and the Zelee,
239 incessantly tossed about by the hurricane, could not be worth the
240 Nautilus, quiet **repository** of labour that she is, truly motionless
241 in the midst of the waters.

242 "To-morrow," added the Captain, rising, "to-morrow, at twenty
243 minutes to three p.m., the Nautilus shall float, and leave the Strait
244 of Torres uninjured."

245 Having curtly pronounced these words, Captain Nemo bowed
246 slightly. This was to dismiss me, and I went back to my room.

247 There I found Conseil, who wished to know the result of my
248 interview with the Captain.

249 "My boy," said I, "when I **feigned** to believe that his Nautilus
250 was threatened by the natives of Papua, the Captain answered
251 me very sarcastically. I have but one thing to say to you: Have
252 confidence in him, and go to sleep in peace."

253 "Have you no need of my services, sir?"

254 "No, my friend. What is Ned Land doing?"

255 "If you will excuse me, sir," answered Conseil, "friend Ned is busy
256 making a kangaroo-pie which will be a marvel."

257 I remained alone and went to bed, but slept indifferently. I heard
258 the noise of the savages, who stamped on the platform, uttering
259 deafening cries. The night passed thus, without disturbing the
260 ordinary repose of the crew. The presence of these cannibals
261 affected them no more than the soldiers of a masked battery care
262 for the ants that crawl over its front.

263 At six in the morning I rose. The hatches had not been opened.
264 The inner air was not renewed, but the reservoirs, filled ready
265 for any emergency, were now resorted to, and discharged several
266 cubic feet of oxygen into the exhausted atmosphere of the
267 Nautilus.

268 I worked in my room till noon, without having seen Captain
269 Nemo, even for an instant. On board no preparations for
270 departure were visible.

271 I waited still some time, then went into the large saloon. The
272 clock marked half-past two. In ten minutes it would be high-
273 tide: and, if Captain Nemo had not made a rash promise, the
274 Nautilus would be immediately detached. If not, many months
275 would pass **ere** she could leave her bed of coral.

276 However, some warning vibrations began to be felt in the vessel.
277 I heard the keel grating against the rough calcareous bottom of
278 the coral reef.

279 At five-and-twenty minutes to three, Captain Nemo appeared in
280 the saloon.

281 "We are going to start," said he.

282 "Ah!" replied I.

283 "I have given the order to open the hatches."

284 "And the Papuans?"

285 "The Papuans?" answered Captain Nemo, slightly shrugging his
286 shoulders.

287 "Will they not come inside the Nautilus?"

288 "How?"

289 "Only by leaping over the hatches you have opened."

290 "M. Aronnax," quietly answered Captain Nemo, "they will not
291 enter the hatches of the Nautilus in that way, even if they were
292 open."

293 I looked at the Captain.

294 "You do not understand?" said he.

295 "Hardly."

296 "Well, come and you will see."

297 I directed my steps towards the central staircase. There Ned
298 Land and Conseil were slyly watching some of the ship's crew,
299 who were opening the hatches, while cries of rage and fearful
300 **vociferations** resounded outside.

301 The port lids were pulled down outside. Twenty horrible faces
302 appeared. But the first native who placed his hand on the stair-
303 rail, struck from behind by some invisible force, I know not
304 what, fled, uttering the most fearful cries and making the wildest
305 contortions.

306 Ten of his companions followed him. They met with the same
307 fate.

Conseil was in ecstasy. Ned Land, carried away by his violent instincts, rushed on to the staircase. But the moment he seized the rail with both hands, he, in his turn, was overthrown.

"I am struck by a thunderbolt," cried he, with an oath.

This explained all. It was no rail; but a metallic cable charged with electricity from the deck communicating with the platform. Whoever touched it felt a powerful shock—and this shock would have been mortal if Captain Nemo had discharged into the conductor the whole force of the current. It might truly be said that between his assailants and himself he had stretched a network of electricity which none could pass with **impunity**.

Meanwhile, the exasperated Papuans had beaten a retreat paralyzed with terror. As for us, half laughing, we consoled and rubbed the unfortunate Ned Land, who swore like one possessed.

But at this moment the Nautilus, raised by the last waves of the tide, quitted her coral bed exactly at the fortieth minute fixed by the Captain. Her screw swept the waters slowly and majestically. Her speed increased gradually, and, sailing on the surface of the ocean, she quitted safe and sound the dangerous passes of the Straits of Torres.

Vocabulary part 1 Chapters 20-21

anthropophagy, circumspection, disposition, aerial, trifles, declivities, intemperance, depopulate, moored, gesticulating, parry, viands, repository, feigned, ere, vociferations, impunity

Questions for part 1 chapters 20-21

1. What do the trio first find on the island?

2. How did the group manage to catch the "Bird of Paradise"?

3. In chapter 20 lines 202-204 it states "Yes, sir; drunk with the nutmegs that it devoured under the nutmeg-tree, under which I found it. See, friend Ned, see the monstrous effects of intemperance." What lesson does Conseil derive from seeing a drunk bird that he wishes to serve as a lesson to Ned Land?

4. In chapter 20 lines 259-261 it says: "Suppose we do not return to the Nautilus this evening?" said Conseil. "Suppose we never return?" added Ned Land." What is the meaning of Ned Land here?

5. In chapter 21 lines 10-12 the author writes: "Are they apes?" cried Ned Land. "Very nearly—they are savages. "To the boat!" I said, hurrying to the sea." What does the Professor mean when he says "very nearly- they are savages"? Would someone speak like that today about natives of another country? Why yes or not? Would the Torah approve of such speech?

____

____

____

6. In chapter 21 lines 45-48, Captain Nemo addressing the Professor states "So you are astonished, Professor, at having set foot on a strange land and finding savages? Savages! where are there not any? Besides, are they worse than others, these whom you call savages?". What does the Captain possibly mean by this? What kind of statement about people, in general, is the Captain making? What do you think is the Torah's position on this association between savages and people?

____

____

____

7. In chapter 21 lines 135-155, the Professor and Conseil go fishing for shells and the Professor makes a discovery. What was it and how is it destroyed?

____

____

8. In chapter 21 lines 152-157 it states: Conseil!" cried I. "Conseil!" "Well, sir! do you not see that the cannibal has commenced the attack?" "A shell is not worth the life of a man," said I." Is the Professor right in his response? Why or why not? What do you think the Torah would say?

____

____

____

____

____

9. In the next line it states: "Ah! the scoundrel!" cried Conseil; "I would rather he had broken my shoulder!" Conseil was in earnest, but I was not of his opinion." What do these phrases mean, and how does it represent a philosophical difference between the two?

____

____

10. In chapter 21 lines 222-229 Captain Nemo discusses the life and tragic death of a certain French Captain D'Urville. What is ironic about the life and death of this Captain?

____

____

11. What two aspects stopped the natives from entering the submarine?

____

____

12. How did the submarine get unstuck and sail free?

____

____

Chapter 22

"AEGRI SOMNIA"

The following day 10th January, the Nautilus continued her course between two seas, but with such remarkable speed that I could not estimate it at less than thirty-five miles an hour. The rapidity of her screw was such that I could neither follow nor count its revolutions. When I reflected that this marvelous electric agent, after having afforded motion, heat, and light to the Nautilus, still protected her from outward attack, and transformed her into an ark of safety which no profane hand might touch without being thunderstricken, my admiration was unbounded, and from the structure it extended to the engineer who had called it into existence.

Our course was directed to the west, and on the 11th of January we doubled Cape Wessel, situation in 135° long. and 10° S. lat., which forms the east point of the Gulf of Carpentaria. The reefs were still numerous, but more equalized, and marked on the chart with extreme precision. The Nautilus easily avoided the breakers of Money to port and the Victoria reefs to starboard, placed at 130° long. and on the 10th parallel, which we strictly followed.

On the 13th of January, Captain Nemo arrived in the Sea of Timor, and recognized the island of that name in 122° long.

From this point the direction of the Nautilus inclined towards the south-west. Her head was set for the Indian Ocean. Where would the fancy of Captain Nemo carry us next? Would he return to the coast of Asia or would he approach again the shores of Europe? **Improbable conjectures** both, to a man who fled from inhabited continents. Then would he descend to the south? Was he going to double the Cape of Good Hope, then Cape Horn, and finally go as far as the Antarctic pole? Would he come back at last to the Pacific, where his Nautilus could sail free and independently? Time would show.

32 After having skirted the sands of Cartier, of Hibernia,
33 Seringapatam, and Scott, last efforts of the solid against the
34 liquid element, on the 14th of January we lost sight of land
35 altogether. The speed of the Nautilus was considerably abated,
36 and with irregular course she sometimes swam in the bosom of
37 the waters, sometimes floated on their surface.

38 During this period of the voyage, Captain Nemo made some
39 interesting experiments on the varied temperature of the sea,
40 in different beds. Under ordinary conditions these observations
41 are made by means of rather complicated instruments, and
42 with somewhat doubtful results, by means of thermometrical
43 sounding-leads, the glasses often breaking under the pressure
44 of the water, or an apparatus grounded on the variations of the
45 resistance of metals to the electric currents. Results so obtained
46 could not be correctly calculated. On the contrary, Captain Nemo
47 went himself to test the temperature in the depths of the sea, and
48 his thermometer, placed in communication with the different
49 sheets of water, gave him the required degree immediately and
50 accurately.

51 It was thus that, either by overloading her reservoirs or by
52 descending obliquely by means of her inclined planes, the
53 Nautilus successively attained the depth of three, four, five,
54 seven, nine, and ten thousand yards, and the definite result of this
55 experience was that the sea preserved an average temperature of
56 four degrees and a half at a depth of five thousand fathoms under
57 all latitudes.

58 On the 16th of January, the Nautilus seemed becalmed only a few
59 yards beneath the surface of the waves. Her electric apparatus
60 remained inactive and her motionless screw left her to drift at
61 the mercy of the currents. I supposed that the crew was occupied
62 with interior repairs, rendered necessary by the violence of the
63 mechanical movements of the machine.

64 My companions and I then witnessed a curious spectacle. The
65 hatches of the saloon were open, and, as the beacon light of
66 the Nautilus was not in action, a dim **obscurity** reigned in the

67 midst of the waters. I observed the state of the sea, under these
68 conditions, and the largest fish appeared to me no more than
69 scarcely defined shadows, when the Nautilus found herself
70 suddenly transported into full light. I thought at first that the
71 beacon had been lighted, and was casting its electric radiance
72 into the liquid mass. I was mistaken, and after a rapid survey
73 perceived my error.

74 The Nautilus floated in the midst of a phosphorescent bed
75 which, in this obscurity, became quite dazzling. It was produced
76 by myriads of luminous animalculae, whose brilliancy was
77 increased as they glided over the metallic hull of the vessel. I
78 was surprised by lightning in the midst of these luminous sheets,
79 as though they had been rivulets of lead melted in an **ardent**
80 furnace or metallic masses brought to a white heat, so that, by
81 force of contrast, certain portions of light appeared to cast a
82 shade in the midst of the general ignition, from which all shade
83 seemed banished. No; this was not the calm irradiation of our
84 ordinary lightning. There was unusual life and vigour: this was
85 truly living light!

86 In reality, it was an infinite **agglomeration** of colored infusoria,
87 of veritable globules of jelly, provided with a threadlike tentacle,
88 and of which as many as twenty-five thousand have been counted
89 in less than two cubic half-inches of water.

90 During several hours the Nautilus floated in these brilliant
91 waves, and our admiration increased as we watched the marine
92 monsters disporting themselves like salamanders. I saw there in
93 the midst of this fire that burns not the swift and elegant porpoise
94 (the indefatigable clown of the ocean), and some swordfish
95 ten feet long, those prophetic heralds of the hurricane whose
96 formidable sword would now and then strike the glass of the
97 saloon. Then appeared the smaller fish, the balista, the leaping
98 mackerel, wolf-thorn-tails, and a hundred others which striped
99 the luminous atmosphere as they swam. This dazzling spectacle
100 was enchanting! Perhaps some atmospheric condition increased
101 the intensity of this phenomenon. Perhaps some storm agitated

102 the surface of the waves. But at this depth of some yards, the
103 Nautilus was unmoved by its fury and reposed peacefully in still
104 water.

105 So we progressed, incessantly charmed by some new marvel.
106 The days passed rapidly away, and I took no account of them.
107 Ned, according to habit, tried to vary the diet on board. Like
108 snails, we were fixed to our shells, and I declare it is easy to lead
109 a snail's life.

110 Thus this life seemed easy and natural, and we thought no longer
111 of the life we led on land; but something happened to recall us to
112 the strangeness of our situation.

113 On the 18th of January, the Nautilus was in 105° long. and 15°
114 S. lat. The weather was threatening, the sea rough and rolling.
115 There was a strong east wind. The barometer, which had been
116 going down for some days, foreboded a coming storm. I went
117 up on to the platform just as the second lieutenant was taking
118 the measure of the horary angles, and waited, according to habit
119 till the daily phrase was said. But on this day it was exchanged
120 for another phrase not less **incomprehensible**. Almost directly,
121 I saw Captain Nemo appear with a glass, looking towards the
122 horizon.

123 For some minutes he was **immovable**, without taking his eye off
124 the point of observation. Then he lowered his glass and exchanged
125 a few words with his lieutenant. The latter seemed to be a victim
126 to some emotion that he tried in vain to repress. Captain Nemo,
127 having more command over himself, was cool. He seemed, too,
128 to be making some objections to which the lieutenant replied
129 by formal assurances. At least I concluded so by the difference
130 of their tones and gestures. For myself, I had looked carefully
131 in the direction indicated without seeing anything. The sky and
132 water were lost in the clear line of the horizon.

133 However, Captain Nemo walked from one end of the platform
134 to the other, without looking at me, perhaps without seeing
135 me. His step was firm, but less regular than usual. He stopped

136 sometimes, crossed his arms, and observed the sea. What could
137 he be looking for on that immense expanse?

138 The Nautilus was then some hundreds of miles from the nearest
139 coast.

140 The lieutenant had taken up the glass and examined the horizon
141 steadfastly, going and coming, stamping his foot and showing
142 more nervous agitation than his superior officer. Besides, this
143 mystery must necessarily be solved, and before long; for, upon an
144 order from Captain Nemo, the engine, increasing its propelling
145 power, made the screw turn more rapidly.

146 Just then the lieutenant drew the Captain's attention again.
147 The latter stopped walking and directed his glass towards the
148 place indicated. He looked long. I felt very much puzzled,
149 and descended to the drawing-room, and took out an excellent
150 telescope that I generally used. Then, leaning on the cage of the
151 watch-light that jutted out from the front of the platform, set
152 myself to look over all the line of the sky and sea.

153 But my eye was no sooner applied to the glass than it was quickly
154 snatched out of my hands.

155 I turned round. Captain Nemo was before me, but I did not know
156 him. His face was **transfigured**. His eyes flashed **sullenly**; his
157 teeth were set; his stiff body, clenched fists, and head shrunk
158 between his shoulders, betrayed the violent agitation that
159 pervaded his whole frame. He did not move. My glass, fallen
160 from his hands, had rolled at his feet.

161 Had I unwittingly provoked this fit of anger? Did this
162 incomprehensible person imagine that I had discovered some
163 forbidden secret? No; I was not the object of this hatred, for
164 he was not looking at me; his eye was steadily fixed upon
165 the **impenetrable** point of the horizon. At last Captain Nemo
166 recovered himself. His agitation subsided. He addressed some
167 words in a foreign language to his lieutenant, then turned to me.
168 "M. Aronnax," he said, in rather an imperious tone, "I require

169   you to keep one of the conditions that bind you to me."

170   "What is it, Captain?"

171   "You must be confined, with your companions, until I think fit
172   to release you."

173   "You are the master," I replied, looking steadily at him. "But
174   may I ask you one question?"

175   "None, sir."

176   There was no resisting this **imperious** command, it would have
177   been useless. I went down to the cabin occupied by Ned Land
178   and Conseil, and told them the Captain's determination. You may
179   judge how this communication was received by the Canadian.

180   But there was not time for **altercation**. Four of the crew waited
181   at the door, and conducted us to that cell where we had passed
182   our first night on board the Nautilus.

183   Ned Land would have **remonstrated**, but the door was shut
184   upon him.

185   "Will master tell me what this means?" asked Conseil.

186   I told my companions what had passed. They were as much
187   astonished as I, and equally at a loss how to account for it.

188   Meanwhile, I was absorbed in my own reflections, and could
189   think of nothing but the strange fear **depicted** in the Captain's
190   **countenance**. I was utterly at a loss to account for it, when my
191   cogitations were disturbed by these words from Ned Land:

192   "Hallo! breakfast is ready."

193   And indeed the table was laid. Evidently Captain Nemo had
194   given this order at the same time that he had hastened the speed
195   of the Nautilus.

196   "Will master permit me to make a recommendation?" asked
197   Conseil.

198 "Yes, my boy."

199 "Well, it is that master breakfasts. It is **prudent**, for we do not
200 know what may happen."

201 "You are right, Conseil."

202 "Unfortunately," said Ned Land, "they have only given us the
203 ship's fare."

204 "Friend Ned," asked Conseil, "what would you have said if the
205 breakfast had been entirely forgotten?"

206 This argument cut short the harpooner's recriminations.

207 We sat down to table. The meal was eaten in silence.

208 Just then the luminous globe that lighted the cell went out,
209 and left us in total darkness. Ned Land was soon asleep, and
210 what astonished me was that Conseil went off into a heavy
211 slumber. I was thinking what could have caused his **irresistible**
212 drowsiness, when I felt my brain becoming **stupefied**. In spite
213 of my efforts to keep my eyes open, they would close. A painful
214 suspicion seized me. Evidently **soporific** substances had been
215 mixed with the food we had just taken. Imprisonment was not
216 enough to conceal Captain Nemo's projects from us, sleep was
217 more necessary. I then heard the panels shut. The **undulations**
218 of the sea, which caused a slight rolling motion, ceased. Had
219 the Nautilus quitted the surface of the ocean? Had it gone back
220 to the motionless bed of water? I tried to resist sleep. It was
221 impossible. My breathing grew weak. I felt a mortal cold freeze
222 my stiffened and half-paralysed limbs. My eye lids, like leaden
223 caps, fell over my eyes. I could not raise them; a morbid sleep,
224 full of hallucinations, bereft me of my being. Then the visions
225 disappeared, and left me in complete **insensibility**.

Vocabulary part 1 Chapter 22

immovable, agglomeration, transfigured, sullenly, impenetrable, imperious, altercation, remonstrated, depicted, prudent, irresistible, soporific, undulations, insensibility

Questions

1. What does the Professor express his admiration for in lines 5-11 and then for whom? Upon whom do frum Jews express admiration for in such gushing tones?

    ____

    ____

2. What jolts the Professor back to reality in realizing how strange his and his companions' existence is?

    ____

3. What do you think the Captain sees and doesn't want the Professor to see?

    ____

4. Why do you think Conseil tells the Professor it may be wise to eat breakfast in lines 199-200? What do you think he had in mind might possibly happen?

    ____

    ____

5. What does the Captain do to stop the Professor from knowing what is happening?

    ____

    ____

Chapter 23

THE CORAL KINGDOM

The next day I woke with my head singularly clear. To my great surprise, I was in my own room. My companions, no doubt, had been reinstated in their cabin, without having perceived it any more than I. Of what had passed during the night they were as ignorant as I was, and to penetrate this mystery I only **reckoned** upon the chances of the future.

I then thought of quitting my room. Was I free again or a prisoner? Quite free. I opened the door, went to the half-deck, went up the central stairs. The panels, shut the evening before, were open. I went on to the platform.

Ned Land and Conseil waited there for me. I questioned them; they knew nothing. Lost in a heavy sleep in which they had been totally unconscious, they had been astonished at finding themselves in their cabin.

As for the Nautilus, it seemed quiet and mysterious as ever. It floated on the surface of the waves at a moderate pace. Nothing seemed changed on board.

The second lieutenant then came on to the platform, and gave the usual order below.

As for Captain Nemo, he did not appear.

Of the people on board, I only saw the **impassive** steward, who served me with his usual dumb regularity.

About two o'clock, I was in the drawing-room, busied in arranging my notes, when the Captain opened the door and appeared. I bowed. He made a slight **inclination** in return, without speaking. I resumed my work, hoping that he would perhaps give me some explanation of the events of the preceding night. He made none. I looked at him. He seemed fatigued; his heavy eyes had not been refreshed by sleep; his face looked very sorrowful. He walked to

30 and fro, sat down and got up again, took a chance book, put it
31 down, consulted his instruments without taking his habitual
32 notes, and seemed restless and uneasy. At last, he came up to me,
33 and said:

34 "Are you a doctor, M. Aronnax?"

35 I so little expected such a question that I stared some time at him
36 without answering.

37 "Are you a doctor?" he repeated. "Several of your colleagues have
38 studied medicine."

39 "Well," said I, "I am a doctor and resident surgeon to the hospital.
40 I practiced several years before entering the museum."

41 "Very well, sir."

42 My answer had evidently satisfied the Captain. But, not knowing
43 what he would say next, I waited for other questions, reserving
44 my answers according to circumstances.

45 "M. Aronnax, will you consent to **prescribe** for one of my men?"
46 he asked.

47 "Is he ill?"

48 "Yes."

49 "I am ready to follow you."

50 "Come, then."

51 *I own my heart beat,* I do not know why. I saw certain connection
52 between the illness of one of the crew and the events of the day
53 before; and this mystery interested me at least as much as the
54 sick man.

55 Captain Nemo conducted me to the poop of the Nautilus, and
56 took me into a cabin situated near the sailors' quarters.

57 There, on a bed, lay a man about forty years of age, with a resolute
58 expression of countenance, a true type of an Anglo-Saxon.

59   I leant over him. He was not only ill, he was wounded. His head,
60   swathed in bandages covered with blood, lay on a pillow. I undid
61   the bandages, and the wounded man looked at me with his large
62   eyes and gave no sign of pain as I did it. It was a horrible wound.
63   The skull, shattered by some deadly weapon, left the brain
64   exposed, which was much injured. Clots of blood had formed
65   in the bruised and broken mass, in color like the dregs of wine.

66   There was both **contusion** and **suffusion** of the brain. His
67   breathing was slow, and some **spasmodic** movements of the
68   muscles agitated his face. I felt his pulse. It was **intermittent**.
69   The extremities of the body were growing cold already, and I
70   saw death must **inevitably ensue**. After dressing the unfortunate
71   man's wounds, I readjusted the bandages on his head, and turned
72   to Captain Nemo.

73   "What caused this wound?" I asked.

74   "What does it signify?" he replied, **evasively**. "A shock has broken
75   one of the levers of the engine, which struck myself. But your
76   opinion as to his state?"

77   I hesitated before giving it.

78   "You may speak," said the Captain. "This man does not understand
79   French."

80   I gave a last look at the wounded man.

81   "He will be dead in two hours."

82   "Can nothing save him?"

83   "Nothing."

84   Captain Nemo's hand contracted, and some tears glistened in his
85   eyes, which I thought incapable of shedding any.

86   For some moments I still watched the dying man, whose life
87   ebbed slowly. His **pallor** increased under the electric light that
88   was shed over his death-bed. I looked at his intelligent forehead,
89   furrowed with premature wrinkles, produced probably by

90 misfortune and sorrow. I tried to learn the secret of his life from
91 the last words that escaped his lips.

92 "You can go now, M. Aronnax," said the Captain.

93 I left him in the dying man's cabin, and returned to my room
94 much affected by this scene. During the whole day, I was haunted
95 by uncomfortable suspicions, and at night I slept badly, and
96 between my broken dreams I fancied I heard distant sighs like
97 the notes of a funeral psalm. Were they the prayers of the dead,
98 murmured in that language that I could not understand?

99 The next morning I went on to the bridge. Captain Nemo was
100 there before me. As soon as he **perceived** me he came to me.

101 "Professor, will it be convenient to you to make a submarine
102 excursion to-day?"

103 "With my companions?" I asked.

104 "If they like."

105 "We obey your orders, Captain."

106 "Will you be so good then as to put on your cork jackets?"

107 It was not a question of dead or dying. I rejoined Ned Land and
108 Conseil, and told them of Captain Nemo's **proposition**. Conseil
109 **hastened** to accept it, and this time the Canadian seemed quite
110 willing to follow our example.

111 It was eight o'clock in the morning. At half-past eight we
112 were equipped for this new excursion, and provided with two
113 contrivances for light and breathing. The double door was open;
114 and, accompanied by Captain Nemo, who was followed by a
115 dozen of the crew, we set foot, at a depth of about thirty feet, on
116 the solid bottom on which the Nautilus rested.

117 A slight **declivity** ended in an uneven bottom, at fifteen fathoms
118 depth. This bottom differed entirely from the one I had visited on
119 my first excursion under the waters of the Pacific Ocean. Here,
120 there was no fine sand, no submarine prairies, no sea-forest. I

121 immediately recognized that marvelous region in which, on that
122 day, the Captain did the honors to us. It was the coral kingdom.

123 The light produced a thousand charming varieties, playing in the
124 midst of the branches that were so vividly coloured. I seemed
125 to see the membraneous and cylindrical tubes tremble beneath
126 the undulation of the waters. I was tempted to gather their fresh
127 petals, ornamented with delicate tentacles, some just blown, the
128 others budding, while a small fish, swimming swiftly, touched
129 them slightly, like flights of birds. But if my hand approached
130 these living flowers, these animated, sensitive plants, the whole
131 colony took alarm. The white petals re-entered their red cases,
132 the flowers faded as I looked, and the bush changed into a block
133 of stony knobs.

134 Chance had thrown me just by the most precious specimens of
135 the zoophyte. This coral was more valuable than that found in
136 the Mediterranean, on the coasts of France, Italy and Barbary. Its
137 tints justified the poetical names of "Flower of Blood," and "Froth
138 of Blood," that trade has given to its most beautiful productions.
139 Coral is sold for L20 per ounce; and in this place the watery beds
140 would make the fortunes of a company of coral-divers. This
141 precious matter, often confused with other polypi, formed then
142 the **inextricable** plots called "macciota," and on which I noticed
143 several beautiful specimens of pink coral.

144 But soon the bushes contract, and the arborisations increase.
145 Real petrified thickets, long joints of fantastic architecture,
146 were disclosed before us. Captain Nemo placed himself under
147 a dark gallery, where by a slight declivity we reached a depth of
148 a hundred yards. The light from our lamps produced sometimes
149 magical effects, following the rough outlines of the natural arches
150 and **pendants** disposed like lustres, that were tipped with points
151 of fire.

152 At last, after walking two hours, we had attained a depth of about
153 three hundred yards, that is to say, the extreme limit on which
154 coral begins to form. But there was no isolated bush, nor modest
155 brushwood, at the bottom of lofty trees. It was an immense forest

156 of large mineral vegetations, enormous petrified trees, united by
157 garlands of elegant sea-bindweed, all adorned with clouds and
158 reflections. We passed freely under their high branches, lost in
159 the shade of the waves.

160 Captain Nemo had stopped. I and my companions halted, and,
161 turning round, I saw his men were forming a semi-circle round
162 their chief. Watching attentively, I observed that four of them
163 carried on their shoulders an object of an oblong shape.

164 We occupied, in this place, the center of a vast glade surrounded
165 by the lofty foliage of the submarine forest. Our lamps threw
166 over this place a sort of clear twilight that singularly elongated
167 the shadows on the ground. At the end of the glade the darkness
168 increased, and was only relieved by little sparks reflected by the
169 points of coral.

170 Ned Land and Conseil were near me. We watched, and I thought
171 I was going to witness a strange scene. On observing the ground,
172 I saw that it was raised in certain places by slight **excrescences**
173 encrusted with limy deposits, and disposed with a regularity that
174 betrayed the hand of man.

175 In the midst of the glade, on a pedestal of rocks roughly piled
176 up... Upon a sign from Captain Nemo one of the men advanced;
177 and..began to dig a hole with a pickaxe that he took from his belt.
178 I understood all! This glade was a cemetery, this hole a tomb, this
179 oblong object the body of the man who had died in the night!
180 The Captain and his men had come to bury their companion
181 in this general resting-place, at the bottom of this inaccessible
182 ocean!

183 The grave was being dug slowly; the fish fled on all sides while
184 their retreat was being thus disturbed; I heard the strokes of the
185 pickaxe, which sparkled when it hit upon some flint lost at the
186 bottom of the waters. The hole was soon large and deep enough
187 to receive the body. Then the bearers approached; the body,
188 enveloped in a tissue of white linen, was lowered into the damp
189 grave...

190 The grave was then filled in with the rubbish taken from the
191 ground, which formed a slight mound. When this was done,
192 Captain Nemo and his men rose; then, approaching the grave, …
193 all extended their hands in sign of a last adieu. Then the funeral
194 procession returned to the Nautilus, passing under the arches of
195 the forest, in the midst of thickets, along the coral bushes, and
196 still on the ascent. At last the light of the ship appeared, and its
197 luminous track guided us to the Nautilus. At one o'clock we had
198 returned.

199 As soon as I had changed my clothes I went up on to the platform,
200 and, a prey to conflicting emotions, I sat down near the **binnacle**.
201 Captain Nemo joined me. I rose and said to him:

202 "So, as I said he would, this man died in the night?"

203 "Yes, M. Aronnax."

204 "And he rests now, near his companions, in the coral cemetery?"

205 "Yes, forgotten by all else, but not by us. We dug the grave, and
206 the polypi undertake to seal our dead for eternity." And, burying
207 his face quickly in his hands, he tried in vain to suppress a sob.
208 Then he added: "Our peaceful cemetery is there, some hundred
209 feet below the surface of the waves."

210 "Your dead sleep quietly, at least, Captain, out of the reach of
211 sharks."

212 "Yes, sir, of sharks and men," gravely replied the Captain.

Vocabulary part 1 chapter 23

impassive, inclination, prescribe, contusion, suffusion, spasmodic, inevitably, ensue, evasively, pallor, perceived, inextricable, pendants, excrescences, binnacle

Questions for part 1 chapter 23

1. In line 51, the Professor says, "I own my heart beat"… What does this phrase mean?

2. What do you think happened during the night? Do you believe the Captain's story of how this young man was injured?

3. Do you think what occurred at night has to do with the fact that they were put to sleep? Why?

4. What do you think Captain Nemo means in the last line of the chapter? Based on the various statements made by Captain Nemo regarding the nature of people, how does this statement fit in with his views on people in general? Explain

Part Two

Chapter 1

THE INDIAN OCEAN

We now come to the second part of our journey under the sea. The first ended with the moving scene in the coral cemetery which left such a deep impression on my mind. Thus, in the midst of this great sea, Captain Nemo's life was passing, even to his grave, which he had prepared in one of its deepest **abysses**. There, not one of the ocean's monsters could trouble the last sleep of the crew of the Nautilus, of those friends **riveted** to each other in death as in life. "Nor any man, either," had added the Captain. Still the same fierce, **implacable defiance** towards human society!

I could no longer **content** myself with the theory which satisfied Conseil.

That worthy fellow persisted in seeing in the Commander of the Nautilus one of those unknown **savants** who return mankind contempt for **indifference**. For him, he was a misunderstood genius who, tired of earth's **deceptions**, had taken **refuge** in this **inaccessible medium**, where he might follow his instincts freely. To my mind, this explains but one side of Captain Nemo's character. Indeed, the mystery of that last night during which we had been chained in prison, the sleep, and the precaution so violently taken by the Captain of snatching from my eyes the glass I had raised to sweep the horizon, the **mortal** wound of the man, due to an unaccountable shock of the Nautilus, all put me on a new track. No; Captain Nemo was not satisfied with **shunning** man. His formidable **apparatus** not only suited his instinct of freedom, but perhaps also the design of some terrible **retaliation**.

At this moment nothing is clear to me; I catch but a glimpse of light amidst all the darkness, and I must confine myself to

30 writing as events shall dictate.

31 That day, the 24th of January, 1868, at noon, the second officer
32 came to take the **altitude** of the sun. I mounted the platform, lit
33 a cigar, and watched the operation. It seemed to me that the man
34 did not understand French; for several times I made remarks in a
35 loud voice, which must have drawn from him some involuntary
36 sign of attention, if he had understood them; but he remained
37 undisturbed and **dumb**.

38 As he was taking observations with the **sextant**, one of the sailors
39 of the Nautilus (the strong man who had accompanied us on
40 our first submarine excursion to the Island of Crespo) came to
41 clean the glasses of the lantern. I examined the fittings of the
42 apparatus, the strength of which was increased a hundredfold
43 by **lenticular** rings, placed similar to those in a lighthouse, and
44 which projected their brilliance in a horizontal plane. The electric
45 lamp was combined in such a way as to give its most powerful
46 light. Indeed, it was produced in **vacuo**, which insured both its
47 steadiness and its intensity. This vacuum economized the graphite
48 points between which the luminous arc was developed—an
49 important point of economy for Captain Nemo, who could not
50 easily have replaced them; and under these conditions their waste
51 was imperceptible. When the Nautilus was ready to continue its
52 submarine journey, I went down to the **saloon**. The panel was
53 closed, and the course marked direct west.

54 We were **furrowing** the waters of the Indian Ocean, a vast liquid
55 plain, with a surface of 1,200,000,000 of acres, and whose waters
56 are so clear and **transparent** that any one leaning over them
57 would turn **giddy**. The Nautilus usually floated between fifty
58 and a hundred **fathoms** deep. We went on so for some days. To
59 anyone but myself, who had a great love for the sea, the hours
60 would have seemed long and **monotonous**; but the daily walks
61 on the platform, when I steeped myself in the reviving air of the
62 ocean, the sight of the rich waters through the windows of the
63 saloon, the books in the library, the **compiling** of my **memoirs**,
64 took up all my time, and left me not a moment of **ennui** or
65 weariness.

66 For some days we saw a great number of aquatic birds, sea-mews
67 or gulls. Some were cleverly killed and, prepared in a certain
68 way, made very acceptable **water-game**. Amongst large-winged
69 birds, carried a long distance from all lands and resting upon the
70 waves from the **fatigue** of their flight, I saw some magnificent
71 **albatrosses, uttering discordant** cries…, and birds belonging to
72 the family of the long-wings.

73 As to the fish, they always provoked our admiration when we
74 surprised the secrets of their aquatic life through the open
75 panels. I saw many kinds which I never before had a chance of
76 observing.

77 I shall notice chiefly **ostracions** peculiar to the Red Sea, the Indian
78 Ocean, and that part which washes the coast of tropical America.
79 …I would also mention quadrangular ostracions, having on the
80 back four large **tubercles**; some dotted over with white spots on
81 the lower part of the body, and which may be tamed like birds;
82 **trigons** provided with spikes formed by the lengthening of their
83 bony shell, and which, from their strange **gruntings**, are called
84 "seapigs"; also **dromedaries** with large humps in the shape of a
85 cone, whose flesh is very tough and leathery.

86 From the 21st to the 23rd of January the Nautilus went at the
87 rate of two hundred and fifty leagues in twenty-four hours, being
88 five hundred and forty miles, or twenty-two miles an hour. If
89 we recognized so many different varieties of fish, it was because,
90 attracted by the electric light, they tried to follow us; the greater
91 part, however, were soon distanced by our speed, though some
92 kept their place in the waters of the Nautilus for a time. The
93 morning of the 24th, in 12° 5' S. lat., and 94° 33' long., we observed
94 Keeling Island, a coral formation, planted with magnificent
95 **cocos**, and which had been visited by Mr. Darwin and Captain
96 Fitzroy. The Nautilus skirted the shores of this desert island for a
97 little distance. Its nets brought up numerous specimens of **polypi**
98 and curious shells of Mollusca. Some precious productions of the
99 species of **delphinulae** enriched the treasures of Captain Nemo,
100 to which I added an **astraea punctifera**, a kind of **parasite**
101 **polypus** often found fixed to a shell.

Soon Keeling Island disappeared from the horizon, and our course was directed to the north-west in the direction of the Indian Peninsula.

From Keeling Island our course was slower and more variable, often taking us into great depths. Several times they made use of the **inclined planes**, which certain internal levers placed **obliquely** to the waterline. In that way we went about two miles, but without ever obtaining the greatest depths of the Indian Sea, which soundings of seven thousand fathoms have never reached. As to the temperature of the lower strata, the thermometer invariably indicated 4° above zero. I only observed that in the upper regions the water was always colder in the high levels than at the surface of the sea.

On the 25th of January the ocean was entirely deserted; the Nautilus passed the day on the surface, beating the waves with its powerful screw and making them rebound to a great height. Who under such circumstances would not have taken it for a gigantic **cetacean**? Three parts of this day I spent on the platform. I watched the sea. Nothing on the horizon, till about four o'clock a steamer running west on our counter. Her **masts** were visible for an instant, but she could not see the Nautilus, being too low in the water. I fancied this steamboat belonged to the P.O. Company, which runs from **Ceylon** to **Sydney**, touching at King George's Point and **Melbourne**.

At five o'clock in the evening, before that fleeting twilight which binds night to day in tropical zones, Conseil and I were astonished by a curious spectacle.

It was a **shoal** of **argonauts** travelling along on the surface of the ocean. We could count several hundreds. They belonged to the tubercle kind which are peculiar to the Indian seas.

These graceful mollusks moved backwards by means of their **locomotive** tube, through which they propelled the water already drawn in. Of their eight **tentacles**, six were **elongated**, and stretched out floating on the water, whilst the other two, rolled up flat, were spread to the wing like a light sail. I saw their spiral-shaped and fluted shells, which Cuvier justly compares to an elegant skiff. A boat indeed! It bears the creature which secretes it without its adhering to it.

For nearly an hour the Nautilus floated in the midst of this shoal of mollusks. Then I know not what sudden fright they took. But as if at a signal every sail was furled, the arms folded, the body drawn in, the shells turned over, changing their center of gravity, and the whole fleet disappeared under the waves. Never did the ships of a **squadron maneuver** with more unity.

At that moment night fell suddenly, and the reeds, scarcely raised by the breeze, lay peaceably under the sides of the Nautilus.

The next day, 26th of January, we cut the equator at the eighty-second **meridian** and entered the northern hemisphere. During the day a formidable troop of sharks accompanied us, terrible creatures, which multiply in these seas and make them very dangerous. They were "cestracio philippi" sharks, with brown backs and whitish bellies, armed with eleven rows of teeth—eyed sharks—their throat being marked with a large black spot surrounded with white like an eye. There were also some Isabella sharks, with rounded **snouts** marked with dark spots. These powerful creatures often hurled themselves at the windows of the **saloon** with such violence as to make us feel very **insecure**. At such times Ned Land was no longer master of himself. He wanted to go to the surface and harpoon the monsters, particularly certain smooth-hound sharks, whose mouth is studded with teeth like a **mosaic**; and large tiger-sharks nearly six yards long, the last named of which seemed to excite him more particularly. But the Nautilus, accelerating her speed, easily left the most rapid of them behind.

The 27th of January, at the entrance of the vast of **Bay of Bengal**, we met repeatedly a **forbidding spectacle**, dead bodies floating on the surface of the water. They were the dead of the Indian villages, carried by the Ganges to the level of the sea, and which the **vultures**, the only **undertakers** of the country, had not been able to devour. But the sharks did not fail to help them at their funeral work.

About seven o'clock in the evening, the Nautilus, half-**immersed**, was sailing in a sea of milk. At first sight the ocean seemed **lactified**. Was it the effect of the **lunar** rays? No; for the moon, scarcely two days old, was still lying hidden under the horizon in the rays of the sun. The whole sky, though lit by the **sidereal** rays, seemed black by contrast with the whiteness of the waters.

Conseil could not believe his eyes, and questioned me as to the cause of this strange phenomenon. Happily I was able to answer him.

"It is called a milk sea," I explained. "A large extent of white **wavelets** often to be seen on the coasts of Amboyna, and in these parts of the sea."

"But, sir," said Conseil, "can you tell me what causes such an effect? for I suppose the water is not really turned into milk."

"No, my boy; and the whiteness which surprises you is caused only by the presence of **myriads** of **infusoria**, a sort of **luminous** little worm, **gelatinous** and without color, of the thickness of a hair, and whose length is not more than seven-thousandths of an inch. These insects adhere to one another sometimes for several leagues."

"Several leagues!" exclaimed Conseil.

"Yes, my boy; and you need not try to compute the number of these **infusoria**. You will not be able, for, if I am not mistaken, ships have floated on these milk seas for more than forty miles."

Towards midnight the sea suddenly resumed its usual color; but behind us, even to the limits of the horizon, the sky reflected the whitened waves, and for a long time seemed **impregnated** with the **vague** glimmerings of an **aurora borealis**.

Vocabulary Part 2 Ch. 1

riveted, implacable, defiance, savants, indifference, deceptions, refuge, inaccessible, shunning, retaliation, altitude, lenticular, furrowing, transparent, giddy, monotonous, compiling, memoirs

Questions part 2 ch. 1

1. What does the author mean in line 9 when he says, "Still the same fierce, implacable defiance towards human society"?

2. What does the author mean in lines 11-12 when he says, "I could no longer content myself with the theory which satisfied Conseil"?

3. What does the sentence on lines 25-27 mean?

4. Why did the Professor say he was not bored in lines 58-65? Why did he enjoy being in the Nautilus?

5. In lines 80-85 the author mentions that some fish in
    the ocean resemble some animals on earth. What do
    Chaza"l say about this phenomenon?

    ____

    ____

    ____

6. What does the author mean in line 170 that the vultures
    were "the only undertakers of the country"? How did
    the sharks help with the dead?

    ____

    ____

    ____

7. What does the author mean in line 174 that the Nautilus
    was "sailing in a sea of milk"?

    ____

    ____

    ____

    ____

Chapter 2
A NOVEL PROPOSAL OF CAPTAIN NEMO'S

On the 28th of February, when at noon the Nautilus came to the surface of the sea, in 9° 4' N. lat., there was land in sight about eight miles to westward. The first thing I noticed was a range of mountains about two thousand feet high, the shapes of which were most **capricious**. On taking the **bearings**, I knew that we were nearing the island of Ceylon, the pearl which hangs from the **lobe** of the Indian Peninsula.

Captain Nemo and his second appeared at this moment. The Captain glanced at the map. Then turning to me, said:

"The Island of Ceylon, noted for its pearl-fisheries. Would you like to visit one of them, M. Aronnax?"

"Certainly, Captain."

"Well, the thing is easy. Though, if we see the **fisheries**, we shall not see the fishermen. The annual **exportation** has not yet begun. Never mind, I will give orders to make for the Gulf of Manaar, where we shall arrive in the night."

The Captain said something to his second, who immediately went out. Soon the Nautilus returned to her native element, and the **manometer** showed that she was about thirty feet deep.

"Well, sir," said Captain Nemo, "you and your companions shall visit the Bank of Manaar, and if by chance some fisherman should be there, we shall see him at work."

"Agreed, Captain!"

"By the bye, M. Aronnax you are not afraid of sharks?"

"Sharks!" exclaimed I.

26 This question seemed a very hard one.

27 "Well?" continued Captain Nemo.

28 "I admit, Captain, that I am not yet very familiar with that kind
29 of fish."

30 "We are accustomed to them," replied Captain Nemo, "and in
31 time you will be too. However, we shall be armed, and on the
32 road we may be able to hunt some of the tribe. It is interesting.
33 So, till to-morrow, sir, and early."

34 This said in a careless tone, Captain Nemo left the saloon.
35 Now, if you were invited to hunt the bear in the mountains of
36 Switzerland, what would you say?

37 "Very well! to-morrow we will go and hunt the bear." If you
38 were asked to hunt the lion in the plains of Atlas, or the tiger in
39 the Indian jungles, what would you say?

40 "Ha! ha! it seems we are going to hunt the tiger or the lion!" But
41 when you are invited to hunt the shark in its natural element,
42 you would perhaps reflect before accepting the invitation. As for
43 myself, I passed my hand over my forehead, on which stood large
44 drops of cold perspiration. "Let us reflect," said I, "and take our
45 time. Hunting otters in submarine forests, as we did in the Island
46 of Crespo, will pass; but going up and down at the bottom of the
47 sea, where one is almost certain to meet sharks, is quite another
48 thing! I know well that in certain countries, particularly in the
49 Andaman Islands, the **negroes** never hesitate to attack them with
50 a **dagger** in one hand and a running **noose** in the other; but I
51 also know that few who affront those creatures ever return alive.
52 However, I am not a negro, and if I were I think a little hesitation
53 in this case would not be ill-timed."

54 At this moment Conseil and the Canadian entered, quite
55 composed, and even joyous. They knew not what awaited them.

56 "Faith, sir," said Ned Land, "your Captain Nemo—the devil
57 take him!—has just made us a very pleasant offer."

58   "Ah!" said I, "you know?"

59   "If agreeable to you, sir," interrupted Conseil, "the commander
60   of the Nautilus has invited us to visit the magnificent Ceylon
61   fisheries to-morrow, in your company; he did it kindly, and
62   behaved like a real gentleman."

63   "He said nothing more?"

64   "Nothing more, sir, except that he had already spoken to you of
65   this little walk."

66   "Sir," said Conseil, "would you give us some details of the pearl
67   fishery?"

68   "As to the fishing itself," I asked, "or the incidents, which?"

69   "On the fishing," replied the Canadian; "before entering upon
70   the ground, it is as well to know something about it."

71   "Very well; sit down, my friends, and I will teach you."

72   Ned and Conseil seated themselves on an **ottoman**, and the first
73   thing the Canadian asked was:

74   "Sir, what is a pearl?"

75   "My worthy Ned," I answered, "to the poet, a pearl is a tear of the
76   sea; to the Orientals, it is a drop of dew solidified; to the ladies, it
77   is a jewel of an oblong shape, of a brilliancy of mother-of-pearl
78   substance, which they wear on their fingers, their necks, or their
79   ears; for the chemist it is a mixture of **phosphate** and **carbonate**
80   of **lime**, with a little **gelatine**; and lastly, for naturalists, it is
81   simply a **morbid** secretion of the organ that produces the mother-
82   of-pearl amongst certain **bivalves**."

83   "Branch of mollusks," said Conseil.

84   "Precisely so, my learned Conseil; and, amongst these **testacea**
85   the **earshell**, the **tridacnae**, the turbots, in a word, all those
86   which secrete mother-of-pearl, that is, the blue, bluish, violet,

87 or white substance which lines the interior of their shells, are
88 capable of producing pearls.”

89 “Mussels too?” asked the Canadian.

90 “Yes, mussels of certain waters in Scotland, Wales, Ireland,
91 Saxony, Bohemia, and France.”

92 “Good! For the future I shall pay attention,” replied the Canadian.

93 “But,” I continued, “the particular mollusk which secretes
94 the pearl is the pearl-oyster, the **meleagrina margaritiferct**,
95 that precious **pintadine**. The pearl is nothing but a **nacreous**
96 formation, deposited in a globular form, either adhering to the
97 oyster shell, or buried in the folds of the creature. On the shell it
98 is fast; in the flesh it is loose; but always has for a kernel a small
99 hard substance, may be a barren egg, may be a grain of sand,
100 around which the pearly matter deposits itself year after year
101 successively, and by thin concentric layers.”

102 “Are many pearls found in the same oyster?” asked Conseil.

103 “Yes, my boy. Some are a perfect **casket**. One oyster has been
104 mentioned, though I allow myself to doubt it, as having contained
105 no less than a hundred and fifty sharks.”

106 “A hundred and fifty sharks!” exclaimed Ned Land.

107 “Did I say sharks?” said I hurriedly. “I meant to say a hundred
108 and fifty pearls. Sharks would not be sense.”

109 “Certainly not,” said Conseil; “but will you tell us now by what
110 means they extract these pearls?”

111 “They proceed in various ways. When they adhere to the shell,
112 the fishermen often pull them off with **pincers**; but the most
113 common way is to lay the oysters on mats of the seaweed which
114 covers the banks. Thus they die in the open air; and at the end of
115 ten days they are in a forward state of decomposition. They are
116 then plunged into large **reservoirs** of sea-water; then they are

117 opened and washed.”

118 “The price of these pearls varies according to their size?” asked
119 Conseil.

120 “Not only according to their size,” I answered, “but also according
121 to their shape, their water (that is, their color), and their **luster**:
122 that is, that bright and diapered sparkle which makes them so
123 charming to the eye. The most beautiful are called virgin pearls,
124 or **paragons**. They are formed alone in the tissue of the mollusk,
125 are white, often opaque, and sometimes have the transparency
126 of an opal; they are generally round or oval. The round are made
127 into bracelets, the oval into pendants, and, being more precious,
128 are sold singly. Those adhering to the shell of the oyster are more
129 irregular in shape, and are sold by weight. Lastly, in a lower
130 order are classed those small pearls known under the name of
131 seed-pearls; they are sold by measure, and are especially used in
132 embroidery for church ornaments.”

133 “But,” said Conseil, “is this pearl-fishery dangerous?”

134 “No,” I answered, quickly; “particularly if certain precautions
135 are taken.”

136 “What does one risk in such a calling?” said Ned Land, “the
137 swallowing of some mouthfuls of sea-water?”

138 “As you say, Ned. By the bye,” said I, trying to take Captain
139 Nemo’s careless tone, “are you afraid of sharks, brave Ned?”

140 “I!” replied the Canadian; “a harpooner by profession? It is my
141 trade to make light of them.”

142 “But,” said I, “it is not a question of fishing for them with an
143 iron-swivel, hoisting them into the vessel, cutting off their tails
144 with a blow of a chopper, ripping them up, and throwing their
145 heart into the sea!”

146 “Then, it is a question of——”

147 "Precisely."

148 "In the water?"

149 "In the water."

150 "Faith, with a good harpoon! You know, sir, these sharks are ill-
151 fashioned beasts. They turn on their bellies to seize you, and in
152 that time——"

153 Ned Land had a way of saying "seize" which made my blood
154 run cold.

155 "Well, and you, Conseil, what do you think of sharks?"

156 "Me!" said Conseil. "I will be **frank**, sir."

157 "So much the better," thought I.

158 "If you, sir, mean to face the sharks, I do not see why your
159 faithful servant should not face them with you."

𝔙𝔬𝔠𝔞𝔟𝔲𝔩𝔞𝔯𝔶 𝔓𝔞𝔯𝔱 2 𝔠𝔥. 2

lobe, fisheries, exportation, noose, morbid, reservoirs, luster, precautions, frank

Questions part 2 ch. 2

1. What does the author mean in line 18, "the Nautilus returned to her native element"?

2. In lines 75-82, how does the author describe what the pearl is to different people?

3. How do they remove the pearls from the oyster (lines 111-117)?

4. What influences the price of the pearl? (lines 120-132)

5. Are the Professor and Conseil frightened by sharks? How about Ned Land: Is he afraid? How do you know?

Chapter 3
A PEARL OF TEN MILLIONS

The next morning at four o'clock I was awakened by the steward whom Captain Nemo had placed at my service. I rose hurriedly, dressed, and went into the saloon.

Captain Nemo was awaiting me.

"M. Aronnax," said he, "are you ready to start?"

"I am ready."

"Then please to follow me."

"And my companions, Captain?"

"They have been told and are waiting."

"Are we not to put on our diver's dresses?" asked I.

"Not yet. I have not allowed the Nautilus to come too near this coast, and we are some distance from the Manaar Bank; but the boat is ready, and will take us to the exact point of, which will save us a long way. It carries our diving apparatus, which we will put on when we begin our submarine journey."

Captain Nemo conducted me to the central staircase, which led on the platform. Ned and Conseil were already there, delighted at the idea of the "pleasure party" which was preparing. Five sailors from the Nautilus, with their oars, waited in the boat, which had been made fast against the side.

The night was still dark. Layers of clouds covered the sky, allowing but few stars to be seen. I looked on the side where the land lay, and saw nothing but a dark line enclosing three parts of the horizon, from south-west to north west. The Nautilus, having returned during the night up the western coast of Ceylon, was now west of the bay, or rather gulf, formed by the mainland and the Island of Manaar. There, under the dark waters, stretched the

28 pintadine bank, an **inexhaustible** field of pearls, the length of
29 which is more than twenty miles.

30 Captain Nemo, Ned Land, Conseil, and I took our places in
31 the stern of the boat. The master went to the tiller; his four
32 companions leaned on their oars, the painter was cast off, and
33 we **sheared** off.

34 The boat went towards the south; the oarsmen did not hurry.
35 I noticed that their strokes, strong in the water, only followed
36 each other every ten seconds, according to the method generally
37 adopted in the navy. Whilst the craft was running by its own
38 velocity, the liquid drops struck the dark depths of the waves
39 crisply like spats of melted lead. A little billow, spreading wide,
40 gave a slight roll to the boat, and some samphire reeds flapped
41 before it.

42 We were silent. What was Captain Nemo thinking of? Perhaps
43 of the land he was approaching, and which he found too near to
44 him, contrary to the Canadian's opinion, who thought it too far
45 off. As to Conseil, he was merely there from curiosity.

46 About half-past five the first tints on the horizon showed the
47 upper line of coast more distinctly. Flat enough in the east, it
48 rose a little to the south. Five miles still lay between us, and it
49 was **indistinct** owing to the mist on the water. At six o'clock
50 it became suddenly daylight, with that **rapidity peculiar** to
51 tropical regions, which know neither dawn nor twilight. The
52 solar rays pierced the curtain of clouds, piled up on the eastern
53 horizon, and the **radiant orb** rose rapidly. I saw land **distinctly**,
54 with a few trees scattered here and there. The boat neared
55 Manaar Island, which was rounded to the south. Captain Nemo
56 rose from his seat and watched the sea.

57 At a sign from him the anchor was dropped, but the chain
58 scarcely ran, for it was little more than a yard deep, and this spot
59 was one of the highest points of the bank of pintadines.

60 "Here we are, M. Aronnax," said Captain Nemo. "You see that

61 enclosed bay? Here, in a month will be assembled the numerous
62 fishing boats of the exporters, and these are the waters their
63 divers will ransack so boldly. Happily, this bay is well situated
64 for that kind of fishing. It is sheltered from the strongest winds;
65 the sea is never very rough here, which makes it favorable for
66 the diver's work. We will now put on our dresses, and begin our
67 walk."

68 I did not answer, and, while watching the suspected waves,
69 began with the help of the sailors to put on my heavy sea-dress.
70 Captain Nemo and my companions were also dressing. None of
71 the Nautilus men were to accompany us on this new excursion.

72 Soon we were enveloped to the throat in india-rubber clothing;
73 the air apparatus fixed to our backs by braces. As to the Ruhmkorff
74 apparatus, there was no necessity for it. Before putting my head
75 into the copper cap, I had asked the question of the Captain.

76 "They would be useless," he replied. "We are going to no great
77 depth, and the solar rays will be enough to light our walk.
78 Besides, it would not be prudent to carry the electric light in
79 these waters; its brilliancy might attract some of the dangerous
80 inhabitants of the coast most **inopportunely**."

81 As Captain Nemo pronounced these words, I turned to Conseil
82 and Ned Land. But my two friends had already **encased** their
83 heads in the metal cap, and they could neither hear nor answer.

84 One last question remained to ask of Captain Nemo.

85 "And our arms?" asked I; "our guns?"

86 "Guns! What for? Do not mountaineers attack the bear with a
87 dagger in their hand, and is not steel surer than lead? Here is a
88 strong blade; put it in your belt, and we start."

89 I looked at my companions; they were armed like us, and, more
90 than that, Ned Land was brandishing an enormous harpoon,
91 which he had placed in the boat before leaving the Nautilus.

92 Then, following the Captain's example, I allowed myself to be

93 dressed in the heavy copper helmet, and our reservoirs of air
94 were at once in activity. An instant after we were landed, one
95 after the other, in about two yards of water upon an even sand.
96 Captain Nemo made a sign with his hand, and we followed him
97 by a gentle declivity till we disappeared under the waves.

98 Over our feet, like coveys of snipe in a bog, rose shoals of fish, of
99 the genus monoptera, which have no other fins but their tail....
100 The heightening sun lit the mass of waters more and more. The
101 soil changed by degrees. To the fine sand succeeded a perfect
102 causeway of boulders, covered with a carpet of molluscs and
103 zoophytes....

104 At about seven o'clock we found ourselves at last surveying the
105 oyster-banks on which the pearl-oysters are reproduced by
106 millions.

107 Captain Nemo pointed with his hand to the enormous heap
108 of oysters; and I could well understand that this mine was
109 inexhaustible, for Nature's creative power is far beyond man's
110 instinct of destruction. Ned Land, faithful to his instinct, **hastened**
111 to fill a net which he carried by his side with some of the finest
112 specimens. But we could not stop. We must follow the Captain,
113 who seemed to guide him self by paths known only to himself.
114 The ground was sensibly rising, and sometimes, on holding up
115 my arm, it was above the surface of the sea. Then the level of
116 the bank would sink **capriciously**. Often we rounded high rocks
117 **scarped** into pyramids. In their dark fractures huge crustacea,
118 perched upon their high claws like some war-machine, watched
119 us with fixed eyes, and under our feet crawled various kinds of
120 annelides.

121 At this moment there opened before us a large grotto dug in a
122 picturesque heap of rocks and carpeted with all the thick warp of
123 the submarine flora. At first it seemed very dark to me. The solar
124 rays seemed to be extinguished by successive **gradations**, until
125 its vague transparency became nothing more than drowned light.
126 Captain Nemo entered; we followed. My eyes soon accustomed
127 themselves to this relative state of darkness. I could distinguish

128 the arches springing capriciously from natural pillars, standing
129 broad upon their granite base, like the heavy columns of Tuscan
130 architecture. Why had our **incomprehensible** guide led us to
131 the bottom of this submarine **crypt**? I was soon to know. After
132 descending a rather sharp declivity, our feet trod the bottom of
133 a kind of circular pit. There Captain Nemo stopped, and with
134 his hand indicated an object I had not yet perceived. It was an
135 oyster of extraordinary dimensions, a gigantic tridacne, a goblet
136 which could have contained a whole lake of holy-water, a basin
137 the breadth of which was more than two yards and a half, and
138 consequently larger than that ornamenting the saloon of the
139 Nautilus. I approached this extraordinary mollusc. It adhered by
140 its filaments to a table of granite, and there, isolated, it developed
141 itself in the calm waters of the grotto. I estimated the weight of
142 this tridacne at 600 lb. Such an oyster would contain 30 lb. of
143 meat; and one must have the stomach of a Gargantua to demolish
144 some dozens of them.

145 Captain Nemo was evidently **acquainted** with the existence of
146 this bivalve, and seemed to have a particular motive in verifying
147 the actual state of this tridacne. The shells were a little open; the
148 Captain came near and put his dagger between to prevent them
149 from closing; then with his hand he raised the membrane with
150 its fringed edges, which formed a cloak for the creature. There,
151 between the folded plaits, I saw a loose pearl, whose size equaled
152 that of a coco-nut. Its globular shape, perfect clearness, and
153 admirable lustre made it altogether a jewel of inestimable value.
154 Carried away by my curiosity, I stretched out my hand to seize it,
155 weigh it, and touch it; but the Captain stopped me, made a sign
156 of refusal, and quickly withdrew his dagger, and the two shells
157 closed suddenly. I then understood Captain Nemo's intention.
158 In leaving this pearl hidden in the mantle of the tridacne he
159 was allowing it to grow slowly. Each year the secretions of the
160 mollusc would add new concentric circles. I estimated its value
161 at L500,000 at least.

162 After ten minutes Captain Nemo stopped suddenly. I thought he
163 had halted previously to returning. No; by a gesture he bade us

164 crouch beside him in a deep fracture of the rock, his hand pointed
165 to one part of the liquid mass, which I watched attentively.

166 About five yards from me a shadow appeared, and sank to the
167 ground. The **disquieting** idea of sharks shot through my mind,
168 but I was mistaken; and once again it was not a monster of the
169 ocean that we had anything to do with.

170 It was a man, a living man, an Indian, a fisherman, a poor devil
171 who, I suppose, had come to glean before the harvest. I could
172 see the bottom of his canoe anchored some feet above his head.
173 He dived and went up successively. A stone held between his
174 feet, cut in the shape of a sugar loaf, whilst a rope fastened him
175 to his boat, helped him to descend more rapidly. This was all his
176 apparatus. Reaching the bottom, about five yards deep, he went
177 on his knees and filled his bag with oysters picked up at random.
178 Then he went up, emptied it, pulled up his stone, and began the
179 operation once more, which lasted thirty seconds.

180 The diver did not see us. The shadow of the rock hid us from
181 sight. And how should this poor Indian ever dream that men,
182 beings like himself, should be there under the water watching
183 his movements and losing no detail of the fishing? Several times
184 he went up in this way, and dived again. He did not carry away
185 more than ten at each plunge, for he was obliged to pull them
186 from the bank to which they adhered by means of their strong
187 byssus. And how many of those oysters for which he risked his
188 life had no pearl in them! I watched him closely; his maneuvers
189 were regular; and for the space of half an hour no danger
190 appeared to threaten him.

191 I was beginning to accustom myself to the sight of this interesting
192 fishing, when suddenly, as the Indian was on the ground, I saw
193 him make a gesture of terror, rise, and make a spring to return to
194 the surface of the sea.

195 I understood his dread. A gigantic shadow appeared just above
196 the unfortunate diver. It was a shark of enormous size advancing
197 diagonally, his eyes on fire, and his jaws open. I was mute with

198 horror and unable to move.

199 The voracious creature shot towards the Indian, who threw
200 himself on one side to avoid the shark's fins; but not its tail, for
201 it struck his chest and stretched him on the ground.

202 This scene lasted but a few seconds: the shark returned, and,
203 turning on his back, prepared himself for cutting the Indian in
204 two, when I saw Captain Nemo rise suddenly, and then, dagger
205 in hand, walk straight to the monster, ready to fight face to face
206 with him. The very moment the shark was going to snap the
207 unhappy fisherman in two, he perceived his new adversary, and,
208 turning over, made straight towards him.

209 I can still see Captain Nemo's position. Holding himself well
210 together, he waited for the shark with admirable coolness; and,
211 when it rushed at him, threw himself on one side with wonderful
212 quickness, avoiding the shock, and burying his dagger deep into
213 its side. But it was not all over. A terrible combat ensued.

214 The shark had seemed to roar, if I might say so. The blood rushed
215 in torrents from its wound. The sea was dyed red, and through
216 the opaque liquid I could distinguish nothing more. Nothing
217 more until the moment when, like lightning, I saw the undaunted
218 Captain hanging on to one of the creature's fins, struggling, as
219 it were, hand to hand with the monster, and dealing successive
220 blows at his enemy, yet still unable to give a **decisive** one.

221 The shark's struggles agitated the water with such fury that the
222 rocking threatened to upset me.

223 I wanted to go to the Captain's assistance, but, nailed to the spot
224 with horror, I could not stir.

225 I saw the haggard eye; I saw the different phases of the fight. The
226 Captain fell to the earth, upset by the enormous mass which leant
227 upon him. The shark's jaws opened wide, like a pair of factory
228 shears, and it would have been all over with the Captain; but,
229 quick as thought, harpoon in hand, Ned Land rushed towards the
230 shark and struck it with its sharp point.

The waves were impregnated with a mass of blood. They rocked under the shark's movements, which beat them with **indescribable** fury. Ned Land had not missed his aim. It was the monster's death-rattle. Struck to the heart, it struggled in dreadful **convulsions**, the shock of which overthrew Conseil.

But Ned Land had disentangled the Captain, who, getting up without any wound, went straight to the Indian, quickly cut the cord which held him to his stone, took him in his arms, and, with a sharp blow of his heel, mounted to the surface.

We all three followed in a few seconds, saved by a miracle, and reached the fisherman's boat.

Captain Nemo's first care was to recall the unfortunate man to life again. I did not think he could succeed. I hoped so, for the poor creature's immersion was not long; but the blow from the shark's tail might have been his death-blow.

Happily, with the Captain's and Conseil's sharp friction, I saw consciousness return by degrees. He opened his eyes. What was his surprise, his terror even, at seeing four great copper heads leaning over him! And, above all, what must he have thought when Captain Nemo, drawing from the pocket of his dress a bag of pearls, placed it in his hand! This **munificent** charity from the man of the waters to the poor Cingalese was accepted with a trembling hand. His wondering eyes showed that he knew not to what super-human beings he owed both fortune and life.

At a sign from the Captain we regained the bank, and, following the road already traversed, came in about half an hour to the anchor which held the canoe of the Nautilus to the earth.

Once on board, we each, with the help of the sailors, got rid of the heavy copper helmet.

Captain Nemo's first word was to the Canadian

"Thank you, Master Land," said he.

"It was in revenge, Captain," replied Ned Land. "I owed you that."

A ghastly smile passed across the Captain's lips, and that was all.

"To the Nautilus," said he.

The boat flew over the waves. Some minutes after we met the shark's dead body floating. By the black marking of the extremity of its fins, I recognized the terrible melanopteron of the Indian Seas, of the species of shark so properly called. It was more than twenty-five feet long; its enormous mouth occupied one-third of its body. It was an adult, as was known by its six rows of teeth placed in an isosceles triangle in the upper jaw.

Whilst I was contemplating this inert mass, a dozen of these voracious beasts appeared round the boat; and, without noticing us, threw themselves upon the dead body and fought with one another for the pieces.

At half-past eight we were again on board the Nautilus. There I reflected on the incidents which had taken place in our excursion to the Manaar Bank.

Two conclusions I must **inevitably** draw from it—one bearing upon the unparalleled courage of Captain Nemo, the other upon his devotion to a human being, a representative of that race from which he fled beneath the sea. Whatever he might say, this strange man had not yet succeeded in entirely crushing his heart.

When I made this observation to him, he answered in a slightly moved tone:

"That Indian, sir, is an inhabitant of an oppressed country; and I am still, and shall be, to my last breath, one of them!"

$\mathfrak{Vocabulary\ Part\ 2\ Ch.\ 3}$

disembarking inexhaustible sheared, radiant, distinctly, inopportunely, crypt, acquainted

Questions part 2 chapter 3

1. What is meant in line 109-110 when the authors states, "for Nature's creative power is far beyond man's instinct of destruction." What moral point do you think the author is alluding to here?

____

____

____

2. Why do you think the Captain did not want the Professor to touch "the pearl" (lines 154-157)?

____

____

____

3. In lines 181-183 the author writes "And how should this poor Indian ever dream that men, beings like himself, should be there under the water watching his movements and losing no detail of the fishing?" What sort of contrast is the author drawing upon here?

____

____

____

4. In lines 187-188 the author remarks, "And how many of those oysters for which he risked his life had no pearl in them". Why would a person be willing to risk his life for money? Is this sentiment something that Chaza"l already noticed? If yes, where?

____

____

____

5. In lines 288-289, the author remarks, "That Indian, sir,

is an inhabitant of an oppressed country; and I am still, and shall be, to my last breath, one of them". What do you think this statement means?

____

____

____

Chapter 4

THE RED SEA

In the course of the day of the 29th of January, the island of Ceylon disappeared under the horizon, and the Nautilus, at a speed of twenty miles an hour, slid into the **labyrinth** of canals which separate the Maldives from the Laccadives. It coasted even the Island of Kiltan, a land originally coraline, discovered by Vasco da Gama in 1499, and one of the nineteen principal islands of the Laccadive Archipelago, situated between 10° and 14° 30' N. lat., and 69° 50' 72" E. long.

We had made 16,220 miles, or 7,500 (French) leagues from our starting-point in the Japanese Seas.

The next day (30th January), when the Nautilus went to the surface of the ocean there was no land in sight. Its course was N.N.E., in the direction of the Sea of Oman, between Arabia and the Indian Peninsula, which serves as an outlet to the Persian Gulf. It was evidently a block without any possible egress. Where was Captain Nemo taking us to? I could not say. This, however, did not satisfy the Canadian, who that day came to me asking where we were going.

"We are going where our Captain's fancy takes us, Master Ned."

"His fancy cannot take us far, then," said the Canadian. "The Persian Gulf has no outlet: and, if we do go in, it will not be long before we are out again."

"Very well, then, we will come out again, Master Land; and if, after the Persian Gulf, the Nautilus would like to visit the Red Sea, the Straits of Bab-el-mandeb are there to give us entrance."

"I need not tell you, sir," said Ned Land, "that the Red Sea is as much closed as the Gulf, as the Isthmus of Suez is not yet cut; and, if it was, a boat as mysterious as ours would not risk itself in a canal cut with sluices. And again, the Red Sea is not the road to take us back to Europe."

31 "But I never said we were going back to Europe."

32 "What do you suppose, then?"

33 "I suppose that, after visiting the curious coasts of Arabia and
34 Egypt, the Nautilus will go down the Indian Ocean again, perhaps
35 cross the Channel of Mozambique, perhaps off the Mascarenhas,
36 so as to gain the Cape of Good Hope."

37 "And once at the Cape of Good Hope?" asked the Canadian, with
38 peculiar emphasis.

39 "Well, we shall penetrate into that Atlantic which we do not yet
40 know. Ah! friend Ned, you are getting tired of this journey under
41 the sea; you are **surfeited** with the **incessantly** varying spectacle
42 of submarine wonders. For my part, I shall be sorry to see the
43 end of a voyage which it is given to so few men to make."

44 For four days, till the 3rd of February, the Nautilus scoured the
45 Sea of Oman, at various speeds and at various depths. It seemed
46 to go at random, as if hesitating as to which road it should follow,
47 but we never passed the Tropic of Cancer.

48 In quitting this sea we sighted Muscat for an instant, one of the
49 most important towns of the country of Oman. I admired its
50 strange aspect, surrounded by black rocks upon which its white
51 houses and forts stood in relief. I saw the rounded domes of its
52 mosques, the elegant points of its minarets, its fresh and **verdant**
53 terraces. But it was only a vision! The Nautilus soon sank under
54 the waves of that part of the sea.

55 We passed along the Arabian coast of Mahrah and Hadramaut,
56 for a distance of six miles, its **undulating** line of mountains
57 being occasionally relieved by some ancient ruin. The 5th of
58 February we at last entered the Gulf of Aden, a perfect funnel
59 introduced into the neck of Bab-el-mandeb, through which the
60 Indian waters entered the Red Sea.

61 The 6th of February, the Nautilus floated in sight of Aden,
62 perched upon a **promontory** which a narrow isthmus joins to
63 the mainland, a kind of inaccessible Gibraltar, the fortifications

64 of which were rebuilt by the English after taking possession in
65 1839. I caught a glimpse of the octagon minarets of this town,
66 which was at one time the richest commercial magazine on the
67 coast.

68 I certainly thought that Captain Nemo, arrived at this point,
69 would back out again; but I was mistaken, for he did no such
70 thing, much to my surprise.

71 The next day, the 7th of February, we entered the Straits of Bab-
72 el-mandeb, the name of which, in the Arab tongue, means The
73 Gate of Tears.

74 To twenty miles in breadth, it is only thirty-two in length. And for
75 the Nautilus, starting at full speed, the crossing was scarcely the
76 work of an hour. But I saw nothing, not even the Island of Perim,
77 with which the British Government has fortified the position
78 of Aden. There were too many English or French steamers of
79 the line of Suez to Bombay, Calcutta to Melbourne, and from
80 Bourbon to the Mauritius, furrowing this narrow passage, for
81 the Nautilus to venture to show itself. So it remained **prudently**
82 below. At last about noon, we were in the waters of the Red Sea.

83 I would not even seek to understand the **caprice** which had
84 decided Captain Nemo upon entering the gulf. But I quite
85 approved of the Nautilus entering it. Its speed was lessened:
86 sometimes it kept on the surface, sometimes it dived to avoid a
87 vessel, and thus I was able to observe the upper and lower parts
88 of this curious sea.

89 The 8th of February, from the first dawn of day, Mocha came in
90 sight, now a ruined town, whose walls would fall at a gunshot,
91 yet which shelters here and there some verdant date-trees; once
92 an important city, containing six public markets, and twenty-six
93 mosques, and whose walls, defended by fourteen forts, formed a
94 girdle of two miles in circumference.

95 The Nautilus then approached the African shore, where the
96 depth of the sea was greater. There, between two waters

97 clear as crystal, through the open panels we were allowed to
98 contemplate the beautiful bushes of brilliant coral and large
99 blocks of rock clothed with a splendid fur of green variety of
100 sites and landscapes along these sandbanks and algae and fuci.
101 What an indescribable spectacle, and what variety of sites and
102 landscapes along these sandbanks and volcanic islands which
103 bound the Libyan coast! But where these shrubs appeared in all
104 their beauty was on the eastern coast, which the Nautilus soon
105 gained. It was on the coast of Tehama, for there not only did
106 this display of zoophytes flourish beneath the level of the sea,
107 but they also formed picturesque interlacing's which unfolded
108 themselves about sixty feet above the surface, more capricious
109 but less highly colored than those whose freshness was kept up
110 by the vital power of the waters.

111 What charming hours I passed thus at the window of the saloon!
112 What new specimens of submarine flora and fauna did I admire
113 under the brightness of our electric lantern!

114 The 9th of February the Nautilus floated in the broadest part of
115 the Red Sea, which is comprised between Souakin, on the west
116 coast, and Komfidah, on the east coast, with a diameter of ninety
117 miles.

118 That day at noon, after the bearings were taken, Captain
119 Nemo mounted the platform, where I happened to be, and I
120 was determined not to let him go down again without at least
121 pressing him regarding his ulterior projects. As soon as he saw
122 me he approached and graciously offered me a cigar.

123 "Well, sir, does this Red Sea please you? Have you sufficiently
124 observed the wonders it covers, its fishes, its zoophytes, its
125 parterres of sponges, and its forests of coral? Did you catch a
126 glimpse of the towns on its borders?"

127 "Yes, Captain Nemo," I replied; "and the Nautilus is wonderfully
128 fitted for such a study. Ah! it is an intelligent boat!"

129 "Yes, sir, intelligent and **invulnerable**. It fears neither the terrible

130 tempests of the Red Sea, nor its currents, nor its sandbanks."

131 "Certainly," said I, "this sea is quoted as one of the worst, and in
132 the time of the ancients, if I am not mistaken, its reputation was
133 **detestable**."

134 "Detestable, M. Aronnax. The Greek and Latin historians do not
135 speak favorably of it, and Strabo says it is very dangerous during
136 the Etesian winds and in the rainy season. The Arabian Edrisi
137 portrays it under the name of the Gulf of Colzoum, and relates
138 that vessels perished there in great numbers on the sandbanks
139 and that no one would risk sailing in the night. It is, he pretends,
140 a sea subject to fearful hurricanes, strewn with inhospitable
141 islands, and 'which offers nothing good either on its surface or
142 in its depths.'"

143 "One may see," I replied, "that these historians never sailed on
144 board the Nautilus."

145 "Just so," replied the Captain, smiling; "and in that respect
146 moderns are not more advanced than the ancients. It required
147 many ages to find out the mechanical power of steam. Who
148 knows if, in another hundred years, we may not see a second
149 Nautilus? Progress is slow, M. Aronnax."

150 "It is true," I answered; "your boat is at least a century before its
151 time, perhaps an era. What a misfortune that the secret of such
152 an invention should die with its inventor!"

153 Captain Nemo did not reply. After some minutes' silence he
154 continued:

155 "You were speaking of the opinions of ancient historians upon
156 the dangerous navigation of the Red Sea."

157 "It is true," said I; "but were not their fears exaggerated?"

158 "Yes and no, M. Aronnax," replied Captain Nemo, who seemed
159 to know the Red Sea by heart. "That which is no longer
160 dangerous for a modern vessel, well rigged, strongly built, and

161 master of its own course, thanks to obedient steam, offered all
162 sorts of perils to the ships of the ancients. Picture to yourself
163 those first navigators venturing in ships made of planks sewn
164 with the cords of the palmtree, saturated with the grease of the
165 seadog, and covered with powdered resin! They had not even
166 instruments wherewith to take their bearings, and they went by
167 guess amongst currents of which they scarcely knew anything.
168 Under such conditions shipwrecks were, and must have been,
169 numerous. But in our time, steamers running between Suez and
170 the South Seas have nothing more to fear from the fury of this
171 gulf, in spite of contrary trade-winds…

172 "I agree with you," said I; "and steam seems to have killed all
173 gratitude in the hearts of sailors. …

174 "The ancients well understood the utility of a communication
175 between the Red Sea and the Mediterranean for their commercial
176 affairs: but they did not think of digging a canal direct, and took
177 the Nile as an intermediate….

178 "Well, Captain, what the ancients dared not undertake, this
179 junction between the two seas, which will shorten the road from
180 Cadiz to India, M. Lesseps has succeeded in doing; and before
181 long he will have changed Africa into an immense island."

182 "Yes, M. Aronnax; you have the right to be proud of your
183 countryman. Such a man brings more honor to a nation than
184 great captains. He began, like so many others, with disgust and
185 rebuffs; but he has triumphed, for he has the genius of will. And
186 it is sad to think that a work like that, which ought to have been
187 an international work and which would have sufficed to make
188 a reign illustrious, should have succeeded by the energy of one
189 man. All honor to M. Lesseps!"

190 "Yes! honor to the great citizen," I replied, surprised by the
191 manner in which Captain Nemo had just spoken.

192 "Unfortunately," he continued, "I cannot take you through the
193 Suez Canal; but you will be able to see the long **jetty** of Port

194 Said after to-morrow, when we shall be in the Mediterranean."

195 "The Mediterranean!" I exclaimed.

196 "Yes, sir; does that **astonish** you?"

197 "What astonishes me is to think that we shall be there the day
198 after to-morrow."

199 "Indeed?"

200 "Yes, Captain, although by this time I ought to have accustomed
201 myself to be surprised at nothing since I have been on board
202 your boat."

203 "But the cause of this surprise?"

204 "Well! it is the fearful speed you will have to put on the Nautilus,
205 if the day after to-morrow she is to be in the Mediterranean,
206 having made the round of Africa, and doubled the Cape of Good
207 Hope!"

208 "Who told you that she would make the round of Africa and
209 double the Cape of Good Hope, sir?"

210 "Well, unless the Nautilus sails on dry land, and passes above
211 the isthmus——"

212 "Or beneath it, M. Aronnax."

213 "Beneath it?"

214 "Certainly," replied Captain Nemo quietly. "A long time ago
215 Nature made under this tongue of land what man has this day
216 made on its surface."

217 "What! such a passage exists?"

218 "Yes; a subterranean passage, which I have named the Arabian
219 Tunnel. It takes us beneath Suez and opens into the Gulf of
220 Pelusium."

221 "But this isthmus is composed of nothing but quick sands?"

222 "To a certain depth. But at fifty-five yards only there is a solid
223 layer of rock."

224 "Did you discover this passage by chance?" I asked more and
225 more surprised.

226 "Chance and reasoning, sir; and by reasoning even more than
227 by chance. Not only does this passage exist, but I have profited
228 by it several times. Without that I should not have ventured this
229 day into the impassable Red Sea. I noticed that in the Red Sea
230 and in the Mediterranean there existed a certain number of fishes
231 of a kind perfectly identical. Certain of the fact, I asked myself
232 was it possible that there was no communication between the
233 two seas? If there was, the subterranean current must necessarily
234 run from the Red Sea to the Mediterranean, from the sole cause
235 of difference of level. I caught a large number of fishes in the
236 neighborhood of Suez. I passed a copper ring through their tails,
237 and threw them back into the sea. Some months later, on the
238 coast of Syria, I caught some of my fish ornamented with the
239 ring. Thus the communication between the two was proved. I
240 then sought for it with my Nautilus; I discovered it, ventured
241 into it, and before long, sir, you too will have passed through my
242 Arabian tunnel!"

labyrinth, surfeited, incessantly, undulating, caprice, invulnerable, detestable, jetty, astonish

Questions part 2 ch. 4

1. What is the Professor's response when he sees the marvels of the Red Sea?

    ____

2. In lines 129-130, Captain Nemo states: "Yes, sir, intelligent and invulnerable. It fears neither the terrible tempests of the Red Sea, nor its currents, nor its sandbanks." What does this statement reveal to us about the Captain's character?

    ____

    ____

    ____

3. In lines 151-52, the Professor goads the Captain into responding about the nature of the boat by saying: "What a misfortune that the secret of such an invention should die with its inventor." What does the Professor hope the Captain responds? Why do you think he would like to understand more about the Captain?

    ____

    ____

    ____

4. In lines 172-173, the Professor remarks that "I agree with you," said I; "and steam seems to have killed all gratitude in the hearts of sailors" How would a Torah Jew look at this statement?

    ____

    ____

    ____

5. How does the last few lines of the chapter completely change the perspective of the reader from what he thought might happen at the outset of the chapter?

Chapter 5

THE ARABIAN TUNNEL
(amended and abridged)

That same evening, in 21° 30' N. lat., the Nautilus floated on the surface of the sea, approaching the Arabian coast. I saw Djeddah, the most important counting-house of Egypt, Syria, Turkey, and India. I **distinguished** clearly enough its buildings, the vessels anchored at the quays, and those whose **draught** of water obliged them to anchor in the roads. The sun, rather low on the horizon, struck full on the houses of the town, bringing out their whiteness. Outside, some wooden cabins, and some made of reeds, showed the quarter inhabited by the Bedouins. Soon Djeddah was shut out from view by the shadows of night, and the Nautilus found herself under water slightly phosphorescent.

The next day, the 10th of February, we sighted several ships running to windward. The Nautilus returned to its submarine navigation; but at noon, when her bearings were taken, the sea being deserted, she rose again to her waterline.

Accompanied by Ned and Conseil, I seated myself on the platform. The coast on the eastern side looked like a mass faintly printed upon a damp fog.

We were leaning on the sides of the pinnace[62], talking of one thing and another, when Ned Land, stretching out his hand towards a spot on the sea, said:

"Do you see anything there, sir?"

"No, Ned," I replied; "but I have not your eyes, you know."

"Look well," said Ned, "there, on the starboard beam, about the height of the lantern! Do you not see a mass which seems to move?"

---

62   a small boat, with sails or oars, forming part of the equipment of a warship or other large vessel.

27 "Certainly," said I, after close attention; "I see something like a
28 long black body on the top of the water."

29 And certainly before long the black object was not more than a
30 mile from us. It looked like a great sandbank deposited in the
31 open sea. It was a gigantic dugong!

32 Ned Land looked eagerly. His eyes shone with **covetousness** at
33 the sight of the animal. His hand seemed ready to harpoon it.
34 One would have thought he was awaiting the moment to throw
35 himself into the sea and attack it in its element.

36 At this instant Captain Nemo appeared on the platform. He saw
37 the dugong, understood the Canadian's attitude, and, addressing
38 him, said:

39 "If you held a harpoon just now, Master Land, would it not burn
40 your hand?"

41 "Just so, sir."

42 "And you would not be sorry to go back, for one day, to your
43 trade of a fisherman and to add this cetacean to the list of those
44 you have already killed?"

45 "I should not, sir."

46 "Well, you can try."

47 "Thank you, sir," said Ned Land, his eyes flaming.

48 "Only," continued the Captain, "I advise you for your own sake
49 not to miss the creature."

50 "Is the dugong dangerous to attack?" I asked, in spite of the
51 Canadian's shrug of the shoulders.

52 "Yes," replied the Captain; "sometimes the animal turns upon
53 its **assailants** and overturns their boat. But for Master Land this
54 danger is not to be feared. His eye is prompt, his arm sure."

55 At this moment seven men of the crew, mute and immovable as
56 ever, mounted the platform. One carried a harpoon and a line
57 similar to those employed in catching whales. The pinnace was
58 lifted from the bridge, pulled from its socket, and let down into
59 the sea. Six oarsmen took their seats, and the coxswain[63] went to
60 the tiller. Ned, Conseil, and I went to the back of the boat.

61 "You are not coming, Captain?" I asked.

62 "No, sir; but I wish you good sport."

63 The boat put off, and, lifted by the six rowers, drew rapidly
64 towards the dugong, which floated about two miles from the
65 Nautilus.

66 Arrived some cables-length from the cetacean, the speed
67 slackened, and the oars dipped noiselessly into the quiet waters.
68 Ned Land, harpoon in hand, stood in the fore part of the boat.
69 The harpoon used for striking the whale is generally attached to
70 a very long cord which runs out rapidly as the wounded creature
71 draws it after him. But here the cord was not more than ten
72 fathoms long, and the extremity was attached to a small barrel
73 which, by floating, was to show the course the dugong took
74 under the water.

75 I stood and carefully watched the Canadian's **adversary**.
76 This dugong, which also bears the name of the halicore,
77 closely resembles the manatee; its **oblong** body **terminated**
78 in a lengthened tail, and its lateral[64] fins in perfect fingers. Its
79 difference from the manatee consisted in its upper jaw, which
80 was armed with two long and pointed teeth which formed on
81 each side **diverging** tusks.

82 This dugong which Ned Land was preparing to attack was of
83 **colossal** dimensions; it was more than seven yards long. It
84 did not move, and seemed to be sleeping on the waves, which
85 circumstance made it easier to capture.

---

63   the steersman of a ship's boat, lifeboat, racing boat, or other boat.
64   of, at, toward, or from the side or sides.

86 The boat approached within six yards of the animal. The oars
87 rested on the rowlocks. I half rose. Ned Land, his body thrown
88 a little back, brandished the harpoon in his experienced hand.

89 Suddenly a hissing noise was heard, and the dugong disappeared.
90 The harpoon, although thrown with great force; had apparently
91 only struck the water.

92 "Curse it!" exclaimed the Canadian furiously; "I have missed
93 it!"

94 "No," said I; "the creature is wounded—look at the blood; but
95 your weapon has not stuck in his body."

96 "My harpoon! my harpoon!" cried Ned Land.

97 The sailors rowed on, and the coxswain made for the floating
98 barrel. The harpoon regained, we followed in pursuit of the
99 animal.

100 The latter came now and then to the surface to breathe. Its wound
101 had not weakened it, for it shot onwards with great rapidity.

102 The boat, rowed by strong arms, flew on its track. Several times
103 it approached within some few yards, and the Canadian was
104 ready to strike, but the dugong made off with a sudden plunge,
105 and it was impossible to reach it.

106 Imagine the passion which excited impatient Ned Land! He
107 hurled at the unfortunate creature the most energetic expletives
108 in the English tongue. For my part, I was only **vexed** to see the
109 dugong escape all our attacks.

110 We pursued it without relaxation for an hour, and I began to think
111 it would prove difficult to capture, when the animal, possessed
112 with the perverse idea of **vengeance** of which he had cause to
113 repent, turned upon the pinnace and assailed us in its turn.

114 This maneuver did not escape the Canadian.

115 "Look out!" he cried.

116 The coxswain said some words in his **outlandish** tongue,
117 doubtless warning the men to keep on their guard.

118 The dugong came within twenty feet of the boat, stopped, sniffed
119 the air briskly with its large nostrils (not pierced at the extremity,
120 but in the upper part of its muzzle). Then, taking a spring, he
121 threw himself upon us.

122 The pinnace could not avoid the shock, and half upset, shipped at
123 least two tons of water, which had to be emptied; but, thanks to
124 the coxswain, we caught it sideways, not full front, so we were
125 not quite overturned. While Ned Land, clinging to the bows,
126 belabored the gigantic animal with blows from his harpoon,
127 the creature's teeth were buried in the gunwale, and it lifted the
128 whole thing out of the water, as a lion does a roebuck. We were
129 upset over one another, and I know not how the adventure would
130 have ended, if the Canadian, still enraged with the beast, had not
131 struck it to the heart.

132 I heard its teeth grind on the iron plate, and the dugong
133 disappeared, carrying the harpoon with him. But the barrel soon
134 returned to the surface, and shortly after the body of the animal,
135 turned on its back. The boat came up with it, took it in tow, and
136 made straight for the Nautilus.

137 It required tackle of enormous strength to hoist the dugong on to
138 the platform. It weighed 10,000 lb.

139 The next day, 11th February, the larder of the Nautilus was
140 enriched by some more delicate game. A flight of sea-swallows
141 rested on the Nautilus. It was a species of the Sterna nilotica,
142 peculiar to Egypt; its beak is black, head grey and pointed, the
143 eye surrounded by white spots, the back, wings, and tail of a
144 greyish color, the belly and throat white, and claws red. They
145 also took some dozen of Nile ducks, a wild bird of high flavor,
146 its throat and upper part of the head white with black spots.

147 About five o'clock in the evening we sighted to the north the
148 Cape of Ras-Mohammed. This cape forms the extremity of

149 Arabia Petraea, comprised between the Gulf of Suez and the
150 Gulf of Acabah.

151 The Nautilus penetrated into the Straits of Jubal, which leads
152 to the Gulf of Suez. I distinctly saw a high mountain, towering
153 between the two gulfs of Ras-Mohammed. It was Mount Horeb,
154 that Sinai at the top of which Moses saw the almighty face to
155 face.

156 At six o'clock the Nautilus, sometimes floating, sometimes
157 immersed, passed some distance from Tor, situated at the end
158 of the bay, the waters of which seemed tinted with red, an
159 observation already made by Captain Nemo. Then night fell in
160 the midst of a heavy silence, sometimes broken by the cries of
161 the pelican and other night-birds, and the noise of the waves
162 breaking upon the shore, chafing against the rocks, or the panting
163 of some far-off steamer beating the waters of the Gulf with its
164 noisy paddles.

165 From eight to nine o'clock the Nautilus remained some fathoms
166 under the water. According to my calculation we must have
167 been very near Suez. Through the panel of the saloon, I saw the
168 bottom of the rocks brilliantly lit up by our electric lamp. We
169 seemed to be leaving the Straits behind us more and more.

170 At a quarter-past nine, the vessel having returned to the surface,
171 I mounted the platform. Most impatient to pass through Captain
172 Nemo's tunnel, I could not stay in one place, so came to breathe
173 the fresh night air.

174 Soon in the shadow I saw a pale light, half discolored by the fog,
175 shining about a mile from us.

176 "A floating lighthouse!" said someone near me.

177 I turned, and saw the Captain.

178 "It is the floating light of Suez," he continued. "It will not be
179 long before we gain the entrance of the tunnel."

180   "The entrance cannot be easy?"

181   "No, sir; for that reason I am accustomed to go into the
182   steersman's cage and myself direct our course. And now, if
183   you will go down, M. Aronnax, the Nautilus is going under the
184   waves, and will not return to the surface until we have passed
185   through the Arabian Tunnel."

186   Captain Nemo led me towards the central staircase; half way
187   down he opened a door, traversed the upper deck, and landed in
188   the pilot's cage, which it may be remembered rose at the extremity
189   of the platform. It was a cabin measuring six feet square, very
190   much like that occupied by the pilot on the steamboats of the
191   Mississippi or Hudson. In the midst worked a wheel, placed
192   vertically, and caught to the tiller-rope, which ran to the back
193   of the Nautilus. Four light-ports with lenticular glasses, let in a
194   groove in the partition of the cabin, allowed the man at the wheel
195   to see in all directions.

196   This cabin was dark; but soon my eyes accustomed themselves
197   to the obscurity, and I perceived the pilot, a strong man, with
198   his hands resting on the spokes of the wheel. Outside, the sea
199   appeared vividly lit up by the lantern, which shed its rays from
200   the back of the cabin to the other extremity of the platform.

201   "Now," said Captain Nemo, "let us try to make our passage."

202   Electric wires connected the pilot's cage with the machinery room,
203   and from there the Captain could communicate simultaneously
204   to his Nautilus the direction and the speed. He pressed a metal
205   knob, and at once the speed of the screw diminished.

206   I looked in silence at the high straight wall we were running by
207   at this moment, the immovable base of a massive sandy coast.
208   We followed it thus for an hour only some few yards off.

209   Captain Nemo did not take his eye from the knob, suspended by
210   its two concentric circles in the cabin. At a simple gesture, the
211   pilot modified the course of the Nautilus every instant.

212 I had placed myself at the port-scuttle, and saw some magnificent
213 substructures of coral, zoophytes, seaweed, and fucus, agitating
214 their enormous claws, which stretched out from the fissures of
215 the rock.

216 At a quarter-past ten, the Captain himself took the helm. A large
217 gallery, black and deep, opened before us. The Nautilus went
218 boldly into it. A strange roaring was heard round its sides. It
219 was the waters of the Red Sea, which the incline of the tunnel
220 **precipitated** violently towards the Mediterranean. The Nautilus
221 went with the torrent, rapid as an arrow, in spite of the efforts of
222 the machinery, which, in order to offer more effective resistance,
223 beat the waves with reversed screw.

224 On the walls of the narrow passage I could see nothing but
225 brilliant rays, straight lines, furrows of fire, traced by the great
226 speed, under the brilliant electric light. My heart beat fast.

227 At thirty-five minutes past ten, Captain Nemo quitted the helm,
228 and, turning to me, said:

229 "The Mediterranean!"

230 In less than twenty minutes, the Nautilus, carried along by the
231 torrent, had passed through the Isthmus of Suez.

Vocabulary part 2 ch. 5

distinguished, draught, covetousness, assailants, prompt, adversary, oblong, terminated, diverging, colossal, vexed, vengeance, outlandish, precipitated

Questions part 2 ch. 5

1. In lines 111-113, what does the phrase "possessed with the perverse idea of **vengeance** of which he had cause to repent" mean? How is this an example of anthropomorphism?

2. Why do you think the Captain gives Ned Land the choice of killing the dugong?

3. What happened to the dugong, and what happened to the travelers who were trying to kill it?

4. How does the Nautilus get from the Red Sea to the Mediterranean Sea?

5. Who takes the submarine through the tunnel, and why do you think he does?

6. Why doesn't the Captain need to turn the propeller on the submarine to make it move through the tunnel?

Chapter 6
THE GRECIAN ARCHIPELAGO

The next day, the 12th of February, at the dawn of day, the Nautilus rose to the surface. I hastened on to the platform. Three miles to the south the dim outline of Pelusium was to be seen. A torrent had carried us from one sea to another. About seven o'clock Ned and Conseil joined me.

"Well, Sir Naturalist," said the Canadian, in a slightly jovial tone, "and the Mediterranean?"

"We are floating on its surface, friend Ned."

"What!" said Conseil, "this very night."

"Yes, this very night; in a few minutes we have passed this **impassable** isthmus."

"I do not believe it," replied the Canadian.

"Then you are wrong, Master Land," I continued; "this low coast which rounds off to the south is the Egyptian coast. And you who have such good eyes, Ned, you can see the jetty of Port Said stretching into the sea."

The Canadian looked **attentively**.

"Certainly you are right, sir, and your Captain is a first-rate man. We are in the Mediterranean. Good! Now, if you please, let us talk of our own little affair, but so that no one hears us."

I saw what the Canadian wanted, and, in any case, I thought it better to let him talk, as he wished it; so we all three went and sat down near the lantern, where we were less exposed to the spray of the blades.

"Now, Ned, we listen; what have you to tell us?"

"What I have to tell you is very simple. We are in Europe;

27 and before Captain Nemo's **caprices** drag us once more to the
28 bottom of the Polar Seas, or lead us into Oceania, I ask to leave
29 the Nautilus."

30 I wished in no way to **shackle** the liberty of my companions, but
31 I certainly felt no desire to leave Captain Nemo.

32 Thanks to him, and thanks to his apparatus, I was each day nearer
33 the completion of my submarine studies; and I was rewriting
34 my book of submarine depths in its very element. Should I ever
35 again have such an opportunity of observing the wonders of the
36 ocean? No, certainly not! And I could not bring myself to the
37 idea of abandoning the Nautilus before the cycle of investigation
38 was accomplished.

39 "Friend Ned, answer me frankly, are you tired of being on board?
40 Are you sorry that **destiny** has thrown us into Captain Nemo's
41 hands?"

42 The Canadian remained some moments without answering.
43 Then, crossing his arms, he said:

44 "Frankly, I do not regret this journey under the seas. I shall be
45 glad to have made it; but, now that it is made, let us have done
46 with it. That is my idea."

47 "It will come to an end, Ned."

48 "Where and when?"

49 "Where I do not know—when I cannot say; or, rather, I suppose
50 it will end when these seas have nothing more to teach us."

51 "Then what do you hope for?" demanded the Canadian.

52 "That circumstances may occur as well six months hence as now
53 by which we may and ought to profit."

54 "Oh!" said Ned Land, "and where shall we be in six months, if
55 you please, Sir Naturalist?"

56 "Perhaps in China; you know the Nautilus is a rapid traveler. It
57 goes through water as swallows through the air, or as an express
58 on the land. It does not fear frequented seas; who can say that
59 it may not beat the coasts of France, England, or America, on
60 which flight may be attempted as **advantageously** as here."

61 "M. Aronnax," replied the Canadian, "your arguments are rotten
62 at the foundation. You speak in the future, `We shall be there! we
63 shall be here!' I speak in the present, `We are here, and we must
64 profit by it.'"

65 Ned Land's logic pressed me hard, and I felt myself beaten on
66 that ground. I knew not what argument would now tell in my
67 favor.

68 "Sir," continued Ned, "let us suppose an impossibility: if Captain
69 Nemo should this day offer you your liberty; would you accept
70 it?"

71 "I do not know," I answered.

72 "And if," he added, "the offer made you this day was never to be
73 renewed, would you accept it?"

74 "Friend Ned, this is my answer. Your reasoning is against me. We
75 must not rely on Captain Nemo's good-will. Common **prudence**
76 forbids him to set us at liberty. On the other side, prudence bids
77 us profit by the first opportunity to leave the Nautilus."

78 "Well, M. Aronnax, that is wisely said."

79 "Only one observation—just one. The occasion must be serious,
80 and our first attempt must succeed; if it fails, we shall never find
81 another, and Captain Nemo will never forgive us."

82 "All that is true," replied the Canadian. "But your observation
83 applies equally to all attempts at flight, whether in two years'
84 time, or in two days'. But the question is still this: If a favorable
85 opportunity presents itself, it must be seized."

86 "Agreed! And now, Ned, will you tell me what you mean by a
87 favorable opportunity?"

88 "It will be that which, on a dark night, will bring the Nautilus a
89 short distance from some European coast."

90 "And you will try and save yourself by swimming?"

91 "Yes, if we were near enough to the bank, and if the vessel was
92 floating at the time. Not if the bank was far away, and the boat
93 was under the water."

94 "And in that case?"

95 "In that case, I should seek to make myself master of the pinnace.
96 I know how it is worked. We must get inside, and the bolts once
97 drawn, we shall come to the surface of the water, without even
98 the pilot, who is in the bows, perceiving our flight."

99 "Well, Ned, watch for the opportunity; but do not forget that a
100 hitch will ruin us."

101 "I will not forget, sir."

102 "And now, Ned, would you like to know what I think of your
103 project?"

104 "Certainly, M. Aronnax."

105 "Well, I think—I do not say I hope—I think that this favorable
106 opportunity will never present itself."

107 "Why not?"

108 "Because Captain Nemo cannot hide from himself that we have
109 not given up all hope of regaining our liberty, and he will be on
110 his guard, above all, in the seas and in the sight of European
111 coasts."

112 "We shall see," replied Ned Land, shaking his head determinedly.

113 "And now, Ned Land," I added, "let us stop here. Not another

114 word on the subject. The day that you are ready, come and let us
115 know, and we will follow you. I rely entirely upon you."

116 Thus ended a conversation which, at no very distant time,
117 led to such grave results. I must say here that facts seemed
118 to confirm my foresight, to the Canadian's great despair. Did
119 Captain Nemo distrust us in these frequented seas? or did he
120 only wish to hide himself from the numerous vessels, of all
121 nations, which ploughed the Mediterranean? I could not tell; but
122 we were oftener between waters and far from the coast. Or, if the
123 Nautilus did emerge, nothing was to be seen but the pilot's cage;
124 and sometimes it went to great depths, for, between the Grecian
125 Archipelago and Asia Minor we could not touch the bottom by
126 more than a thousand fathoms.

127 Thus I only knew we were near the Island of Carpathos, one of
128 the Sporades, by Captain Nemo reciting these lines from Virgil:

129 «Est   Carpathio   Neptuni   gurgite   vates,
130 Caeruleus Proteus,»

131 as he pointed to a spot on the planisphere.

132 It was indeed the ancient abode of Proteus, the old shepherd of
133 Neptune's flocks, now the Island of Scarpanto, situated between
134 Rhodes and Crete. I saw nothing but the granite base through the
135 glass panels of the saloon.

136 The next day, the 14th of February, I resolved to employ
137 some hours in studying the fishes of the Archipelago; but for
138 some reason or other the panels remained hermetically sealed.
139 Upon taking the course of the Nautilus, I found that we were
140 going towards Candia, the ancient Isle of Crete. At the time I
141 embarked on the Abraham Lincoln, the whole of this island had
142 risen in insurrection against the despotism of the Turks. But
143 how the **insurgents** had fared since that time I was absolutely
144 ignorant, and it was not Captain Nemo, deprived of all land
145 communications, who could tell me.

146 I made no **allusion** to this event when that night I found myself

alone with him in the saloon. Besides, he seemed to be **taciturn** and preoccupied. Then, contrary to his custom, he ordered both panels to be opened, and, going from one to the other, observed the mass of waters attentively. To what end I could not guess; so, on my side, I employed my time in studying the fish passing before my eyes.

In the midst of the waters a man appeared, a diver, carrying at his belt a leathern purse. It was not a body abandoned to the waves; it was a living man, swimming with a strong hand, disappearing occasionally to take breath at the surface.

I turned towards Captain Nemo, and in an **agitated** voice exclaimed:

"A man shipwrecked! He must be saved at any price!"

The Captain did not answer me, but came and leaned against the panel.

The man had approached, and, with his face flattened against the glass, was looking at us.

To my great amazement, Captain Nemo signed to him. The diver answered with his hand, mounted immediately to the surface of the water, and did not appear again.

"Do not be uncomfortable," said Captain Nemo. "It is Nicholas of Cape Matapan, surnamed Pesca. He is well known in all the Cyclades. A bold diver! water is his element, and he lives more in it than on land, going continually from one island to another, even as far as Crete."

"You know him, Captain?"

"Why not, M. Aronnax?"

Saying which, Captain Nemo went towards a piece of furniture standing near the left panel of the saloon. Near this piece of furniture, I saw a chest bound with iron, on the cover of which

177 was a copper plate, bearing the cypher of the Nautilus with its
178 device.

179 At that moment, the Captain, without noticing my presence,
180 opened the piece of furniture, a sort of strong box, which held a
181 great many ingots.

182 They were ingots of gold. From whence came this precious
183 metal, which represented an enormous sum? Where did the
184 Captain gather this gold from? and what was he going to do with
185 it?

186 I did not say one word. I looked. Captain Nemo took the ingots
187 one by one, and arranged them methodically in the chest, which
188 he filled entirely. I estimated the contents at more than 4,000 lb.
189 weight of gold, that is to say, nearly L200,000.

190 The chest was securely fastened, and the Captain wrote an
191 address on the lid, in characters which must have belonged to
192 Modern Greece.

193 This done, Captain Nemo pressed a knob, the wire of which
194 communicated with the quarters of the crew. Four men appeared,
195 and, not without some trouble, pushed the chest out of the saloon.
196 Then I heard them hoisting it up the iron staircase by means of
197 pulleys.

198 At that moment, Captain Nemo turned to me.

199 "And you were saying, sir?" said he.

200 "I was saying nothing, Captain."

201 "Then, sir, if you will allow me, I will wish you good night."

202 Whereupon he turned and left the saloon.

203 I returned to my room much troubled, as one may believe. I
204 vainly tried to sleep—I sought the connecting link between the
205 apparition of the diver and the chest filled with gold. Soon, I felt
206 by certain movements of pitching and tossing that the Nautilus

207 was leaving the depths and returning to the surface.

208 Then I heard steps upon the platform; and I knew they were
209 unfastening the pinnace and launching it upon the waves. For
210 one instant it struck the side of the Nautilus, then all noise ceased.

211 Two hours after, the same noise, the same going and coming was
212 renewed; the boat was hoisted on board, replaced in its socket,
213 and the Nautilus again plunged under the waves.

214 So these millions had been transported to their address. To what
215 point of the continent? Who was Captain Nemo's correspondent?

216 The next day I related to Conseil and the Canadian the events of
217 the night, which had excited my curiosity to the highest degree.
218 My companions were not less surprised than myself.

219 "But where does he take his millions to?" asked Ned Land.

220 To that there was no possible answer. I returned to the saloon after
221 having breakfast and set to work. Till five o'clock in the evening
222 I employed myself in arranging my notes. At that moment—
223 (ought I to attribute it to some peculiar **idiosyncrasy**)—I felt
224 so great a heat that I was obliged to take off my coat. It was
225 strange, for we were under low latitudes; and even then the
226 Nautilus, submerged as it was, ought to experience no change
227 of temperature. I looked at the manometer; it showed a depth of
228 sixty feet, to which atmospheric heat could never attain.

229 I continued my work, but the temperature rose to such a pitch as
230 to be intolerable.

231 "Could there be fire on board?" I asked myself.

232 I was leaving the saloon, when Captain Nemo entered; he
233 approached the thermometer, consulted it, and, turning to me,
234 said:

235 "Forty-two degrees."

236 "I have noticed it, Captain," I replied; "and if it gets much hotter

237 we cannot bear it.”

238 “Oh, sir, it will not get better if we do not wish it.”

239 “You can reduce it as you please, then?”

240 “No; but I can go farther from the stove which produces it.”

241 “It is outward, then!”

242 “Certainly; we are floating in a current of boiling water.”

243 “Is it possible!” I exclaimed.

244 “Look.”

245 The panels opened, and I saw the sea entirely white all round.
246 A sulphurous smoke was curling amid the waves, which boiled
247 like water in a copper. I placed my hand on one of the panes of
248 glass, but the heat was so great that I quickly took it off again.

249 “Where are we?” I asked.

250 “Near the Island of Santorin, sir,” replied the Captain. “I wished
251 to give you a sight of the curious spectacle of a submarine
252 eruption.”

253 “I thought,” said I, “that the formation of these new islands was
254 ended.”

255 “Nothing is ever ended in the volcanic parts of the sea,” replied
256 Captain Nemo; “and the globe is always being worked by
257 subterranean fires…

258 “And the canal in which we are at this moment?” I asked.

259 “Here it is,” replied Captain Nemo, showing me a map of the
260 Archipelago. “You see, I have marked the new islands.”

261 I returned to the glass. The Nautilus was no longer moving, the
262 heat was becoming unbearable. The sea, which till now had been
263 white, was red, owing to the presence of salts of iron. In spite of

the ship's being hermetically sealed, an **insupportable** smell of sulphur filled the saloon, and the brilliancy of the electricity was entirely extinguished by bright scarlet flames. I was in a bath, I was choking, I was broiled.

"We can remain no longer in this boiling water," said I to the Captain.

"It would not be prudent," replied the impassive Captain Nemo.

An order was given; the Nautilus tacked about and left the furnace it could not brave with **impunity**. A quarter of an hour after we were breathing fresh air on the surface. The thought then struck me that, if Ned Land had chosen this part of the sea for our flight, we should never have come alive out of this sea of fire.

The next day, the 16th of February, we left the basin which, between Rhodes and Alexandria, is reckoned about 1,500 fathoms in depth, and the Nautilus, passing some distance from Ccrigo, quitted the Grecian Archipelago after having doubled Cape Matapan.

𝔙ocabulary 𝔓art 2 𝔠h. 6

impassable, shackle, destiny, advantageously, prudence, insurgents, ingots, idiosyncrasy, insupportable

Questions part 2 ch. 6

1. Why isn't the Professor interested in leaving the boat at this time?

   ____

   ____

2. How much longer does the Professor want to stay on the boat and is Ned Land in favor of this?

   ____

   ____

3. What does the Professor say regarding the choice he would make if the Captain gave him the ability to leave the boat? What would you have done if you were the Professor and were given only one chance at leaving? As a Torah Jew-how would the Torah influence your decision?

   ____

   ____

   ____

   ____

4. What do you make of the strange encounter between the diver and the Nautilus, and do you think it may have something to do with the insurrection going on in Crete? Why or why not?

   ____

   ____

   ____

5. Has the Captain totally cut off ties to the land? Prove it
    one way or another.

Chapter 7

THE MEDITERRANEAN IN FORTY-EIGHT HOURS

The Mediterranean, the blue sea par excellence, "the great sea" of the Hebrews, "the sea" of the Greeks, the "mare nostrum" of the Romans, bordered by orange-trees, aloes, cacti, and sea-pines; **embalmed** with the perfume of the myrtle, surrounded by rude mountains, **saturated** with pure and **transparent** air, but **incessantly** worked by underground fires…

It is upon these banks, and on these waters, says Michelet, that man is renewed in one of the most powerful climates of the globe. But, beautiful as it was, I could only take a rapid glance at the basin whose superficial area is two million of square yards. Even Captain Nemo's knowledge was lost to me, for this puzzling person did not appear once during our passage at full speed. I estimated the course which the Nautilus took under the waves of the sea at about six hundred leagues, and it was accomplished in forty-eight hours. Starting on the morning of the 16th of February from the shores of Greece, we had crossed the Straits of Gibraltar by sunrise on the 18th.

It was plain to me that this Mediterranean, enclosed in the midst of those countries which he wished to avoid, was distasteful to Captain Nemo. Those waves and those breezes brought back too many remembrances, if not too many regrets. Here he had no longer that independence and that liberty of **gait** which he had when in the open seas, and his Nautilus felt itself cramped between the close shores of Africa and Europe.

Our speed was now twenty-five miles an hour. It may be well understood that Ned Land, to his great disgust, was **obliged** to renounce his intended flight. He could not launch the pinnace, going at the rate of twelve or thirteen yards every second. To quit the Nautilus under such conditions would be as bad as jumping from a train going at full speed—an **imprudent** thing, to say the

31 least of it. Besides, our vessel only mounted to the surface of the
32 waves at night to renew its stock of air; it was steered entirely by
33 the compass and the log.

34 I saw no more of the interior of this Mediterranean than a traveller
35 by express train perceives of the landscape which flies before his
36 eyes; that is to say, the distant horizon, and not the nearer objects
37 which pass like a flash of lightning.

38 We were then passing between Sicily and the coast of Tunis. In
39 the narrow space between Cape Bon and the Straits of Messina
40 the bottom of the sea rose almost suddenly. There was a perfect
41 bank, on which there was not more than nine fathoms of water,
42 whilst on either side the depth was ninety fathoms.

43 The Nautilus had to maneuver very carefully so as not to strike
44 against this submarine barrier.

45 I showed Conseil, on the map of the Mediterranean, the spot
46 occupied by this reef.

47 "But if you please, sir," observed Conseil, "it is like a real
48 **isthmus** joining Europe to Africa."

49 "Yes, my boy, it forms a perfect bar to the Straits of Lybia, and
50 the soundings of Smith have proved that in former times the
51 continents between Cape Boco and Cape Furina were joined."

52 "I can well believe it," said Conseil.

53 "I will add," I continued, "that a similar barrier exists between
54 Gibraltar and Ceuta, which in geological times formed the entire
55 Mediterranean."

56 "What if some volcanic burst should one day raise these two
57 barriers above the waves?"

58 "It is not probable, Conseil."

59 "Well, but allow me to finish, please, sir; if this phenomenon
60 should take place, it will be troublesome for M. Lesseps, who

61 has taken so much pains to pierce the isthmus."

62 "I agree with you; but I repeat, Conseil, this phenomenon
63 will never happen. The violence of subterranean force is ever
64 diminishing….

65 During the night of the 16th and 17th February we had entered
66 the second Mediterranean basin, the greatest depth of which was
67 1,450 fathoms. The Nautilus, by the action of its crew, slid down
68 the inclined planes and buried itself in the lowest depths of the
69 sea.

70 On the 18th of February, about three o'clock in the morning, we
71 were at the entrance of the Straits of Gibraltar. There once existed
72 two currents: an upper one, long since recognized, which conveys
73 the waters of the ocean into the basin of the Mediterranean; and a
74 lower counter-current, which reasoning has now shown to exist.
75 Indeed, the volume of water in the Mediterranean, incessantly
76 added to by the waves of the Atlantic and by rivers falling into
77 it, would each year raise the level of this sea, for its evaporation
78 is not sufficient to restore the equilibrium. As it is not so, we
79 must necessarily admit the existence of an under-current, which
80 empties into the basin of the Atlantic through the Straits of
81 Gibraltar the surplus waters of the Mediterranean. A fact indeed;
82 and it was this counter-current by which the Nautilus profited. It
83 advanced rapidly by the narrow pass. For one instant I caught a
84 glimpse of the beautiful ruins of the temple of Hercules, buried
85 in the ground, according to Pliny, and with the low island which
86 supports it; and a few minutes later we were floating on the
87 Atlantic.

For questions and vocabulary on chapter 7 -
see the end of chapter 8.

Chapter 8

VIGO BAY

1 **The Atlantic!** a vast sheet of water whose superficial area covers twenty-five millions of square miles, the length of which is nine thousand miles, with a **mean breadth** of two thousand seven hundred—an ocean whose parallel winding shores embrace an immense circumference, watered by the largest rivers of the world, the St. Lawrence, the Mississippi, the Amazon, the Plata, the Orinoco, the Niger, the Senegal, the Elbe, the Loire, and the Rhine, which carry water from the most civilized, as well as from the most savage, countries! Magnificent field of water, **incessantly ploughed** by vessels of every nation, sheltered by the flags of every nation, and which terminates in those two terrible points so dreaded by mariners, Cape Horn and the Cape of Tempests.

The Nautilus was piercing the water with its sharp spur, after having accomplished nearly ten thousand leagues in three months and a half, a distance greater than the great circle of the earth. Where were we going now, and what was reserved for the future? The Nautilus, leaving the Straits of Gibraltar, had gone far out. It returned to the surface of the waves, and our daily walks on the platform were restored to us.

I mounted at once, accompanied by Ned Land and Conseil. At a distance of about twelve miles, Cape St. Vincent was dimly to be seen, forming the south-western point of the Spanish peninsula. A strong southerly gale was blowing. The sea was swollen and billowy; it made the Nautilus rock violently. It was almost impossible to keep one's foot on the platform, which the heavy rolls of the sea beat over every instant. So we descended after inhaling some mouthfuls of fresh air.

I returned to my room, Conseil to his cabin; but the Canadian, with a **preoccupied** air, followed me. Our rapid passage across the Mediterranean had not allowed him to put his project into execution, and he could not help showing his disappointment.

33 When the door of my room was shut, he sat down and looked at
34 me silently.

35 "Friend Ned," said I, "I understand you; but you cannot **reproach**
36 yourself. To have attempted to leave the Nautilus under the
37 circumstances would have been folly."

38 Ned Land did not answer; his **compressed** lips and frowning
39 brow showed with him the violent possession this fixed idea had
40 taken of his mind.

41 "Let us see," I continued; "we need not despair yet. We are going
42 up the coast of Portugal again; France and England are not far off,
43 where we can easily find refuge. Now if the Nautilus, on leaving
44 the Straits of Gibraltar, had gone to the south, if it had carried us
45 towards regions where there were no continents, I should share
46 your uneasiness. But we know now that Captain Nemo does not
47 fly from civilized seas, and in some days I think you can act with
48 security."

49 Ned Land still looked at me fixedly; at length his fixed lips parted,
50 and he said, "It is for to-night."

51 I drew myself up suddenly. I was, I admit, little prepared for this
52 communication. I wanted to answer the Canadian, but words
53 would not come.

54 "We agreed to wait for an opportunity," continued Ned Land,
55 "and the opportunity has arrived. This night we shall be but a few
56 miles from the Spanish coast. It is cloudy. The wind blows freely.
57 I have your word, M. Aronnax, and I rely upon you."

58 As I was silent, the Canadian approached me.

59 "To-night, at nine o'clock," said he. "I have warned Conseil.
60 At that moment Captain Nemo will be shut up in his room,
61 probably in bed. Neither the engineers nor the ship's crew can
62 see us. Conseil and I will gain the central staircase, and you, M.
63 Aronnax, will remain in the library, two steps from us, waiting
64 my signal. The oars, the mast, and the sail are in the canoe. I have

even succeeded in getting some provisions. I have procured an English wrench, to unfasten the bolts which attach it to the shell of the Nautilus. So all is ready, till to-night."

"The sea is bad."

"That I allow," replied the Canadian; "but we must risk that. Liberty is worth paying for; besides, the boat is strong, and a few miles with a fair wind to carry us is no great thing. Who knows but by to-morrow we may be a hundred leagues away? Let circumstances only favor us, and by ten or eleven o'clock we shall have landed on some spot of terra firma, alive or dead. But adieu now till to-night."

With these words the Canadian withdrew, leaving me almost dumb. I had imagined that, the chance gone, I should have time to reflect and discuss the matter. My obstinate companion had given me no time; and, after all, what could I have said to him? Ned Land was perfectly right. There was almost the opportunity to profit by. Could I retract my word, and take upon myself the responsibility of compromising the future of my companions? To-morrow Captain Nemo might take us far from all land.

At that moment a rather loud hissing noise told me that the reservoirs were filling, and that the Nautilus was sinking under the waves of the Atlantic.

A sad day I passed, between the desire of regaining my liberty of action and of abandoning the wonderful Nautilus, and leaving my submarine studies incomplete.

What dreadful hours I passed thus! Sometimes seeing myself and companions safely landed, sometimes wishing, in spite of my reason, that some unforeseen circumstance, would prevent the realization of Ned Land's project.

Twice I went to the saloon. I wished to consult the compass. I wished to see if the direction the Nautilus was taking was bringing us nearer or taking us farther from the coast. But no; the Nautilus kept in Portuguese waters.

98 I must therefore take my part and prepare for flight. My luggage
99 was not heavy; my notes, nothing more.

100 As to Captain Nemo, I asked myself what he would think of
101 our escape; what trouble, what wrong it might cause him and
102 what he might do in case of its discovery or failure. Certainly
103 I had no cause to complain of him; on the contrary, never was
104 hospitality freer than his. In leaving him I could not be taxed
105 with ingratitude. No oath bound us to him. It was on the strength
106 of circumstances he relied, and not upon our word, to fix us for
107 ever.

108 I had not seen the Captain since our visit to the Island of
109 Santorin. Would chance bring me to his presence before our
110 departure? I wished it, and I feared it at the same time. I listened
111 if I could hear him walking the room **contiguous** to mine. No
112 sound reached my ear. I felt an unbearable uneasiness. This day
113 of waiting seemed eternal. Hours struck too slowly to keep pace
114 with my impatience.

115 My dinner was served in my room as usual. I ate but little; I
116 was too preoccupied. I left the table at seven o'clock. A hundred
117 and twenty minutes (I counted them) still separated me from
118 the moment in which I was to join Ned Land. My **agitation**
119 redoubled. My pulse beat violently. I could not remain quiet. I
120 went and came, hoping to calm my troubled spirit by constant
121 movement. The idea of failure in our bold enterprise was the least
122 painful of my anxieties; but the thought of seeing our project
123 discovered before leaving the Nautilus, of being brought before
124 Captain Nemo, irritated, or (what was worse) saddened, at my
125 desertion, made my heart beat.

126 I wanted to see the saloon for the last time. I descended the stairs
127 and arrived in the museum, where I had passed so many useful
128 and agreeable hours. I looked at all its riches, all its treasures, like
129 a man on the eve of an eternal exile, who was leaving never to
130 return.

131 These wonders of Nature, these masterpieces of art, amongst

132 which for so many days my life had been concentrated, I was
133 going to abandon them for ever! I should like to have taken a last
134 look through the windows of the saloon into the waters of the
135 Atlantic: but the panels were hermetically closed, and a cloak of
136 steel separated me from that ocean which I had not yet explored.

137 In passing through the saloon, I came near the door let into
138 the angle which opened into the Captain's room. To my great
139 surprise, this door was ajar. I drew back involuntarily. If Captain
140 Nemo should be in his room, he could see me. But, hearing no
141 sound, I drew nearer. The room was deserted. I pushed open
142 the door and took some steps forward. Still the same monklike
143 severity of aspect.

144 Suddenly the clock struck eight. The first beat of the hammer on
145 the bell awoke me from my dreams. I trembled as if an invisible
146 eye had plunged into my most secret thoughts, and I hurried
147 from the room.

148 There my eye fell upon the compass. Our course was still north.
149 The log indicated moderate speed, the manometer a depth of
150 about sixty feet.

151 I returned to my room, clothed myself warmly—sea boots, an
152 otterskin cap, a great coat of byssus, lined with sealskin; I was
153 ready, I was waiting. The vibration of the screw alone broke
154 the deep silence which reigned on board. I listened attentively.
155 Would no loud voice suddenly inform me that Ned Land had
156 been surprised in his projected flight. A mortal dread hung over
157 me, and I vainly tried to regain my accustomed coolness.

158 At a few minutes to nine, I put my ear to the Captain's door. No
159 noise. I left my room and returned to the saloon, which was half
160 in obscurity, but deserted.

161 I opened the door communicating with the library. The same
162 insufficient light, the same solitude. I placed myself near the door
163 leading to the central staircase, and there waited for Ned Land's
164 signal.

At that moment the trembling of the screw sensibly diminished, then it stopped entirely. The silence was now only disturbed by the beatings of my own heart. Suddenly a slight shock was felt; and I knew that the Nautilus had stopped at the bottom of the ocean. My uneasiness increased. The Canadian's signal did not come. I felt inclined to join Ned Land and beg of him to put off his attempt. I felt that we were not sailing under our usual conditions.

At this moment the door of the large saloon opened, and Captain Nemo appeared. He saw me, and without further preamble began in an amiable tone of voice:

"Ah, sir! I have been looking for you. Do you know the history of Spain?"

Now, one might know the history of one's own country by heart; but in the condition I was at the time, with troubled mind and head quite lost, I could not have said a word of it.

"Well," continued Captain Nemo, "you heard my question! Do you know the history of Spain?"

"Very slightly," I answered.

"Well, here are learned men having to learn," said the Captain. "Come, sit down, and I will tell you a curious episode in this history. Sir, listen well," said he; "this history will interest you on one side, for it will answer a question which doubtless you have not been able to solve."

"I listen, Captain," said I, not knowing what my interlocutor was driving at, and asking myself if this incident was bearing on our projected flight.

"Sir, if you have no objection, we will go back to 1702. You cannot be ignorant that your king, Louis XIV, thinking that the gesture of a potentate was sufficient to bring the Pyrenees under his yoke, had imposed the Duke of Anjou, his grandson, on the Spaniards. This prince reigned more or less badly under the name of Philip V, and had a strong party against him abroad. Indeed, the preceding year, the royal houses of Holland, Austria, and England had concluded a treaty of alliance at the Hague, with the intention of plucking the crown of Spain from the head of Philip V, and placing it on that of an archduke to whom they prematurely gave the title of Charles III.

"Spain must resist this coalition; but she was almost entirely unprovided with either soldiers or sailors. However, money would not fail them, provided that their galleons, laden with gold and silver from America, once entered their ports. And about the end of 1702 they expected a rich convoy which France was escorting with a fleet of twenty-three vessels, commanded by Admiral Chateau-Renaud, for the ships of the coalition were already beating the Atlantic. This convoy was to go to Cadiz, but the Admiral, hearing that an English fleet was cruising in those waters, resolved to make for a French port.

"The Spanish commanders of the convoy objected to this decision. They wanted to be taken to a Spanish port, and, if not to Cadiz, into Vigo Bay, situated on the northwest coast of Spain, and which was not blocked.

"Admiral Chateau-Renaud had the rashness to obey this injunction, and the galleons entered Vigo Bay.

"Unfortunately, it formed an open road which could not be defended in any way. They must therefore hasten to unload the galleons before the arrival of the combined fleet; and time would not have failed them had not a miserable question of rivalry suddenly arisen.

"You are following the chain of events?" asked Captain Nemo.

"Perfectly," said I, not knowing the end proposed by this historical lesson.

"I will continue. This is what passed. The merchants of Cadiz had a privilege by which they had the right of receiving all merchandise coming from the West Indies. Now, to disembark these ingots at the port of Vigo was depriving them of their rights. They complained at Madrid, and obtained the consent of the weak-minded Philip that the convoy, without discharging its cargo, should remain sequestered in the roads of Vigo until the enemy had disappeared.

"But whilst coming to this decision, on the 22nd of October, 1702, the English vessels arrived in Vigo Bay, when Admiral Chateau-Renaud, in spite of inferior forces, fought bravely. But, seeing that the treasure must fall into the enemy's hands, he burnt and scuttled every galleon, which went to the bottom with their immense riches."

Captain Nemo stopped. I admit I could not see yet why this history should interest me.

"Well?" I asked.

"Well, M. Aronnax," replied Captain Nemo, "we are in that Vigo Bay; and it rests with yourself whether you will penetrate its mysteries."

The Captain rose, telling me to follow him. I had had time to recover. I obeyed. The saloon was dark, but through the transparent glass the waves were sparkling. I looked.

For half a mile around the Nautilus, the waters seemed bathed in electric light. The sandy bottom was clean and bright. Some of the ship's crew in their diving-dresses were clearing away half-rotten barrels and empty cases from the midst of the blackened wrecks. From these cases and from these barrels escaped ingots of gold and silver, cascades of piastres and jewels. The sand was heaped up with them. Laden with their precious booty, the men returned to the Nautilus, disposed of their burden, and went back to this inexhaustible fishery of gold and silver.

I understood now. This was the scene of the battle of the 22nd of October, 1702. Here on this very spot the galleons laden for the Spanish Government had sunk. Here Captain Nemo came, according to his wants, to pack up those millions with which he

263 burdened the Nautilus. It was for him and him alone America
264 had given up her precious metals. He was heir direct, without
265 anyone to share, in those treasures torn from the Incas and from
266 the conquered of Ferdinand Cortez.

267 "Did you know, sir," he asked, smiling, "that the sea contained
268 such riches?"

269 "I knew," I answered, "that they value money held in suspension
270 in these waters at two millions."

271 "Doubtless; but to extract this money the expense would be
272 greater than the profit. Here, on the contrary, I have but to
273 pick up what man has lost—and not only in Vigo Bay, but in
274 a thousand other ports where shipwrecks have happened, and
275 which are marked on my submarine map. Can you understand
276 now the source of the millions I am worth?"

277 "I understand, Captain. But allow me to tell you that in exploring
278 Vigo Bay you have only been beforehand with a rival society."

279 "And which?"

280 "A society which has received from the Spanish Government the
281 privilege of seeking those buried galleons. The shareholders are
282 led on by the **allurement** of an enormous bounty, for they value
283 these rich shipwrecks at five hundred millions."

284 "Five hundred millions they were," answered Captain Nemo,
285 "but they are so no longer."

286 "Just so," said I; "and a warning to those shareholders would be
287 an act of charity. But who knows if it would be well received?
288 What gamblers usually regret above all is less the loss of their
289 money than of their foolish hopes. After all, I pity them less than
290 the thousands of unfortunates to whom so much riches well-
291 distributed would have been profitable, whilst for them they will
292 be forever barren."

293 I had no sooner expressed this regret than I felt that it must have
294 wounded Captain Nemo.

"Barren!" he exclaimed, with animation. "Do you think then, sir, that these riches are lost because I gather them? Is it for myself alone, according to your idea, that I take the trouble to collect these treasures? Who told you that I did not make a good use of it? Do you think I am ignorant that there are suffering beings and oppressed races on this earth, miserable creatures to console, victims to avenge? Do you not understand?"

Captain Nemo stopped at these last words, regretting perhaps that he had spoken so much. But I had guessed that, whatever the motive which had forced him to seek independence under the sea, it had left him still a man, that his heart still beat for the sufferings of humanity, and that his immense charity was for oppressed races as well as individuals. And I then understood for whom those millions were destined which were forwarded by Captain Nemo when the Nautilus was cruising in the waters of Crete.

𝕍𝕠𝕔𝕒𝕓𝕦𝕝𝕒𝕣𝕪

embalmed, gait, imprudent, isthmus, mean, breadth, ploughed, preoccupied, compressed, contiguous, agitation, allurement

Questions

1. Why do you think Captain Nemo was racing through the Mediterranean? What does the author suggest?

2. What is the proof the author brings that proves that there is a countercurrent going underneath the straits of Gibraltar and into the Atlantic ocean?

3. Explain what lines 104-105 (chapter 8) mean when it says: "I could not be taxed with ingratitude".

4. In line 110 the professor thinks: "I wished it, and I feared it at the same time?" Why?

5. What happens when the ship travels through the Mediterranean and exits into the Atlantic Ocean?

6. What is Ned Land's plan?

7. Is the Professor happy about leaving? Why or why not?
    Explain his hesitations.

8. What happens to hinder the plans of Ned Land?

9. What does the accumulation of gold by the divers
    answer for the Professor?

10. What are the meaning of lines 286-292 in your own
    terms?

11. What new insight does the Professor have about
    Captain Nemo?

Chapter 9
A VANISHED CONTINENT

The next morning, the 19th of February, I saw the Canadian enter my room. I expected this visit. He looked very disappointed.

"Well, sir?" said he.

"Well, Ned, fortune was against us yesterday."

"Yes; that Captain must needs stop exactly at the hour we intended leaving his vessel."

"Yes, Ned, he had business at his bankers."

"His bankers!"

"Or rather his banking-house; by that I mean the ocean, where his riches are safer than in the chests of the State."

I then related to the Canadian the incidents of the preceding night, hoping to bring him back to the idea of not abandoning the Captain; but my recital had no other result than an energetically expressed regret from Ned that he had not been able to take a walk on the battlefield of Vigo on his own account.

"However," said he, "all is not ended. It is only a blow of the harpoon lost. Another time we must succeed; and to-night, if necessary——"

"In what direction is the Nautilus going?" I asked.

"I do not know," replied Ned.

"Well, at noon we shall see the point."

The Canadian returned to Conseil. As soon as I was dressed, I went into the saloon. The compass was not reassuring. The course of the Nautilus was S.S.W. We were turning our backs on Europe.

I waited with some impatience till the ship's place was pricked on the chart. At about half-past eleven the reservoirs were emptied,

27 and our vessel rose to the surface of the ocean. I rushed towards
28 the platform. Ned Land had preceded me. No more land in
29 sight. Nothing but an immense sea. Some sails on the horizon,
30 doubtless those going to San Roque in search of favorable winds
31 for doubling the Cape of Good Hope. The weather was cloudy.
32 A gale of wind was preparing. Ned raved, and tried to pierce the
33 cloudy horizon. He still hoped that behind all that fog stretched
34 the land he so longed for.

35 At noon the sun showed itself for an instant. The second profited
36 by this brightness to take its height. Then, the sea becoming more
37 **billowy**, we descended, and the panel closed.

38 An hour after, upon consulting the chart, I saw the position of
39 the Nautilus was marked at 16° 17' long., and 33° 22' lat., at 150
40 leagues from the nearest coast. There was no means of flight, and
41 I leave you to imagine the rage of the Canadian when I informed
42 him of our situation.

43 For myself, I was not particularly sorry. I felt lightened of the
44 load which had oppressed me, and was able to return with some
45 degree of calmness to my accustomed work.

46 That night, about eleven o'clock, I received a most unexpected
47 visit from Captain Nemo. He asked me very graciously if I felt
48 fatigued from my watch of the preceding night. I answered in the
49 negative.

50 "Then, M. Aronnax, I propose a curious **excursion**."

51 "Propose, Captain?"

52 "You have **hitherto** only visited the submarine depths by daylight,
53 under the brightness of the sun. Would it suit you to see them in
54 the darkness of the night?"

55 "Most willingly."

56 "I warn you, the way will be tiring. We shall have far to walk, and
57 must climb a mountain. The roads are not well kept."

58 "What you say, Captain, only heightens my curiosity; I am ready
59 to follow you."

60 "Come then, sir, we will put on our diving-dresses."

61 Arrived at the robing-room, I saw that neither of my companions
62 nor any of the ship's crew were to follow us on this excursion.
63 Captain Nemo had not even proposed my taking with me either
64 Ned or Conseil.

65 In a few moments we had put on our diving-dresses; they placed
66 on our backs the reservoirs, abundantly filled with air, but no
67 electric lamps were prepared. I called the Captain's attention to
68 the fact.

69 "They will be useless," he replied.

70 I thought I had not heard aright, but I could not repeat my
71 observation, for the Captain's head had already disappeared in its
72 metal case. I finished harnessing myself. I felt them put an iron-
73 pointed stick into my hand, and some minutes later, after going
74 through the usual form, we set foot on the bottom of the Atlantic
75 at a depth of 150 fathoms. Midnight was near. The waters were
76 profoundly dark, but Captain Nemo pointed out in the distance
77 a reddish spot, a sort of large light shining brilliantly about two
78 miles from the Nautilus. What this fire might be, what could feed
79 it, why and how it lit up the liquid mass, I could not say. In any
80 case, it did light our way, vaguely, it is true, but I soon accustomed
81 myself to the peculiar darkness, and I understood, under such
82 circumstances, the uselessness of the Ruhmkorff apparatus.

83 As we advanced, I heard a kind of pattering above my head. The
84 noise redoubling, sometimes producing a continual shower,
85 I soon understood the cause. It was rain falling violently, and
86 crisping the surface of the waves. Instinctively the thought flashed
87 across my mind that I should be wet through! By the water! in
88 the midst of the water! I could not help laughing at the odd idea.
89 But, indeed, in the thick diving-dress, the liquid element is no
90 longer felt, and one only seems to be in an atmosphere somewhat
91 denser than the terrestrial atmosphere. Nothing more.

92 After half an hour's walk the soil became stony. Medusae,
93 microscopic crustacea, and pennatules lit it slightly with their
94 phosphorescent gleam. I caught a glimpse of pieces of stone
95 covered with millions of zoophytes and masses of sea weed.
96 My feet often slipped upon this sticky carpet of sea weed, and
97 without my iron-tipped stick I should have fallen more than
98 once. In turning round, I could still see the whitish lantern of the
99 Nautilus beginning to pale in the distance.

100 But the rosy light which guided us increased and lit up the
101 horizon. The presence of this fire under water puzzled me in
102 the highest degree. Was I going towards a natural phenomenon
103 as yet unknown to the *savants* of the earth? Or even (for this
104 thought crossed my brain) had the hand of man ought to do with
105 this conflagration? Had he fanned this flame? Was I to meet in
106 these depths companions and friends of Captain Nemo whom he
107 was going to visit, and who, like him, led this strange existence?
108 Should I find down there a whole colony of exiles who, weary of
109 the miseries of this earth, had sought and found independence
110 in the deep ocean? All these foolish and unreasonable ideas
111 pursued me. And in this condition of mind, over-excited by
112 the succession of wonders continually passing before my eyes, I
113 should not have been surprised to meet at the bottom of the sea
114 one of those submarine towns of which Captain Nemo dreamed.

115 Our road grew lighter and lighter. The white glimmer came in
116 rays from the summit of a mountain about 800 feet high. But
117 what I saw was simply a reflection, developed by the clearness of
118 the waters. The source of this inexplicable light was a fire on the
119 opposite side of the mountain.

120 In the midst of this stony maze furrowing the bottom of the
121 Atlantic, Captain Nemo advanced without hesitation. He knew
122 this dreary road. Doubtless he had often travelled over it, and
123 could not lose himself. I followed him with unshaken confidence.
124 He seemed to me like a **genie** of the sea; and, as he walked before
125 me, I could not help admiring his stature, which was outlined in
126 black on the luminous horizon.

127 It was one in the morning when we arrived at the first slopes
128 of the mountain; but to gain access to them we must venture
129 through the difficult paths of a vast copse.

130 Yes; a copse of dead trees, without leaves, without sap, trees
131 petrified by the action of the water and here and there overtopped
132 by gigantic pines. It was like a coal-pit still standing, holding by
133 the roots to the broken soil, and whose branches, like fine black
134 paper cuttings, showed distinctly on the watery ceiling. Picture
135 to yourself a forest in the Hartz hanging on to the sides of the
136 mountain, but a forest swallowed up. The paths were encumbered
137 with seaweed and fucus, between which grovelled a whole world
138 of crustacea. I went along, climbing the rocks, striding over
139 extended trunks, breaking the sea bind-weed which hung from
140 one tree to the other; and frightening the fishes, which flew from
141 branch to branch. Pressing onward, I felt no fatigue. I followed
142 my guide, who was never tired. What a spectacle! How can I
143 express it? how paint the aspect of those woods and rocks in this
144 medium—their under parts dark and wild, the upper coloured
145 with red tints, by that light which the reflecting powers of the
146 waters doubled? We climbed rocks which fell directly after with
147 gigantic bounds and the low growling of an avalanche. To right
148 and left ran long, dark galleries, where sight was lost. Here opened
149 vast glades which the hand of man seemed to have worked; and
150 I sometimes asked myself if some inhabitant of these submarine
151 regions would not suddenly appear to me.

152 But Captain Nemo was still mounting. I could not stay behind. I
153 followed boldly. My stick gave me good help. A false step would
154 have been dangerous on the narrow passes sloping down to the
155 sides of the gulfs; but I walked with firm step, without feeling any
156 **giddiness**. Now I jumped a crevice, the depth of which would
157 have made me hesitate had it been among the glaciers on the
158 land; now I ventured on the unsteady trunk of a tree thrown
159 across from one abyss to the other, without looking under my
160 feet, having only eyes to admire the wild sites of this region.

161 There, monumental rocks, leaning on their regularly-cut bases,
162 seemed to defy all laws of equilibrium. From between their

163 stony knees trees sprang, like a jet under heavy pressure, and
164 upheld others which upheld them. Natural towers, large scarps,
165 cut perpendicularly, like a "curtain," inclined at an angle which
166 the laws of gravitation could never have tolerated in terrestrial
167 regions.

168 Two hours after quitting the Nautilus we had crossed the line
169 of trees, and a hundred feet above our heads rose the top of the
170 mountain, which cast a shadow on the brilliant irradiation of
171 the opposite slope. Some petrified shrubs ran fantastically here
172 and there. Fishes got up under our feet like birds in the long
173 grass. The massive rocks were **rent** with impenetrable fractures,
174 deep **grottos**, and unfathomable holes, at the bottom of which
175 formidable creatures might be heard moving. My blood curdled
176 when I saw enormous antennae blocking my road, or some
177 frightful claw closing with a noise in the shadow of some cavity.
178 Millions of luminous spots shone brightly in the midst of the
179 darkness. They were the eyes of giant crustacea crouched in their
180 holes; giant lobsters setting themselves up like halberdiers[65], and
181 moving their claws with the clicking sound of pincers; titanic
182 crabs, pointed like a gun on its carriage; and frightful-looking
183 poulps, interweaving their tentacles like a living nest of serpents.

184 We had now arrived on the first platform, where other surprises
185 awaited me. Before us lay some picturesque ruins, which betrayed
186 the hand of man and not that of the Creator. There were vast
187 heaps of stone, amongst which might be traced the vague and
188 shadowy forms of castles and temples, clothed with a world of
189 blossoming zoophytes, and over which, instead of ivy, sea-weed
190 and fucus threw a thick vegetable mantle. But what was this
191 portion of the globe which had been swallowed by **cataclysms**?
192 Who had placed those rocks and stones like cromlechs[66] of
193 prehistoric times? Where was I? Whither had Captain Nemo's
194 fancy hurried me?

---

65   A halberd is a two-handed pole weapon used in late medieval
times
66   (in Wales) a megalithic tomb consisting of a large flat stone laid
on upright ones.

195 I would **fain** have asked him; not being able to, I stopped him—I
196 seized his arm. But, shaking his head, and pointing to the highest
197 point of the mountain, he seemed to say:

198 "Come, come along; come higher!"

199 I followed, and in a few minutes I had climbed to the top, which
200 for a circle of ten yards commanded the whole mass of rock.

201 I looked down the side we had just climbed. The mountain did
202 not rise more than seven or eight hundred feet above the level
203 of the plain; but on the opposite side it commanded from twice
204 that height the depths of this part of the Atlantic. My eyes ranged
205 far over a large space lit by a violent **fulguration**. In fact, the
206 mountain was a volcano.

207 At fifty feet above the peak, in the midst of a rain of stones and
208 scoriae, a large crater was vomiting forth torrents of lava which
209 fell in a cascade of fire into the bosom of the liquid mass. Thus
210 situated, this volcano lit the lower plain like an immense torch,
211 even to the extreme limits of the horizon. I said that the submarine
212 crater threw up lava, but no flames. Flames require the oxygen
213 of the air to feed upon and cannot be developed under water;
214 but streams of lava, having in themselves the principles of their
215 incandescence, can attain a white heat, fight vigorously against
216 the liquid element, and turn it to vapor by contact.

217 Rapid currents bearing all these gases in diffusion and torrents
218 of lava slid to the bottom of the mountain like an eruption of
219 Vesuvius on another Terra del Greco.

220 There indeed under my eyes, ruined, destroyed, lay a town—its
221 roofs open to the sky, its temples fallen, its arches dislocated,
222 its columns lying on the ground, from which one would still
223 recognize the massive character of Tuscan architecture. Further
224 on, some remains of a gigantic aqueduct; here the high base of
225 an Acropolis, with the floating outline of a Parthenon; there
226 traces of a quay, as if an ancient port had formerly abutted on the
227 borders of the ocean, and disappeared with its merchant vessels
228 and its war-galleys. Farther on again, long lines of sunken walls

and broad, deserted streets—a perfect Pompeii escaped beneath the waters. Such was the sight that Captain Nemo brought before my eyes!

Where was I? Where was I? I must know at any cost. I tried to speak, but Captain Nemo stopped me by a gesture, and, picking up a piece of chalk-stone, advanced to a rock of black basalt, and traced the one word:

ATLANTIS

What a light shot through my mind! Atlantis! the Atlantis of Plato, that continent denied by Origen and Humboldt, who placed its disappearance amongst the legendary tales. I had it there now before my eyes, bearing upon it the **unexceptionable** testimony of its catastrophe. The region thus engulfed was beyond Europe, Asia, and Lybia, beyond the columns of Hercules, where those powerful people, the Atlantides, lived, against whom the first wars of ancient Greeks were waged.

Thus, led by the strangest destiny, I was treading under foot the mountains of this continent, touching with my hand those ruins a thousand generations old and contemporary with the geological epochs. I was walking on the very spot where the contemporaries of the first man had walked.

Whilst I was trying to fix in my mind every detail of this grand landscape, Captain Nemo remained motionless, as if petrified in mute ecstasy, leaning on a mossy stone. Was he dreaming of those generations long since disappeared? Was he asking them the secret of human destiny? Was it here this strange man came to steep himself in historical recollections, and live again this ancient life—he who wanted no modern one? What would I not have given to know his thoughts, to share them, to understand them! We remained for an hour at this place, contemplating the vast plains under the brightness of the lava, which was some times wonderfully intense. Rapid tremblings ran along the mountain caused by internal bubblings, deep noise, distinctly transmitted through the liquid medium were echoed with **majestic** grandeur.

263 At this moment the moon appeared through the mass of waters
264 and threw her pale rays on the buried continent. It was but a
265 gleam, but what an indescribable effect! The Captain rose, cast
266 one last look on the immense plain, and then bade me follow
267 him.

268 We descended the mountain rapidly, and, the mineral forest
269 once passed, I saw the lantern of the Nautilus shining like a star.
270 The Captain walked straight to it, and we got on board as the first
271 rays of light whitened the surface of the ocean.

Vocabulary Part 2 Ch. 9

excursion, billowy, hitherto, savant's, genie, giddiness, rent, grotto, cataclysm, fain, fulguration, unexceptionable, majestic

Questions Part 2 Ch. 9

1. What does the word "fortune" in line 4 mean?
    a. Wealth,
    b. opulence,
    c. prosperity
    d. luck

2. What does this sentence (lines 16-17) mean, "It is only a blow of the harpoon lost"?

    ____

    ____

3. What makes the Professor laugh at the sound of rain hitting the waves (lines 85-88)?

    ____

    ____

4. In line 130, the Professor is surprised by lots of dead trees. What is so surprising about this group of dead trees?

    ____

    ____

5. What is witty about lines 140-141 which state: "and frightening the fishes, which flew from branch to branch."

    ____

    ____

6. What does the strange orange glow turn out to be from?

    ____

    ____

7. On their underwater excursion, what historical truth is revealed to the Professor?

8. What is meant by the sentence: (lines 254-256) "Was it here this strange man came to steep himself in historical recollections, and live again this ancient life—he who wanted no modern one?"

Chapter 10

THE SUBMARINE COAL-MINES

The next day, the 20th of February, I awoke very late: the fatigues of the previous night had prolonged my sleep until eleven o'clock. I dressed quickly, and hastened to find the course the Nautilus was taking. The instruments showed it to be still toward the south, with a speed of twenty miles an hour and a depth of fifty fathoms.

The species of fishes here did not differ much from those already noticed. There were rays of giant size, five yards long, and endowed with great muscular strength, which enabled them to shoot above the waves; sharks of many kinds; amongst others, one fifteen feet long, with triangular sharp teeth, and whose transparency rendered it almost invisible in the water.

Amongst bony fish Conseil noticed some about three yards long, armed at the upper jaw with a piercing sword; other bright-coloured creatures, known in the time of Aristotle by the name of the sea-dragon, which are dangerous to capture on account of the spikes on their back.

About four o'clock, the soil, generally composed of a thick mud mixed with petrified wood, changed by degrees, and it became more stony, and seemed strewn with conglomerate and pieces of basalt, with a sprinkling of lava. I thought that a mountainous region was succeeding the long plains; and accordingly, after a few evolutions of the Nautilus, I saw the southerly horizon blocked by a high wall which seemed to close all exit. Its summit evidently passed the level of the ocean. It must be a continent, or at least an island—one of the Canaries, or of the Cape Verde Islands. The bearings not being yet taken, perhaps **designedly**, I was ignorant of our exact position. In any case, such a wall seemed to me to mark the limits of that Atlantis, of which we had in reality passed over only the smallest part.

31 Much longer should I have remained at the window admiring the
32 beauties of sea and sky, but the panels closed. At this moment
33 the Nautilus arrived at the side of this high, perpendicular wall.
34 What it would do, I could not guess. I returned to my room; it
35 no longer moved. I laid myself down with the full intention of
36 waking after a few hours' sleep; but it was eight o'clock the
37 next day when I entered the saloon. I looked at the manometer.
38 It told me that the Nautilus was floating on the surface of the
39 ocean. Besides, I heard steps on the platform. I went to the
40 panel. It was open; but, instead of broad daylight, as I expected,
41 I was surrounded by profound darkness. Where were we? Was I
42 mistaken? Was it still night? No; not a star was shining and night
43 has not that utter darkness.

44 I knew not what to think, when a voice near me said:

45 "Is that you, Professor?"

46 "Ah! Captain," I answered, "where are we?"

47 "Underground, sir."

48 "Underground!" I exclaimed. "And the Nautilus floating still?"

49 "It always floats."

50 "But I do not understand."

51 "Wait a few minutes, our lantern will be lit, and, if you like light
52 places, you will be satisfied."

53 I stood on the platform and waited. The darkness was so
54 complete that I could not even see Captain Nemo; but, looking
55 to the zenith, exactly above my head, I seemed to catch an
56 undecided gleam, a kind of twilight filling a circular hole. At this
57 instant the lantern was lit, and its vividness dispelled the faint
58 light. I closed my dazzled eyes for an instant, and then looked
59 again. The Nautilus was stationary, floating near a mountain
60 which formed a sort of quay[67]. The lake, then, supporting it was

67   a concrete, stone, or metal platform lying alongside or projecting
into water for loading and unloading ships.

61 a lake imprisoned by a circle of walls, measuring two miles in
62 diameter and six in circumference. Its level (the manometer
63 showed) could only be the same as the outside level, for there
64 must necessarily be a communication between the lake and the
65 sea. The high partitions, leaning forward on their base, grew into
66 a vaulted roof bearing the shape of an immense funnel turned
67 upside down, the height being about five or six hundred yards.
68 At the summit was a circular orifice, by which I had caught the
69 slight gleam of light, evidently daylight.

70 "Where are we?" I asked.

71 "In the very heart of an extinct volcano, the interior of which
72 has been invaded by the sea, after some great convulsion of
73 the earth. Whilst you were sleeping, Professor, the Nautilus
74 penetrated to this lagoon by a natural canal, which opens about
75 ten yards beneath the surface of the ocean. This is its harbor
76 of refuge, a sure, commodious, and mysterious one, sheltered
77 from all gales. Show me, if you can, on the coasts of any of your
78 continents or islands, a road which can give such perfect refuge
79 from all storms."

80 "Certainly," I replied, "you are in safety here, Captain Nemo.
81 Who could reach you in the heart of a volcano? But did I not see
82 an opening at its summit?"

83 "Yes; its crater, formerly filled with lava, vapour, and flames,
84 and which now gives entrance to the life-giving air we breathe."

85 "But what is this volcanic mountain?"

86 "It belongs to one of the numerous islands with which this sea
87 is strewn—to vessels a simple sandbank—to us an immense
88 cavern. Chance led me to discover it, and chance served me
89 well."

90 "But of what use is this refuge, Captain? The Nautilus wants no
91 port."

92 "No, sir; but it wants electricity to make it move, and the

93 wherewithal to make the electricity—sodium to feed the elements,
94 coal from which to get the sodium, and a coal-mine to supply
95 the coal. And exactly on this spot the sea covers entire forests
96 embedded during the geological periods, now mineralized and
97 transformed into coal; for me they are an **inexhaustible** mine."

98 "Your men follow the trade of miners here, then, Captain?"

99 "Exactly so. These mines extend under the waves like the mines
100 of Newcastle. Here, in their diving-dresses, pick axe and shovel
101 in hand, my men extract the coal, which I do not even ask from
102 the mines of the earth. When I burn this combustible for the
103 manufacture of sodium, the smoke, escaping from the crater of
104 the mountain, gives it the appearance of a still-active volcano."

105 "And we shall see your companions at work?"

106 "No; not this time at least; for I am in a hurry to continue our
107 submarine tour of the earth. So I shall content myself with
108 drawing from the reserve of sodium I already possess. The time
109 for loading is one day only, and we continue our voyage. So,
110 if you wish to go over the cavern and make the round of the
111 lagoon, you must take advantage of to-day, M. Aronnax."

112 I thanked the Captain and went to look for my companions, who
113 had not yet left their cabin. I invited them to follow me without
114 saying where we were. They mounted the platform. Conseil,
115 who was astonished at nothing, seemed to look upon it as quite
116 natural that he should wake under a mountain, after having fallen
117 asleep under the waves. But Ned Land thought of nothing but
118 finding whether the cavern had any exit. After breakfast, about
119 ten o'clock, we went down on to the mountain.

120 "Here we are, once more on land," said Conseil.

121 "I do not call this land," said the Canadian. "And besides, we are
122 not on it, but beneath it."

123 Between the walls of the mountains and the waters of the lake
124 lay a sandy shore which, at its greatest breadth, measured five

hundred feet. On this soil one might easily make the tour of the lake. But the base of the high partitions was stony ground, with volcanic locks and enormous pumice-stones lying in picturesque heaps. All these detached masses, covered with enamel, polished by the action of the subterraneous fires, shone **resplendent** by the light of our electric lantern. The mica dust from the shore, rising under our feet, flew like a cloud of sparks. The bottom now rose sensibly, and we soon arrived at long **circuitous** slopes, or inclined planes, which took us higher by degrees; but we were obliged to walk carefully among these conglomerates, bound by no cement, the feet slipping on the glassy crystal, felspar, and quartz.

The volcanic nature of this enormous excavation was confirmed on all sides, and I pointed it out to my companions.

"Picture to yourselves," said I, "what this crater must have been when filled with boiling lava, and when the level of the incandescent liquid rose to the orifice of the mountain, as though melted on the top of a hot plate."

"I can picture it perfectly," said Conseil. "But, sir, will you tell me why the Great Architect has suspended operations, and how it is that the furnace is replaced by the quiet waters of the lake?"

"Most probably, Conseil, because some convulsion beneath the ocean produced that very opening which has served as a passage for the Nautilus. Then the waters of the Atlantic rushed into the interior of the mountain. There must have been a terrible struggle between the two elements…

"Very well," replied Ned Land; "I accept the explanation, sir; but, in our own interests, I regret that the opening of which you speak was not made above the level of the sea."

"But, friend Ned," said Conseil, "if the passage had not been under the sea, the Nautilus could not have gone through it."

We continued ascending. The steps became more and more perpendicular and narrow. Deep excavations, which we were

158 obliged to cross, cut them here and there; sloping masses had
159 to be turned. We slid upon our knees and crawled along. But
160 Conseil's dexterity and the Canadian's strength surmounted
161 all obstacles. At a height of about 31 feet the nature of the
162 ground changed without becoming more practicable. To the
163 conglomerate and trachyte succeeded black basalt, the first
164 dispread in layers full of bubbles, the latter forming regular
165 prisms, placed like a colonnade supporting the spring of the
166 immense vault, an admirable specimen of natural architecture.
167 Between the blocks of basalt wound long streams of lava,
168 long since grown cold, encrusted with bituminous rays; and in
169 some places there were spread large carpets of sulphur. A more
170 powerful light shone through the upper crater, shedding a vague
171 glimmer over these volcanic depressions for ever buried in the
172 bosom of this extinguished mountain. But our upward march
173 was soon stopped at a height of about two hundred and fifty
174 feet by impassable obstacles. There was a complete vaulted
175 arch overhanging us, and our ascent was changed to a circular
176 walk. At the last change vegetable life began to struggle with
177 the mineral. Some shrubs, and even some trees, grew from the
178 fractures of the walls. I recognized some euphorbias, with the
179 caustic sugar coming from them; heliotropes, quite incapable of
180 justifying their name, sadly drooped their clusters of flowers,
181 both their color and perfume half gone. Here and there some
182 chrysanthemums grew timidly at the foot of an aloe with long,
183 sickly-looking leaves. But between the streams of lava, I saw
184 some little violets still slightly perfumed, and I admit that I smelt
185 them with delight. Perfume is the soul of the flower, and sea-
186 flowers have no soul.

187 We had arrived at the foot of some sturdy dragon-trees, which
188 had pushed aside the rocks with their strong roots, when Ned
189 Land exclaimed:

190 "Ah! sir, a hive! a hive!"

191 "A hive!" I replied, with a gesture of **incredulity**.

192 "Yes, a hive," repeated the Canadian, "and bees humming round

193 it."

194 I approached, and was bound to believe my own eyes. There at
195 a hole bored in one of the dragon-trees were some thousands
196 of these **ingenious** insects, so common in all the Canaries,
197 and whose produce is so much esteemed. Naturally enough,
198 the Canadian wished to gather the honey, and I could not well
199 oppose his wish. A quantity of dry leaves, mixed with sulphur,
200 he lit with a spark from his flint, and he began to smoke out the
201 bees. The humming ceased by degrees, and the hive eventually
202 yielded several pounds of the sweetest honey, with which Ned
203 Land filled his haversack.

204 "When I have mixed this honey with the paste of the bread-
205 fruit," said he, "I shall be able to offer you a succulent cake."

206 [Transcriber's Note: 'bread-fruit' has been substituted for
207 'artocarpus' in this ed.]

208 "'Pon my word," said Conseil, "it will be gingerbread."

209 "Never mind the gingerbread," said I; "let us continue our
210 interesting walk."

211 At every turn of the path we were following, the lake appeared
212 in all its length and breadth. The lantern lit up the whole of
213 its peaceable surface, which knew neither ripple nor wave.
214 The Nautilus remained perfectly immovable. On the platform,
215 and on the mountain, the ship's crew were working like black
216 shadows clearly carved against the luminous atmosphere. We
217 were now going round the highest crest of the first layers of
218 rock which upheld the roof. I then saw that bees were not the
219 only representatives of the animal kingdom in the interior of this
220 volcano. Birds of prey hovered here and there in the shadows, or
221 fled from their nests on the top of the rocks. There were sparrow
222 hawks, with white breasts, and kestrels, and down the slopes
223 scampered, with their long legs, several fine fat bustards. I leave
224 anyone to imagine the **covetousness** of the Canadian at the sight
225 of this savory game, and whether he did not regret having no gun.

226 But he did his best to replace the lead by stones, and, after several
227 fruitless attempts, he succeeded in wounding a magnificent bird.
228 To say that he risked his life twenty times before reaching it is
229 but the truth; but he managed so well that the creature joined
230 the honey-cakes in his bag. We were now obliged to descend
231 toward the shore, the crest becoming impracticable. Above us
232 the crater seemed to gape like the mouth of a well. From this
233 place the sky could be clearly seen, and clouds, **dissipated** by
234 the west wind, leaving behind them, even on the summit of the
235 mountain, their misty **remnants**—certain proof that they were
236 only moderately high, for the volcano did not rise more than
237 eight hundred feet above the level of the ocean. Half an hour
238 after the Canadian's last exploit we had regained the inner shore.
239 Here the flora was represented by large carpets of marine crystal,
240 a little umbelliferous plant very good to pickle, which also bears
241 the name of pierce-stone and sea-fennel. Conseil gathered some
242 bundles of it. As to the fauna, it might be counted by thousands
243 of crustacea of all sorts, lobsters, crabs, spider-crabs, chameleon
244 shrimps, and a large number of shells, rockfish, and limpets.
245 Three-quarters of an hour later we had finished our circuitous
246 walk and were on board. The crew had just finished loading the
247 sodium, and the Nautilus could have left that instant. But Captain
248 Nemo gave no order. Did he wish to wait until night, and leave
249 the submarine passage secretly? Perhaps so. Whatever it might
250 be, the next day, the Nautilus, having left its port, steered clear of
251 all land at a few yards beneath the waves of the Atlantic.

Vocabulary Part 2 Ch. 10

designedly, commodious, resplendent, circuitous, incredulity, ingenious, dissipated, remnants

Questions part 2 ch. 10

1. What does the word "fatigues" in line # 2 mean?
   a. Wearisome
   b. Battle clothing
   c. Tiredness
   d. Comfortability

2. What do lines 88-89 say about Captain Nemo's belief in Divine Providence (*hashgacha pratis*) "Chance led me to discover it, and chance served me well"

   ____

   ____

   ____

   ____

3. Who does Conseil refer to (line 144) when he talks about the "Great Architect"?

   ____

4. Why does the Captain go to the lake inside a mountain?

   ____

   ____

   ____

5. What unique item do the trio find on their tour of the inside of the mountain?

   ____

Chapter 11

THE SARGASSO SEA

That day the Nautilus crossed a singular part of the Atlantic Ocean. No one can be ignorant of the existence of a current of warm water known by the name of the Gulf Stream. After leaving the Gulf of Florida, we went in the direction of Spitzbergen. But before entering the Gulf of Mexico, about 45° of N. lat., this current divides into two arms, the principal one going towards the coast of Ireland and Norway, whilst the second bends to the south about the height of the Azores; then, touching the African shore, and describing a lengthened oval, returns to the Antilles. This second arm—it is rather a collar than an arm—surrounds with its circles of warm water that portion of the cold, quiet, immovable ocean called the Sargasso Sea, a perfect lake in the open Atlantic: it takes no less than three years for the great current to pass round it. Such was the region the Nautilus was now visiting, a perfect meadow, a close carpet of seaweed, fucus, and tropical berries, so thick and so compact that the stem of a vessel could hardly tear its way through it. And Captain Nemo, not wishing to entangle his screw in this **herbaceous** mass, kept some yards beneath the surface of the waves. The name Sargasso comes from the Spanish word "sargazzo" which signifies kelp. This kelp, or berry-plant, is the principal formation of this immense bank. And this is the reason why these plants unite in the peaceful basin of the Atlantic. The only explanation which can be given, he says, seems to me to result from the experience known to all the world. Place in a vase some fragments of cork or other floating body, and give to the water in the vase a circular movement, the scattered fragments will unite in a group in the center of the liquid surface, that is to say, in the part least agitated. In the phenomenon we are considering, the Atlantic is the vase, the Gulf Stream the circular current, and the Sargasso Sea the central point at which the floating bodies unite.

I share Maury's opinion, and I was able to study the phenomenon in the very midst, where vessels rarely penetrate. Above us floated

34 products of all kinds, heaped up among these brownish plants;
35 trunks of trees torn from the Andes or the Rocky Mountains,
36 and floated by the Amazon or the Mississippi; numerous wrecks,
37 remains of keels, or ships' bottoms, side-planks stove in, and
38 so weighted with shells and barnacles that they could not again
39 rise to the surface. And time will one day justify Maury's other
40 opinion, that these substances thus accumulated for ages will
41 become petrified by the action of the water and will then form
42 inexhaustible coal-mines—a precious reserve prepared by far-
43 seeing Nature for the moment when men shall have exhausted
44 the mines of continents.

45 In the midst of this **inextricable** mass of plants and sea weed,
46 I noticed some charming pink halcyons and actiniae, with their
47 long tentacles trailing after them, and medusae, green, red, and
48 blue.

49 All the day of the 22nd of February we passed in the Sargasso
50 Sea, where such fish as are partial to marine plants find abundant
51 nourishment. The next, the ocean had returned to its accustomed
52 aspect. From this time for nineteen days, from the 23rd of
53 February to the 12th of March, the Nautilus kept in the middle
54 of the Atlantic, carrying us at a constant speed of a hundred
55 leagues in twenty-four hours. Captain Nemo **evidently** intended
56 accomplishing his submarine program, and I imagined that he
57 intended, after doubling Cape Horn, to return to the Australian
58 seas of the Pacific. Ned Land had cause for fear. In these large
59 seas, void of islands, we could not attempt to leave the boat. Nor
60 had we any means of opposing Captain Nemo's will. Our only
61 course was to submit; but what we could neither gain by force
62 nor **cunning**, I liked to think might be obtained by **persuasion**.
63 This voyage ended, would he not consent to restore our liberty,
64 under an oath never to reveal his existence? —an oath of honor
65 which we should have religiously kept. But we must consider
66 that delicate question with the Captain. But was I free to claim
67 this liberty? Had he not himself said from the beginning, in the
68 firmest manner, that the secret of his life exacted from him our
69 lasting imprisonment on board the Nautilus? And would not my

70 four months' silence appear to him a **tacit** acceptance of our
71 situation? And would not a return to the subject result in raising
72 suspicions which might be hurtful to our projects, if at some
73 future time a favorable opportunity offered to return to them?

74 During the nineteen days mentioned above, no incident of any
75 kind happened to signalize our voyage. I saw little of the Captain;
76 he was at work. In the library I often found his books left open,
77 especially those on natural history. My work on submarine
78 depths, conned over by him, was covered with marginal notes,
79 often contradicting my theories and systems; but the Captain
80 contented himself with thus **purging** my work; it was very rare
81 for him to discuss it with me. Sometimes I heard the **melancholy**
82 tones of his organ; but only at night, in the midst of the deepest
83 **obscurity**, when the Nautilus slept upon the deserted ocean.
84 During this part of our voyage we sailed whole days on the
85 surface of the waves. The sea seemed abandoned. A few sailing-
86 vessels, on the road to India, were making for the Cape of Good
87 Hope. One day we were followed by the boats of a whaler, who,
88 no doubt, took us for some enormous whale of great price; but
89 Captain Nemo did not wish the worthy fellows to lose their time
90 and trouble, so ended the chase by plunging under the water.
91 Our navigation continued until the 13th of March; that day
92 the Nautilus was employed in taking soundings, which greatly
93 interested me. We had then made about 13,000 leagues since our
94 departure from the high seas of the Pacific. The bearings gave
95 us 45° 37' S. lat., and 37° 53' W. long. It was the same water in
96 which Captain Denham of the Herald sounded 7,000 fathoms
97 without finding the bottom. There, too, Lieutenant Parker, of
98 the American frigate Congress, could not touch the bottom with
99 15,140 fathoms. Captain Nemo intended seeking the bottom
100 of the ocean by a diagonal sufficiently lengthened by means of
101 lateral planes placed at an angle of 45° with the water-line of the
102 Nautilus. Then the screw set to work at its maximum speed, its
103 four blades beating the waves with indescribable force. Under
104 this powerful pressure, the hull of the Nautilus quivered like a
105 **sonorous** chord and sank regularly under the water.

At 7,000 fathoms I saw some blackish tops rising from the midst of the waters; but these summits might belong to high mountains like the Himalayas or Mont Blanc, even higher; and the depth of the **abyss** remained **incalculable**. The Nautilus descended still lower, in spite of the great pressure. I felt the steel plates tremble at the fastenings of the bolts; its bars bent, its partitions groaned; the windows of the saloon seemed to curve under the pressure of the waters. And this firm structure would doubtless have yielded, if, as its Captain had said, it had not been capable of resistance like a solid block. We had attained a depth of 16,000 yards (four leagues), and the sides of the Nautilus then bore a pressure of 1,600 atmospheres, that is to say, 3,200 lb. to each square two-fifths of an inch of its surface.

"What a situation to be in!" I exclaimed. "To overrun these deep regions where man has never trod! Look, Captain, look at these magnificent rocks, these uninhabited grottoes, these lowest receptacles of the globe, where life is no longer possible! What unknown sights are here! Why should we be unable to preserve a remembrance of them?"

"Would you like to carry away more than the remembrance?" said Captain Nemo.

"What do you mean by those words?"

"I mean to say that nothing is easier than to make a photographic view of this submarine region."

I had not time to express my surprise at this new proposition, when, at Captain Nemo's call, an objective was brought into the saloon. Through the widely-opened panel, the liquid mass was bright with electricity, which was distributed with such uniformity that not a shadow, not a **gradation**, was to be seen in our manufactured light. The Nautilus remained motionless, the force of its screw subdued by the inclination of its planes: the instrument was propped on the bottom of the oceanic site, and in a few seconds we had obtained a perfect negative.

139 But, the operation being over, Captain Nemo said, "Let us go up;
140 we must not abuse our position, nor expose the Nautilus too long
141 to such great pressure."

142 "Go up again!" I exclaimed.

143 "Hold well on."

144 I had not time to understand why the Captain cautioned me
145 thus, when I was thrown forward on to the carpet. At a signal
146 from the Captain, its screw was shipped, and its blades raised
147 vertically; the Nautilus shot into the air like a balloon, rising
148 with stunning rapidity, and cutting the mass of waters with a
149 sonorous **agitation**. Nothing was visible; and in four minutes
150 it had shot through the four leagues which separated it from the
151 ocean, and, after emerging like a flying-fish, fell, making the
152 waves rebound to an enormous height.

Vocabulary Part 2, Ch. 11

herbaceous, evidently, persuasion, tacit, purging, melancholy, obscurity, sonorous, incalculable, gradation,

Questions Part 2 Ch.11

1. What is the Sargasso Sea? Where is it? What floats in it? What is the theory why it forms?

   ____

   ____

   ____

2. In lines 60-73 the Professor ponders his options of leaving the vessel. He devises a plan but then doubts it. What is his plan, and what makes him think it would not work?

   ____

   ____

   ____

3. In lines 90-110, what does the Captain do when nothing of interest is going on?

   ____

   ____

4. What does the Captain do to preserve the memory of the great oceanic depths?

   ____

   ____

5. Why did the Captain not want to stay long on the bottom of the ocean?

   ____

   ____

6. Why do you think the submarine shot out of the water when rising from the depths?

   ____

   ____

Chapter 12
CACHALOTS AND WHALES

1 **During the nights** of the 13th and 14th of March, the Nautilus
2 returned to its southerly course. I fancied that, when on a level
3 with Cape Horn, he would turn the helm westward, in order to
4 beat the Pacific seas, and so complete the tour of the world. He
5 did nothing of the kind, but continued on his way to the southern
6 regions. Where was he going to? To the pole? It was madness! I
7 began to think that the Captain's **temerity** justified Ned Land's
8 fears. For some time past the Canadian had not spoken to me of
9 his projects of flight; he was less communicative, almost silent. I
10 could see that this lengthened imprisonment was weighing upon
11 him, and I felt that rage was burning within him. When he met
12 the Captain, his eyes lit up with **suppressed** anger; and I feared
13 that his natural violence would lead him into some extreme. That
14 day, the 14th of March, Conseil and he came to me in my room.
15 I inquired the cause of their visit.

16 "A simple question to ask you, sir," replied the Canadian.

17 "Speak, Ned."

18 "How many men are there on board the Nautilus, do you think?"

19 "I cannot tell, my friend."

20 "I should say that its working does not require a large crew."

21 "Certainly, under existing conditions, ten men, at the most,
22 ought to be enough."

23 "Well, why should there be any more?"

24 "Why?" I replied, looking fixedly at Ned Land, whose meaning
25 was easy to guess. "Because," I added, "if my **surmises** are correct,
26 and if I have well understood the Captain's existence, the Nautilus
27 is not only a vessel: it is also a place of refuge for those who, like
28 its commander, have broken every tie upon earth."

29 "Perhaps so," said Conseil; "but, in any case, the Nautilus can only
30 contain a certain number of men. Could not you, sir, estimate
31 their maximum?"

32 "How, Conseil?"

33 "By calculation; given the size of the vessel, which you know,
34 sir, and consequently the quantity of air it contains, knowing
35 also how much each man expends at a breath, and comparing
36 these results with the fact that the Nautilus is obliged to go to the
37 surface every twenty-four hours."

38 Conseil had not finished the sentence before I saw what he was
39 driving at.

40 "I understand," said I; "but that calculation, though simple
41 enough, can give but a very uncertain result."

42 "Never mind," said Ned Land urgently.

43 "Here it is, then," said I. "In one hour each man consumes the
44 oxygen contained in twenty gallons of air; and in twenty-four,
45 that contained in 480 gallons. We must, therefore find how many
46 times 480 gallons of air the Nautilus contains."

47 "Just so," said Conseil.

48 "Or," I continued, "the size of the Nautilus being 1,500 tons; and
49 one ton holding 200 gallons, it contains 300,000 gallons of air,
50 which, divided by 480, gives a quotient of 625. Which means
51 to say, strictly speaking, that the air contained in the Nautilus
52 would suffice for 625 men for twenty-four hours."

53 "Six hundred and twenty-five!" repeated Ned.

54 "But remember that all of us, passengers, sailors, and officers
55 included, would not form a tenth part of that number."

56 "Still too many for three men," murmured Conseil.

57 The Canadian shook his head, passed his hand across his
58 forehead, and left the room without answering.

59 "Will you allow me to make one observation, sir?" said Conseil.
60 "Poor Ned is longing for everything that he can not have. His past
61 life is always present to him; everything that we are forbidden
62 he regrets. His head is full of old **recollections**. And we must
63 understand him. What has he to do here? Nothing; he is not
64 learned like you, sir; and has not the same taste for the beauties
65 of the sea that we have. He would risk everything to be able to go
66 once more into a tavern in his own country."

67 Certainly the **monotony** on board must seem **intolerable** to the
68 Canadian, accustomed as he was to a life of liberty and activity.
69 Events were rare which could **rouse** him to any show of spirit;
70 but that day an event did happen which recalled the bright days
71 of the harpooner. About eleven in the morning, being on the
72 surface of the ocean, the Nautilus fell in with a troop of whales—
73 an encounter which did not astonish me, knowing that these
74 creatures, hunted to death, had taken refuge in high latitudes.

75 We were seated on the platform, with a quiet sea. The month of
76 October in those latitudes gave us some lovely autumnal days.
77 It was the Canadian—he could not be mistaken—who signaled
78 a whale on the eastern horizon. Looking attentively, one might
79 see its black back rise and fall with the waves five miles from the
80 Nautilus.

81 "Ah!" exclaimed Ned Land, "if I was on board a whaler, now such
82 a meeting would give me pleasure. It is one of large size. See with
83 what strength its blow-holes throw up columns of air and steam!
84 Confound it, why am I bound to these steel plates?"

85 "What, Ned," said I, "you have not forgotten your old ideas of
86 fishing?"

87 "Can a whale-fisher ever forget his old trade, sir? Can he ever tire
88 of the emotions caused by such a chase?"

89 "You have never fished in these seas, Ned?"

90 "Never, sir; in the northern only, and as much in Behring as in
91 Davis Straits."

92 "Then the southern whale is still unknown to you. It is the
93 Greenland whale you have hunted up to this time, and that would
94 not risk passing through the warm waters of the equator. Whales
95 are localized, according to their kinds, in certain seas which they
96 never leave. And if one of these creatures went from Behring to
97 Davis Straits, it must be simply because there is a passage from
98 one sea to the other, either on the American or the Asiatic side."

99 "In that case, as I have never fished in these seas, I do not know
100 the kind of whale frequenting them!"

101 "I have told you, Ned."

102 "A greater reason for making their acquaintance," said Conseil.

103 "Look! look!" exclaimed the Canadian, "they approach: they
104 aggravate me; they know that I cannot get at them!"

105 Ned stamped his feet. His hand trembled, as he grasped an
106 imaginary harpoon.

107 "Are these cetaceans as large as those of the northern seas?"
108 asked he.

109 "Very nearly, Ned."

110 "Because I have seen large whales, sir, whales measuring a
111 hundred feet. I have even been told that those of Hullamoch and
112 Umgallick, of the Aleutian Islands, are sometimes a hundred and
113 fifty feet long."

114 "That seems to me exaggeration. These creatures are only
115 balaeaopterons, provided with dorsal fins; and, like the cachalots,
116 are generally much smaller than the Greenland whale."

117 "Ah!" exclaimed the Canadian, whose eyes had never left the
118 ocean, "they are coming nearer; they are in the same water as the
119 Nautilus."

120 Then, returning to the conversation, he said:

121 "You spoke of the cachalot as a small creature. I have heard of

gigantic ones. They are intelligent cetacea. It is said of some that they cover themselves with seaweed and fucus, and then are taken for islands. People encamp upon them, and settle there; lights a fire——"

"And build houses," said Conseil.

"Yes, joker," said Ned Land. "And one fine day the creature plunges, carrying with it all the inhabitants to the bottom of the sea."

"Something like the travels of Sinbad the Sailor," I replied, laughing.

"Ah!" suddenly exclaimed Ned Land, "it is not one whale; there are ten—there are twenty—it is a whole troop! And I not able to do anything! hands and feet tied!"

"But, friend Ned," said Conseil, "why do you not ask Captain Nemo's permission to chase them?"

Conseil had not finished his sentence when Ned Land had lowered himself through the panel to seek the Captain. A few minutes afterwards the two appeared together on the platform.

Captain Nemo watched the troop of cetacea playing on the waters about a mile from the Nautilus.

"They are southern whales," said he; "there goes the fortune of a whole fleet of whalers."

"Well, sir," asked the Canadian, "can I not chase them, if only to remind me of my old trade of harpooner?"

"And to what purpose?" replied Captain Nemo; "only to destroy! We have nothing to do with the whale-oil on board."

"But, sir," continued the Canadian, "in the Red Sea you allowed us to follow the dugong."

"Then it was to procure fresh meat for my crew. Here it would be killing for killing's sake. I know that is a privilege reserved for man, but I do not approve of such murderous pastime. In destroying the southern whale (like the Greenland whale, an inoffensive creature), your traders do a **culpable** action, Master Land. They have already **depopulated** the whole of Baffin's Bay, and are **annihilating** a class of useful animals. Leave the unfortunate cetacea alone. They have plenty of natural enemies—cachalots, swordfish, and sawfish—without you troubling them."

The Captain was right. The **barbarous** and **inconsiderate greed** of these fishermen will one day cause the disappearance of the last whale in the ocean. Ned Land whistled "Yankee-doodle" between his teeth, thrust his hands into his pockets, and turned his back upon us. But Captain Nemo watched the troop of cetacea, and, addressing me, said:

"I was right in saying that whales had natural enemies enough, without counting man. These will have plenty to do before long. Do you see, M. Aronnax, about eight miles to leeward, those blackish moving points?"

"Yes, Captain," I replied.

"Those are cachalots[68]—terrible animals, which I have met in troops of two or three hundred. As to those, they are cruel, mischievous creatures; they would be right in exterminating them."

The Canadian turned quickly at the last words.

"Well, Captain," said he, "it is still time, in the interest of the whales."

"It is useless to expose one's self, Professor. The Nautilus will **disperse** them. It is armed with a steel spur as good as Master Land's harpoon, I imagine."

The Canadian did not put himself out enough to shrug his shoulders. Attack cetacea with blows of a spur! Who had ever heard of such a thing?

68   Is called the sperm whale and is the largest of the toothed whales and the largest toothed predator.

183 "Wait, M. Aronnax," said Captain Nemo. "We will show you
184 something you have never yet seen. We have no pity for these
185 ferocious creatures. They are nothing but mouth and teeth."

186 Mouth and teeth! No one could better describe the
187 macrocephalous[69] cachalot, which is sometimes more than
188 seventy-five feet long. Its enormous head occupies one-third of
189 its entire body. Better armed than the whale, whose upper jaw is
190 furnished only with whalebone, it is supplied with twenty-five
191 large tusks, about eight inches long, cylindrical and conical at
192 the top, each weighing two pounds. It is in the upper part of this
193 enormous head, in great cavities divided by cartilages, that is to be
194 found from six to eight hundred pounds of that precious oil called
195 spermaceti. The cachalot is a disagreeable creature, more tadpole
196 than fish, according to Fredol's description. It is badly formed,
197 the whole of its left side being (if we may say it), a "failure," and
198 being only able to see with its right eye. But the formidable troop
199 was nearing us. They had seen the whales and were preparing
200 to attack them. One could judge beforehand that the cachalots
201 would be victorious, not only because they were better built for
202 attack than their inoffensive adversaries, but also because they
203 could remain longer under water without coming to the surface.
204 There was only just time to go to the help of the whales. The
205 Nautilus went under water. Conseil, Ned Land, and I took our
206 places before the window in the saloon, and Captain Nemo
207 joined the pilot in his cage to work his apparatus as an engine
208 of destruction. Soon I felt the beatings of the screw quicken, and
209 our speed increased. The battle between the cachalots and the
210 whales had already begun when the Nautilus arrived. They did
211 not at first show any fear at the sight of this new monster joining
212 in the conflict. But they soon had to guard against its blows. What
213 a battle! The Nautilus was nothing but a formidable harpoon,
214 brandished by the hand of its Captain. It hurled itself against the
215 fleshy mass, passing through from one part to the other, leaving
216 behind it two **quivering** halves of the animal. It could not feel the
217 formidable blows from their tails upon its sides, nor the shock
218 which it produced itself, much more. One cachalot killed, it ran at

69	having or being an exceptionally large head or cranium.

219 the next, tacked on the spot that it might not miss its prey, going
220 forwards and backwards, answering to its helm, plunging when
221 the cetacean dived into the deep waters, coming up with it when
222 it returned to the surface, striking it front or sideways, cutting or
223 tearing in all directions and at any pace, piercing it with its terrible
224 spur. What carnage! What a noise on the surface of the waves!
225 What sharp hissing, and what snorting peculiar to these enraged
226 animals! In the midst of these waters, generally so peaceful, their
227 tails made perfect billows. For one hour this wholesale massacre
228 continued, from which the cachalots could not escape. Several
229 times ten or twelve united tried to crush the Nautilus by their
230 weight. From the window we could see their enormous mouths,
231 studded with tusks, and their formidable eyes. Ned Land could
232 not contain himself; he threatened and swore at them. We could
233 feel them clinging to our vessel like dogs worrying a wild boar in
234 a copse. But the Nautilus, working its screw, carried them here
235 and there, or to the upper levels of the ocean, without caring for
236 their enormous weight, nor the powerful strain on the vessel. At
237 length the mass of cachalots broke up, the waves became quiet,
238 and I felt that we were rising to the surface. The panel opened,
239 and we hurried on to the platform. The sea was covered with
240 mutilated bodies. A formidable explosion could not have divided
241 and torn this fleshy mass with more violence. We were floating
242 amid gigantic bodies, bluish on the back and white underneath,
243 covered with enormous **protuberances**. Some terrified cachalots
244 were flying towards the horizon. The waves were dyed red for
245 several miles, and the Nautilus floated in a sea of blood: Captain
246 Nemo joined us.

247 "Well, Master Land?" said he.

248 "Well, sir," replied the Canadian, whose enthusiasm had
249 somewhat calmed; "it is a terrible spectacle, certainly. But I am
250 not a butcher. I am a hunter, and I call this a butchery."

251 "It is a massacre of **mischievous** creatures," replied the Captain;
252 "and the Nautilus is not a butcher's knife."

253 "I like my harpoon better," said the Canadian.

"Every one to his own," answered the Captain, looking fixedly at Ned Land.

I feared he would commit some act of violence, which would end in sad consequences. But his anger was turned by the sight of a whale which the Nautilus had just come up with. The creature had not quite escaped from the cachalot's teeth. I recognized the southern whale by its flat head, which is entirely black. **Anatomically**, it is distinguished from the white whale and the North Cape whale by the seven cervical vertebrae, and it has two more ribs than its congeners. The unfortunate cetacean was lying on its side, riddled with holes from the bites, and quite dead. From its **mutilated** fin still hung a young whale which it could not save from the massacre. Its open mouth let the water flow in and out, murmuring like the waves breaking on the shore. Captain Nemo steered close to the corpse of the creature. Two of his men mounted its side, and I saw, not without surprise, that they were drawing from its..milk.., that is to say, about two or three tons. The Captain offered me a cup of the milk, which was still warm. I could not help showing my **repugnance** to the drink; but he assured me that it was excellent, and not to be distinguished from cow's milk. I tasted it, and was of his opinion. It was a useful reserve to us, for in the shape of salt butter or cheese it would form an agreeable variety from our ordinary food. From that day I noticed with uneasiness that Ned Land's ill-will towards Captain Nemo increased, and I resolved to watch the Canadian's gestures closely.

Vocabulary Part 2 Ch. 12

temerity, suppressed, surmises, recollections, monotony, intolerable, rouse, culpable, annihilating, barbarous, inconsiderate, greed, disperse, quivering, protuberances, mischievous, Anatomically, mutilated, repugnance

Questions Part 2 Ch. 12

1. What two high school subjects does the Professor use to estimate the maximum crew onboard the Nautilus?

2. What does Conseil say is the cause of Ned Land's distress for being on the vessel (lines 60-66)

3. In what way is the Professor so much more fitting for this voyage than Ned Land? Based on your answer, why do you think the author added a character like Ned Land to the story?

4. Why does the Captain at first not wish to give Ned Land any chance to kill the whales? From the perspective of Judaism, does the Captain have a point? Why or why not?

5. How does the Captain seem to "play Hashem" in lines 144-158? Who in the end disagrees with the Captain? Do you agree with the Captain here? Why or why not?

6. In lines (272-274) the Professor, when offered the whale's milk, says, " I could not help showing my repugnance to the drink; but he assured me that it was excellent, and not to be distinguished from cow's milk." Why do you think the milk repulsed him?

Chapter 13

THE ICEBERG

1 **The Nautilus was** steadily pursuing its southerly course,
following the fiftieth meridian with considerable speed. Did
he wish to reach the pole? I did not think so, for every attempt
to reach that point had **hitherto** failed. Again, the season was
far advanced, for in the Antarctic regions the 13th of March
corresponds with the 13th of September of northern regions,
which begin at the equinoctial[70] season. On the 14th of March I
saw floating ice in latitude 55°, merely pale bits of debris from
twenty to twenty-five feet long, forming banks over which the
sea curled. The Nautilus remained on the surface of the ocean.
Ned Land, who had fished in the Arctic Seas, was familiar with
its icebergs; but Conseil and I admired them for the first time. In
the atmosphere towards the southern horizon stretched a white
dazzling band. English whalers have given it the name of "ice
blink." However thick the clouds may be, it is always visible,
and announces the presence of an ice pack or bank. Accordingly,
larger blocks soon appeared, whose brilliancy changed with the
caprices of the fog. Some of these masses showed green veins,
as if long undulating lines had been traced with sulphate of
copper; others resembled enormous amethysts[71] with the light
shining through them. Some reflected the light of day upon a
thousand crystal facets. Others shaded with **vivid** calcareous[72]
reflections resembled a perfect town of marble. The more we
neared the south the more these floating islands increased both
in number and importance.

At 60° lat. every pass had disappeared. But, seeking carefully,
Captain Nemo soon found a narrow opening, through which he
boldly slipped, knowing, however, that it would close behind
him. Thus, guided by this clever hand, the Nautilus passed
through all the ice with a precision which quite charmed Conseil;

---

70   happening at or near the time of an equinox
71   Amethyst is a violet variety of quartz
72   containing calcium carbonate; chalky.

31 icebergs or mountains, ice-fields or smooth plains, seeming to
32 have no limits, drift-ice or floating ice-packs, plains broken up,
33 called palchs when they are circular, and streams when they
34 are made up of long strips. The temperature was very low; the
35 thermometer exposed to the air marked 2 deg. or 3° below zero,
36 but we were warmly clad with fur, at the expense of the sea-
37 bear and seal. The interior of the Nautilus, warmed regularly by
38 its electric apparatus, **defied** the most intense cold. Besides, it
39 would only have been necessary to go some yards beneath the
40 waves to find a more bearable temperature. Two months earlier
41 we should have had **perpetual** daylight in these latitudes; but
42 already we had had three or four hours of night, and by and
43 by there would be six months of darkness in these circumpolar
44 regions. On the 15th of March we were in the latitude of New
45 Shetland and South Orkney. The Captain told me that formerly
46 numerous tribes of seals inhabited them; but that English and
47 American whalers, in their rage for destruction, massacred both
48 old and young; thus, where there was once life and animation,
49 they had left silence and death.

50 About eight o'clock on the morning of the 16th of March the
51 Nautilus, following the fifty-fifth meridian, cut the Antarctic
52 polar circle. Ice surrounded us on all sides, and closed the horizon.
53 But Captain Nemo went from one opening to another, still going
54 higher. I cannot express my astonishment at the beauties of
55 these new regions. The ice took most surprising forms. Here the
56 grouping formed an oriental town, with innumerable mosques
57 and minarets; there a fallen city thrown to the earth, as it were,
58 by some **convulsion** of nature. The whole aspect was constantly
59 changed by the oblique rays of the sun, or lost in the greyish
60 fog amidst hurricanes of snow. **Detonations** and falls were
61 heard on all sides, great overthrows of icebergs, which altered
62 the whole landscape like a diorama[73]. Often seeing no exit, I
63 thought we were definitely prisoners; but, instinct guiding him
64 at the slightest **indication**, Captain Nemo would discover a new
65 pass. He was never mistaken when he saw the thin threads of

____

73   a model representing a scene with three-dimensional figures,
either in miniature or as a large-scale museum exhibit.

66 bluish water trickling along the ice-fields; and I had no doubt
67 that he had already ventured into the midst of these Antarctic
68 seas before. On the 16th of March, however, the ice-fields
69 absolutely blocked our road. It was not the iceberg itself, as yet,
70 but vast fields cemented by the cold. But this obstacle could not
71 stop Captain Nemo: he hurled himself against it with frightful
72 violence. The Nautilus entered the **brittle** mass like a wedge,
73 and split it with frightful crackings. It was the battering ram of
74 the ancients hurled by infinite strength. The ice, thrown high in
75 the air, fell like hail around us. By its own power of **impulsion**
76 our apparatus made a canal for itself; sometimes carried away
77 by its own **impetus**, it lodged on the ice-field, crushing it with
78 its weight, and sometimes buried beneath it, dividing it by a
79 simple pitching movement, producing large **rents** in it. Violent
80 **gales assailed** us at this time, accompanied by thick fogs,
81 through which, from one end of the platform to the other, we
82 could see nothing. The wind blew sharply from all parts of the
83 compass, and the snow lay in such hard heaps that we had to
84 break it with blows of a pickaxe. The temperature was always
85 at 5 deg. below zero; every outward part of the Nautilus was
86 covered with ice. A rigged vessel would have been entangled in
87 the blocked up gorges. A vessel without sails, with electricity
88 for its **motive** power, and wanting no coal, could alone brave
89 such high latitudes. At length, on the 18th of March, after many
90 useless assaults, the Nautilus was positively blocked. It was no
91 longer either streams, packs, or ice-fields, but an **interminable**
92 and immovable barrier, formed by mountains soldered together.

93 "An iceberg!" said the Canadian to me.

94 I knew that to Ned Land, as well as to all other navigators
95 who had preceded us, this was an **inevitable** obstacle. The
96 sun appearing for an instant at noon, Captain Nemo took an
97 observation as near as possible, which gave our situation at 51°
98 30' long. and 67° 39' of S. lat. We had advanced one degree
99 more in this Antarctic region. Of the liquid surface of the sea
100 there was no longer a glimpse. Under the spur of the Nautilus
101 lay stretched a vast plain, entangled with confused blocks. Here

102 and there sharp points and slender needles rising to a height of
103 200 feet; further on a steep shore, hewn as it were with an axe
104 and clothed with greyish tints; huge mirrors, reflecting a few
105 rays of sunshine, half drowned in the fog. And over this desolate
106 face of nature a stern silence reigned, scarcely broken by the
107 flapping of the wings of petrels and puffins. Everything was
108 frozen—even the noise. The Nautilus was then obliged to stop
109 in its adventurous course amid these fields of ice. In spite of our
110 efforts, in spite of the powerful means employed to break up
111 the ice, the Nautilus remained immovable. Generally, when we
112 can proceed no further, we have return still open to us; but here
113 return was as impossible as advance, for every pass had closed
114 behind us; and for the few moments when we were stationary,
115 we were likely to be entirely blocked, which did indeed happen
116 about two o'clock in the afternoon, the fresh ice forming around
117 its sides with astonishing rapidity. I was obliged to admit that
118 Captain Nemo was more than **imprudent**. I was on the platform
119 at that moment. The Captain had been observing our situation
120 for some time past, when he said to me:

121 "Well, sir, what do you think of this?"

122 "I think that we are caught, Captain."

123 "So, M. Aronnax, you really think that the Nautilus cannot
124 disengage itself?"

125 "With difficulty, Captain; for the season is already too far
126 advanced for you to **reckon** on the breaking of the ice."

127 "Ah! sir," said Captain Nemo, in an ironical tone, "you will
128 always be the same. You see nothing but difficulties and
129 obstacles. I affirm that not only can the Nautilus disengage itself,
130 but also that it can go further still."

131 "Further to the South?" I asked, looking at the Captain.

132 "Yes, sir; it shall go to the pole."

133 "To the pole!" I exclaimed, unable to repress a gesture of

134   incredulity.

135   "Yes," replied the Captain, coldly, "to the Antarctic pole—to
136   that unknown point from whence springs every meridian of the
137   globe. You know whether I can do as I please with the Nautilus!"

138   Yes, I knew that. I knew that this man was bold, even to
139   **rashness**. But to conquer those obstacles which **bristled** round
140   the South Pole, rendering it more inaccessible than the North,
141   which had not yet been reached by the boldest navigators—was
142   it not a mad enterprise, one which only a **maniac** would have
143   conceived? It then came into my head to ask Captain Nemo if he
144   had ever discovered that pole which had never yet been **trodden**
145   by a human creature?

146   "No, sir," he replied; "but we will discover it together. Where
147   others have failed, I will not fail. I have never yet led my Nautilus
148   so far into southern seas; but, I repeat, it shall go further yet."

149   "I can well believe you, Captain," said I, in a slightly ironical
150   tone. "I believe you! Let us go ahead! There are no obstacles for
151   us! Let us smash this iceberg! Let us blow it up; and, if it resists,
152   let us give the Nautilus wings to fly over it!"

153   "Over it, sir!" said Captain Nemo, quietly; "no, not over it, but
154   under it!"

155   "Under it!" I exclaimed, a sudden idea of the Captain's projects
156   flashing upon my mind. I understood; the wonderful qualities
157   of the Nautilus were going to serve us in this superhuman
158   enterprise.

159   "I see we are beginning to understand one another, sir," said the
160   Captain, half smiling. "You begin to see the possibility—I should
161   say the success—of this attempt. That which is impossible for an
162   ordinary vessel is easy to the Nautilus. If a continent lies before
163   the pole, it must stop before the continent; but if, on the contrary,
164   the pole is washed by open sea, it will go even to the pole."

165   "Certainly," said I, carried away by the Captain's reasoning; "if

166 the surface of the sea is solidified by the ice, the lower depths
167 are free by the Providential law which has placed the maximum
168 of density of the waters of the ocean one degree higher than
169 freezing-point; and, if I am not mistaken, the portion of this
170 iceberg which is above the water is as one to four to that which
171 is below."

172 "Very nearly, sir; for one foot of iceberg above the sea there are
173 three below it. If these ice mountains are not more than 300 feet
174 above the surface, they are not more than 900 beneath. And what
175 are 900 feet to the Nautilus?"

176 "Nothing, sir."

177 "It could even seek at greater depths that uniform temperature
178 of sea-water, and there brave with **impunity** the thirty or forty
179 degrees of surface cold."

180 "Just so, sir—just so," I replied, getting **animated**.

181 "The only difficulty," continued Captain Nemo, "is that of
182 remaining several days without renewing our provision of air."

183 "Is that all? The Nautilus has vast reservoirs; we can fill them,
184 and they will supply us with all the oxygen we want."

185 "Well thought of, M. Aronnax," replied the Captain, smiling.
186 "But, not wishing you to accuse me of rashness, I will first give
187 you all my objections."

188 "Have you any more to make?"

189 "Only one. It is possible, if the sea exists at the South Pole, that it
190 may be covered; and, consequently, we shall be unable to come
191 to the surface."

192 "Good, sir! but do you forget that the Nautilus is armed with a
193 powerful spur, and could we not send it diagonally against these
194 fields of ice, which would open at the shocks."

195 "Ah! sir, you are full of ideas to-day."

196 "Besides, Captain," I added, enthusiastically, "why should we
197 not find the sea open at the South Pole as well as at the North?
198 The frozen poles of the earth do not coincide, either in the
199 southern or in the northern regions; and, until it is proved to the
200 **contrary**, we may suppose either a continent or an ocean free
201 from ice at these two points of the globe."

202 "I think so too, M. Aronnax," replied Captain Nemo. "I only
203 wish you to observe that, after having made so many objections
204 to my project, you are now crushing me with arguments in its
205 favor!"

206 The preparations for this **audacious** attempt now began. The
207 powerful pumps of the Nautilus were working air into the
208 reservoirs and storing it at high pressure. About four o'clock,
209 Captain Nemo announced the closing of the panels on the
210 platform. I threw one last look at the massive iceberg which we
211 were going to cross. The weather was clear, the atmosphere pure
212 enough, the cold very great, being 12° below zero; but, the wind
213 having gone down, this temperature was not so unbearable. About
214 ten men mounted the sides of the Nautilus, armed with pickaxes
215 to break the ice around the vessel, which was soon free. The
216 operation was quickly performed, for the fresh ice was still very
217 thin. We all went below. The usual reservoirs were filled with
218 the newly-liberated water, and the Nautilus soon descended. I
219 had taken my place with Conseil in the saloon; through the open
220 window we could see the lower beds of the Southern Ocean.
221 The thermometer went up, the needle of the compass **deviated**
222 on the dial. At about 900 feet, as Captain Nemo had foreseen,
223 we were floating beneath the undulating bottom of the iceberg.
224 But the Nautilus went lower still—it went to the depth of four
225 hundred fathoms. The temperature of the water at the surface
226 showed twelve degrees, it was now only ten; we had gained two.
227 I need not say the temperature of the Nautilus was raised by its
228 heating apparatus to a much higher degree; every maneuver was
229 accomplished with wonderful precision.

230 "We shall pass it, if you please, sir," said Conseil.

231 "I believe we shall," I said, in a tone of firm conviction.

232 In this open sea, the Nautilus had taken its course direct to the
233 pole, without leaving the fifty-second meridian. From 67° 30'
234 to 90 deg., twenty-two degrees and a half of latitude remained
235 to travel; that is, about five hundred leagues. The Nautilus kept
236 up a mean speed of twenty-six miles an hour—the speed of an
237 express train. If that was kept up, in forty hours we should reach
238 the pole.

239 For a part of the night the novelty of the situation kept us at
240 the window. The sea was lit with the electric lantern; but it was
241 deserted; fishes did not sojourn in these imprisoned waters;
242 they only found there a passage to take them from the Antarctic
243 Ocean to the open polar sea. Our pace was rapid; we could feel
244 it by the **quivering** of the long steel body. About two in the
245 morning I took some hours' repose, and Conseil did the same. In
246 crossing the waist I did not meet Captain Nemo: I supposed him
247 to be in the pilot's cage. The next morning, the 19th of March, I
248 took my post once more in the saloon. The electric log told me
249 that the speed of the Nautilus had been slackened. It was then
250 going towards the surface; but prudently emptying its reservoirs
251 very slowly. My heart beat fast. Were we going to emerge and
252 regain the open polar atmosphere? No! A shock told me that the
253 Nautilus had struck the bottom of the iceberg, still very thick,
254 judging from the deadened sound. We had in deed "struck," to
255 use a sea expression, but in an inverse sense, and at a thousand
256 feet deep. This would give three thousand feet of ice above us;
257 one thousand being above the water-mark. The iceberg was then
258 higher than at its borders—not a very reassuring fact. Several
259 times that day the Nautilus tried again, and every time it struck
260 the wall which lay like a ceiling above it. Sometimes it met with
261 but 900 yards, only 200 of which rose above the surface. It was
262 twice the height it was when the Nautilus had gone under the
263 waves. I carefully noted the different depths, and thus obtained
264 a submarine profile of the chain as it was developed under the
265 water. That night no change had taken place in our situation.
266 Still ice between four and five hundred yards in depth! It was

evidently diminishing, but, still, what a thickness between us and the surface of the ocean! It was then eight. According to the daily custom on board the Nautilus, its air should have been renewed four hours ago; but I did not suffer much, although Captain Nemo had not yet made any demand upon his reserve of oxygen. My sleep was painful that night; hope and fear besieged me by turns: I rose several times. The groping of the Nautilus continued. About three in the morning, I noticed that the lower surface of the iceberg was only about fifty feet deep. One hundred and fifty feet now separated us from the surface of the waters. The iceberg was by degrees becoming an ice-field, the mountain a plain. My eyes never left the manometer. We were still rising diagonally to the surface, which sparkled under the electric rays. The iceberg was stretching both above and beneath into lengthening slopes; mile after mile it was getting thinner. At length, at six in the morning of that memorable day, the 19th of March, the door of the saloon opened, and Captain Nemo appeared.

"The sea is open!!" was all he said.

𝔙𝔬𝔠𝔞𝔟𝔲𝔩𝔞𝔯𝔶 𝔓𝔯𝔱 2 𝔠𝔥. 13

vivid, defied, perpetual, convulsion, detonation, indication, brittle, impulsion, impetus, rents, gales, assailed, interminable, inevitable

Questions Part 2 Ch. 13

1. What is the difference between an ice bank and an ice field?

2. Where does Captain Nemo plan to go to?

3. What does the Professor think about Captain Nemo's plan to go to the south Pole?

4. What does the metaphor in lines 73-74, "It was the battering ram of the ancients hurled by infinite strength", refer to?

5. Does the Professor think the South Pole is a solid continent or an open sea?

6. In lines 146-47, Captain Nemo says: "Where others have failed, I will not fail". What does this line tell us about his character?

7. What does the "Providential law", alluded to in line 167, mean?

8. What is the danger(s) of going to the pole?

9. How does a Torah Jew think about putting oneself in

danger for the sake of knowledge?

Chapter 14

THE SOUTH POLE

1 **I rushed on** to the platform. Yes! the open sea, with but a few
2 scattered pieces of ice and moving icebergs—a long stretch of
3 sea; a world of birds in the air, and myriads of fishes under those
4 waters, which varied from intense blue to olive green, according
5 to the bottom. The thermometer marked 3° C. above zero. It was
6 **comparatively** spring, shut up as we were behind this iceberg,
7 whose lengthened mass was dimly seen on our northern horizon.

8 "Are we at the pole?" I asked the Captain, with a beating heart.

9 "I do not know," he replied. "At noon I will take our bearings."

10 "But will the sun show himself through this fog?" said I, looking
11 at the **leaden** sky.

12 "However little it shows, it will be enough," replied the Captain.

13 About ten miles south a **solitary** island rose to a height of one
14 hundred and four yards. We made for it, but carefully, for the sea
15 might be strewn with banks. One hour afterwards we had reached
16 it, two hours later we had made the round of it. It measured
17 four or five miles in circumference. A narrow canal separated
18 it from a considerable stretch of land, perhaps a continent, for
19 we could not see its limits. The existence of this land seemed
20 to give some color to Maury's theory. The **ingenious** American
21 has remarked that, between the South Pole and the sixtieth
22 parallel, the sea is covered with floating ice of enormous size,
23 which is never met with in the North Atlantic. From this fact
24 he has drawn the conclusion that the Antarctic Circle **encloses**
25 considerable continents, as icebergs cannot form in open sea,
26 but only on the coasts. According to these calculations, the
27 mass of ice surrounding the southern pole forms a vast cap, the
28 circumference of which must be, at least, 2,500 miles. But the
29 Nautilus, for fear of running aground, had stopped about three
30 cable-lengths from a strand over which reared a superb heap

31 of rocks. The boat was launched; the Captain, two of his men,
32 bearing instruments, Conseil, and myself were in it. It was ten in
33 the morning. I had not seen Ned Land. Doubtless the Canadian
34 did not wish to admit the presence of the South Pole. A few
35 strokes of the oar brought us to the sand, where we ran ashore.
36 Conseil was going to jump on to the land, when I held him back.

37 "Sir," said I to Captain Nemo, "to you belongs the honor of first
38 setting foot on this land."

39 "Yes, sir," said the Captain, "and if I do not hesitate to tread this
40 South Pole, it is because, up to this time, no human being has
41 left a trace there."

42 Saying this, he jumped lightly on to the sand. His heart beat with
43 emotion. He climbed a rock, sloping to a little promontory[74],
44 and there, with his arms crossed, mute and motionless, and with
45 an eager look, he seemed to take possession of these southern
46 regions. After five minutes passed in this ecstasy, he turned to
47 us.

48 "When you like, sir."

49 I landed, followed by Conseil, leaving the two men in the boat.
50 For a long way the soil was composed of a reddish sandy stone,
51 something like crushed brick, scoriae, streams of lava, and
52 pumice-stones. One could not mistake its volcanic origin. In
53 some parts, slight curls of smoke emitted a sulphureous smell,
54 proving that the internal fires had lost nothing of their expansive
55 powers, though, having climbed a high acclivity[75], I could see
56 no volcano for a radius of several miles. We know that in those
57 Antarctic countries, James Ross found two craters, the Erebus
58 and Terror, in full activity, on the 167th meridian, latitude 77°
59 32'. The vegetation of this desolate continent seemed to me
60 much restricted…

61 There appeared on the high bottoms some coral shrubs, of the

74   a point of high land that juts out into a large body of water; a
headland.
75   an upward slope

62 kind which, according to James Ross, live in the Antarctic seas
63 to the depth of more than 1,000 yards. Then there were little
64 kingfishers and starfish studding the soil. But where life abounded
65 most was in the air. There thousands of birds fluttered and flew
66 of all kinds, deafening us with their cries; others crowded the
67 rock, looking at us as we passed by without fear, and pressing
68 familiarly close by our feet. There were penguins, so agile in
69 the water, heavy and awkward as they are on the ground; they
70 were uttering harsh cries, a large assembly, sober in gesture, but
71 extravagant in clamor. Albatrosses passed in the air, the expanse
72 of their wings being at least four yards and a half, and justly
73 called the vultures of the ocean; some gigantic petrels, and some
74 damiers, a kind of small duck, the underpart of whose body is
75 black and white; then there were a whole series of petrels, some
76 whitish, with brown-bordered wings, others blue, peculiar to the
77 Antarctic seas, and so oily, as I told Conseil, that the inhabitants
78 of the Ferroe Islands had nothing to do before lighting them but
79 to put a wick in.

80 "A little more," said Conseil, "and they would be perfect lamps!
81 After that, we cannot expect Nature to have previously furnished
82 them with wicks!"

83 About half a mile farther on the soil was riddled with ruffs' nests,
84 a sort of laying-ground, out of which many birds were issuing.
85 Captain Nemo had some hundreds hunted. They uttered a cry…
86 were about the size of a goose, slate-color on the body, white
87 beneath, with a yellow line round their throats; they allowed
88 themselves to be killed with a stone, never trying to escape. But
89 the fog did not lift, and at eleven the sun had not yet shown itself.
90 Its absence made me uneasy. Without it no observations were
91 possible. How, then, could we decide whether we had reached
92 the pole? When I rejoined Captain Nemo, I found him leaning on
93 a piece of rock, silently watching the sky. He seemed impatient
94 and **vexed**. But what was to be done? This rash and powerful
95 man could not command the sun as he did the sea. Noon arrived
96 without the orb of day showing itself for an instant. We could
97 not even tell its position behind the curtain of fog; and soon the

98   fog turned to snow.

99   "Till to-morrow," said the Captain, quietly, and we returned to
100 the Nautilus amid these atmospheric disturbances.

101 The tempest of snow continued till the next day. It was impossible
102 to remain on the platform. From the saloon, where I was taking
103 notes of incidents happening during this excursion to the polar
104 continent, I could hear the cries of petrels and albatrosses
105 sporting in the midst of this violent storm. The Nautilus did not
106 remain motionless, but skirted the coast, advancing ten miles
107 more to the south in the half-light left by the sun as it skirted
108 the edge of the horizon. The next day, the 20th of March, the
109 snow had ceased. The cold was a little greater, the thermometer
110 showing 2° below zero. The fog was rising, and I hoped that that
111 day our observations might be taken. Captain Nemo not having
112 yet appeared, the boat took Conseil and myself to land. The soil
113 was still of the same volcanic nature; everywhere were traces of
114 lava, scoriae, and basalt; but the crater which had vomited them
115 I could not see. Here, as lower down, this continent was alive
116 with myriads of birds. But their rule was now divided with large
117 troops of sea-mammals, looking at us with their soft eyes. There
118 were several kinds of seals, some stretched on the earth, some
119 on flakes of ice, many going in and out of the sea. They did not
120 flee at our approach, never having had anything to do with man;
121 and I reckoned that there were provisions there for hundreds of
122 vessels.

123 "Sir," said Conseil, "will you tell me the names of these
124 creatures?"

125 "They are seals and morses."

126 It was now eight in the morning. Four hours remained to us
127 before the sun could be observed with advantage. I directed our
128 steps towards a vast bay cut in the steep granite shore. There,
129 I can aver that earth and ice were lost to sight by the numbers
130 of sea-mammals covering them… There were more seals than
131 anything else, forming distinct groups, male and female, the

132 father watching over his family, the mother suckling her little
133 ones, some already strong enough to go a few steps. When they
134 wished to change their place, they took little jumps, made by the
135 contraction of their bodies, and helped awkwardly enough by
136 their imperfect fin, which, as with the lamantin, their cousins,
137 forms a perfect forearm. I should say that, in the water, which
138 is their element—the spine of these creatures is flexible; with
139 smooth and close skin and webbed feet—they swim admirably.
140 In resting on the earth they take the most graceful attitudes…I
141 made Conseil notice the considerable development of the lobes
142 of the brain in these interesting cetaceans. No mammal, except
143 man, has such a quantity of brain matter; they are also capable of
144 receiving a certain amount of education, are easily domesticated,
145 and I think, with other naturalists, that if properly taught they
146 would be of great service as fishing-dogs. The greater part of
147 them slept on the rocks or on the sand. Amongst these seals,
148 properly so called, which have no external ears (in which they
149 differ from the otter, whose ears are prominent), I noticed several
150 varieties of seals about three yards long, with a white coat,
151 bulldog heads, armed with teeth in both jaws, four incisors at
152 the top and four at the bottom, and two large canine teeth in the
153 shape of a fleur-de-lis[76]. Amongst them glided sea-elephants, a
154 kind of seal, with short, flexible trunks. The giants of this species
155 measured twenty feet round and ten yards and a half in length;
156 but they did not move as we approached.

157 "These creatures are not dangerous?" asked Conseil.

158 "No; not unless you attack them. When they have to defend their
159 young their rage is terrible, and it is not uncommon for them to
160 break the fishing-boats to pieces."

161 "They are quite right," said Conseil.

162 "I do not say they are not."

163 Two miles farther on we were stopped by the promontory which

---

76   a stylized lily composed of three petals bound together near their
bases

164 shelters the bay from the southerly winds. Beyond it we heard
165 loud bellowings such as a troop of **ruminants** would produce.

166 "Good!" said Conseil; "a concert of bulls!"

167 "No; a concert of morses."

168 "They are fighting!"

169 "They are either fighting or playing."

170 We now began to climb the blackish rocks, amid unforeseen
171 stumbles, and over stones which the ice made slippery. More
172 than once I rolled over at the expense of my loins. Conseil, more
173 **prudent** or more steady, did not stumble, and helped me up,
174 saying:

175 "If, sir, you would have the kindness to take wider steps, you
176 would preserve your **equilibrium** better."

177 Arrived at the upper ridge of the promontory, I saw a vast
178 white plain covered with morses. They were playing amongst
179 themselves, and what we heard were bellowings of pleasure, not
180 of anger.

181 As I passed these curious animals I could examine them
182 leisurely, for they did not move. Their skins were thick and
183 rugged, of a yellowish tint, approaching to red; their hair was
184 short and scant. Some of them were four yards and a quarter
185 long. Quieter and less timid than their cousins of the north, they
186 did not, like them, place sentinels round the outskirts of their
187 encampment. After examining this city of morses, I began to
188 think of returning. It was eleven o'clock, and, if Captain Nemo
189 found the conditions favorable for observations, I wished to be
190 present at the operation. We followed a narrow pathway running
191 along the summit of the steep shore. At half-past eleven we had
192 reached the place where we landed. The boat had run aground,
193 bringing the Captain. I saw him standing on a block of basalt,
194 his instruments near him, his eyes fixed on the northern horizon,
195 near which the sun was then describing a lengthened curve. I

took my place beside him, and waited without speaking. Noon arrived, and, as before, the sun did not appear. It was a fatality. Observations were still wanting. If not accomplished to-morrow, we must give up all idea of taking any. We were indeed exactly at the 20th of March. To-morrow, the 21st, would be the equinox; the sun would disappear behind the horizon for six months, and with its disappearance the long polar night would begin. Since the September equinox it had emerged from the northern horizon, rising by lengthened spirals up to the 21st of December. At this period, the summer solstice of the northern regions, it had begun to descend; and to-morrow was to shed its last rays upon them. I communicated my fears and observations to Captain Nemo.

"You are right, M. Aronnax," said he; "if to-morrow I cannot take the altitude of the sun, I shall not be able to do it for six months. But precisely because chance has led me into these seas on the 21st of March, my bearings will be easy to take, if at twelve we can see the sun."

"Why, Captain?"

"Because then the orb of day described such lengthened curves that it is difficult to measure exactly its height above the horizon, and grave errors may be made with instruments."

"What will you do then?"

"I shall only use my chronometer," replied Captain Nemo. "If to-morrow, the 21st of March, the disc of the sun, allowing for refraction, is exactly cut by the northern horizon, it will show that I am at the South Pole."

"Just so," said I. "But this statement is not mathematically correct, because the equinox does not necessarily begin at noon."

"Very likely, sir; but the error will not be a hundred yards and we do not want more. Till to-morrow, then!"

Captain Nemo returned on board. Conseil and I remained to survey the shore, observing and studying until five o'clock.

228 Then I went to bed, not, however, without **invoking**, like the
229 Indian, the favor of the radiant orb. The next day, the 21st of
230 March, at five in the morning, I mounted the platform. I found
231 Captain Nemo there.

232 "The weather is lightening a little," said he. "I have some
233 hope. After breakfast we will go on shore and choose a post for
234 observation."

235 That point settled, I sought Ned Land. I wanted to take him
236 with me. But the **obstinate** Canadian refused, and I saw that
237 his taciturnity[77] and his bad humor grew day by day. After all, I
238 was not sorry for his obstinacy under the circumstances. Indeed,
239 there were too many seals on shore, and we ought not to lay such
240 temptation in this unreflecting fisherman's way. Breakfast over,
241 we went on shore. The Nautilus had gone some miles further
242 up in the night. It was a whole league from the coast, above
243 which reared a sharp peak about five hundred yards high. The
244 boat took with me Captain Nemo, two men of the crew, and the
245 instruments, which consisted of a chronometer, a telescope, and
246 a barometer. While crossing, I saw numerous whales belonging
247 to the three kinds peculiar to the southern seas; the whale, or the
248 English "right whale," which has no dorsal fin; the "humpback,"
249 with reeved chest and large, whitish fins, which, in spite of
250 its name, do not form wings; and the fin-back, of a yellowish
251 brown, the liveliest of all the cetacea. This powerful creature is
252 heard a long way off when he throws to a great height columns
253 of air and vapor, which look like whirlwinds of smoke. These
254 different mammals were **disporting** themselves in troops in the
255 quiet waters; and I could see that this basin of the Antarctic Pole
256 serves as a place of refuge to the cetacea too closely tracked by
257 the hunters. I also noticed large medusae floating between the
258 reeds.

259 At nine we landed; the sky was brightening, the clouds were
260 flying to the south, and the fog seemed to be leaving the cold
261 surface of the waters. Captain Nemo went towards the peak,
262 which he doubtless meant to be his observatory. It was a

77   (of a person) reserved or uncommunicative in speech; saying little.

painful ascent over the sharp lava and the pumice-stones, in an atmosphere often impregnated with a sulphureous smell from the smoking cracks. For a man unaccustomed to walk on land, the Captain climbed the steep slopes with an agility I never saw equaled and which a hunter would have envied. We were two hours getting to the summit of this peak, which was half porphyry and half basalt. From thence we looked upon a vast sea which, towards the north, distinctly traced its boundary line upon the sky. At our feet lay fields of dazzling whiteness. Over our heads a pale azure, free from fog. To the north the disc of the sun seemed like a ball of fire, already horned by the cutting of the horizon. From the bosom of the water rose sheaves of liquid jets by hundreds. In the distance lay the Nautilus like a cetacean asleep on the water. Behind us, to the south and east, an immense country and a **chaotic** heap of rocks and ice, the limits of which were not visible. On arriving at the summit Captain Nemo carefully took the mean height of the barometer, for he would have to consider that in taking his observations. At a quarter to twelve the sun, then seen only by refraction, looked like a golden disc shedding its last rays upon this deserted continent and seas which never man had yet ploughed. Captain Nemo, furnished with a lenticular glass which, by means of a mirror, corrected the refraction, watched the orb sinking below the horizon by degrees, following a lengthened diagonal. I held the chronometer. My heart beat fast. If the disappearance of the half-disc of the sun **coincided** with twelve o'clock on the chronometer, we were at the pole itself.

"Twelve!" I exclaimed.

"The South Pole!" replied Captain Nemo, in a grave voice, handing me the glass, which showed the orb cut in exactly equal parts by the horizon.

I looked at the last rays crowning the peak, and the shadows mounting by degrees up its slopes. At that moment Captain Nemo, resting with his hand on my shoulder, said:

"I, Captain Nemo, on this 21st day of March, 1868, have reached

298 the South Pole on the ninetieth degree; and I take possession of
299 this part of the globe, equal to one-sixth of the known continents."

300 "In whose name, Captain?"

301 "In my own, sir!"

302 Saying which, Captain Nemo unfurled a black banner, bearing
303 an "N" in gold quartered on its bunting. Then, turning towards
304 the orb of day, whose last rays lapped the horizon of the sea, he
305 exclaimed:

306 "**Adieu**, sun! Disappear, thou **radiant orb**! rest beneath this
307 open sea, and let a night of six months spread its shadows over
308 my new domains!"

comparatively, encloses, ruminant, equilibrium, invoking, disporting, chaotic, coincided, adieu, orb

Questions Part 2 Ch. 14

1. What prevented the adventurers at first from knowing whether they reached the south pole or not?

2. Explain Conseil's comment on lines 80-82.

3. Did they end up reaching the South Pole? How do they know

4. What is remarkable about the behavior of the large animals on the south pole?

5. What is meant by lines 239-240? "Indeed, there were too many seals on shore, and we ought not to lay such temptation in this unreflecting fisherman's way."

6. Why do you think the Professor asks Captain Nemo in whose name does he take possession of the land of Antarctica, and why does the Captain take possession for himself?

Chapter 15

ACCIDENT OR INCIDENT?

The next day, the 22nd of March, at six in the morning, preparations for departure were begun. The last **gleams** of twilight were melting into night. The cold was great, the constellations shone with wonderful intensity. In the **zenith** glittered that wondrous Southern Cross[78]—the polar bear of Antarctic regions. The thermometer showed 120 below zero, and when the wind freshened it was most biting. Flakes of ice increased on the open water. The sea seemed everywhere alike. Numerous blackish patches spread on the surface, showing the formation of fresh ice. Evidently the southern basin, frozen during the six winter months, was absolutely **inaccessible**. What became of the whales in that time? Doubtless they went beneath the icebergs, seeking more **practicable** seas. As to the seals and morses[79], accustomed to live in a hard climate, they remained on these icy shores. These creatures have the instinct to break holes in the ice-field and to keep them open. To these holes they come for breath; when the birds, driven away by the cold, have emigrated to the north, these sea mammals remain sole masters of the polar continent. But the reservoirs were filling with water, and the Nautilus was slowly descending. At 1,000 feet deep it stopped; its screw beat the waves, and it advanced straight towards the north at a speed of fifteen miles an hour. Towards night it was already floating under the immense body of the iceberg. At three in the morning I was awakened by a violent shock. I sat up in my bed and listened in the darkness, when I was thrown into the middle of the room. The Nautilus, after having struck, had **rebounded** violently. I groped along the partition, and by the staircase to the saloon, which was lit by the luminous ceiling. The furniture was upset. Fortunately the windows were firmly set, and had held fast. The pictures on

---

78 the smallest constellation (the Crux or Cross), but the most familiar one to observers in the southern hemisphere. It contains the bright star Acrux, the "Jewel Box" star cluster, and most of the Coalsack nebula

79 Commonly referred to as a walrus today

31 the **starboard** side, from being no longer vertical, were clinging
32 to the paper, whilst those of the port side were hanging at least
33 a foot from the wall. The Nautilus was lying on its starboard
34 side perfectly motionless. I heard footsteps, and a confusion of
35 voices; but Captain Nemo did not appear. As I was leaving the
36 saloon, Ned Land and Conseil entered.

37 "What is the matter?" said I, at once.

38 "I came to ask you, sir," replied Conseil.

39 "**Confound** it!" exclaimed the Canadian, "I know well enough!
40 The Nautilus has struck; and, judging by the way she lies, I do
41 not think she will right herself as she did the first time in Torres
42 Straits."

43 "But," I asked, "has she at least come to the surface of the sea?"

44 "We do not know," said Conseil.

45 "It is easy to decide," I answered. I consulted the **manometer**. To
46 my great surprise, it showed a depth of more than 180 fathoms.
47 "What does that mean?" I exclaimed.

48 "We must ask Captain Nemo," said Conseil.

49 "But where shall we find him?" said Ned Land.

50 "Follow me," said I, to my companions.

51 We left the saloon. There was no one in the library. At the centre
52 staircase, by the berths of the ship's crew, there was no one. I
53 thought that Captain Nemo must be in the pilot's cage. It was
54 best to wait. We all returned to the saloon. For twenty minutes
55 we remained thus, trying to hear the slightest noise which might
56 be made on board the Nautilus, when Captain Nemo entered. He
57 seemed not to see us; his face, generally so **impassive**, showed
58 signs of uneasiness. He watched the compass silently, then the
59 manometer; and, going to the **planisphere**, placed his finger
60 on a spot representing the southern seas. I would not interrupt

61 him; but, some minutes later, when he turned towards me, I said,
62 using one of his own expressions in the Torres Straits:

63 "An incident, Captain?"

64 "No, sir; an accident this time."

65 "Serious?"

66 "Perhaps."

67 "Is the danger immediate?"

68 "No."

69 "The Nautilus has **stranded**?"

70 "Yes."

71 "And this has happened—how?"

72 "From a **caprice** of nature, not from the ignorance of man. Not
73 a mistake has been made in the working. But we cannot prevent
74 equilibrium from producing its effects. We may brave human
75 laws, but we cannot resist natural ones."

76 Captain Nemo had chosen a strange moment for uttering this
77 philosophical reflection. On the whole, his answer helped me
78 little.

79 "May I ask, sir, the cause of this accident?"

80 "An enormous block of ice, a whole mountain, has turned over,"
81 he replied. "When icebergs are undermined at their base by
82 warmer water or **reiterated** shocks their center of gravity rises,
83 and the whole thing turns over. This is what has happened; one
84 of these blocks, as it fell, struck the Nautilus, then, gliding under
85 its hull, raised it with irresistible force, bringing it into beds
86 which are not so thick, where it is lying on its side."

87 "But can we not get the Nautilus off by emptying its reservoirs,
88 that it might regain its equilibrium?"

89 "That, sir, is being done at this moment. You can hear the pump
90 working. Look at the needle of the manometer; it shows that
91 the Nautilus is rising, but the block of ice is floating with it;
92 and, until some obstacle stops its ascending motion, our position
93 cannot be altered."

94 Indeed, the Nautilus still held the same position to starboard;
95 doubtless it would right itself when the block stopped. But
96 at this moment who knows if we may not be frightfully
97 crushed between the two glassy surfaces? I reflected on all the
98 consequences of our position. Captain Nemo never took his eyes
99 off the manometer. Since the fall of the iceberg, the Nautilus had
100 risen about a hundred and fifty feet, but it still made the same
101 angle with the perpendicular. Suddenly a slight movement was
102 felt in the hold. Evidently it was righting a little. Things hanging
103 in the saloon were sensibly returning to their normal position.
104 The partitions were nearing the upright. No one spoke. With
105 beating hearts we watched and felt the straightening. The boards
106 became horizontal under our feet. Ten minutes passed.

107 "At last we have righted!" I exclaimed.

108 "Yes," said Captain Nemo, going to the door of the saloon.

109 "But are we floating?" I asked.

110 "Certainly," he replied; "since the reservoirs are not empty; and,
111 when empty, the Nautilus must rise to the surface of the sea."

112 We were in open sea; but at a distance of about ten yards, on
113 either side of the Nautilus, rose a dazzling wall of ice. Above
114 and beneath the same wall. Above, because the lower surface of
115 the iceberg stretched over us like an immense ceiling. Beneath,
116 because the overturned block, having slid by degrees, had found
117 a resting-place on the lateral walls, which kept it in that position.
118 The Nautilus was really imprisoned in a perfect tunnel of ice
119 more than twenty yards in breadth, filled with quiet water. It
120 was easy to get out of it by going either forward or backward,
121 and then make a free passage under the iceberg, some hundreds

of yards deeper. The **luminous** ceiling had been extinguished, but the saloon was still **resplendent** with intense light. It was the powerful reflection from the glass partition sent violently back to the sheets of the lantern. I cannot describe the effect of the **voltaic** rays upon the great blocks so **capriciously** cut; upon every angle, every **ridge**, every facet was thrown a different light, according to the nature of the veins running through the ice; a dazzling mine of gems, particularly of sapphires, their blue rays crossing with the green of the emerald. Here and there were opal shades of wonderful softness, running through bright spots like diamonds of fire, the brilliancy of which the eye could not bear. The power of the lantern seemed increased a hundredfold, like a lamp through the **lenticular** plates of a first-class lighthouse.

"How beautiful! how beautiful!" cried Conseil.

"Yes," I said, "it is a wonderful sight. Is it not, Ned?"

"Yes, confound it! Yes," answered Ned Land, "it is superb! I am mad at being obliged to admit it. No one has ever seen anything like it; but the sight may cost us dear. And, if I must say all, I think we are seeing here things which God never intended man to see."

Ned was right, it was too beautiful. Suddenly a cry from Conseil made me turn.

"What is it?" I asked.

"Shut your eyes, sir! Do not look, sir!" Saying which, Conseil clapped his hands over his eyes.

"But what is the matter, my boy?"

"I am dazzled, blinded."

My eyes turned involuntarily towards the glass, but I could not stand the fire which seemed to devour them. I understood what had happened. The Nautilus had put on full speed. All the quiet luster of the ice-walls was at once changed into flashes of

153 lightning. The fire from these myriads of diamonds was blinding.
154 It required some time to calm our troubled looks. At last the
155 hands were taken down.

156 "Faith, I should never have believed it," said Conseil.

157 It was then five in the morning; and at that moment a shock
158 was felt at the bows of the Nautilus. I knew that its spur had
159 struck a block of ice. It must have been a false manoeuvre, for
160 this submarine tunnel, obstructed by blocks, was not very easy
161 navigation. I thought that Captain Nemo, by changing his course,
162 would either turn these obstacles or else follow the windings of
163 the tunnel. In any case, the road before us could not be entirely
164 blocked. But, contrary to my expectations, the Nautilus took a
165 decided **retrograde** motion.

166 "We are going backwards?" said Conseil.

167 "Yes," I replied. "This end of the tunnel can have no **egress**."

168 "And then?"

169 "Then," said I, "the working is easy. We must go back again, and
170 go out at the southern opening. That is all."

171 In speaking thus, I wished to appear more confident than I really
172 was. But the retrograde motion of the Nautilus was increasing;
173 and, reversing the screw, it carried us at great speed.

174 "It will be a **hindrance**," said Ned.

175 "What does it matter, some hours more or less, provided we get
176 out at last?"

177 "Yes," repeated Ned Land, "provided we do get out at last!"

178 For a short time I walked from the saloon to the library. My
179 companions were silent. I soon threw myself on an **ottoman**,
180 and took a book, which my eyes overran mechanically. A quarter
181 of an hour after, Conseil, approaching me, said, "Is what you are
182 reading very interesting, sir?"

183 "Very interesting!" I replied.

184 "I should think so, sir. It is your own book you are reading."

185 "My book?"

186 And indeed I was holding in my hand the work on the Great
187 Submarine Depths. I did not even dream of it. I closed the book
188 and returned to my walk. Ned and Conseil rose to go.

189 "Stay here, my friends," said I, detaining them. "Let us remain
190 together until we are out of this block."

191 "As you please, sir," Conseil replied.

192 Some hours passed. I often looked at the instruments hanging
193 from the partition. The manometer showed that the Nautilus
194 kept at a constant depth of more than three hundred yards; the
195 compass still pointed to south; the log indicated a speed of twenty
196 miles an hour, which, in such a cramped space, was very great.
197 But Captain Nemo knew that he could not **hasten** too much, and
198 that minutes were worth ages to us. At twenty-five minutes past
199 eight a second shock took place, this time from behind. I turned
200 pale. My companions were close by my side. I seized Conseil's
201 hand. Our looks expressed our feelings better than words. At this
202 moment the Captain entered the saloon. I went up to him.

203 "Our course is barred southward?" I asked.

204 "Yes, sir. The iceberg has shifted and closed every outlet."

205 "We are blocked up then?"

206 "Yes."

Chapter 15

Vocabulary Part 2 Ch. 15

gleams, zenith, practicable, starboard, manometer, planisphere, stranded, reiterated

Questions Part 2 Ch. 15

1. In lines 63-64, the Captain discusses what has happened to the Nautilus. What was the reason given for the problem with the Nautilus? Is it explained as a natural phenomenon? Is Hashem in the picture? How would a Torah Jew react if he were the Captain?

2. What happened to tip the Nautilus?

3. Describe what the iceberg looked like from the inside.

4. What makes Conseil clap his hands over his eyes in lines 145-146?

5. What new problem arises in lines 203-206?

6. What do you imagine will happen in the next chapter?

Chapter 16

WANT OF AIR

1 **Thus, around the** Nautilus, above and below, was an
2 impenetrable wall of ice. We were prisoners to the iceberg. I
3 watched the Captain. His countenance had resumed its habitual
4 **imperturbability**.

5 "Gentlemen," he said calmly, "there are two ways of dying in the
6 circumstances in which we are placed." (This puzzling person
7 had the air of a mathematical Professor lecturing to his pupils.)
8 "The first is to be crushed; the second is to die of suffocation. I
9 do not speak of the possibility of dying of hunger, for the supply
10 of **provisions** in the Nautilus will certainly last longer than we
11 shall. Let us, then, calculate our chances."

12 "As to suffocation, Captain," I replied, "that is not to be feared,
13 because our reservoirs are full."

14 "Just so; but they will only yield two days' supply of air. Now,
15 for thirty-six hours we have been hidden under the water, and
16 already the heavy atmosphere of the Nautilus requires renewal.
17 In forty-eight hours our reserve will be exhausted."

18 "Well, Captain, can we be delivered before forty-eight hours?"

19 "We will attempt it, at least, by piercing the wall that surrounds
20 us."

21 "On which side?"

22 "Sound will tell us. I am going to run the Nautilus aground on
23 the lower bank, and my men will attack the iceberg on the side
24 that is least thick."

25 Captain Nemo went out. Soon I discovered by a hissing noise
26 that the water was entering the reservoirs. The Nautilus sank
27 slowly, and rested on the ice at a depth of 350 yards, the depth at
28 which the lower bank was immersed.

29 "My friends," I said, "our situation is serious, but I rely on your
30 courage and energy."

31 "Sir," replied the Canadian, "I am ready to do anything for the
32 general safety."

33 "Good! Ned," and I held out my hand to the Canadian.

34 "I will add," he continued, "that, being as handy with the pickaxe
35 as with the harpoon, if I can be useful to the Captain, he can
36 command my services."

37 "He will not refuse your help. Come, Ned!"

38 I led him to the room where the crew of the Nautilus were putting
39 on their cork-jackets. I told the Captain of Ned's proposal, which
40 he accepted. The Canadian put on his sea-costume, and was ready
41 as soon as his companions. When Ned was dressed, I re-entered
42 the drawing-room, where the panes of glass were open, and,
43 posted near Conseil, I examined the ambient beds that supported
44 the Nautilus. Some instants after, we saw a dozen of the crew set
45 foot on the bank of ice, and among them Ned Land, easily known
46 by his stature. Captain Nemo was with them. Before proceeding
47 to dig the walls, he took the soundings, to be sure of working in
48 the right direction. Long sounding lines were sunk in the side
49 walls, but after fifteen yards they were again stopped by the
50 thick wall. It was useless to attack it on the ceiling-like surface,
51 since the iceberg itself measured more than 400 yards in height.
52 Captain Nemo then sounded the lower surface. There ten yards
53 of wall separated us from the water, so great was the thickness
54 of the ice-field. It was necessary, therefore, to cut from it a piece
55 equal in extent to the waterline of the Nautilus. There were about
56 6,000 cubic yards to detach, so as to dig a hole by which we
57 could descend to the ice-field. The work had begun immediately
58 and carried on with **indefatigable** energy. Instead of digging
59 round the Nautilus which would have involved greater difficulty,
60 Captain Nemo had an immense **trench** made at eight yards from
61 the port-quarter. Then the men set to work simultaneously with
62 their screws on several points of its circumference. Presently

63 the pickaxe attacked this compact matter vigorously, and large
64 blocks were detached from the mass. By a curious effect of
65 specific gravity, these blocks, lighter than water, fled, so to
66 speak, to the vault of the tunnel, that increased in thickness at the
67 top in proportion as it diminished at the base. But that mattered
68 little, so long as the lower part grew thinner. After two hours'
69 hard work, Ned Land came in exhausted. He and his comrades
70 were replaced by new workers, whom Conseil and I joined.
71 The second lieutenant of the Nautilus **superintended** us. The
72 water seemed singularly cold, but I soon got warm handling
73 the pickaxe. My movements were free enough, although they
74 were made under a pressure of thirty atmospheres. When I re-
75 entered, after working two hours, to take some food and rest, I
76 found a perceptible difference between the pure fluid with which
77 the Rouquayrol engine supplied me and the atmosphere of the
78 Nautilus, already charged with carbonic acid. The air had not
79 been renewed for forty-eight hours, and its vivifying qualities
80 were considerably enfeebled. However, after a lapse of twelve
81 hours, we had only raised a block of ice one yard thick, on the
82 marked surface, which was about 600 cubic yards! Reckoning
83 that it took twelve hours to accomplish this much it would take
84 five nights and four days to bring this enterprise to a satisfactory
85 conclusion. Five nights and four days! And we have only air
86 enough for two days in the reservoirs! "Without taking into
87 account," said Ned, "that, even if we get out of this infernal
88 prison, we shall also be imprisoned under the iceberg, shut out
89 from all possible communication with the atmosphere." True
90 enough! Who could then foresee the minimum of time necessary
91 for our deliverance? We might be suffocated before the Nautilus
92 could regain the surface of the waves? Was it destined to perish
93 in this ice-tomb, with all those it enclosed? The situation was
94 terrible. But everyone had looked the danger in the face, and
95 each was determined to do his duty to the last.

96 As I expected, during the night a new block a yard square was
97 carried away, and still further sank the immense hollow. But in
98 the morning when, dressed in my cork-jacket, I traversed the
99 slushy mass at a temperature of six or seven degrees below zero,

100   I remarked that the side walls were gradually closing in. The
101   beds of water farthest from the trench, that were not warmed by
102   the men's work, showed a tendency to solidification. In presence
103   of this new and **imminent** danger, what would become of our
104   chances of safety, and how hinder the solidification of this liquid
105   medium, that would burst the partitions of the Nautilus like
106   glass?

107   I did not tell my companions of this new danger. What was the
108   good of damping the energy they displayed in the painful work
109   of escape? But when I went on board again, I told Captain Nemo
110   of this grave complication.

111   "I know it," he said, in that calm tone which could counteract
112   the most terrible apprehensions. "It is one danger more; but I see
113   no way of escaping it; the only chance of safety is to go quicker
114   than solidification. We must be beforehand with it, that is all."

115   On this day for several hours I used my pickaxe vigorously. The
116   work kept me up. Besides, to work was to quit the Nautilus,
117   and breathe directly the pure air drawn from the reservoirs, and
118   supplied by our apparatus, and to quit the **impoverished** and
119   vitiated atmosphere. Towards evening the trench was dug one
120   yard deeper. When I returned on board, I was nearly suffocated
121   by the carbonic acid with which the air was filled—ah! if we had
122   only the chemical means to drive away this deleterious gas. We
123   had plenty of oxygen; all this water contained a considerable
124   quantity, and by dissolving it with our powerful piles, it would
125   restore the **vivifying** fluid. I had thought well over it; but of
126   what good was that, since the carbonic acid produced by our
127   respiration had invaded every part of the vessel? To absorb it, it
128   was necessary to fill some jars with caustic potash, and to shake
129   them incessantly. Now this substance was wanting on board, and
130   nothing could replace it. On that evening, Captain Nemo ought
131   to open the taps of his reservoirs, and let some pure air into the
132   interior of the Nautilus; without this precaution we could not
133   get rid of the sense of suffocation. The next day, March 26th, I
134   resumed my miner's work in beginning the fifth yard. The side

walls and the lower surface of the iceberg thickened visibly. It was evident that they would meet before the Nautilus was able to disengage itself. Despair seized me for an instant; my pickaxe nearly fell from my hands. What was the good of digging if I must be suffocated, crushed by the water that was turning into stone?—a punishment that the ferocity of the savages even would not have invented! Just then Captain Nemo passed near me. I touched his hand and showed him the walls of our prison. The wall to port had advanced to at least four yards from the hull of the Nautilus. The Captain understood me, and signed me to follow him. We went on board. I took off my cork-jacket and accompanied him into the drawing-room.

"M. Aronnax, we must attempt some desperate means, or we shall be sealed up in this solidified water as in cement."

"Yes; but what is to be done?"

"Ah! if my Nautilus were strong enough to bear this pressure without being crushed!"

"Well?" I asked, not catching the Captain's idea.

"Do you not understand," he replied, "that this congelation of water will help us? Do you not see that by its solidification, it would burst through this field of ice that imprisons us, as, when it freezes, it bursts the hardest stones? Do you not perceive that it would be an agent of safety instead of destruction?"

"Yes, Captain, perhaps. But, whatever resistance to crushing the Nautilus possesses, it could not support this terrible pressure, and would be flattened like an iron plate."

"I know it, sir. Therefore we must not reckon on the aid of nature, but on our own exertions. We must stop this solidification. Not only will the side walls be pressed together; but there is not ten feet of water before or behind the Nautilus. The **congelation** gains on us on all sides."

"How long will the air in the reservoirs last for us to breathe on

167 board?”

168 The Captain looked in my face. “After to-morrow they will be
169 empty!”

170 A cold sweat came over me. However, ought I to have been
171 astonished at the answer? On March 22, the Nautilus was in the
172 open polar seas. We were at 26°. For five days we had lived on
173 the reserve on board. And what was left of the respirable air must
174 be kept for the workers. Even now, as I write, my recollection is
175 still so vivid that an involuntary terror seizes me and my lungs
176 seem to be without air. Meanwhile, Captain Nemo reflected
177 silently, and evidently an idea had struck him; but he seemed to
178 reject it. At last, these words escaped his lips:

179 “Boiling water!” he muttered.

180 “Boiling water?” I cried.

181 “Yes, sir. We are enclosed in a space that is relatively confined.
182 Would not jets of boiling water, constantly injected by the pumps,
183 raise the temperature in this part and stay the congelation?”

184 “Let us try it,” I said resolutely.

185 “Let us try it, Professor.”

186 The thermometer then stood at 7° outside. Captain Nemo took
187 me to the galleys, where the vast distillatory machines stood that
188 furnished the drinkable water by evaporation. They filled these
189 with water, and all the electric heat from the piles was thrown
190 through the worms bathed in the liquid. In a few minutes this
191 water reached 100°. It was directed towards the pumps, while
192 fresh water replaced it in proportion. The heat developed by the
193 troughs was such that cold water, drawn up from the sea after
194 only having gone through the machines, came boiling into the
195 body of the pump. The injection was begun, and three hours
196 after the thermometer marked 6° below zero outside. One degree
197 was gained. Two hours later the thermometer only marked 4°.

198 "We shall succeed," I said to the Captain, after having anxiously
199 watched the result of the operation.

200 "I think," he answered, "that we shall not be crushed. We have
201 no more suffocation to fear."

202 During the night the temperature of the water rose to 1° below
203 zero. The injections could not carry it to a higher point. But, as
204 the congelation of the sea-water produces at least 2°, I was at
205 least reassured against the dangers of solidification.

206 The next day, March 27th, six yards of ice had been cleared,
207 twelve feet only remaining to be cleared away. There was yet
208 forty-eight hours' work. The air could not be renewed in the
209 interior of the Nautilus. And this day would make it worse. An
210 intolerable weight oppressed me. Towards three o'clock in the
211 evening this feeling rose to a violent degree. Yawns dislocated
212 my jaws. My lungs panted as they inhaled this burning fluid,
213 which became rarefied more and more. A moral torpor took hold
214 of me. I was powerless, almost unconscious. My brave Conseil,
215 though exhibiting the same symptoms and suffering in the same
216 manner, never left me. He took my hand and encouraged me,
217 and I heard him murmur, "Oh! if I could only not breathe, so as
218 to leave more air for my master!"

219 Tears came into my eyes on hearing him speak thus. If our
220 situation to all was intolerable in the interior, with what haste
221 and gladness would we put on our cork-jackets to work in our
222 turn! Pickaxes sounded on the frozen ice-beds. Our arms ached,
223 the skin was torn off our hands. But what were these fatigues,
224 what did the wounds matter? Vital air came to the lungs! We
225 breathed! we breathed!

226 All this time no one prolonged his voluntary task beyond the
227 prescribed time. His task accomplished, each one handed in
228 turn to his panting companions the apparatus that supplied him
229 with life. Captain Nemo set the example, and submitted first
230 to this severe discipline. When the time came, he gave up his
231 apparatus to another and returned to the vitiated air on board,

232 calm, **unflinching**, unmurmuring.

233 On that day the ordinary work was accomplished with unusual
234 vigor. Only two yards remained to be raised from the surface.
235 Two yards only separated us from the open sea. But the reservoirs
236 were nearly emptied of air. The little that remained ought to be
237 kept for the workers; not a particle for the Nautilus. When I went
238 back on board, I was half suffocated. What a night! I know not
239 how to describe it. The next day my breathing was oppressed.
240 Dizziness accompanied the pain in my head and made me like
241 a drunken man. My companions showed the same symptoms.
242 Some of the crew had rattling in the throat.

243 On that day, the sixth of our imprisonment, Captain Nemo,
244 finding the pickaxes work too slowly, resolved to crush the
245 ice-bed that still separated us from the liquid sheet. This man's
246 coolness and energy never forsook him. He subdued his physical
247 pains by moral force.

248 By his orders the vessel was lightened, that is to say, raised from
249 the ice-bed by a change of specific gravity. When it floated they
250 towed it so as to bring it above the immense trench made on the
251 level of the water-line. Then, filling his reservoirs of water, he
252 descended and shut himself up in the hole.

253 Just then all the crew came on board, and the double door of
254 communication was shut. The Nautilus then rested on the bed of
255 ice, which was not one yard thick, and which the sounding leads
256 had perforated in a thousand places. The taps of the reservoirs
257 were then opened, and a hundred cubic yards of water was
258 let in, increasing the weight of the Nautilus to 1,800 tons. We
259 waited, we listened, forgetting our sufferings in hope. Our safety
260 depended on this last chance. Notwithstanding the buzzing in
261 my head, I soon heard the humming sound under the hull of
262 the Nautilus. The ice cracked with a singular noise, like tearing
263 paper, and the Nautilus sank.

264 "We are off!" murmured Conseil in my ear.

265 I could not answer him. I seized his hand, and pressed it
266 convulsively. All at once, carried away by its frightful overcharge,
267 the Nautilus sank like a bullet under the waters, that is to say, it
268 fell as if it was in a vacuum. Then all the electric force was
269 put on the pumps, that soon began to let the water out of the
270 reservoirs. After some minutes, our fall was stopped. Soon, too,
271 the manometer indicated an ascending movement. The screw,
272 going at full speed, made the iron hull tremble to its very bolts
273 and drew us towards the north. But if this floating under the
274 iceberg is to last another day before we reach the open sea, I
275 shall be dead first.

276 Half stretched upon a divan in the library, I was suffocating.
277 My face was purple, my lips blue, my faculties suspended. I
278 neither saw nor heard. All notion of time had gone from my
279 mind. My muscles could not contract. I do not know how many
280 hours passed thus, but I was conscious of the agony that was
281 coming over me. I felt as if I was going to die. Suddenly I came
282 to. Some breaths of air penetrated my lungs. Had we risen to
283 the surface of the waves? Were we free of the iceberg? No! Ned
284 and Conseil, my two brave friends, were sacrificing themselves
285 to save me. Some particles of air still remained at the bottom
286 of one apparatus. Instead of using it, they had kept it for me,
287 and, while they were being suffocated, they gave me life, drop
288 by drop. I wanted to push back the thing; they held my hands,
289 and for some moments I breathed freely. I looked at the clock;
290 it was eleven in the morning. It ought to be the 28th of March.
291 The Nautilus went at a frightful pace, forty miles an hour. It
292 literally tore through the water. Where was Captain Nemo? Had
293 he **succumbed**? Were his companions dead with him? At the
294 moment the manometer indicated that we were not more than
295 twenty feet from the surface. A mere plate of ice separated us
296 from the atmosphere. Could we not break it? Perhaps. In any
297 case the Nautilus was going to attempt it. I felt that it was in
298 an oblique position, lowering the stern, and raising the bows.
299 The introduction of water had been the means of disturbing its
300 equilibrium. Then, impelled by its powerful screw, it attacked
301 the ice-field from beneath like a **formidable** battering-ram. It

302   broke it by backing and then rushing forward against the field,
303   which gradually gave way; and at last, dashing suddenly against
304   it, shot forwards on the ice-field, that crushed beneath its weight.
305   The panel was opened—one might say torn off—and the pure air
306   came in in **abundance** to all parts of the Nautilus.

Vocabulary Part 2 Ch. 16

imperturbability, indefatigable, trench, superintended, imminent, vivifying, congelation, unflinching, succumbed, abundance

Questions part 2 Ch. 16

1. In lines 29-30, it states: "My friends," I said, "our situation is serious, but I rely on your courage and energy". As a Torah Jew, what is missing from this statement?

2. What is the solution suggested to get out of their ice imprisonment?

3. What is the problem noted in lines 85-86 with the plan?

4. What plan does the Captain come up with to prevent the walls from closing in on the Nautilus?

5. In lines 217-218, Conseil says: "Oh! if I could only not breathe, so as to leave more air for my master!". What character trait is exhibited here? Is it positive or negative?

6. In lines 245-247, the author describes Captain Nemo's actions. What positive character traits are discussed in these lines?

Chapter 17

FROM CAPE HORN TO THE AMAZON

How I got on to the platform, I have no idea; perhaps the Canadian had carried me there. But I breathed, I inhaled the vivifying sea-air. My two companions were getting drunk with the fresh particles. The other unhappy men had been so long without food, that they could not with **impunity indulge** in the simplest **aliments** that were given them. We, on the **contrary**, had no end to restrain ourselves; we could draw this air freely into our lungs, and it was the breeze, the breeze alone, that filled us with this **keen** enjoyment.

"Ah!" said Conseil, "how delightful this oxygen is! Master need not fear to breathe it. There is enough for everybody."

Ned Land did not speak, but he opened his jaws wide enough to frighten a shark. Our strength soon returned, and, when I looked round me, I saw we were alone on the platform. The foreign seamen in the Nautilus were contented with the air that circulated in the interior; none of them had come to drink in the open air.

The first words I spoke were words of gratitude and thankfulness to my two companions. Ned and Conseil had prolonged my life during the last hours of this long agony. All my gratitude could not repay such devotion.

"My friends," said I, "we are bound one to the other forever, and I am under infinite obligations to you."

"Which I shall take advantage of," exclaimed the Canadian.

"What do you mean?" said Conseil.

"I mean that I shall take you with me when I leave this infernal Nautilus."

28 "Well," said Conseil, "after all this, are we going right?"

29 "Yes," I replied, "for we are going the way of the sun, and here
30 the sun is in the north."

31 "No doubt," said Ned Land; "but it remains to be seen whether
32 he will bring the ship into the Pacific or the Atlantic Ocean, that
33 is, into frequented or deserted seas."

34 I could not answer that question, and I feared that Captain Nemo
35 would rather take us to the vast ocean that touches the coasts
36 of Asia and America at the same time. He would thus complete
37 the tour round the submarine world, and return to those waters
38 in which the Nautilus could sail freely. We ought, before long,
39 to settle this important point. The Nautilus went at a rapid pace.
40 The polar circle was soon passed, and the course shaped for
41 Cape Horn. We were off the American point, March 31st, at
42 seven o'clock in the evening. Then all our past sufferings were
43 forgotten. The remembrance of that imprisonment in the ice was
44 **effaced** from our minds. We only thought of the future. Captain
45 Nemo did not appear again either in the drawing-room or on
46 the platform. The point shown each day on the planisphere,
47 and, marked by the lieutenant, showed me the exact direction
48 of the Nautilus. Now, on that evening, it was evident, to, my
49 great satisfaction, that we were going back to the North by the
50 Atlantic. The next day, April 1st, when the Nautilus ascended
51 to the surface some minutes before noon, we sighted land to
52 the west. It was Terra del Fuego, which the first navigators
53 named thus from seeing the quantity of smoke that rose from the
54 natives' huts. The coast seemed low to me, but in the distance
55 rose high mountains. I even thought I had a glimpse of Mount
56 Sarmiento, that rises 2,070 yards above the level of the sea, with
57 a very pointed summit, which, according as it is misty or clear,
58 is a sign of fine or of wet weather. At this moment the peak
59 was clearly defined against the sky. The Nautilus, diving again
60 under the water, approached the coast, which was only some
61 few miles off. From the glass windows in the drawing-room, I
62 saw long seaweeds and gigantic fuci and varech, of which the

63 open polar sea contains so many specimens, with their sharp
64 polished filaments; they measured about 300 yards in length—
65 real cables, thicker than one's thumb; and, having great tenacity,
66 they are often used as ropes for vessels. Another weed known as
67 velp, with leaves four feet long, buried in the coral concretions,
68 hung at the bottom. It served as nest and food for myriads of
69 crustacea and molluscs, crabs, and cuttlefish. There seals and
70 otters had splendid **repasts**, eating the flesh of fish with sea-
71 vegetables, according to the English fashion. Over this fertile
72 and luxuriant ground the Nautilus passed with great rapidity.
73 Towards evening it approached the Falkland group, the rough
74 summits of which I recognized the following day. The depth of
75 the sea was moderate. On the shores our nets brought in beautiful
76 specimens of sea weed, and particularly a certain fucus, the roots
77 of which were filled with the best mussels in the world. Geese
78 and ducks fell by dozens on the platform, and soon took their
79 places in the pantry on board.

80 When the last heights of the Falklands had disappeared from the
81 horizon, the Nautilus sank to between twenty and twenty-five
82 yards, and followed the American coast. Captain Nemo did not
83 show himself. Until the 3rd of April we did not quit the shores of
84 Patagonia, sometimes under the ocean, sometimes at the surface.
85 The Nautilus passed beyond the large estuary formed by the
86 Uruguay. Its direction was northwards, and followed the long
87 windings of the coast of South America. We had then made 1,600
88 miles since our embarkation in the seas of Japan. About eleven
89 o'clock in the morning the Tropic of Capricorn was crossed on
90 the thirty-seventh meridian, and we passed Cape Frio standing
91 out to sea. Captain Nemo, to Ned Land's great displeasure, did
92 not like the neighborhood of the inhabited coasts of Brazil, for
93 we went at a **giddy** speed. Not a fish, not a bird of the swiftest
94 kind could follow us, and the natural curiosities of these seas
95 escaped all observation.

96 This speed was kept up for several days, and in the evening of the
97 9th of April we sighted the most westerly point of South America
98 that forms Cape San Roque. But then the Nautilus swerved

99   again, and sought the lowest depth of a submarine valley which
100 is between this Cape and Sierra Leone on the African coast. This
101 valley bifurcates[80] to the parallel of the Antilles, and terminates
102 at the mouth by the enormous depression of 9,000 yards. In this
103 place, the geological basin of the ocean forms, as far as the Lesser
104 Antilles, a cliff to three and a half miles perpendicular in height,
105 and, at the parallel of the Cape Verde Islands, another wall not
106 less considerable, that encloses thus all the sunk continent of the
107 Atlantic. The bottom of this immense valley is dotted with some
108 mountains, that give to these submarine places a picturesque
109 aspect. I speak, moreover, from the manuscript charts that were
110 in the library of the Nautilus—charts evidently due to Captain
111 Nemo's hand, and made after his personal observations. For two
112 days the desert and deep waters were visited by means of the
113 inclined planes. The Nautilus was furnished with long diagonal
114 broadsides which carried it to all elevations. But on the 11th of
115 April it rose suddenly, and land appeared at the mouth of the
116 Amazon River, a vast estuary[81], the embouchure[82] of which is
117 so considerable that it freshens the sea-water for the distance of
118 several leagues.

119 The equator was crossed. Twenty miles to the west were the
120 Guianas, a French territory, on which we could have found
121 an easy refuge; but a stiff breeze was blowing, and the furious
122 waves would not have allowed a single boat to face them. Ned
123 Land understood that, no doubt, for he spoke not a word about
124 it. For my part, I made no **allusion** to his schemes of flight, for
125 I would not urge him to make an attempt that must **inevitably**
126 fail. I made the time pass pleasantly by interesting studies....
127 fish... I observed in passing belonging to the apteronotes, and
128 whose snout is white as snow, the body of a beautiful black,
129 marked with a very long loose fleshy strip; odontognathes,
130 armed with spikes; ...maigres, with gold caudal fins, dark thorn-
131 tails, anableps of Surinam, etc.

---

80   divide into two branches or forks
81   the tidal mouth of a large river, where the tide meets the stream.
82   the way in which a player applies the mouth to the mouthpiece of
a brass or wind instrument.

Notwithstanding this "et cetera," I must not omit to mention fish that Conseil will long remember, and with good reason. One of our nets had hauled up a sort of very flat ray fish, which, with the tail cut off, formed a perfect disc, and weighed twenty ounces. It was white underneath, red above, with large round spots of dark blue encircled with black, very glossy skin, **terminating** in a bilobed fin. Laid out on the platform, it struggled, tried to turn itself by **convulsive** movements, and made so many efforts, that one last turn had nearly sent it into the sea. But Conseil, not wishing to let the fish go, rushed to it, and, before I could prevent him, had seized it with both hands. In a moment he was overthrown, his legs in the air, and half his body paralyzed, crying—

"Oh! master, master! help me!"

It was the first time the poor boy had spoken to me so familiarly. The Canadian and I took him up, and rubbed his contracted arms till he became sensible. The unfortunate Conseil had attacked a cramp-fish of the most dangerous kind, the cumana. This odd animal, in a medium conductor like water, strikes fish at several yards' distance, so great is the power of its electric organ, the two principal surfaces of which do not measure less than twenty-seven square feet. The next day, April 12th, the Nautilus approached the Dutch coast, near the mouth of the Maroni. There several groups of sea-cows herded together; they were manatees, that, like the dugong and the stellera, belong to the skenian order. These beautiful animals, peaceable and inoffensive, from eighteen to twenty-one feet in length, weigh at least sixteen hundredweight. I told Ned Land and Conseil that provident nature had assigned an important role to these mammalia. Indeed, they, like the seals, are designed to graze on the submarine prairies, and thus destroy the accumulation of weed that obstructs the tropical rivers.

"And do you know," I added, "what has been the result since men have almost entirely annihilated this useful race? That the **putrefied** weeds have poisoned the air, and the poisoned air

167 causes the yellow fever, that desolates these beautiful countries.
168 Enormous vegetations are multiplied under the torrid seas, and
169 the evil is **irresistibly** developed from the mouth of the Rio de
170 la Plata to Florida. If we are to believe Toussenel, this plague is
171 nothing to what it would be if the seas were cleaned of whales
172 and seals. Then, infested with poulps, medusae, and cuttle-fish,
173 they would become immense centers of infection, since their
174 waves would not possess 'these vast stomachs that G-d had
175 charged to infest the surface of the seas.'"

Vocabulary For Part 2 Ch, 17

indulge, contrary, keen, convulsive, terminating, putrefied, irresistibly

Questions Part 2 Ch. 17

1. In line 11, Conseil says to his master: "how delightful this oxygen is!" What did it take for Conseil to say this? Why don't people say that regularly? How should a Torah Jew look at oxygen?

2. In lines 20-21, the Professor says: "All my gratitude could not repay such devotion." What middah is expressed here? Is it a good midah?

3. In lines 22-23, the Professor continues and says: "My friends," said I, "we are bound one to the other forever, and I am under infinite obligations to you". What does this statement express about how strong bonds of friendship are established?

4. What is the role of the manatees in keeping the oceans' ecosystem healthy? State two effects that have occurred due to people hunting down these manatees.

Chapter 18

THE POULPS

For several days the Nautilus kept off from the American coast. **Evidently** it did not wish to risk the tides of the Gulf of Mexico or of the sea of the Antilles. April 16th, we sighted Martinique and Guadaloupe from a distance of about thirty miles. I saw their tall peaks for an instant. The Canadian, who counted on carrying out his projects in the Gulf, by either landing or hailing one of the numerous boats that coast from one island to another, was quite **disheartened**. Flight would have been quite practicable, if Ned Land had been able to take possession of the boat without the Captain's knowledge. But in the open sea it could not be thought of. The Canadian, Conseil, and I had a long conversation on this subject. For six months we had been prisoners on board the Nautilus. We had travelled 17,000 leagues; and, as Ned Land said, there was no reason why it should come to an end. We could hope nothing from the Captain of the Nautilus, but only from ourselves. Besides, for some time past he had become graver, more retired, less sociable. He seemed to shun me. I met him rarely. Formerly he was pleased to explain the submarine marvels to me; now he left me to my studies, and came no more to the saloon. What change had come over him? For what cause? For my part, I did not wish to bury with me my curious and novel studies. I had now the power to write the true book of the sea; and this book, sooner or later, I wished to see daylight. The land nearest us was the archipelago of the Bahamas. There rose high submarine cliffs covered with large weeds. It was about eleven o'clock when Ned Land drew my attention to a formidable pricking, like the sting of an ant, which was produced by means of large seaweeds.

"Well," I said, "these are proper caverns for poulps[83], and I should not be astonished to see some of these monsters."

83
Animals) a cephalopod such as an octopus, <u>cuttlefish</u> or squid

31 "What!" said Conseil; "cuttlefish, real cuttlefish of the
32 cephalopod class?"

33 "No," I said, "poulps of huge dimensions."

34 "I will never believe that such animals exist," said Ned.

35 "Well," said Conseil, with the most serious air in the world, "I
36 remember perfectly to have seen a large vessel drawn under the
37 waves by an octopus's arm."

38 "You saw that?" said the Canadian.

39 "Yes, Ned."

40 "With your own eyes?"

41 "With my own eyes."

42 "Where, pray, might that be?"

43 "At St. Malo," answered Conseil.

44 "In the port?" said Ned, ironically.

45 "No; in a church," replied Conseil.

46 "In a church!" cried the Canadian.

47 "Yes; friend Ned. In a picture representing the poulp in question."

48 "Good!" said Ned Land, bursting out laughing.

49 "He is quite right," I said. "I have heard of this picture; but the
50 subject represented is taken from a legend, and you know what
51 to think of legends in the matter of natural history. Besides,
52 when it is a question of monsters, the imagination is apt to run
53 wild. Not only is it supposed that these poulps can draw down
54 vessels, but a certain Olaus Magnus speaks of an octopus a mile
55 long that is more like an island than an animal. It is also said
56 that the Bishop of Nidros was building an altar on an immense
57 rock. Mass finished, the rock began to walk, and returned to the

58 sea. The rock was a poulp. Another Bishop, Pontoppidan, speaks
59 also of a poulp on which a regiment of cavalry could maneuver.
60 Lastly, the ancient naturalists speak of monsters whose mouths
61 were like gulfs, and which were too large to pass through the
62 Straits of Gibraltar."

63 "But how much is true of these stories?" asked Conseil.

64 "Nothing, my friends; at least of that which passes the limit
65 of truth to get to **fable** or legend. Nevertheless, there must be
66 some ground for the imagination of the story-tellers. One cannot
67 deny that poulps and cuttlefish exist of a large species, **inferior**,
68 however, to the cetaceans. Aristotle has stated the dimensions of
69 a cuttlefish as five cubits, or nine feet two inches. Our fishermen
70 frequently see some that are more than four feet long. Some
71 skeletons of poulps are preserved in the museums of Trieste and
72 Montpelier, that measure two yards in length. Besides, according
73 to the calculations of some naturalists, one of these animals only
74 six feet long would have tentacles twenty-seven feet long. That
75 would suffice to make a formidable monster."

76 "Do they fish for them in these days?" asked Ned.

77 "If they do not fish for them, sailors see them at least. One of my
78 friends, Captain Paul Bos of Havre, has often **affirmed** that he
79 met one of these monsters of **colossal** dimensions in the Indian
80 seas. But the most astonishing fact, and which does not permit of
81 the denial of the existence of these gigantic animals, happened
82 some years ago, in 1861."

83 "What is the fact?" asked Ned Land.

84 "This is it. In 1861, to the north-east of Teneriffe, very nearly
85 in the same latitude we are in now, the crew of the dispatch-
86 boat Alector perceived a monstrous cuttlefish swimming in the
87 waters. Captain Bouguer went near to the animal, and attacked
88 it with harpoon and guns, without much success, for balls
89 and harpoons glided over the soft flesh. After several fruitless
90 attempts the crew tried to pass a slip-knot round the body of

91   the mollusc. The noose slipped as far as the tail fins and there
92   stopped. They tried then to haul it on board, but its weight was
93   so considerable that the tightness of the cord separated the tail
94   from the body, and, deprived of this ornament, he disappeared
95   under the water.”

96   “Indeed! is that a fact?”

97   “An indisputable fact, my good Ned. They proposed to name
98   this poulp ‘Bouguer’s cuttlefish.’”

99   “What length was it?” asked the Canadian.

100   “Did it not measure about six yards?” said Conseil, who, posted
101   at the window, was examining again the irregular windings of
102   the cliff.

103   “Precisely,” I replied.

104   “Its head,” rejoined Conseil, “was it not crowned with eight
105   tentacles, that beat the water like a nest of serpents?”

106   “Precisely.”

107   “Had not its eyes, placed at the back of its head, considerable
108   development?”

109   “Yes, Conseil.”

110   “And was not its mouth like a parrot’s beak?”

111   “Exactly, Conseil.”

112   “Very well! no offence to master,” he replied, quietly; “if this is
113   not Bouguer’s cuttlefish, it is, at least, one of its brothers.”

114   I looked at Conseil. Ned Land hurried to the window.

115   “What a horrible beast!” he cried.

116   I looked in my turn, and could not repress a gesture of disgust.
117   Before my eyes was a horrible monster worthy to figure in the

118 legends of the marvelous. It was an immense cuttlefish, being
119 eight yards long. It swam crossways in the direction of the
120 Nautilus with great speed, watching us with its enormous staring
121 green eyes. Its eight arms, or rather feet, fixed to its head, that
122 have given the name of cephalopod to these animals, were twice
123 as long as its body, and were twisted like the furies' hair. One
124 could see the 250 air holes on the inner side of the tentacles.
125 The monster's mouth, a horned beak like a parrot's, opened and
126 shut vertically. Its tongue, a horned substance, furnished with
127 several rows of pointed teeth, came out **quivering** from this
128 **veritable** pair of shears. What a freak of nature, a bird's beak
129 on a mollusk! Its spindle-like body formed a fleshy mass that
130 might weigh 4,000 to 5,000 lb.; the, varying color changing with
131 great rapidity, according to the irritation of the animal, passed
132 successively from livid grey to reddish brown. What irritated
133 this mollusk? No doubt the presence of the Nautilus, more
134 formidable than itself, and on which its suckers or its jaws had
135 no hold. Yet, what monsters these poulps are! what vitality the
136 Creator has given them! what vigor in their movements! and
137 they possess three hearts! Chance had brought us in presence
138 of this cuttlefish, and I did not wish to lose the opportunity of
139 carefully studying this specimen of cephalopods. I overcame the
140 horror that inspired me, and, taking a pencil, began to draw it.

141 "Perhaps this is the same which the Alector saw," said Conseil.

142 "No," replied the Canadian; "for this is whole, and the other had
143 lost its tail."

144 "That is no reason," I replied. "The arms and tails of these
145 animals are re-formed by renewal; and in seven years the tail of
146 Bouguer's cuttlefish has no doubt had time to grow."

147 By this time other poulps appeared at the port light. I counted
148 seven. They formed a procession after the Nautilus, and I heard
149 their beaks gnashing against the iron hull. I continued my work.
150 These monsters kept in the water with such precision that they
151 seemed immovable. Suddenly the Nautilus stopped. A shock
152 made it tremble in every plate.

153 "Have we struck anything?" I asked.

154 "In any case," replied the Canadian, "we shall be free, for we
155 are floating."

156 The Nautilus was floating, no doubt, but it did not move. A
157 minute passed. Captain Nemo, followed by his lieutenant,
158 entered the drawing-room. I had not seen him for some time. He
159 seemed dull. Without noticing or speaking to us, he went to the
160 panel, looked at the poulps, and said something to his lieutenant.
161 The latter went out. Soon the panels were shut. The ceiling was
162 lighted. I went towards the Captain.

163 "A curious collection of poulps?" I said.

164 "Yes, indeed, Mr. Naturalist," he replied; "and we are going to
165 fight them, man to beast."

166 I looked at him. I thought I had not heard aright.

167 "Man to beast?" I repeated.

168 "Yes, sir. The screw is stopped. I think that the horny jaws of one
169 of the cuttlefish is entangled in the blades. That is what prevents
170 our moving."

171 "What are you going to do?"

172 "Rise to the surface, and slaughter this **vermin**."

173 "A difficult enterprise."

174 "Yes, indeed. The electric bullets are powerless against the soft
175 flesh, where they do not find resistance enough to go off. But we
176 shall attack them with the hatchet."

177 "And the harpoon, sir," said the Canadian, "if you do not refuse
178 my help."

179 "I will accept it, Master Land."

180 "We will follow you," I said, and, following Captain Nemo, we

181   went towards the central staircase.

182   There, about ten men with boarding-hatchets were ready for
183   the attack. Conseil and I took two hatchets; Ned Land seized
184   a harpoon. The Nautilus had then risen to the surface. One of
185   the sailors, posted on the top ladderstep, unscrewed the bolts of
186   the panels. But hardly were the screws loosed, when the panel
187   rose with great violence, evidently drawn by the suckers of a
188   poulp's arm. Immediately one of these arms slid like a serpent
189   down the opening and twenty others were above. With one blow
190   of the axe, Captain Nemo cut this formidable tentacle, that slid
191   wriggling down the ladder. Just as we were pressing one on the
192   other to reach the platform, two other arms, lashing the air, came
193   down on the seaman placed before Captain Nemo, and lifted
194   him up with irresistible power. Captain Nemo uttered a cry, and
195   rushed out. We hurried after him.

196   What a scene! The unhappy man, seized by the tentacle and
197   fixed to the suckers, was balanced in the air at the **caprice** of
198   this enormous trunk. He rattled in his throat, he was stifled, he
199   cried, "Help! help!" These words, spoken in French, startled
200   me! I had a fellow-countryman on board, perhaps several! That
201   heart-rending cry! I shall hear it all my life. The unfortunate man
202   was lost. Who could rescue him from that powerful pressure?
203   However, Captain Nemo had rushed to the poulp, and with one
204   blow of the axe had cut through one arm. His lieutenant struggled
205   furiously against other monsters that crept on the flanks of
206   the Nautilus. The crew fought with their axes. The Canadian,
207   Conseil, and I buried our weapons in the fleshy masses; a strong
208   smell of musk penetrated the atmosphere. It was horrible!

209   For one instant, I thought the unhappy man, entangled with
210   the poulp, would be torn from its powerful suction. Seven of
211   the eight arms had been cut off. One only wriggled in the air,
212   **brandishing** the victim like a feather. But just as Captain Nemo
213   and his lieutenant threw themselves on it, the animal ejected a
214   stream of black liquid. We were blinded with it. When the cloud
215   dispersed, the cuttlefish had disappeared, and my unfortunate

216 countryman with it. Ten or twelve poulps now invaded the
217 platform and sides of the Nautilus. We rolled pell-mell into the
218 midst of this nest of serpents, that wriggled on the platform in
219 the waves of blood and ink. It seemed as though these slimy
220 tentacles sprang up like the hydra's heads. Ned Land's harpoon,
221 at each stroke, was plunged into the staring eyes of the cuttle
222 fish. But my bold companion was suddenly overturned by the
223 tentacles of a monster he had not been able to avoid.

224 Ah! how my heart beat with emotion and horror! The formidable
225 beak of a cuttlefish was open over Ned Land. The unhappy man
226 would be cut in two. I rushed to his succor. But Captain Nemo
227 was before me; his axe disappeared between the two enormous
228 jaws, and, miraculously saved, the Canadian, rising, plunged his
229 harpoon deep into the triple heart of the poulp.

230 "I owed myself this revenge!" said the Captain to the Canadian.

231 Ned bowed without replying. The combat had lasted a quarter of
232 an hour. The monsters, **vanquished** and **mutilated**, left us at last,
233 and disappeared under the waves. Captain Nemo, covered with
234 blood, nearly exhausted, gazed upon the sea that had swallowed
235 up one of his companions, and great tears gathered in his eyes.

𝔙ocabulary 𝔓art 2 𝔠h. 18

disheartened, fable, inferior, veritable, vermin, brandishing, vanquished

Questions Part 2 Ch. 18

1. Do the Poulp look frightening to the passengers aboard the Nautilus?

2. What do the Poulp do to stop the Nautilus?

3. How do you think Captain Nemo responded to the Poulp stopping his seemingly invincible craft? What point may the author be trying to make about the power of nature over man in this event?

4. What does the Poulp do to one of the crew members?

5. What almost occurs to Ned Land and who saves him? What reason is given for saving Ned Land? What middah does Ned Land's savior express when stating why he saved him.

6. Why do you think the Frenchmen (line 199), when thrown into the mouth of the Poulp, suddenly spoke in his native language?

Chapter 19

THE GULF STREAM

This terrible scene of the 20th of April none of us can ever forget. I have written it under the influence of violent emotion. Since then I have revised the **recital**; I have read it to Conseil and to the Canadian. They found it exact as to facts, but **insufficient** as to effect. To paint such pictures, one must have the pen of the most illustrious of our poets, the author of The Toilers of the Deep.

I have said that Captain Nemo wept while watching the waves; his **grief** was great. It was the second companion he had lost since our arrival on board, and what a death! That friend, crushed, **stifled**, bruised by the dreadful arms of a poulp, pounded by his iron jaws, would not rest with his comrades in the peaceful coral cemetery! In the midst of the struggle, it was the **despairing** cry uttered by the unfortunate man that had torn my heart. The poor Frenchman, forgetting his conventional language, had taken to his own mother tongue, to utter a last appeal! Amongst the crew of the Nautilus, associated with the body and soul of the Captain, recoiling like him from all contact with men, I had a fellow-countryman. Did he alone represent France in this mysterious association, evidently composed of individuals of diverse nationalities? It was one of these **insoluble** problems that rose up **unceasingly** before my mind!

Captain Nemo entered his room, and I saw him no more for some time. But that he was sad and **irresolute** I could see by the vessel, of which he was the soul, and which received all his impressions. The Nautilus did not keep on in its settled course; it floated about like a corpse at the will of the waves. It went at random. He could not tear himself away from the scene of the last struggle, from this sea that had **devoured** one of his men. Ten days passed thus. It was not till the 1st of May that the Nautilus resumed its northerly course, after having sighted the Bahamas at the mouth of the Bahama Canal. We were then

33 following the current from the largest river to the sea, that has
34 its banks, its fish, and its proper temperatures. I mean the Gulf
35 Stream. It is really a river, that flows freely to the middle of the
36 Atlantic, and whose waters do not mix with the ocean waters.
37 It is a salt river, salter than the surrounding sea. Its mean depth
38 is 1,500 fathoms, its mean breadth ten miles. In certain places
39 the current flows with the speed of two miles and a half an hour.
40 The body of its waters is more considerable than that of all the
41 rivers in the globe. It was on this ocean river that the Nautilus
42 then sailed.

43 I must add that, during the night, the phosphorescent waters of
44 the Gulf Stream rivalled the electric power of our watch-light,
45 especially in the stormy weather that threatened us so frequently.
46 May 8th, we were still crossing Cape Hatteras, at the height
47 of the North Caroline. The width of the Gulf Stream there is
48 seventy-five miles, and its depth 210 yards. The Nautilus still
49 went at random; all supervision seemed abandoned. I thought
50 that, under these circumstances, escape would be possible.
51 Indeed, the inhabited shores offered anywhere an easy refuge.
52 The sea was incessantly ploughed by the steamers that ply
53 between New York or Boston and the Gulf of Mexico, and
54 overrun day and night by the little schooners coasting about
55 the several parts of the American coast. We could hope to be
56 picked up. It was a favorable opportunity, **notwithstanding** the
57 thirty miles that separated the Nautilus from the coasts of the
58 Union. One unfortunate circumstance thwarted the Canadian's
59 plans. The weather was very bad. We were nearing those shores
60 where tempests are so frequent, that country of waterspouts and
61 cyclones actually engendered by the current of the Gulf Stream.
62 To tempt the sea in a frail boat was certain destruction. Ned Land
63 owned this himself. He **fretted**, seized with **nostalgia** that flight
64 only could cure.

65 "Master," he said that day to me, "this must come to an end. I
66 must make a clean breast of it. This Nemo is leaving land and
67 going up to the north. But I declare to you that I have had enough
68 of the South Pole, and I will not follow him to the North."

69 "What is to be done, Ned, since flight is **impracticable** just
70 now?"

71 "We must speak to the Captain," said he; "you said nothing
72 when we were in your native seas. I will speak, now we are
73 in mine. When I think that before long the Nautilus will be by
74 Nova Scotia, and that there near New Foundland is a large bay,
75 and into that bay the St. Lawrence empties itself, and that the St.
76 Lawrence is my river, the river by Quebec, my native town—
77 when I think of this, I feel furious, it makes my hair stand on
78 end. Sir, I would rather throw myself into the sea! I will not stay
79 here! I am stifled!"

80 The Canadian was evidently losing all patience. His vigorous
81 nature could not stand this prolonged imprisonment. His face
82 altered daily; his temper became more surly. I knew what he
83 must suffer, for I was seized with home-sickness myself. Nearly
84 seven months had passed without our having had any news from
85 land; Captain Nemo's isolation, his altered spirits, especially
86 since the fight with the poulps, his **taciturnity**, all made me
87 view things in a different light.

88 "Well, sir?" said Ned, seeing I did not reply.

89 "Well, Ned, do you wish me to ask Captain Nemo his intentions
90 concerning us?"

91 "Yes, sir."

92 "Although he has already made them known?"

93 "Yes; I wish it settled finally. Speak for me, in my name only, if
94 you like."

95 "But I so seldom meet him. He avoids me."

96 "That is all the more reason for you to go to see him."

97 I went to my room. From thence I meant to go to Captain Nemo's.
98 It would not do to let this opportunity of meeting him slip. I

99 knocked at the door. No answer. I knocked again, then turned
100 the handle. The door opened, I went in. The Captain was there.
101 Bending over his work-table, he had not heard me. **Resolved**
102 not to go without having spoken, I approached him. He raised
103 his head quickly, frowned, and said roughly, "You here! What
104 do you want?"

105 "To speak to you, Captain."

106 "But I am busy, sir; I am working. I leave you at liberty to shut
107 yourself up; cannot I be allowed the same?"

108 This reception was not encouraging; but I was determined to
109 hear and answer everything.

110 "Sir," I said coldly, "I have to speak to you on a matter that
111 admits of no delay."

112 "What is that, sir?" he replied, ironically. "Have you discovered
113 something that has escaped me, or has the sea delivered up any
114 new secrets?"

115 We were at cross-purposes. But, before I could reply, he showed
116 me an open manuscript on his table, and said, in a more serious
117 tone, "Here, M. Aronnax, is a manuscript written in several
118 languages. It contains the sum of my studies of the sea; and, if it
119 please God, it shall not perish with me. This manuscript, signed
120 with my name, complete with the history of my life, will be
121 shut up in a little floating case. The last survivor of all of us on
122 board the Nautilus will throw this case into the sea, and it will go
123 **whither** it is **borne** by the waves."

124 This man's name! his history written by himself! His mystery
125 would then be revealed some day.

126 "Captain," I said, "I can but approve of the idea that makes you
127 act thus. The result of your studies must not be lost. But the
128 means you employ seem to me to be **primitive**. Who knows
129 where the winds will carry this case, and in whose hands it will
130 fall? Could you not use some other means? Could not you, or

131   one of yours——"

132   "Never, sir!" he said, **hastily** interrupting me.

133   "But I and my companions are ready to keep this manuscript in
134   store; and, if you will put us at liberty——"

135   "At liberty?" said the Captain, rising.

136   "Yes, sir; that is the subject on which I wish to question you. For
137   seven months we have been here on board, and I ask you to-day,
138   in the name of my companions and in my own, if your intention
139   is to keep us here always?"

140   "M. Aronnax, I will answer you to-day as I did seven months
141   ago: Whoever enters the Nautilus, must never quit it."

142   "You impose actual slavery upon us!"

143   "Give it what name you please."

144   "But everywhere the slave has the right to regain his liberty."

145   "Who denies you this right? Have I ever tried to chain you with
146   an oath?"

147   He looked at me with his arms crossed.

148   "Sir," I said, "to return a second time to this subject will be
149   neither to your nor to my taste; but, as we have entered upon
150   it, let us go through with it. I repeat, it is not only myself whom
151   it concerns. Study is to me a relief, a **diversion**, a passion that
152   could make me forget everything. Like you, I am willing to live
153   **obscure**, in the frail hope of **bequeathing** one day, to future
154   time, the result of my labors. But it is otherwise with Ned Land.
155   Every man, worthy of the name, deserves some consideration.
156   Have you thought that love of liberty, hatred of slavery, can give
157   rise to schemes of revenge in a nature like the Canadian's; that
158   he could think, attempt, and try——"

159   I was silenced; Captain Nemo rose.

"Whatever Ned Land thinks of, attempts, or tries, what does it matter to me? I did not seek him! It is not for my pleasure that I keep him on board! As for you, M. Aronnax, you are one of those who can understand everything, even silence. I have nothing more to say to you. Let this first time you have come to treat of this subject be the last, for a second time I will not listen to you."

I retired. Our situation was critical. I related my conversation to my two companions.

"We know now," said Ned, "that we can expect nothing from this man. The Nautilus is nearing Long Island. We will escape, whatever the weather may be."

But the sky became more and more threatening. Symptoms of a hurricane became **manifest**. The atmosphere was becoming white and misty. On the horizon fine streaks of cirrhous clouds were succeeded by masses of cumuli. Other low clouds passed swiftly by. The swollen sea rose in huge billows. The birds disappeared with the exception of the petrels, those friends of the storm. The barometer fell sensibly, and indicated an extreme extension of the vapors. The mixture of the storm glass was decomposed under the influence of the electricity that pervaded the atmosphere. The tempest burst on the 18th of May, just as the Nautilus was floating off Long Island, some miles from the port of New York. I can describe this strife of the elements! for, instead of fleeing to the depths of the sea, Captain Nemo, by an unaccountable **caprice**, would brave it at the surface. The wind blew from the south-west at first. Captain Nemo, during the squalls, had taken his place on the platform. He had made himself fast, to prevent being washed overboard by the monstrous waves. I had hoisted myself up, and made myself fast also, dividing my admiration between the tempest and this extraordinary man who was coping with it. The raging sea was swept by huge cloud-drifts, which were actually saturated with the waves. The Nautilus, sometimes lying on its side, sometimes standing up like a mast, rolled and pitched terribly. About five

195 o'clock a torrent of rain fell, that lulled neither sea nor wind. The
196 hurricane blew nearly forty leagues an hour. It is under these
197 conditions that it overturns houses, breaks iron gates, displaces
198 twenty-four pounders. However, the Nautilus, in the midst of
199 the tempest, confirmed the words of a clever engineer, "There is
200 no well-constructed hull that cannot defy the sea." This was not
201 a resisting rock; it was a steel spindle, obedient and movable,
202 without rigging or masts, that braved its fury with impunity.
203 However, I watched these raging waves attentively. They
204 measured fifteen feet in height, and 150 to 175 yards long, and
205 their speed of propagation was thirty feet per second. Their bulk
206 and power increased with the depth of the water. Such waves as
207 these, at the Hebrides, have displaced a mass weighing 8,400 lb.
208 They are they which, in the tempest of December 23rd, 1864,
209 after destroying the town of Yeddo, in Japan, broke the same day
210 on the shores of America. The intensity of the tempest increased
211 with the night. The barometer, as in 1860 at Reunion during a
212 cyclone, fell seven-tenths at the close of day. I saw a large vessel
213 pass the horizon struggling painfully. She was trying to lie to
214 under half steam, to keep up above the waves. It was probably
215 one of the steamers of the line from New York to Liverpool, or
216 Havre. It soon disappeared in the gloom. At ten o'clock in the
217 evening the sky was on fire. The atmosphere was streaked with
218 vivid lightning. I could not bear the brightness of it; while the
219 captain, looking at it, seemed to envy the spirit of the tempest.
220 A terrible noise filled the air, a complex noise, made up of the
221 howls of the crushed waves, the roaring of the wind, and the
222 claps of thunder. The wind veered suddenly to all points of the
223 horizon; and the cyclone, rising in the east, returned after passing
224 by the north, west, and south, in the inverse course pursued by
225 the circular storm of the southern hemisphere. Ah, that Gulf
226 Stream! It deserves its name of the King of Tempests. It is that
227 which causes those formidable cyclones, by the difference of
228 temperature between its air and its currents. A shower of fire
229 had succeeded the rain. The drops of water were changed to
230 sharp spikes. One would have thought that Captain Nemo was
231 **courting** a death worthy of himself, a death by lightning. As the

232 Nautilus, pitching dreadfully, raised its steel spur in the air, it
233 seemed to act as a conductor, and I saw long sparks burst from
234 it. Crushed and without strength I crawled to the panel, opened
235 it, and descended to the saloon. The storm was then at its height.
236 It was impossible to stand upright in the interior of the Nautilus.
237 Captain Nemo came down about twelve. I heard the reservoirs
238 filling by degrees, and the Nautilus sank slowly beneath the
239 waves. Through the open windows in the saloon I saw large fish
240 terrified, passing like **phantoms** in the water. Some were struck
241 before my eyes. The Nautilus was still descending. I thought
242 that at about eight fathoms deep we should find a calm. But no!
243 the upper beds were too violently agitated for that. We had to
244 seek repose at more than twenty-five fathoms in the bowels of
245 the deep. But there, what quiet, what silence, what peace! Who
246 could have told that such a hurricane had been let loose on the
247 surface of that ocean?

Vocabulary Part 2 Ch. 19

insufficient, stifled, grief, insoluble, unceasingly, irresolute, fretted, nostalgia, impracticable, taciturnity, whither, borne, primitive

Questions part 2 Ch. 19

1. Why do you think the Nautilus floundered after the death of one of its crew members?

    ____

    ____

    ____

2. What is the gulf stream?

    ____

    ____

3. How does the Captain plan to keep his name alive for many years to come even after he perishes?

    ____

    ____

4. Why do you think the Captain stood on top of the deck during the hurricane?

    ____

    ____

    ____

5. From the fact that the author uses the words-"chain" (line 145) when referring to a person who made an oath (*shvua*)-what what can be deduced about the nature of people's respect then regarding the binding nature of an oath?

    ____

    ____

Chapter 20

FROM LATITUDE 47° 24' TO LONGITUDE 17° 28'

In consequence of the storm, we had been thrown eastward once more. All hope of escape on the shores of New York or St. Lawrence had faded away; and poor Ned, in despair, had isolated himself like Captain Nemo. Conseil and I, however, never left each other. I said that the Nautilus had gone aside to the east. I should have said (to be more exact) the north-east. For some days, it wandered first on the surface, and then beneath it, amid those fogs so dreaded by sailors. What accidents are due to these thick fogs! What shocks upon these reefs when the wind drowns the breaking of the waves! What collisions between vessels, in spite of their warning lights, whistles, and alarm bells! And the bottoms of these seas look like a field of battle, where still lie all the conquered of the ocean; some old and already encrusted, others fresh and reflecting from their iron bands and copper plates the brilliancy of our lantern.

On the 15th of May we were at the extreme south of the Bank of Newfoundland. This bank consists of alluvia, or large heaps of organic matter, brought either from the Equator by the Gulf Stream, or from the North Pole by the counter-current of cold water which skirts the American coast. There also are heaped up those erratic blocks which are carried along by the broken ice; and close by, a vast charnel-house of molluscs, which perish here by millions. The depth of the sea is not great at Newfoundland— not more than some hundreds of fathoms; but towards the south is a depression of 1,500 fathoms. There the Gulf Stream widens. It loses some of its speed and some of its temperature, but it becomes a sea.

It was on the 17th of May, about 500 miles from Heart's Content, at a depth of more than 1,400 fathoms, that I saw the electric cable lying on the bottom. Conseil, to whom I had not mentioned it, thought at first that it was a gigantic sea-serpent.

32 But I **undeceived** the worthy fellow, and by way of **consolation**
33 related several particulars in the laying of this cable. The first
34 one was laid in the years 1857 and 1858; but, after transmitting
35 about 400 telegrams, would not act any longer. In 1863 the
36 engineers constructed another one, measuring 2,000 miles in
37 length, and weighing 4,500 tons, which was **embarked** on the
38 Great Eastern. This attempt also failed...

39 I did not expect to find the electric cable in its primitive state,
40 such as it was on leaving the **manufactory**. The long serpent,
41 covered with the remains of shells, bristling with foraminiferae,
42 was encrusted with a strong coating which served as a protection
43 against all boring molluscs. It lay quietly sheltered from the
44 motions of the sea, and under a favorable pressure for the
45 transmission of the electric spark which passes from Europe to
46 America in .32 of a second. Doubtless this cable will last for a
47 great length of time, for they find that the gutta-percha covering
48 is improved by the sea-water. Besides, on this level, so well
49 chosen, the cable is never so deeply submerged as to cause it to
50 break. The Nautilus followed it to the lowest depth, which was
51 more than 2,212 fathoms, and there it lay without any anchorage;
52 and then we reached the spot where the accident had taken place
53 in 1863. The bottom of the ocean then formed a valley about
54 100 miles broad, in which Mont Blanc might have been placed
55 without its summit appearing above the waves. This valley is
56 closed at the east by a perpendicular wall more than 2,000 yards
57 high. We arrived there on the 28th of May, and the Nautilus was
58 then not more than 120 miles from Ireland.

59 Was Captain Nemo going to land on the British Isles? No. To
60 my great surprise he made for the south, once more coming back
61 towards European seas. In rounding the Emerald Isle, for one
62 instant I caught sight of Cape Clear, and the light which guides
63 the thousands of vessels leaving Glasgow or Liverpool. An
64 important question then arose in my mind. Did the Nautilus dare
65 entangle itself in the Manche? Ned Land, who had re-appeared
66 since we had been nearing land, did not cease to question me.
67 How could I answer? Captain Nemo remained invisible. After

68 having shown the Canadian a glimpse of American shores, was
69 he going to show me the coast of France?

70 But the Nautilus was still going southward. On the 30th of May,
71 it passed in sight of Land's End, between the extreme point of
72 England and the Scilly Isles, which were left to starboard. If we
73 wished to enter the Manche, he must go straight to the east. He
74 did not do so.

75 During the whole of the 31st of May, the Nautilus described a
76 series of circles on the water, which greatly interested me. It
77 seemed to be seeking a spot it had some trouble in finding. At
78 noon, Captain Nemo himself came to work the ship's log. He
79 spoke no word to me, but seemed gloomier than ever. What could
80 sadden him thus? Was it his proximity to European shores? Had
81 he some recollections of his abandoned country? If not, what
82 did he feel? Remorse or regret? For a long while this thought
83 haunted my mind, and I had a kind of **presentiment** that before
84 long chance would betray the captain's secrets.

85 The next day, the 1st of June, the Nautilus continued the same
86 process. It was evidently seeking some particular spot in the
87 ocean. Captain Nemo took the sun's altitude as he had done the
88 day before. The sea was beautiful, the sky clear. About eight
89 miles to the east, a large steam vessel could be discerned on the
90 horizon. No flag fluttered from its mast, and I could not discover
91 its nationality. Some minutes before the sun passed the meridian,
92 Captain Nemo took his sextant, and watched with great attention.
93 The perfect rest of the water greatly helped the operation. The
94 Nautilus was motionless; it neither rolled nor pitched.

95 I was on the platform when the altitude was taken, and the
96 Captain pronounced these words: "It is here."

97 He turned and went below. Had he seen the vessel which was
98 changing its course and seemed to be nearing us? I could not tell.
99 I returned to the saloon. The panels closed, I heard the hissing of
100 the water in the reservoirs. The Nautilus began to sink, following
101 a vertical line, for its screw communicated no motion to it. Some

102 minutes later it stopped at a depth of more than 420 fathoms,
103 resting on the ground. The luminous ceiling was darkened, then
104 the panels were opened, and through the glass I saw the sea
105 brilliantly illuminated by the rays of our lantern for at least half
106 a mile round us.

107 I looked to the port side, and saw nothing but an immensity of
108 quiet waters. But to starboard, on the bottom appeared a large
109 **protuberance**, which at once attracted my attention. One would
110 have thought it a ruin buried under a coating of white shells,
111 much resembling a covering of snow. Upon examining the
112 mass attentively, I could recognize the ever-thickening form of
113 a vessel bare of its masts, which must have sunk. It certainly
114 belonged to past times. This wreck, to be thus encrusted with
115 the lime of the water, must already be able to count many years
116 passed at the bottom of the ocean.

117 What was this vessel? Why did the Nautilus visit its tomb? Could
118 it have been **aught** but a shipwreck which had drawn it under the
119 water? I knew not what to think, when near me in a slow voice I
120 heard Captain Nemo say:

121 "At one time this ship was called the Marseillais. It carried
122 seventy-four guns, and was launched in 1762. In 1778, the 13th
123 of August, commanded by La Poype-Ver trieux, it fought boldly
124 against the Preston. In 1779, on the 4th of July, it was at the
125 taking of Grenada, with the squadron of Admiral Estaing. In
126 1781, on the 5th of September, it took part in the battle of Comte
127 de Grasse, in Chesapeake Bay. In 1794, the French Republic
128 changed its name. On the 16th of April, in the same year, it
129 joined the squadron of Villaret Joyeuse, at Brest, being entrusted
130 with the escort of a cargo of corn coming from America, under
131 the command of Admiral Van Stebel. On the 11th and 12th
132 Prairal of the second year, this squadron fell in with an English
133 vessel. Sir, to-day is the 13th Prairal, the first of June, 1868. It
134 is now seventy four years ago, day for day on this very spot, in
135 latitude 47° 24', longitude 17° 28', that this vessel, after fighting
136 heroically, losing its three masts, with the water in its hold, and

137 the third of its crew disabled, preferred sinking with its 356 sailors
138 to surrendering; and, nailing its colors to the poop, disappeared
139 under the waves to the cry of `Long live the Republic!'"

140 "The Avenger!" I exclaimed.

141 "Yes, sir, the Avenger! A good name!" muttered Captain Nemo,
142 crossing his arms.

**For vocabulary and questions on Chapter twenty-see the end of
the book**

Chapter 21

A HECATOMB

The way of describing this unlooked-for scene, the history of the patriot ship, told at first so coldly, and the emotion with which this strange man pronounced the last words, the name of the Avenger, the significance of which could not escape me, all impressed itself deeply on my mind. My eyes did not leave the Captain, who, with his hand stretched out to sea, was watching with a glowing eye the glorious wreck. Perhaps I was never to know who he was, from **whence** he came, or where he was going to, but I saw the man move, and apart from the **savant**. It was no common **misanthropy** which had shut Captain Nemo and his companions within the Nautilus, but a hatred, either monstrous or sublime, which time could never weaken. Did this hatred still seek for vengeance? The future would soon teach me that. But the Nautilus was rising slowly to the surface of the sea, and the form of the Avenger disappeared by degrees from my sight. Soon a slight rolling told me that we were in the open air. At that moment a dull boom was heard. I looked at the Captain. He did not move.

"Captain?" said I.

He did not answer. I left him and mounted the platform. Conseil and the Canadian were already there.

"Where did that sound come from?" I asked.

"It was a gunshot," replied Ned Land.

I looked in the direction of the vessel I had already seen. It was nearing the Nautilus, and we could see that it was putting on steam. It was within six miles of us.

"What is that ship, Ned?"

"By its rigging, and the height of its lower masts," said the Canadian, "I bet she is a ship-of-war. May it reach us; and, if

30 necessary, sink this cursed Nautilus.”

31 “Friend Ned,” replied Conseil, “what harm can it do to the
32 Nautilus? Can it attack it beneath the waves? Can its cannonade
33 us at the bottom of the sea?”

34 “Tell me, Ned,” said I, “can you recognize what country she
35 belongs to?”

36 The Canadian knitted his eyebrows, dropped his eyelids, and
37 screwed up the corners of his eyes, and for a few moments fixed
38 a **piercing** look upon the vessel.

39 “No, sir,” he replied; “I cannot tell what nation she belongs to,
40 for she shows no colors. But I can declare she is a man-of-war,
41 for a long **pennant** flutters from her main mast.”

42 For a quarter of an hour we watched the ship which was steaming
43 towards us. I could not, however, believe that she could see the
44 Nautilus from that distance; and still less that she could know
45 what this submarine engine was. Soon the Canadian informed
46 me that she was a large, armored, two-decker ram. A thick black
47 smoke was pouring from her two funnels. Her closely-furled
48 sails were stopped to her yards. She hoisted no flag at her mizzen-
49 peak. The distance prevented us from distinguishing the colors
50 of her pennant, which floated like a thin ribbon. She advanced
51 rapidly. If Captain Nemo allowed her to approach, there was a
52 chance of salvation for us.

53 “Sir,” said Ned Land, “if that vessel passes within a mile of us
54 I shall throw myself into the sea, and I should advise you to do
55 the same.”

56 I did not reply to the Canadian’s suggestion, but continued
57 watching the ship. Whether English, French, American, or
58 Russian, she would be sure to take us in if we could only reach
59 her. Presently a white smoke burst from the fore part of the
60 vessel; some seconds after, the water, agitated by the fall of
61 a heavy body, splashed the stern of the Nautilus, and shortly
62 afterwards a loud explosion struck my ear.

63 "What! they are firing at us!" I exclaimed.

64 "So please you, sir," said Ned, "they have recognized the
65 unicorn, and they are firing at us."

66 "But," I exclaimed, "surely they can see that there are men in
67 the case?"

68 "It is, perhaps, because of that," replied Ned Land, looking at
69 me.

70 A whole flood of light burst upon my mind. Doubtless they
71 knew now how to believe the stories of the pretended monster.
72 No doubt, on board the Abraham Lincoln, when the Canadian
73 struck it with the harpoon, Commander Farragut had recognized
74 in the supposed narwhal a submarine vessel, more dangerous
75 than a supernatural cetacean. Yes, it must have been so; and
76 on every sea they were now seeking this engine of destruction.
77 Terrible indeed! if, as we supposed, Captain Nemo employed
78 the Nautilus in works of **vengeance**. On the night when we were
79 imprisoned in that cell, in the midst of the Indian Ocean, had he
80 not attacked some vessel? The man buried in the coral cemetery,
81 had he not been a victim to the shock caused by the Nautilus?
82 Yes, I repeat it, it must be so. One part of the mysterious existence
83 of Captain Nemo had been unveiled; and, if his identity had not
84 been recognized, at least, the nations united against him were
85 no longer hunting a **chimerical** creature, but a man who had
86 vowed a deadly hatred against them. All the formidable past rose
87 before me. Instead of meeting friends on board the approaching
88 ship, we could only expect **pitiless** enemies. But the shot rattled
89 about us. Some of them struck the sea and **ricocheted**, losing
90 themselves in the distance. But none touched the Nautilus.
91 The vessel was not more than three miles from us. In spite of
92 the serious cannonade, Captain Nemo did not appear on the
93 platform; but, if one of the conical projectiles had struck the
94 shell of the Nautilus, it would have been fatal. The Canadian
95 then said, "Sir, we must do all we can to get out of this **dilemma**.
96 Let us signal them. They will then, perhaps, understand that we
97 are honest folks."

98 Ned Land took his handkerchief to wave in the air; but he had
99 scarcely displayed it, when he was struck down by an iron hand,
100 and fell, in spite of his great strength, upon the deck.

101 "Fool!" exclaimed the Captain, "do you wish to be pierced by
102 the spur of the Nautilus before it is hurled at this vessel?"

103 Captain Nemo was terrible to hear; he was still more terrible
104 to see. His face was deadly pale, with a spasm at his heart. For
105 an instant it must have ceased to beat. His pupils were fearfully
106 contracted. He did not speak, he roared, as, with his body thrown
107 forward, he wrung the Canadian's shoulders. Then, leaving
108 him, and turning to the ship of war, whose shot was still raining
109 around him, he exclaimed, with a powerful voice, "Ah, ship of
110 an accursed nation, you know who I am! I do not want your
111 colors to know you by! Look! and I will show you mine!"

112 And on the fore part of the platform Captain Nemo unfurled a
113 black flag, similar to the one he had placed at the South Pole. At
114 that moment a shot struck the shell of the Nautilus **obliquely**,
115 without piercing it; and, rebounding near the Captain, was lost
116 in the sea. He shrugged his shoulders; and, addressing me, said
117 shortly, "Go down, you and your companions, go down!"

118 "Sir," I cried, "are you going to attack this vessel?"

119 "Sir, I am going to sink it."

120 "You will not do that?"

121 "I shall do it," he replied coldly. "And I advise you not to judge
122 me, sir. Fate has shown you what you ought not to have seen.
123 The attack has begun; go down."

124 "What is this vessel?"

125 "You do not know? Very well! so much the better! Its nationality
126 to you, at least, will be a secret. Go down!"

127 We could but obey. About fifteen of the sailors surrounded the

128 Captain, looking with **implacable** hatred at the vessel nearing
129 them. One could feel that the same desire of vengeance animated
130 every soul. I went down at the moment another projectile struck
131 the Nautilus, and I heard the Captain exclaim:

132 "Strike, mad vessel! Shower your useless shot! And then, you
133 will not escape the spur of the Nautilus. But it is not here that
134 you shall perish! I would not have your ruins **mingle** with those
135 of the Avenger!"

136 I reached my room. The Captain and his second had remained
137 on the platform. The screw was set in motion, and the Nautilus,
138 moving with speed, was soon beyond the reach of the ship's
139 guns. But the pursuit continued, and Captain Nemo contented
140 himself with keeping his distance.

141 About four in the afternoon, being no longer able to contain my
142 impatience, I went to the central staircase. The panel was open,
143 and I ventured on to the platform. The Captain was still walking
144 up and down with an agitated step. He was looking at the ship,
145 which was five or six miles to leeward.

146 He was going round it like a wild beast, and, drawing it eastward,
147 he allowed them to pursue. But he did not attack. Perhaps he still
148 hesitated? I wished to mediate once more. But I had scarcely
149 spoken, when Captain Nemo imposed silence, saying:

150 "I am the law, and I am the judge! I am the oppressed, and
151 there is the oppressor! Through him I have lost all that I loved,
152 cherished, and venerated—country, wife, children, father, and
153 mother. I saw all perish! All that I hate is there! Say no more!"

154 I cast a last look at the man-of-war, which was putting on steam,
155 and rejoined Ned and Conseil.

156 "We will fly!" I exclaimed.

157 "Good!" said Ned. "What is this vessel?"

158 "I do not know; but, whatever it is, it will be sunk before night. In

159 any case, it is better to perish with it, than be made accomplices
160 in a retaliation the justice of which we cannot judge."

161 "That is my opinion too," said Ned Land, coolly. "Let us wait
162 for night."

163 Night arrived. Deep silence reigned on board. The compass
164 showed that the Nautilus had not altered its course. It was on
165 the surface, rolling slightly. My companions and I resolved to
166 fly when the vessel should be near enough either to hear us or to
167 see us; for the moon, which would be full in two or three days,
168 shone brightly. Once on board the ship, if we could not prevent
169 the blow which threatened it, we could, at least we would, do
170 all that circumstances would allow. Several times I thought the
171 Nautilus was preparing for attack; but Captain Nemo contented
172 himself with allowing his adversary to approach, and then fled
173 once more before it.

174 Part of the night passed without any incident. We watched the
175 opportunity for action. We spoke little, for we were too much
176 moved. Ned Land would have thrown himself into the sea, but
177 I forced him to wait. According to my idea, the Nautilus would
178 attack the ship at her waterline, and then it would not only be
179 possible, but easy to fly.

180 At three in the morning, full of uneasiness, I mounted the
181 platform. Captain Nemo had not left it. He was standing at the
182 fore part near his flag, which a slight breeze displayed above his
183 head. He did not take his eyes from the vessel. The intensity of his
184 look seemed to attract, and fascinate, and draw it onward more
185 surely than if he had been towing it. The moon was then passing
186 the meridian. Jupiter was rising in the east. Amid this peaceful
187 scene of nature, sky and ocean rivalled each other in tranquility,
188 the sea offering to the orbs of night the finest mirror they could
189 ever have in which to reflect their image. As I thought of the
190 deep calm of these elements, compared with all those **passions**
191 **brooding imperceptibly** within the Nautilus, I shuddered.

192 The vessel was within two miles of us. It was ever nearing that

phosphorescent light which showed the presence of the Nautilus. I could see its green and red lights, and its white lantern hanging from the large foremast. An indistinct vibration quivered through its rigging, showing that the furnaces were heated to the uttermost. Sheaves of sparks and red ashes flew from the funnels, shining in the atmosphere like stars.

I remained thus until six in the morning, without Captain Nemo noticing me. The ship stood about a mile and a half from us, and with the first dawn of day the firing began afresh. The moment could not be far off when, the Nautilus attacking its adversary, my companions and myself should forever leave this man. I was preparing to go down to remind them, when the second mounted the platform, accompanied by several sailors. Captain Nemo either did not or would not see them. Some steps were taken which might be called the signal for action. They were very simple. The iron balustrade around the platform was lowered, and the lantern and pilot cages were pushed within the shell until they were flush with the deck. The long surface of the steel cigar no longer offered a single point to check its maneuvers. I returned to the saloon. The Nautilus still floated; some streaks of light were filtering through the liquid beds. With the undulations of the waves the windows were brightened by the red streaks of the rising sun, and this dreadful day of the 2nd of June had dawned.

At five o'clock, the log showed that the speed of the Nautilus was slackening, and I knew that it was allowing them to draw nearer. Besides, the reports were heard more distinctly, and the projectiles, laboring through the ambient water, were extinguished with a strange hissing noise.

"My friends," said I, "the moment is come. One grasp of the hand, and may God protect us!"

Ned Land was resolute, Conseil calm, myself so nervous that I knew not how to contain myself. We all passed into the library; but the moment I pushed the door opening on to the central staircase, I heard the upper panel close sharply. The Canadian

228 rushed on to the stairs, but I stopped him. A well-known hissing
229 noise told me that the water was running into the reservoirs,
230 and in a few minutes the Nautilus was some yards beneath the
231 surface of the waves. I understood the maneuver. It was too late
232 to act. The Nautilus did not wish to strike at the impenetrable
233 cuirass, but below the water-line, where the metallic covering
234 no longer protected it.

235 We were again imprisoned, unwilling witnesses of the dreadful
236 drama that was preparing. We had scarcely time to reflect; taking
237 refuge in my room, we looked at each other without speaking.
238 A deep stupor had taken hold of my mind: thought seemed to
239 stand still. I was in that painful state of expectation preceding a
240 dreadful report. I waited, I listened, every sense was merged in
241 that of hearing! The speed of the Nautilus was accelerated. It was
242 preparing to rush. The whole ship trembled. Suddenly I screamed.
243 I felt the shock, but comparatively light. I felt the penetrating
244 power of the steel spur. I heard rattlings and scrapings. But the
245 Nautilus, carried along by its propelling power, passed through
246 the mass of the vessel like a needle through sailcloth!

247 I could stand it no longer. Mad, out of my mind, I rushed from my
248 room into the saloon. Captain Nemo was there, mute, gloomy,
249 implacable; he was looking through the port panel. A large mass
250 cast a shadow on the water; and, that it might lose nothing of her
251 agony, the Nautilus was going down into the abyss with her. Ten
252 yards from me I saw the open shell, through which the water was
253 rushing with the noise of thunder, then the double line of guns
254 and the netting. The bridge was covered with black, **agitated**
255 shadows.

256 The water was rising. The poor creatures were crowding the
257 ratlines, clinging to the masts, struggling under the water. It was
258 a human ant-heap overtaken by the sea. Paralyzed, stiffened
259 with anguish, my hair standing on end, with eyes wide open,
260 panting, without breath, and without voice, I too was watching!
261 An irresistible attraction glued me to the glass! Suddenly an
262 explosion took place. The compressed air blew up her decks, as if

263 the magazines had caught fire. Then the unfortunate vessel sank
264 more rapidly. Her topmast, laden with victims, now appeared;
265 then her spars, bending under the weight of men; and, last of all,
266 the top of her mainmast. Then the dark mass disappeared, and
267 with it the dead crew, drawn down by the strong eddy.

268 I turned to Captain Nemo. That terrible avenger, a perfect
269 archangel of hatred, was still looking. When all was over, he
270 turned to his room, opened the door, and entered. I followed
271 him with my eyes. On the end wall beneath his heroes, I saw the
272 portrait of a woman, still young, and two little children. Captain
273 Nemo looked at them for some moments, stretched his arms
274 towards them, and, kneeling down, burst into deep sobs.

For vocabulary and questions on Chapter twenty one - see the end of the book

Chapter 22

THE LAST WORDS OF CAPTAIN NEMO

The panels had closed on this dreadful vision, but light had
not returned to the saloon: all was silence and darkness within
the Nautilus. At wonderful speed, a hundred feet beneath the
water, it was leaving this desolate spot. Whither was it going?
To the north or south? Where was the man flying to after such
dreadful **retaliation**? I had returned to my room, where Ned and
Conseil had remained silent enough. I felt an **insurmountable**
horror for Captain Nemo. Whatever he had suffered at the hands
of these men, he had no right to punish thus. He had made me,
if not an **accomplice**, at least a witness of his **vengeance**. At
eleven the electric light reappeared. I passed into the saloon. It
was deserted. I consulted the different instruments. The Nautilus
was flying northward at the rate of twenty-five miles an hour,
now on the surface, and now thirty feet below it. On taking the
bearings by the chart, I saw that we were passing the mouth of
the Manche, and that our course was hurrying us towards the
northern seas at a frightful speed. That night we had crossed two
hundred leagues of the Atlantic. The shadows fell, and the sea
was covered with darkness until the rising of the moon. I went
to my room, but could not sleep. I was troubled with dreadful
nightmare. The horrible scene of destruction was continually
before my eyes. From that day, who could tell into what part of
the North Atlantic basin the Nautilus would take us? Still with
unaccountable speed. Still in the midst of these northern fogs.
Would it touch at Spitzbergen, or on the shores of Nova Zembla?
Should we explore those unknown seas, the White Sea, the Sea
of Kara, the Gulf of Obi, the Archipelago of Liarrov, and the
unknown coast of Asia? I could not say. I could no longer judge
of the time that was passing. The clocks had been stopped on
board. It seemed, as in polar countries, that night and day no
longer followed their regular course. I felt myself being drawn
into that strange region where the foundered imagination of

33 Edgar Poe roamed at will. Like the fabulous Gordon Pym, at
34 every moment I expected to see "that veiled human figure, of
35 larger proportions than those of any inhabitant of the earth,
36 thrown across the cataract which defends the approach to the
37 pole." I estimated (though, perhaps, I may be mistaken)—I
38 estimated this adventurous course of the Nautilus to have lasted
39 fifteen or twenty days. And I know not how much longer it might
40 have lasted, had it not been for the catastrophe which ended this
41 voyage. Of Captain Nemo I saw nothing whatever now, nor of
42 his second. Not a man of the crew was visible for an instant.
43 The Nautilus was almost incessantly under water. When we
44 came to the surface to renew the air, the panels opened and shut
45 mechanically. There were no more marks on the planisphere. I
46 knew not where we were. And the Canadian, too, his strength and
47 patience at an end, appeared no more. Conseil could not draw a
48 word from him; and, fearing that, in a dreadful fit of madness,
49 he might kill himself, watched him with constant devotion. One
50 morning (what date it was I could not say) I had fallen into a
51 heavy sleep towards the early hours, a sleep both painful and
52 unhealthy, when I suddenly awoke. Ned Land was leaning over
53 me, saying, in a low voice, "We are going to fly." I sat up.

54 "When shall we go?" I asked.

55 "To-night. All inspection on board the Nautilus seems to have
56 ceased. All appear to be stupefied. You will be ready, sir?"

57 "Yes; where are we?"

58 "In sight of land. I took the reckoning this morning in the fog—
59 twenty miles to the east."

60 "What country is it?"

61 "I do not know; but, whatever it is, we will take refuge there."

62 "Yes, Ned, yes. We will fly to-night, even if the sea should
63 swallow us up."

64 "The sea is bad, the wind violent, but twenty miles in that light

65 boat of the Nautilus does not frighten me. Unknown to the crew,
66 I have been able to procure food and some bottles of water.”

67 “I will follow you.”

68 “But,” continued the Canadian, “if I am surprised, I will defend
69 myself; I will force them to kill me.”

70 “We will die together, friend Ned.”

71 I had made up my mind to all. The Canadian left me. I reached
72 the platform, on which I could with difficulty support myself
73 against the shock of the waves. The sky was threatening; but, as
74 land was in those thick brown shadows, we must fly. I returned to
75 the saloon, fearing and yet hoping to see Captain Nemo, wishing
76 and yet not wishing to see him. What could I have said to him?
77 Could I hide the **involuntary** horror with which he inspired me?
78 No. It was better that I should not meet him face to face; better
79 to forget him. And yet—— How long seemed that day, the last
80 that I should pass in the Nautilus. I remained alone. Ned Land
81 and Conseil avoided speaking, for fear of betraying themselves.
82 At six I dined, but I was not hungry; I forced myself to eat in
83 spite of my disgust, that I might not weaken myself. At half-past
84 six Ned Land came to my room, saying, “We shall not see each
85 other again before our departure. At ten the moon will not be
86 risen. We will profit by the darkness. Come to the boat; Conseil
87 and I will wait for you.”

88 The Canadian went out without giving me time to answer.
89 Wishing to verify the course of the Nautilus, I went to the saloon.
90 We were running N.N.E. at frightful speed, and more than fifty
91 yards deep. I cast a last look on these wonders of nature, on the
92 riches of art heaped up in this museum, upon the **unrivalled**
93 collection destined to perish at the bottom of the sea, with him
94 who had formed it. I wished to fix an indelible impression of it
95 in my mind. I remained an hour thus, bathed in the light of that
96 luminous ceiling, and passing in review those treasures shining
97 under their glasses. Then I returned to my room.

98   I dressed myself in strong sea clothing. I collected my notes,
99   placing them carefully about me. My heart beat loudly. I could
100 not check its pulsations. Certainly my trouble and **agitation**
101 would have betrayed me to Captain Nemo's eyes. What was he
102 doing at this moment? I listened at the door of his room. I heard
103 steps. Captain Nemo was there. He had not gone to rest. At every
104 moment I expected to see him appear, and ask me why I wished
105 to fly. I was constantly on the alert. My imagination magnified
106 everything. The impression became at last so poignant that I
107 asked myself if it would not be better to go to the Captain's
108 room, see him face to face, and brave him with look and gesture.

109 It was the inspiration of a madman; fortunately I resisted the
110 desire, and stretched myself on my bed to quiet my bodily
111 agitation. My nerves were somewhat calmer, but in my excited
112 brain I saw over again all my existence on board the Nautilus;
113 every incident, either happy or unfortunate, which had happened
114 since my disappearance from the Abraham Lincoln—the
115 submarine hunt, the Torres Straits, the savages of Papua, the
116 running ashore, the coral cemetery, the passage of Suez, the
117 Island of Santorin, the Cretan diver, Vigo Bay, Atlantis, the
118 iceberg, the South Pole, the imprisonment in the ice, the fight
119 among the poulps, the storm in the Gulf Stream, the Avenger,
120 and the horrible scene of the vessel sunk with all her crew. All
121 these events passed before my eyes like scenes in a drama.
122 Then Captain Nemo seemed to grow enormously, his features
123 to assume superhuman proportions. He was no longer my equal,
124 but a man of the waters, the **genie** of the sea.

125 It was then half-past nine. I held my head between my hands to
126 keep it from bursting. I closed my eyes; I would not think any
127 longer. There was another half-hour to wait, another half-hour of
128 a nightmare, which might drive me mad.

129 At that moment I heard the distant strains of the organ, a sad
130 harmony to an undefinable chant, the wail of a soul longing to
131 break these earthly bonds. I listened with every sense, scarcely
132 breathing; plunged, like Captain Nemo, in that musical ecstasy,

133   which was drawing him in spirit to the end of life.

134   Then a sudden thought terrified me. Captain Nemo had left his
135   room. He was in the saloon, which I must cross to fly. There I
136   should meet him for the last time. He would see me, perhaps
137   speak to me. A gesture of his might destroy me, a single word
138   chain me on board.

139   But ten was about to strike. The moment had come for me to
140   leave my room, and join my companions.

141   I must not hesitate, even if Captain Nemo himself should rise
142   before me. I opened my door carefully; and even then, as it
143   turned on its hinges, it seemed to me to make a dreadful noise.
144   Perhaps it only existed in my own imagination.

145   I crept along the dark stairs of the Nautilus, stopping at each step
146   to check the beating of my heart. I reached the door of the saloon,
147   and opened it gently. It was plunged in profound darkness. The
148   strains of the organ sounded faintly. Captain Nemo was there.
149   He did not see me. In the full light I do not think he would have
150   noticed me, so entirely was he absorbed in the **ecstasy**.

151   I crept along the carpet, avoiding the slightest sound which
152   might betray my presence. I was at least five minutes reaching
153   the door, at the opposite side, opening into the library.

154   I was going to open it, when a sigh from Captain Nemo nailed
155   me to the spot. I knew that he was rising. I could even see him,
156   for the light from the library came through to the saloon. He
157   came towards me silently, with his arms crossed, gliding like a
158   **specter** rather than walking. His breast was swelling with sobs;
159   and I heard him murmur these words (the last which ever struck
160   my ear):

161   "Almighty God! enough! enough!"

162   Was it a confession of remorse which thus escaped from this
163   man's conscience?

164 In desperation, I rushed through the library, mounted the central
165 staircase, and, following the upper flight, reached the boat. I
166 crept through the opening, which had already admitted my two
167 companions.

168 "Let us go! let us go!" I exclaimed.

169 "Directly!" replied the Canadian.

170 The orifice in the plates of the Nautilus was first closed, and
171 fastened down by means of a false key, with which Ned Land
172 had provided himself; the opening in the boat was also closed.
173 The Canadian began to loosen the bolts which still held us to the
174 submarine boat.

175 Suddenly a noise was heard. Voices were answering each other
176 loudly. What was the matter? Had they discovered our flight? I
177 felt Ned Land slipping a dagger into my hand.

178 "Yes," I murmured, "we know how to die!"

179 The Canadian had stopped in his work. But one word many times
180 repeated, a dreadful word, revealed the cause of the agitation
181 spreading on board the Nautilus. It was not we the crew were
182 looking after!

183 "The **maelstrom**! the maelstrom!" Could a more dreadful word
184 in a more dreadful situation have sounded in our ears! We were
185 then upon the dangerous coast of Norway. Was the Nautilus
186 being drawn into this gulf at the moment our boat was going
187 to leave its sides? We knew that at the tide the pent-up waters
188 between the islands of Ferroe and Loffoden rush with irresistible
189 violence, forming a whirlpool from which no vessel ever escapes.
190 From every point of the horizon enormous waves were meeting,
191 forming a gulf justly called the "Navel of the Ocean," whose
192 power of attraction extends to a distance of twelve miles. There,
193 not only vessels, but whales are sacrificed, as well as white bears
194 from the northern regions.

195 It is thither that the Nautilus, voluntarily or involuntarily, had

196 been run by the Captain.

197 It was describing a spiral, the circumference of which was
198 lessening by degrees, and the boat, which was still fastened to
199 its side, was carried along with giddy speed. I felt that sickly
200 **giddiness** which arises from long-continued whirling round.

201 We were in **dread**. Our horror was at its height, circulation had
202 stopped, all nervous influence was annihilated, and we were
203 covered with cold sweat, like a sweat of agony! And what noise
204 around our frail bark! What roarings repeated by the echo miles
205 away! What an uproar was that of the waters broken on the sharp
206 rocks at the bottom, where the hardest bodies are crushed, and
207 trees worn away, "with all the fur rubbed off," according to the
208 Norwegian phrase!

209 What a situation to be in! We rocked frightfully. The Nautilus
210 defended itself like a human being. Its steel muscles cracked.
211 Sometimes it seemed to stand upright, and we with it!

212 "We must hold on," said Ned, "and look after the bolts. We may
213 still be saved if we stick to the Nautilus."

214 He had not finished the words, when we heard a crashing noise,
215 the bolts gave way, and the boat, torn from its groove, was hurled
216 like a stone from a sling into the midst of the whirlpool.

217 My head struck on a piece of iron, and with the violent shock I
218 lost all consciousness.

For vocabulary and questions on Chapter twenty two - see the end of the book

Chapter 23

CONCLUSION

Thus ends the voyage under the seas. What passed during that night—how the boat escaped from the eddies of the maelstrom— how Ned Land, Conseil, and myself ever came out of the gulf, I cannot tell.

But when I returned to consciousness, I was lying in a fisherman's hut, on the Loffoden Isles. My two companions, safe and sound, were near me holding my hands. We embraced each other heartily.

At that moment we could not think of returning to France. The means of communication between the north of Norway and the south are rare. And I am therefore obliged to wait for the steamboat running monthly from Cape North.

And, among the worthy people who have so kindly received us, I revise my record of these adventures once more. Not a fact has been omitted, not a detail exaggerated. It is a faithful **narrative** of this incredible **expedition** in an element **inaccessible** to man, but to which Progress will one day open a road.

Shall I be believed? I do not know. And it matters little, after all. What I now affirm is, that I have a right to speak of these seas, under which, in less than ten months, I have crossed 20,000 leagues in that submarine tour of the world, which has revealed so many wonders.

But what has become of the Nautilus? Did it resist the pressure of the maelstrom? Does Captain Nemo still live? And does he still follow under the ocean those frightful **retaliations**? Or, did he stop after the last **hecatomb**?

Will the waves one day carry to him this manuscript containing the history of his life? Shall I ever know the name of this man? Will the missing vessel tell us by its nationality that of Captain

30   Nemo?

31   I hope so. And I also hope that his powerful vessel has conquered
32   the sea at its most terrible gulf, and that the Nautilus has survived
33   where so many other vessels have been lost! If it be so—if
34   Captain Nemo still inhabits the ocean, his adopted country, may
35   hatred be **appeased** in that savage heart! May the **contemplation**
36   of so many wonders extinguish forever the spirit of vengeance!
37   May the judge disappear, and the philosopher continue the
38   peaceful exploration of the sea! If his destiny be strange, it is
39   also **sublime**. Have I not understood it myself? Have I not lived
40   ten months of this unnatural life? And to the question asked by
41   Ecclesiastes three thousand years ago, "That which is far off and
42   exceeding deep, who can find it out?" two men alone of all now
43   living have the right to give an answer——

44   CAPTAIN NEMO AND MYSELF.

Vocabulary

undeceived, consolation, embarked, manufactory, presentiment, whence, savant, misanthropy, chimerical, pitiless, ricocheted, dilemma, mingle, passions, brooding, imperceptibly, accomplice, involuntary, maelstrom, dread, hecatomb, appeased, contemplation, sublime

Questions

1. In Chapter 20, what realization regarding the Captain's motives dawns on the Professor?

2. In Chapter 21 line 81, what answer is given to explain the death of a sailor in an earlier chapter?

3. What does the Captain say is the cause for his hatred for the ship's nationality in chapter 21? What right does the Captain claim in sinking that ship?

4. How does the Captain destroy the vessel that attacks him?

5. What is the mood aboard the nautilus after the attack on the ship?

6. What do Ned land and his friends decide to do after the attack on the ship?

____

____

7. Do you think Captain Nemo regrets his actions?

____

____

____

8. How do the captives free themselves of the Nautilus?

____

____

____

9. What do you think of the conclusion of the book?

____

____

____

____

10. How do you feel about the author's decision to obscure the background and the motives of the Capain in doing what he does?

____

____

____

____

11. In numerous instances throughout the book, Ned Land, despite his comparatively smaller knowledge base of natural phenomena compared to the Professor, is right about numerous things. For example, in regards to his doubting that the object attacking ships is a giant Narwhal, it turns out that he is right. Where else in the book is he proven right (hint: part 1, chapter 8), and what does that say about the author's opinion of people

with only "book knowledge"?

____

____

____

____

12. Did you have a feeling that they would eventually get off the ship?

____

____

____

____

13. What did you think about the book as a whole? Was it exciting? Boring? What aspects did you like about the book and which elements were not as appreciated?

____

____

____

____

____

____

____

____